Nancy Butler won the 1998 Golden Leaf Award for Best First Novel for *Lord Monteith's Gift*. Her newest title is *The Ramshackle Suitor.*

Diane Farr, a very talented newcomer, saw her first Regency sell out almost immediately as she became an instant favorite with Regency fans. Her newest novel is *Falling for Chloe.*

Allison Lane won the 1996 *Romantic Times* Reviewers' Choice Award for Best First Regency for *The Rake's Rainbow.* Her newest title is *The Beleaguered Earl.*

Edith Layton, critically acclaimed for her short stories, also writes historicals for HarperCollins, and has won numerous awards. Her last short story appeared in *A Regency Christmas Present.*

Barbara Metzger, one of the stars of the genre, has written over two dozen Regencies and won numerous awards. Her newest title is *Saved by Scandal.*

Coming next month

THE NOTORIOUS WIDOW
by Allison Lane

When a scoundrel tries to tarnish a young widow's reputation, a valiant earl tries to repair the damage–and mend her broken heart as well.

"A formidable talent." —*Romantic Times*

❑ 0-451-20166-3 / $4 99

THE PRODIGAL HERO
by Nancy Butler

MacHeath, a former sailor, regains his honor by rescuing the daughter of his former employer. But he never imagined that he'd also rescue her heart.

"A writer not to be missed." —Mary Balogh

❑ 0-451-20172-8 / $4 99

A GRAND DESIGN
by Emma Jensen

A marquess requires the services of an architect, but is completely unprepared for the audacious charms of the architect's niece.

"One of my favorites." —Barbara Metzger

❑ 0-451-20121-3 / $4 99

To order call: 1-800-788-6262

A Regency Christmas Eve

FIVE STORIES BY

Nancy Butler

Diane Farr

Allison Lane

Edith Layton

Barbara Metzger

A SIGNET BOOK

SIGNET
Published by New American Library, a division of
Penguin Putnam Inc., 375 Hudson Street,
New York, New York 10014, U.S.A.
Penguin Books Ltd, 27 Wrights Lane,
London W8 5TZ, England
Penguin Books Australia Ltd, Ringwood,
Victoria, Australia
Penguin Books Canada Ltd, 10 Alcorn Avenue,
Toronto, Ontario, Canada M4V 3B2
Penguin Books (N.Z.) Ltd, 182–190 Wairau Road,
Auckland 10, New Zealand

Penguin Books Ltd, Registered Offices:
Harmondsworth, Middlesex, England

First published by Signet, an imprint of New American Library,
a division of Penguin Putnam Inc.

First Printing, October 2000
10 9 8 7 6 5 4 3 2 1

Printed in the United States of America

PUBLISHER'S NOTE
These are works of fiction. Names, characters, places, and incidents either are the product of the author's imagination or are used fictitiously, and any resemblance to actual persons, living or dead, business establishments, events, or locales is entirely coincidental.

Contents

Little Miracles

by Barbara Metzger

1

They were as poor as church mice. No, they were the church mice. It was the little stone church that was so poor it could barely sustain a resident family of *Rodentia religiosa.* St. Cecilia's in the Trees was so poor it could have been called St. Cecilia's in the Twigs, for all the nearby oaks had been cut long ago for firewood. The church was so poor that when Portio Mea Domine, named for the page from the *Book of Common Prayers* she was given for bedding, decided to use the alms box for a nursery, nothing disturbed her nestlings. Not a shilling, not a farthing, nary a ha'penny interrupted the infants' rest, not even hungry fingers seeking aid. The parishioners knew better, for they were as poor as the church. Prices were high, incomes were low. Wars and enclosures, bad weather and bad management, influenza and indifference had taken their toll on the entire region of Lower Winfrey. Whole families had moved, seeking better lives in the New World, or in the factory cities of the north.

Whole families of the Churchmouse clan had to move, too. Without the Sunday worshipers, no pockets were filled with crumbled muffins from hurried breakfasts, no childish hands clutched sacks of peppermint drops. The Communion bread barely stretched as far as the few poor congregants who still attended services. Nothing was left for the mice. The gleanings were not enough to fill a flea, much less a family of *Mus ministerus.*

The mice could not even raid the vicarage's paltry pantry, not while the sexton's tomcat, Dread Fred, was on patrol. They lost both little Hope of Redemption and one-eared Abiding Hope to Dread Fred in one week. All hope of continuing the clan, in fact, was nearly gone. What the family had left, though, was a burning, inborn need to propagate their species, and an old secret. The secret of St. Cecilia's hidden wealth had been passed down from father to furry son for generations past counting. Now all they had to do was tell someone about it.

The church clansmice were true believers, of course, and one of their enduring beliefs was in the vow that God had made to the animals one Christmas Eve so long ago. He promised that on every succeeding Christmas Eve, the animals could talk, donkey to dung beetle, hen to horse. Peace would reign among them for that night, the lion lying down with the lamb; they could communicate with one another then, and be understood. This was the Lord's reward to the beasts who shared their humble shelter with the Holy Child.

One Christmas Eve, therefore, the head of the remaining Churchmouse clan, Uncle Nunc Dimittis, begged the nearby creatures to come to the little church. Dread Fred came, and Mrs. Sexton Cotter's chickens, along with the vicar's old horse, a passing fox, an owl, a rabbit, and some sleepy sparrows from the vicarage eaves.

"Why should we help you pesky vermin?" mumbled the horse, unused to speaking since he'd had no stablemates after the vicar sold his carriage pair.

No one wanted to be the one to explain that the richer the church, the fatter the mice, and the more mice, the easier the hunting. The more food for the cat and the fox and the owl, the less they would prey on the chickens and the sparrows. Everyone but the hay-eating horse saw the advantages, but in the blessed spirit of brotherhood, the fox merely said, "Because we are all God's children."

So the creatures agreed to help. Climbing past fallen stones in the walls or under the rotten floorboards or through the holes in the roof, they took up places around the little church and waited for the vicar to come. The horse poked his grizzled muzzle through a broken window.

As was his wont, Vicar Althorpe came to pray after ringing the bells for twelve o'clock. Now the vicar was an old man who had seen his parish and his income decimated, despite his prayers. Tonight they were going to be answered.

"Lord, is that you?" he cried in disbelief or awe.

"Look to St. Francis," he heard again from every corner of the dilapidated church. "Look to St. Francis."

He spun around to see where the voices were coming from, and to find the statue of the saint in its niche. Before he could take a step in that direction, though, he clutched his chest, fell to the floor, and breathed his last, with a smile upon his lips.

The new vicar was a bitter young man, forced by his family into a profession clearly at odds with his predilection for gaming, wenching, and wine. Mr. Rudd was even more incensed when he realized what a meager living his family had found for him. His salary did not half cover his expenses, so he took to selling off the remaining stained glass windows, the last gold offering plate, and even an old hymnal or two. As was *his* wont, he entered the church one Christmas Eve after making sure the sexton rang the midnight bells, since they could be heard by his superior in Upper Winfrey. Rudd was not there to pray, but to see if by some chance some fool of a passerby had left a donation.

"Look to St. Francis," the animals called. The old horse was not among them, since Rudd would rather walk than be seen on such a decrepit beast, nor the rabbit, for Rudd had a rifle. "Look to St. Francis," they all tried to shout louder.

In their eagerness, the animals had forgotten a small technicality of the Christmas miracle: only a righteous man could hear and comprehend their speech. Rudd was so far from righteous he couldn't have heard Gabriel's trumpet.

"Bugger this," Dread Fred muttered. He leaped from the back of a pew onto the molding under St. Francis's niche. Using his well-honed claws, he climbed to the base of the statue and arched his back, making sure the other animals had seen his prowess. "Now watch."

When the vicar turned from the empty poor box, considering whether he could fence the gold chalice, and for how much, Dread Fred nudged the statue so it fell. St. Francis did not, however, land at Rudd's feet. The heavy statue hit the vicar on the head.

"He'd have stolen the thing anyway," the cat hissed as he slinked away.

In the morning the sexton replaced the statue in its niche, then he sent to replace the vicar.

Now the stone church was considered cursed, and was emptier than ever. Every one of the parishioners who could walk, ride, or drive the extra miles traveled to Most Holy Church in Upper Winfrey, with its choir loft and organ, its padded pews and charcoal braziers in winter. Only a few ancient villagers and farm folk came to St. Cecilia's on a Sunday, and then more to visit with one another than to pay homage.

Only two of the Churchmouse clan remained, old Exultemus Domine, who was too old to attract a mate, and young Passeth-All-Understanding, who had nothing to offer a wife, no rich cache of grains, no warm nest. Their prayer book was empty of pages to make a bridal bower, and they were reduced to eating the leather covers. They were out of paper, out of names, and nearly out of time. This would be the last Christmas for the clan, unless a miracle occurred. The other animals refused to help anymore, lest they be persecuted worse than they already were, so Pass and Ed could only huddle together and pray.

". . . Give us this day our daily bread crumbs."

"And lead us not into temptation," the Reverend Mr. Evan Merriweather prayed, with little hope of success. How, by all that was holy and a few things that were not, was he to avoid temptation at Squire Prescott's Sunday dinner? He could easily resist second helpings, although the weekly meal was the only decent food he'd see all week. Compared to what he was served at the vicarage, Squire's mutton was manna. According to Ned Cotter, Mrs. Sexton Cotter had trouble seeing the labels on the spice jars. Evan believed she must have trouble seeing the spice jars at all. Complaining did no good, since Mrs. Cotter heard as well as she saw. The old sexton and his wife had come with the vicarage, and Evan did not have the heart to replace them. He did not have the funds to replace them with more competent help, either.

Still, he was easily able to refuse additional portions at Squire's, knowing the leftovers would be bundled into baskets for him to take round to the parish poor. There were so many poor, and so few baskets, not a single belly would be full, less so if the new vicar stuffed himself at Squire's board.

Mr. Merriweather was not remotely tempted to blow a cloud with Squire after the meal—filthy habit that it was—nor partake of the cognac Prescott pressed on him. Spirits gave Evan the headache, for one, and he did not deem them quite proper for a parson, on a Sunday. He had to set an example for his parishioners, didn't he? What if they saw him staggering back to the vicarage after an afternoon of imbibing?

Lud, how much worse if they saw him lusting after Squire's daughter? Evan ran his hands through his sandy hair and prayed harder, knowing how futile his efforts to avoid her attraction. He simply could not resist Alice Prescott. He was a man, by Heaven, not a monk, nor in his dotage, and she was a beautiful young woman, all rounded and soft, with silky golden curls. Beyond that, Miss Prescott was the sweetest, kindest creature ever put on God's green earth. Evan knew it was she who packed the foodstuffs for the poor, and she who added jams and apples and eggs from Squire's larder. She was the one who insisted the squire and his family attend little St. Cecilia's, rather than join the other gentry at Most Holy, thus putting their pence on the collection plate where they would do most good. Of course the rector at Most Holy still demanded his share of the tithes, likely to gild the baptismal font there, while St. Cecilia's used a chipped porcelain bowl.

Alice—for that's how Evan thought of Miss Prescott, although he would never presume to use her given name—brought flowers and greenery to the church, and embroidered new altar cloths. She visited the sick with broth and restoratives, and she helped teach the village girls skills and letters, so they might better themselves. Her mind and her morals everything admirable, Miss Prescott was as beautiful inside as out.

In other words, words Evan tried not to admit, even to himself, Alice Prescott was everything he could ever want in a wife—a helpmate, the perfect mother to his children, and yes, an alluring lover. She was everything he wanted, and nothing he would ever have. He could never make her an honorable offer, for he honestly had nothing to offer her but a rundown vicarage, an impoverished parish, and a pittance of a salary. Miss Prescott deserved so much more, and her father would insist upon it.

Mr. Merriweather had spent many hours since coming to Lower Winfrey and St. Cecilia's in the Trees three months ago in thinking how he could improve the conditions for his congregation. He'd spent endless hours more once he'd met Miss Prescott in wondering how he could improve his own position enough to be considered an eligible *parti.* His birth was decent, with connections to the current Lord Whittendale, titleholder of note in this area of Sussex, but that would not count with the squire or his wife. It barely counted with Lord Whittendale, who had ignored all of Evan's letters and all the messages sent through his land steward.

Evan could shore up the fallen roof of his church, and he could share his meager rations with the poor, but he could not change a blessed thing for his parishioners. He could tutor the few boys whose parents could afford Latin lessons, and he could scribe letters for the occasional traveler, but he could never afford to take a wife, not while he stayed on at St. Cecilia's.

Sometimes, in the dark of night, Evan thought of leaving. Not of leaving the Church, for unlike many others in orders, he'd never wished to be anything but a cleric, like his own father, may he rest in peace. But he could find another, better post somewhere, he was sure. Evan had taken honors at university, and had recommendations from the archbishop himself. Surely some wealthy parish needed a reverend ready to serve, although none could need him as much as St. Cecilia's. Being needed, Mr. Merriweather was sadly finding, was not the same as being useful. Yet how could he leave, and leave Alice Prescott?

Still on his knees there on the cold floor, making sure his trousers did not snag on any loose boards, for who knew how long before he could replace them, both the boards and the trousers, Evan pondered not going to Squire's for dinner, thus sparing himself the pain of seeing what he could not have. That would mean denying the needy the baskets of food, though, and denying himself the joy of one of Alice's smiles. He could no more stay away than the moth could stay away from the candle, but he could pray for inner peace and acceptance of his place in God's Greater Plan. If He meant His minister to be celibate and sorrowful, well, Evan would do his best, despite pangs for a hunger no mutton could satisfy.

2

The Reverend Mr. Merriweather dressed with care for dinner at the Manor. One did, he told himself, to honor one's hosts, to befit one's position, and to make a good impression on any guests Squire might also have invited. He was not fussing like a belle at her first ball on account of hoping to find favor in a pair of heavenly blue eyes. Of course not. He might be a poor vicar, but he had his dignity.

He had his pride, too. Evan could not help preening a bit in the mirror in the vicarage parlor, noting that all his work resetting the stone walls and sawing boards for the church roof had gained him muscles, as well as calluses. No scholarly stoop for this servant of the Lord. He smoothed his good coat over broader shoulders, and tried to flatten the cowlick at the back of his head.

"What's the lad doing, then, Ned?" Mrs. Cotter called to her husband. "Spitting on his hands?"

"He's trying to fix his hair, Emma, I think. I've got some pig grease I used on the church door, Reverend. Want I should fetch that? That's what I used when I was a-courtin' my Emma." Ned guffawed, then repeated his offer loudly enough for Emma to hear, and the neighbors next door.

"I am not going courting, and I do not wish to arrive at Squire's smelling of bacon, thank you."

"Aye, smelling of April and May is enough." Ned and Emma chuckled again.

So much for his pride and his dignity and his prayers that no one knew of his impossible affection for Miss Alice Prescott. Evan crammed his beaver hat over the offending curl and set off to walk the two miles to Prescott Manor, forlorn hope his only companion.

Squire, at least, was in a jovial mood, welcoming Evan with a glass of sherry before dinner. From his high color and booming voice, it appeared that Prescott had already welcomed the Naysmiths and Colonel Halsey, all of whom attended services at Most Holy Church, with similar glasses of spirits. Evan made his bows, pretending to sip at his wine, pretending not to be watching the door. Then she was there.

Miss Prescott was wearing a blue gown embroidered with tiny flowers. Evan did not think it was the dress she'd worn to church that morning, but he could not be certain, since no one in St. Cecilia's removed their cloaks, not in December. He thought he would have noticed if her eyes were even bluer than usual, though, reflecting the color of her frock. He certainly would have noticed the silk flowers twined in her neatly coiled hair, matching the sprigs on her skirt. Reverend Merriweather decided he did not need dinner if he could feast his eyes on such a delicacy. For sure he'd never manage to swallow, not past the foolish grin on his face. Alice smiled at him and held out her hand. Evan put his glass of sherry in it.

His cheeks redder than Squire's, the vicar took the glass back, recalling courtesy and the company. He bowed to Mrs. Prescott, thanking her for the kind invitation, and inquired after the health of Squire's ancient auntie. Gratified, the antique relative latched onto his sleeve, which was already straining from his newly acquired muscles, and enumerated every ache and pain a person could suffer and still survive. Evan wondered whether his coat or his patience would expire first.

Seated between Aunt Minerva and Mrs. Naysmith, whose husband owned the Winfrey Mercantile, Mr. Merriweather could look directly across the table, over a bowl of fruit, at Alice. He blessed Aunt Minerva and her megrims. Then he blessed the food, after Squire cleared his throat a few times and Alice kicked Evan's ankle, under the table.

As soon as grace was spoken, Squire raised his glass in a toast, to good food, good friends, and good news. "For Colonel Halsey has brought tidings of great import to our little neighborhood. Yes, and the Naysmiths have confirmed it. Lord Whittendale is coming home to White Oaks for Christmas."

"And about time," Aunt Minerva seconded, taking a healthy swig of her wine for such a febrile female.

Viscount Whittendale being Mr. Merriweather's patron, as well as a distant cousin, Evan would never say anything derogatory about the man. There was, however, no denying that Randolph Whitmore was a feckless, reckless here-and-thereian. Bad enough he callously let St. Cecilia's collapse, and the neighboring economy with it, but the viscount was a libertine, a known womanizer, an extravagant gambler, a devil-may-care chaser after the moment's pleasure. For the life of him, Evan could not think why anyone would be in alt to have such a one in their midst.

Sensing Evan's disapproval, the squire explained, "Good for business, don't you see? White Oaks is already ordering goods from the Mercantile, for the house party he'll be bringing with him."

More like an orgy, from what Evan knew of the viscount, but he refrained from comment as Mr. Naysmith raised his own glass. "Linens and toweling, soaps and candles. And his steward is adding on staff."

"And we heard he might hold a ball." Mrs. Naysmith beamed at the Prescott ladies, visions of dress lengths and lace dancing in her eyes.

"Yes, I can see where that can help put some money in local pockets," Evan admitted, "but Lower Winfrey needs more than a fortnight of revelry."

Squire slurped at his soup. "Who's to say Whittendale will be gone after Twelfth Night?"

"Lord Whittendale himself. He told me he despised ruralizing, the one time I met him when I interviewed for this position. He said he hadn't been here in a donkey's age, and didn't intend to visit any time soon." He had not bothered to reply to Evan's pleas for him to visit, to see conditions for himself. "I confess I should like a few moments of my lord's time, but doubt he'll stay even that long."

Prescott waved his spoon in the air, sending droplets of soup toward the centerpiece. Evan decided to forgo the fruit. "Idle chitchat," Squire said, dismissing the vicar's misgivings. "No, word is that Lord Whittendale is ready to settle down."

"About time," Aunt Minerva repeated.

Even Squire's wife looked dubious. She read the London gossip columns as often as her husband. The *on dits* reached Sussex a few days late, but not *that* late.

"Just think," Prescott said around a slab of meat. "The man is thirty if he is a day. Long past time he starts setting up his nursery. He's sown his wild oats, aye, more than his fair share, but he knows what's due his name and his title. *Noblesse oblige* and all that. Asides, all that rushing from party to party and staying out all night grows tiresome. Mark my words, our viscount is coming to look over the country seat, with an eye toward rusticating."

"I hope you may be right, for St. Cecilia's sake, as well as for the rest of the community." Perhaps Evan would even get to ask the viscount for a raise in his salary. While the others speculated on the size and social standing of the viscount's house party, Reverend Merriweather let his mind wander to the size of increase he'd request. His thoughts traveled further afield on paths of gold and landed, as usual, on Alice Prescott—who was looking right at him.

She smiled as if she could see inside his mind and said, "I think we must all benefit from Lord Whittendale's visit, no matter how short."

"Quite right, puss. And I daresay if you play your cards right, you can be a viscountess one day."

Everyone turned to stare at Mr. Merriweather as his fork clattered onto his plate, then skittered to the floor. Mortified, Evan bent to pick it up, bumping his head on the mahogany table. Alice caught her father's attention to cover the vicar's awkwardness. "What fustian nonsense, Papa. As if I ever aspired to such lofty estate."

"And why not, I want to know?" her doting father asked. "You're wellborn enough. Wasn't your mama's grandfather a duke? And I paid enough for that fancy finishing academy to please the highest sticklers. Besides, you're a devilishly pretty chit, if I have to say so myself who shouldn't. Image of your mother at that age, don't you know. And she had beaux swarming at her feet. Could have had an earl, by George, but she chose me." Squire gazed fondly at his wife, the tender sentiments marred only by the gravy dripping down his chin.

"Yes, dearest," Mrs. Prescott said. "But the viscount is so . . . so sophisticated."

"So? Our gal had her London Season. I turned down plenty of offers on her behalf, too. Not like she's some chit fresh out of the schoolroom. Puss mightn't be a dasher, but she'll do, if Whittendale knows what's good for him."

"Doing it too brown, Papa. You know the viscount would never look at me when he has all those elegant females to choose from."

"Now who's talking gammon? A man don't want some pretty wigeon to be mother to his children and to run his household. When he's ready to take on leg shackles, he wants a sensible female, not an ornament. You're a good girl, my Alice, and Whittendale is bound to see that. If he doesn't, I'll bring it to his attention."

Blushing rosily, Alice took a hasty sip of wine. "You'll do nothing of the kind, Papa. Didn't you say that Lady Farnham was to be of the party? Her name was linked with that of the viscount last spring, when we went to London."

"Aye, Farnham's widow is coming along, for all the good it'll do her. A man don't marry his mistress, puss."

Now Evan was blushing, as well as Mrs. Prescott and Mrs. Naysmith. Only Aunt Minerva, used to the freer morals of an earlier age, was unaffected by Squire's bluntness.

The colonel harumphed. "Ladies present, I say."

Ladies were supposed to be conveniently deaf, dumb, and blind to the existence of such creatures, Evan knew, even when their husbands paraded their convenients through the park or at the Opera. That was the kind of marriage Squire wished for his daughter?

It appeared so. "Tender sensibilities be blasted," Squire Prescott said, reaching across the table with his knife to spear another boiled potato. "Everyone knows it's true. A fellow might light on any number of full-blown roses, but he's going to wed the unopened bud."

A virgin, Evan thought. Squire was back to sacrificing virgins on the altar of ambition, like some pot-valiant pagan.

Aunt Minerva was nodding her agreement. "Unless he's dicked in the nob, and no one ever called little Randy Whitmore a slowtop."

Squire passed her the dish of eels in aspic, as reward for agreeing with him. "Right. A chap don't want to worry over his wife's morals, or what cuckoo bird is landing in his nest, especially not the toffs with their generations of blue blood to preserve. He don't want his sons' noses bloodied defending their mum, and he don't want to be forever dueling over rumors of her misconduct, either. There has never been a shred of gossip about my girl, and never will be, do you hear?"

Evan heard the warning, and could only wonder. Did Squire Prescott think *he* would cast dishonor on Alice's name? He'd sooner see his own tongue pickled in that aspic. "Of course not. Miss Prescott is the embodiment of virtue. A perfect lady. More so than many with the title before their names, I daresay."

"Just think, our dear Miss Prescott will be Lady Whittendale." Mrs. Naysmith was already calculating the cachet of having a titled lady as patron.

"My little girl, a viscountess," Mrs. Prescott said with a contented sigh.

Alice was sputtering, trying to topple her parents' air castles before they collapsed around her. She might as well have tried to hold back the tide, for Mrs. Prescott was already wondering where they should hold the wedding ceremony. "Not at St. Cecilia's, that's for certain, not with half the county and all those elegant London guests coming. Perhaps the viscount would prefer to be married in the City after all. I'm sure his town house can easily accommodate the wedding breakfast."

"Mama, there will be no—"

Squire turned to Evan. "So what do you think, eh, Reverend?"

Evan thought the mutton in his mouth tasted like masonry.

3

"I wish you would reconsider your notion to approach Lord Whittendale about a match with Miss Prescott, sir."

"I'll just bet you do, Merriweather. I'll just bet you do." Squire puffed on his cigar, filling the dining room with a blue haze. The ladies had departed for the withdrawing room, and Mr. Naysmith and the colonel had stepped out to use the necessary.

Evan did not want to think of the meaning behind Squire's words. Did everyone know of his calf-love for Alice? Had he been that obvious in his admiration? Evan brushed that dreadful thought aside with a sweep of his hand to clear the smoke. Maybe he could sweep away the fog in his brain box, too, for it was imperative that he think clearly now. Alice's entire future depended on him.

"As . . . as spiritual advisor to your family, I beg you to reexamine your heart. Do you truly think that Lord Whittendale will make your daughter a good husband?"

Squire blew a smoke ring. "As good as any. I never

heard of Whittendale being the brutal sort. He'll not lay a hand on her, not with her papa next door."

"Good grief, I never meant to imply otherwise. I was thinking of her happiness."

"Of course she'll be happy as Viscountess Whittendale. She can have all the pretty dresses she desires, and she can enjoy herself in Town now and again, with invites that would never come her way as some country gentleman's offspring. She'll want for nothing. Rest assured I'll make sure the settlements are generous."

"Those are material things. What of peace of mind? Miss Prescott and my lord have neither interests, experiences, nor friends in common. Heavens, what will they even talk about?"

"The weather, for all I care." Squire's cheeks were getting red again, behind the blue smoke. "Dash it, they'll make friends, learn new interests, same as every married couple. That's what leg shackles are all about, don't you know. No, of course you don't."

Evan bravely persevered. "I know that a couple needs more than a license to make a go of a marriage, sir. You and Mrs. Prescott share a fine affection. Would you wish less for your daughter?"

The squire thought for a moment, swirling his brandy in its glass. "They can ride together, that's what. It's a start. Alice is a notable horsewoman, and Whittendale is renowned for his prowess."

The viscount was known for his neck-or-nothing style of riding. Surely Mr. Prescott did not intend for Alice to take up Lord Whittendale's daredevil ways. Evan's stomach lurched at the thought of gentle Alice riding hell-for-leather through the woods of White Oaks. She'd be tossed, or left behind at the first too-high hedge. He gulped a swallow of the brandy, knowing he'd have a headache later. He already had a heartache, so what was the difference? "He'll abandon her here in the country as soon as she is breeding. You know Lord Whittendale will not give up the pleasures of the City."

"Aye, and her mother will be thrilled to have the infants nearby to spoil. I won't mind dandling a little lordling on my knee either. Wonder if Whittendale has any courtesy titles lying around for his firstborn? Aunt Minerva will know."

Evan almost shouted in desperation. "But what of Alice?"

"She loves children. Always has. Says she wants a bunch of the little blighters. What comes of being an only child, I suppose. Not that Mrs. Prescott and I didn't try, a'course."

"No, I mean, what of Alice's wants and desires?"

"As lady of White Oaks, my gal will be the first female of the neighborhood. She can do all the good deeds she wants. Why, she might just be able to put in a word for you with his lordship, get you a raise in living and fix up the church so folks won't be afraid the roof'll collapse on them."

Evan gave up. "Perhaps his lordship will not be interested," he muttered under his breath. Perhaps pigs would fly, too.

Squire's hearing must have been better than his comprehension. "He'll be interested, by Jupiter. He's not fool enough to turn down the chance to get Prescott Manor when I toddle off."

"Lord Whittendale does not seem terribly concerned with

increasing his holdings. He could make White Oaks a more profitable estate, with better management."

"No matter. Once he takes a gander at my Alice, he'll see all the advantages."

That's what Evan feared, too. How could any man resist her sweet charms? He sighed.

The squire heard that, too. "It's not as though her heart is given to another eligible gentleman, you know. I wouldn't stand in the way if Alice showed a partiality, long as the chap was in a position to make her a decent offer. I don't aim to see my puss living hand to mouth in some ramshackle cottage, you understand."

Evan understood all too well.

"Take a bloke like yourself, hard-working and with a good head on your shoulders. Nice, steady fellow, righteous, even. But you haven't got a pot to piss in, have you?"

Only a chipped, battered bowl, which was how Evan was feeling at this moment.

"No, I've got to look out for my little chick, I do. Asides, you mightn't live past Christmas Eve, what with the day being a tad unhealthy for the vicars of St. Cecilia's, you might say."

With less than a month to live—not that Evan believed in curses or such, of course—the vicar decided to relish what few pleasures came his way. He accepted Miss Prescott's invitation to survey the conservatory. She thought they might decide how best to decorate St. Cecilia's, in case the tonnish guests chose to attend services there. Pine boughs could cover the expanses of missing mortar, and perhaps one of her mother's potted palms or flowering plants could hide that gaping hole in the rear corner.

Evan agreed with whatever Alice suggested, although he doubted that the London party would step foot in his little church, or any church for that matter, sinners that they were. No, he told himself, he should not condemn them without evidence, certainly not while he himself was having impious thoughts of Miss Prescott as she bent over this fern and that flower. Perhaps Lord Whittendale was not a rake, after all, and perhaps Lady Farnham was not his mistress. Victims of vicious tongues, that's what they might be, not villains. Surely they'd attend a few parties, let the locals gawk and gossip, then return to their butterfly lives in London—without Alice.

Before Whittendale left, Evan did mean to show him the disrepair, even if he had to drag his lordship into the church by the silly tassels on the high-polished boots he was sure to be wearing. Once the viscount had made provisions for St. Cecilia's, then Evan would speed him on his way with his blessings. As long as he left without Alice.

The vicar trailed behind Miss Prescott, moving a pot for her, fetching the watering can when she noticed a thirsty plant. Now his head was filled with the scents of warm earth and Alice, instead of Squire's cigar. He still could not think properly.

"There, I think these will do," she finally said. "I'll see that they are brought to the church on Saturday, along with more greens and a ribbon or two. You don't think bows would be too frivolous for church, do you?"

The only bow Evan could think of was the one tied beneath the high waist of Alice's blue gown, right beneath her delectable décolletage. He took a deep breath and blurted: "What do you think of your father's plan?"

She did not pretend to misunderstand. "Oh, I think Papa

is happy in his plotting, but nothing will come of it. Lord Whittendale could have married any number of wellborn beauties with dowries far greater than mine if he wished to be wed at all, which I doubt." She plucked a dead leaf off an ivy.

"But your father is correct; the viscount will have to wed sometime."

"Yes, and I fear Papa will do his best to remind the unfortunate gentleman, as if his own family was not nagging at him enough. But so many snares have been set for Lord Whittendale that by now he must be too downy a bird to fall into any ambitious parent's net."

"If he is ready to start his nursery, however, how can you be so certain he won't be smitten with you?"

Alice chuckled. "Lord Whittendale is not interested in country misses. He was polite enough to attend my come-out ball at Lady Henesley's. That's Mama's godmother, you know. He must have felt duty-bound to come, since our families have known each other for ages, of course, although not on such familiar terms. The viscount brought a crowd of his friends, all gentlemen who rarely accepted such insipid invitations, which quite puffed up Lady Henesley. Whittendale took the floor with me for one set, which inflated my own consequence. Mama was *au anges*. Two days later, when we passed in the park, he did not recognize me as an acquaintance. So no, I do not fear he will be interested in making me an offer."

"Your father is convinced otherwise."

She shrugged and removed another spent bloom. "Papa will have no one to blame but himself when he is disappointed."

Evan had to persist, because he had to know. "What if

he does manage to convince the viscount? Would you be tempted to accept? Your father can be very persuasive." So could the viscount's worldly assets.

"I should hate to go against Papa's wishes, but no, I would never accept an arranged match with Lord Whittendale, no matter the advantages. That is simply not the kind of marriage I want. I would rather remain unwed, in fact, than give myself into the keeping of a man who does not care for me, nor I him."

"Good." Convinced, Evan could breathe again. "You deserve a husband who will cherish and adore you, not merely require a mother for his heirs. You will find such a man, I know it."

She stopped fussing with the flowers and turned to him. "Will I? Where?"

"Where? Um, the assemblies in Upper Winfrey? London in the spring?"

"I have been there. What about here?"

The vicar swallowed. "Here?" He looked around. Here was a dark room that smelled of growing things. The only thing she could find in a place like this was trouble. "Oh, Lord. We really should not be alone like this."

"Nonsense. You are the family's spiritual advisor. Who better to discuss such an important decision?" She turned, and would have tripped on her skirts but for the arm Evan put out to steady her. Then her hand was on his shoulder as she looked up into his eyes. "I think we have both come to the same conclusion, haven't we?"

"Concerning Lord Whittendale?"

"Bother Lord Whittendale." Alice stepped closer still, and licked her lips.

Evan Merriweather was a man of honor, a man of principles, a man of the cloth, by heaven. Hell, he was merely a man. He kissed her. Her lips were as sweet as he'd known they would be; her body as soft in his arms as he'd dreamed it would be; her tiny mews of pleasure as heady as a choir of angels. "The Devil!" He dropped his arms, and nearly dropped Alice. "Good grief, what am I doing?"

"You are kissing me, and about time, sir."

"No, no. I cannot kiss you!"

"But you do it so well," she teased, a tender smile on her pinkened lips.

"No, I mean I cannot compromise you. Your father's trust . . . my calling. This is wrong, my dear."

"Oh, then you do not love me? That would make it wrong indeed. I thought . . . That is, forgive me if I was wrong." A tear trailed down her silky cheek.

"Oh, Lord," he cried, kissing the tear away. "Of course I love you, my angel, more than life. I have from the first minute I saw you. But do you . . . ? That is, could you . . . ?"

"Love you? Of course, silly. Or did you think I kiss every gentleman of my acquaintance in Mama's conservatory?"

So he had to kiss her again, until his conscience pricked him. No, this time it was a cactus. "Thunderation, Alice, you deserve so much better than I can give you."

"Do you mean I deserve a cold and empty marriage, as I would have with Lord Whittendale?"

"Never. But you know it will take an act of divine intervention before your father gives us his blessing."

Alice stood on tiptoe and kissed his cheek. "Well, you are on good terms with the Lord, aren't you?"

4

Evan could speak to God, but he couldn't speak to Squire until he'd spoken to the viscount. Without an improvement in his condition, Mr. Merriweather would not, could not, subject his beloved to life in the vicarage. Alice thought her father would relent and support them, but Evan could not bear to take both Prescott's daughter and his charity. What kind of man battens on his in-laws? Rather he batten on his distant cousin, who could well afford to pay an honest wage.

Dressing with care once more, Evan set out for White Oaks, Lord Whittendale's estate. By the time he got there, though, a cold, windy rain had set in, so he was damp and disheveled, chilled to the bone. The viscount's niffy-naffy London butler made him wait in the unheated hall, dripping on the marble entry, while he inquired if his lordship was receiving. Evan could hear laughter from down the corridor, men's and women's both, so the viscount was already entertaining. Surely a lord's pleasures could be interrupted a moment for the Lord's work?

Feeling more wretched and clumsy with every step, Evan followed the starched-up butler down the hall. If the servant was so top-lofty, he thought, how accommodating could the master be? The majordomo snapped his fingers at a footman to take Merriweather's coat and hat, rather than soil his own immaculate white gloves. Perhaps in similar manner Whittendale would try to relegate Evan to his secretary's care, rather than disturb his revelries. Not this time, the vicar swore to himself.

The company was arrayed as if for portraits, in elegant

groupings of twos and threes. Posed most becomingly, dressed in silks and satins, with jewels sparkling from necks, wrists, and cravats, they all had drinks or cards or each other in hand, and the clock not yet gone on noon. A few looked up from their conversations, then went back to their pastimes, dismissing the rumpled rustic as of no account. One or two of the woman smiled at him speculatively, as if watching his coat stretch across his shoulders. Lud, he thought in panic, what if the seams were finally giving out? He'd be half-naked in the *haute monde*. Evan almost turned and fled back the muddy way he had come. No, he had to speak his piece. For St. Cecilia's. For Alice.

The viscount strode forward, his hand extended. Surprised, Evan shook it, noting his lordship's firm grip. Whittendale was a noted sportsman, after all, so Merriweather should not have been unready, yet he'd been recalling the dissipated, debauched, and drink-sodden spawn of the devil from their previous interview. Instead, the viscount was the picture of good health and good grooming, some few years older than Evan's own six-and-twenty, with black hair that fell in deliberate tousles. Evan was sure the viscount did not have a cowlick, just as he was sure the gentleman's well-fitting, securely stitched coat cost more than his own yearly stipend.

The viscount was about Evan's height, but he seemed of sturdier build, and his brown eyes were laughing at the vicar's inspection. "Do I pass muster, old chap? Or were you expecting that I'd grown horns and a tail since we met last? A bad day, if I recall, after a good night. Never mind. Come stand by the fire and warm yourself. Bea, fetch the good vicar some cognac, will you? No, better make that hot tea, from our visitor's disapproving looks. One of the early martyrs must have worn such an expression on his face just before meeting the lion."

A tall, stunning, auburn-haired woman in a flowing green velvet gown brought Evan a cup of tea. Her smile was enough to warm him to his damp toes, even without the blessedly hot brew. Whittendale's introduction confirmed that this vision was Beatrice, Lady Farnham. The sultry looks that passed between them and the seemingly accidental brushing of her skirts against Whittendale's thighs confirmed that they were lovers.

Embarrassed all over again, Evan stammered, "I . . . I did not mean to intrude, my lord, just to beg a moment of your time."

Whittendale sipped his cognac, his eyes watching Lady Farnham as she joined a pair of Tulips at the pianoforte. "Yes, yes, you are going to shame me into looking over your little church, aren't you? I did read your letters, you know."

He had not answered a one. "The living is in your keeping, my lord," Evan said. "No one else will see to the repairs, and I cannot afford to do more than patchwork with my income."

"Very well, I shall make an inspection. Perhaps I'll bring my guests this Sunday. Heaven knows they could use some religion."

Evan thought he'd start with the seven deadly sins. More than a few were in practice this morning: lust, sloth, avarice, and adultery, unless he missed his guess and a wedding ring or two. "There was another matter, my lord, if we could be private? I could return later if this is not a convenient time?" Evan hated having to make an appointment like some importunate tradesman, and he hated worse the idea of trekking home on such a miserable day and then back again. Still, he would not get the viscount's back up. The reverend realized, belatedly, that he should have sent round a note asking the viscount to name a time for their meeting. Of course, he had no handy footman to carry the message, and he doubted Lord Whittendale would have replied at all.

To Evan's relief, the viscount shook his head. "Nonsense. You are already here. Since my guests and I are forced indoors by the poor weather, this is an opportune moment, although I cannot imagine what's important enough to bring you out in the rain." He pulled a quizzing glass on a ribbon from his pocket and surveyed Evan's wet, muddy boots. "Gads, did you walk the distance?"

"The vicarage has no mount, my lord." In case the not-so-gentle hint irritated his host, Evan added, "Exercise is good for the soul, my lord."

"So is a hot fire on a cold day, dash it. Well, come along, then. We can be private in my book room."

Evan regretfully put down his tea, which he had been letting cool. Thank goodness his hands were no longer numb from holding the fragile cup, he thought. Thank goodness he hadn't dropped the dainty thing. He followed his patron back to the hallway, past the poker-backed butler. Before they could be seated, a footman brought in another tray. "Lady Farnham thought your guest might wish refreshments, my lord."

"How kind of her," Evan said as he accepted a mug of hot lambswool punch, for its warmth and its encouragement. He cleared his throat and began his memorized speech: "You see, my lord, there is more wrong with St.

Cecilia's than a rotted roof and loose floorboards. The whole neighborhood is in difficulties, and I cannot make your steward understand that it is in your interest to meet those needs."

"I'm not sure I understand myself how emptying my coffers to fix highways and drainage ditches is of any benefit to me, but I will look into it. You're late, you see. The squire was already at me about the parish, too, as if I was in short pants again, needing a lecture on my responsibilities. I suppose I can check if my steward is doing a competent job."

"I am sure you will make a fair judgment once you visit the tenant farmers and the villagers."

"Deuce take it, I said I'd look at your church, not spend my time inspecting pig pens and cow byres. That other is my steward's job, and if he is not doing it, I'll find another." His handsome dark eyes narrowed. "You and Squire didn't discuss this between you, did you?"

"No, my lord. Well, yes, but not in so many words, just that we were both pleased to see you in Sussex. We are glad of the opportunity to bring injustices to your notice." He had to add, in all honesty, "Squire did mention he was hoping you'd decide to stay on in the country."

"Not bloody—pardon, not blessed likely. I will see what's to be done, though, just to stop the flow of mail. I'm not Golden Ball, you understand. I cannot fix all the woes of the world with my bank checks."

"Of course not. No one expects that." Evan took another sip of his toddy, feeling the spirits warm him from the inside out. "Simply put, we are hoping that, once you are aware of the deplorable conditions, you will see fit to make an increase in the living wages of those who are dependent upon you." He tacked on a "my lord."

"Like yourself, you mean?"

Evan felt his cheeks growing warm now. "I . . . ah . . ."

Whittendale laughed. "Squire mentioned your plight, too. He sang your praises for what you've tried to do for the people, said you needed some support. I'll look into it."

The viscount was being so reasonable, not at all condescending, that the vicar couldn't help raising his estimation of the man. Why, Evan thought he might even like the gentleman. Until Lord Whittendale said, "Squire mentioned his daughter, too."

Evan detested the dastard. He also dropped his napkin. When he bent to retrieve it, the sound of ripping stitches reverberated through the room.

The viscount had his obnoxious quizzing glass out again. "You are in a sad way, aren't you?"

May he never know how sad, Evan silently prayed around a forced smile.

Whittendale sat back in his chair. "But tell me about Squire's daughter. Little Alice used to be a charmer. Is she still? I know I saw her at some ball or other, but all those chits in their white gowns look alike."

"That would have been Miss Prescott's come-out at Lady Henesley's. And yes, Miss Prescott is still everything pleasing. A fine young woman. A blessing to the neighborhood, in fact."

"I suppose she'd make some chap an admirable wife, then?" His lordship stared into his cup of cheer, without any. "As Prescott and my innumerable female relations keep reminding me, it is past time I considered setting up my nursery. I do not relish shopping the Marriage Mart." He swallowed the contents of his cup and poured another, shuddering. "Almack's, by Hades. Be simpler to take one who's to hand."

Evan felt compelled to defend his Alice as more than just a convenient solution to a pesky problem. "Miss Prescott would make any man an excellent wife. She is kind and intelligent, compassionate to those less fortunate."

Whittendale winced. "A veritable paragon of virtue. Lud, that I've come to this. I suppose that's what parson's mousetrap is all about."

"Not in this parson's book, my lord. What about affection, loyalty, shared interests?" Evan was repeating what he'd told Alice's father, hoping to be heeded this time. "What about love and passion? Do you not want those things from the woman with whom you will spend the rest of your life?"

Whittendale grimaced at the "rest of your life" part. "Hell, no. That's why they make mistresses, don't you know? A chap wouldn't want a wife enacting Cheltenham tragedies every time he decided to attend a mill instead of another blasted musicale, or when he let his eye wander, if you know what I mean." He noted Evan's frown. "No, of course you don't. Forgot your calling. Trust me, Vicar, a well-brought-up miss makes a conformable wife, and a comfortable life, without all those other entanglements."

Knowing he was stepping beyond the line, even for a supposed spiritual advisor, Evan felt he had to say, "Lady Farnham is a beautiful woman who shares your way of life."

Lord Whittendale nodded his agreement, then raised one dark eyebrow. "So?"

"So she would make you a more suitable bride than Alice . . . Miss Prescott."

The viscount threw his head back and laughed. "You really are a green 'un, Merriweather, trying to legitimize a liaison. A man don't marry his mistress. Oh, Prinny might have tried, but the scandal sheets made a laughingstock out of him. Lady Whittendale, when I finally take a bride, will be unsullied, with a spotless reputation, as befits my station in life." He held up a manicured hand with a flashing ruby in his signet ring. "Not that Bea is a lightskirt, mind, or would play me false while we have an understanding. She's a good sort, Beatrice is. Married off to the old windbag at an early age, and never strayed from his side that I ever heard. The thing is, Reverend, with no bark on it, Bea is used goods."

"What, like a carriage discarded for a newer model?" Evan was appalled. "She is a woman, my lord, not an old shoe."

The viscount's eyebrow raised again. "I think you forget who pays your salary, sirrah. The salary you wish increased. Or perhaps you think those clerical collars give you license to poke your nose where it don't belong."

Where he didn't belong was in the profligate's parlor, trying to impart a smidgeon of a scruple. Evan set his cup down and stood. "I have taken enough of your time, my lord. I appreciate your promise to address the needs of our little community."

"Yes, yes. I shall be at the chapel on Sunday, as promised. I suppose the squire's chit will attend, so I can take a look at her then, too." Walking the vicar to the door, Lord Whittendale added, "You know, Merriweather, you ought to consider taking a wife yourself. Find a homely woman with a handsome dowry, and you will be set for life. You won't need to be hanging on my sleeve for every little thing like the carriage I'll send you home in."

Missing windows and rotted pews were no little thing. The viscount would see for himself, so Evan had to be satisfied for now. He bowed his head. "Too kind, my lord. As a matter of fact, I am also considering matrimony."

With the same woman.

They were supposed to be putting flowers in urns, instead of roses in Alice's cheeks. The placement of the wreaths and boughs for Whittendale's impending visit had deteriorated to placing not so chaste kisses. Evan Merriweather was a devilish kisser, for a holy man. In fact, 'twas a good thing mistletoe was considered too pagan for the church, or Heaven alone knew where such goings-on would lead.

The mice knew.

"You see, everyone understands the rules about 'Be fruitful and multiply.' Even human people."

"Aye, and these two need our help, too, so keep gnawing. They can't mate until we rescue the church, no more than we can."

The last remaining St. Cecilia Churchmice were in St. Francis's niche, grinding away at the layers of paint coating their favorite golden statue.

"But we're getting nowhere," Passeth-All-Understanding complained. "My teeth are worn to nubbins, and we'll never have St. Francis shiny enough by Christmas Eve for anyone to notice."

"We will if you stop staring out the crack in the wall at that little field mouse." Exultemus Domine flicked his whiskers clear of paint chips. "Besides, as soon as the vicar and that nice Miss Alice leave, we can go nibble on the meal she brought for us."

"Those are flowers and greens, Ed."

"They call it salad. Not filling, but better than nothing. Keep gnawing."

5

They did not want the church to look shabby and unloved for the London visitors, but Evan and Alice did not want St. Cecilia's to look so festive that Lord Whittendale could ignore the disrepair.

The mice helped. They ate the decorations.

Balancing on that same thin line, Evan spent hours on a sermon that would gently nudge his congregation toward the path of righteousness, without being either censorious of the sinners or accepting of the sins.

The mice helped. They ate his notes.

Reciting from memory, the Reverend Mr. Merriweather first had to master a nearly uncontrollable urge to stare at Alice, who looked enchanting to him in a blue bonnet and a warm red wool cloak. Sitting between her mother and her great-aunt Minerva in the third row, Alice kept her eyes on her prayer book, but a tender smile played upon her lips—the lips he'd been kissing. Evan lost his place and had to start over.

This time he forced his eyes to the rest of the congregation. The few faithful worshipers from the village were sitting in the last rows as usual, ready to bolt if the roof collapsed. They were all wrapped in shawls and mufflers, for the church was as cold as Lord Whittendale's heart this mid-December morning. The White Oaks house party occupied the first two pews, dressed in all their finery, with Lady Farnham at the viscount's side, in a gaily decorated bonnet and fur-lined mantle. Whittendale looked bored, but the beautiful young widow nodded encouragingly, so Evan cleared his throat and began again, trying to inject a bit more fervor, a touch of fire and brimstone along with the—

"Cherries! I see cherries!" Passeth-All-Understanding was jumping up and down on St. Francis's right side.

White-muzzled Exultemus Domine frowned from the statue's other side. "Can't be cherries. Cherries are in summer. This is winter, you catbait."

"Your eyesight is as dull as your teeth, Ed. I tell you, I see cherries on that lady's hat." The younger mouse wrinkled his nose. "It even smells like cherries."

"No, the human people roll in flowers so they don't smell so bad. That's what has you confused."

"I know cherries when I see them!" And Passeth-All-Understanding was going to get himself some. He leaped from the statue's niche to the mildewed molding, then scurried down a warped wall panel and under an equally flawed floorboard, coming up again at the correct crumbling pew. He climbed nimbly up the back of the wooden seat and jumped from there onto Lady Farnham's shoulder, thence to her high collar, just inches away from the cherries on her bonnet. He was just about to reach up for one of the tender delicacies when he realized he was standing on the enemy—an ermine. A jumped-up weasel, to be sure, but still a mouse-menace. So he screamed.

No one heard him, of course, nor the rest of Mr. Merriweather's sermon, for all the ladies were shrieking, the ones who were not swooning, at any rate. Thinking the roof must be falling in, the villagers fled for the door, clogging the exit, only to be shoved aside by the Londoners. Squire Prescott had to half carry his wife out, and Alice, white-faced, supported Aunt Minerva behind him. Shouting "Tallyho," Lord Whittendale and one of his sporting friends took up the hunt after the tiny, terrified culprit, up the aisles and down the pews, until Passeth-All-Understanding passed between the fallen stones in the far corner and bolted for the out-of-doors. The gentlemen charged out the side door, still on the chase.

". . . So go forth and sin no more," Evan concluded to the echoing stones and plaster saints. If the mouse hole were big enough, he'd crawl through it himself.

Then he realized that the church was not entirely evacuated. Lady Farnham remained huddled in her seat, abandoned, ashen, trembling, clutching her Bible as if for defense. He approached her cautiously, lest he frighten the poor woman worse. "My lady, are you injured or unwell? Shall I fetch your maid? Lord Whittendale?"

She shook her head no.

"A glass of water, then? Wine?" He'd give her the sacramental wine, if that would help.

"No. Thank you."

"A vinaigrette?" He dubiously eyed the tiny beaded reticule dangling from her arm. "Smelling salts?"

"No. Please do not concern yourself, Mr. Merriweather. I will recover in a moment."

But Evan could see tears coursing down the widow's high cheekbones. He fumbled in his pocket to find his handkerchief, then debated handing such a plebeian linen square to her, aware that Lady Farnham was used to far finer fabrics. Then again, she was not used to being attacked by maniacal mice.

She accepted his handkerchief with a nod, then clasped it to her mouth in a wad, as if trying to stifle her sobs. Evan had nothing else to offer but comfort. He awkwardly patted her shoulder. "There, there, my dear. You'll feel better in a moment."

"No, I won't," she wailed, flinging herself into the vicar's arms. She clung there, weeping on his chest.

Giving solace to the sorrowful was one thing; holding his patron's mistress was quite another. Mr. Merriweather tried to loosen her arms from around his neck, but Lady Farnham was latched on like a limpet. Lud, how could he explain this to Lord Whittendale? How could he explain it to Alice? He cleared his throat. "My dear lady, I know you were startled, but it was only a mouse."

She laughed, a pitiful keening sound, but sat back, blotting at her eyes and nose. "No, it's not only a mouse. It's a baby."

"A baby? You're . . . ? His? Of course it is. I should not have asked. Have you told him?"

"What for?"

"So he can do the honorable thing, of course."

"Oh, he would do what the polite world considers proper—give me a check and a deed to a little cottage somewhere. He might even come visit now and again when London grew too hot or too cold or too thin of company."

"I meant that he would marry you if he knew about the baby."

She made an unladylike sound. "In your prayers, Reverend. In the real world, a man does not marry his mistress, no matter how much she loves him."

"So everyone keeps telling me. Who makes these wretched rules anyway? An enceinte mistress is precisely whom a man should marry, to give his child a name, to restore his lady's reputation. Especially if he loves her in return."

"I suppose Randolph does love me, in his way. Not enough, however, to risk society's censure." She started to shred Evan's best handkerchief, adding to his misery.

"What shall you do, then?"

Beatrice shrugged. "I cannot go to my family, or the Farnham Dower House, for the shame. I suppose I could travel abroad with the bit of money I inherited from my husband's estate, and I can always sell my jewelry. Randy has been very generous, you know." She choked back a sob. "So I will be able to take up my life anew, after the child is born." She began to weep again. "But without my baby. Only without my child. How can I do that, give up my own flesh and blood?"

Evan could not even fix the church's roof. How could he fix Lady Farnham's troubles? "Perhaps you can convince another man to marry you. A beautiful woman with a bank account ought to have no difficulty finding a husband." Evan knew he was suggesting just the sort of cold-blooded, business-arrangement type of marriage that he deplored, but needs must when the devil drove. No child should be born a bastard.

"Do you think I have not considered such a course? How can I find an eligible *parti* while I am in the Randy's keeping? There is not one man in London brave enough to poach on his preserves. Besides, how can I give myself to another man, knowing that I only want Whittendale, hard as that may be to believe? How unfair to this hypothetical husband, a wife lacking both her virginity and her heart. I could not be that dishonest to any man I cared for enough to marry."

Now she discovered a sense of honor? Evan thought. He shook his head, wishing he had his handkerchief to mop his damp brow. Fornication was acceptable but fabrication was not? He would never understand the *beau monde* and its morality, or lack thereof.

Lady Farnham, meanwhile, had regained some of her composure and was regarding Mr. Merriweather with a speculative eye. She noted that he was thin but nicely muscled, with a full head of sandy hair in need of a trimming. "It seems to me that you could do with a helpmeet, too. Especially one with a bit of blunt. I don't suppose . . . ?"

"M-me?" His voice came out like the bleating of a goat. "That is, I could not offer you the life you are used to, the style you enjoy, not even with your money. I am a simple country vicar, and content to remain as such. I am honored—nay, I am confounded—that you could consider me in your dilemma, but I wish my wife to love me, as I would love her, and no others."

She nodded. "It was a moment's thought, nothing more, but I'd wager you would make a good father."

Evan thought of that quiverful of children Alice wanted, all blue-eyed, blond-haired cherubim. He would love them, every one of them, but he could not feed them or clothe them or send them to school. He sighed. "I fear I might never know, for it is going to take a power greater than mine to see such a thing come to pass. I cannot afford a dog, much less a wife and children."

Now she sighed. "Life seems so unfair sometimes."

"But never hopeless. We'll both come about, I swear. The Lord will provide."

Lady Farnham looked around, noting the angled pole supporting the roof, the boarded-over windows. "It seems the Lord is having troubles enough providing for His own house."

The young church mouse had doubled back through another hole in the stone wall of St. Cecilia's. He was hiding under the floorboards, quivering, catching his breath, and getting lectured.

"For certain you were named rightly." Exultemus Domine was also quivering, in outrage. "For it passes all understanding how you can be as greedy as a fox cub and as stupid as a duck. What if the lady had hit you with her Bible, or one of those panicked fools had stepped on you? What if Dread Fred were on patrol outside? Then what would happen? Our whole line would die out, that's what. Not one Churchmouse would remain to pass on our ancient heritage. Don't you understand responsibility, destiny, Noah-blessed oblige?"

"Oh, stop nattering at me and listen. They're talking about Viscount Whittendale."

After hearing Lady Farnham's tale of woe, Ed wrinkled his nose as if he smelled a ferret. "His lordship is a wicked, wicked man."

"Aye, but he's the one getting to sow his seed."

6

"The devil!" Arriving back inside the church, the viscount was not best pleased to find his mistress nearly in Merriweather's lap.

Misinterpreting his lordship's exclamation, Evan jumped to his feet, explaining, "Lady Farnham is not injured, merely frightened."

Belatedly, Whittendale noticed Beatrice's tear-streaked cheeks and reddened eyes. "Dash it, Bea, it ain't like you to be hen-hearted. You drive with me in my phaeton, don't you?" When she gave him a teary smile, he held out his hand. "There's my girl. Come on now, the others are waiting in the carriages to return to White Oaks."

Instead of mounting his chestnut gelding to ride back alongside the carriage, Whittendale motioned the driver to proceed. He returned to the church, tapping his crop against his leg.

"Blast it, Merriweather, were you trying to make a fool out of me in front of my friends?"

Evan was trying to restore the trampled greenery. "What, do you think I arranged for a mouse to run amok in my church?"

"I am not speaking about your deuced resident rodents. I'm referring to your arms around my *chère ami.* I can just imagine all the talk if any of the fellows had seen that tender little episode. They'd laugh that I was being supplanted in the lady's affections by an impoverished cleric in ill-fitting clothes."

Evan would not be cowed. "She was startled, and you were not here to soothe her, that was all."

"You were holding her hand, by George!" The viscount slapped his crop against the first pew, disturbing the dry rot. "I saw the way you were looking at the little Prescott chit, and you might get away with that until I come to terms with her father, but you have no right to be looking at Bea Farnham, much less touching her."

"As a man of the cloth I have every right to stand as spiritual advisor to whomever needs my comfort and my counsel."

Lord Whittendale recalled Bea's wistful farewell to the vicar, and her promise to visit St. Cecilia's again. "No one comforts my woman but me, do you hear me?"

Evan frowned. "I heard a troubled woman not getting solace from those who should support her in her hour of need."

"Need? Need? Bea wants for nothing. She wouldn't have any need for you if your cheese-paring church wasn't over-ridden by rats!"

The vicar was a forgiving man, but an insult to his church was a slap in the face. Being accused of dalliance with a demi-rep was bad enough; being charged with bad housekeeping in the home of the Lord was too much. Evan squared his shoulders, glad for the extra heft. "What do you know about need? You have never wanted for anything in your life, except for a conscience, perhaps. If you met your responsibilities, the church wouldn't be infested and your lady wouldn't be weeping."

"How dare you lecture me on my duties, you impertinent clod. If you weren't in orders, I'd order you horse-whipped."

Evan snapped back to the man who thought his wealth and title could purchase Alice, "If I weren't in orders, I'd pop your cork for your treatment of those around you, especially women."

"Hah! I'd like to see you try."

Things might have progressed to a bloody, schoolboyish conclusion, but one of the floorboards suddenly shifted with a loud squeak.

Recalled to their location—and their respective dignities—the vicar and the viscount both nodded and stepped back. The reverend knelt to inspect the faulty board, while the lord paced toward the rear door. Before he left, however, Whittendale warned Evan: "I will brook no interference with my females, not the ones I bed nor the one I'll wed. Stay away from Bea Farnham and the Prescott chit or I'll tear this place down with my bare hands."

Evan shifted the board back into alignment with its fellows and straightened up. "You'll never marry Alice Prescott," he told his supposed benefactor, "not after I inform Squire that you intend to litter the countryside with your butter stamps."

"Butter stamps? I have never left a by-blow any— Bea? She is increasing?" Lord Whittendale sat down abruptly in the last row.

Evan blanched. "She did not want to tell you."

"Of course not, the peagoose. She knows I'll send her into the countryside somewhere, and she can't bear to miss a ball. She'll have to forgo the spring Season, I suppose. Can't have a breeding female on my arm."

"That's all you can think of, parties and appearances? What about the child? Have you thought about the child for one instant?"

"I only just heard about the brat this minute, by Jupiter.

I suppose I can find a decent family to take it in. Give it all the best, that kind of thing."

"The best? You'd buy your son a pony and send him to an expensive school. You'd offer your daughter a china doll and a dowry. That's your best. But what about love, what about Lady Farnham's heartache to hold her own babe to her breast?"

"Thunderation, this is none of your concern."

Whittendale stood to leave, but was stopped at the door by the reverend's words: "Can you bear to see another man raise your child? What if he drinks or grows violent? What if the mother tells the poor babe that his own parents did not want him? Is that what you want for your son? Can you truly live with such a decision?"

Whittendale hesitated at the threshold, almost as if he was considering the vicar's questions. Then he straightened his caped riding coat around his shoulders and turned with a sneer. "Stay out of affairs that are beyond your ken, Merriweather. You have a small church and a small mind."

The viscount brushed right past Alice on the church steps without recognizing her. He tipped his hat automatically, but was concentrating too hard on his own thoughts, and on the rickety stairs, to notice that this was the woman he intended to marry.

Alice dropped a curtsey and a murmured "My lord," before hurrying inside. She had seen her mother dosed with the laudanum bottle, her father ensconced with the brandy bottle, and her great-aunt closeted with the ink bottle. Aunt Minerva was writing all of her friends about the debacle, how all those fancified London swells went sprinting for their lives as if the Hounds of Hell were snapping at their heels, instead of a wee bit of whiskers. This was the most entertainment she'd seen in Lower Winfrey in years. Alice, of course, had not shared her relative's delight. Using the usual Sunday food baskets as an excuse, she'd driven her pony cart to the church, and Mr. Merriweather, as soon as she could, just in time to overhear the last of the viscount's conversation.

"Heavens," was all she could say, sinking onto a pew next to Evan, under the statue of St. Francis.

Evan had his head bowed, his hands clenched on the back of the seat in front of him, the picture of despair. He couldn't look at his beloved. "Now I have torn it for sure. I've gone and offended Lord Whittendale so badly that he'll never help us."

Alice put her gloved hand over one of his. "You cannot know that for certain. When he gets over his shock and his anger, perhaps your words will have some better effect on him."

"No. If he thinks about what I said at all, he's liable to replace me as vicar here altogether. Ah, Alice, I am so sorry."

"He's the one who should be sorry, Evan, for planning to abandon his child and its mother."

"You heard, then?"

"Yes, and I think all the less of Lord Whittendale for his cold heart. No matter what happens, if Papa never gives us permission to wed, I would never marry a man who could leave his baby for strangers to rear."

He grasped her hand. "Good, for seeing you as another man's bride would be bad enough, but to think of you going to an arrogant jackass who would not appreciate you as you deserve would break my own heart all over again.

If I cannot have you, I can at least pray for your happiness with an admirable man."

"You are kinder than I, my dearest, for if I cannot marry you, I would despise the woman who did. Nor do I think I could bear to see you happy in such a union, whilst I was steeped in misery. No, I would have to leave, go somewhere I would not be reminded every day of my own loss, if such a place exists."

He had to bring her hand to his lips, he simply had to. "I will have no other woman to wife, I swear." Evan would do nothing more than kiss her gloved fingers, despite the invitation in her blue eyes. In fact, he regretted the kisses they had already shared. No, he did not rue the dishonorable kisses, he regretted that there could never be any more. And that he'd sent Lord Whittendale away in anger.

"I pity the poor female the viscount does marry," he said now, turning the subject from his dismal thoughts. "Such a one as Lord Whittendale would make a wretched husband for any woman."

"And a dreadful father, I should think, even to his legitimate offspring. Why, he'd likely forget his children's names."

"And their birthdays, unless his secretary reminded him," Evan added.

"Or if they threw spots from strawberries, or were afraid of thunder."

"He'd never take his sons fishing, nor share dolls' tea parties with his daughters."

"What, and chance soiling his boots or having his friends see him? Never." Alice squeezed Evan's hand and said, "You, however, would make an excellent father, my dear Mr. Merriweather."

Evan laughed, but without humor. "So everyone seems to think, for all the good anyone's opinions will do. I am afraid it will take a miracle for sure now for me to afford a wife and children."

"We have to have faith, Evan."

"Oh, I do, my dear," he said, brushing flakes of paint off her shoulder. "I do, even with the church falling down around our ears. Nor do I intend to sit around waiting for Lord Whittendale to develop Christmas cheer and a generous spirit. After we deliver your bundles of food, I can start splitting wood for new stair treads this very afternoon, and I can get rid of the mice, at least. I'm sure Mrs. Cotter won't mind if I close her cat in here for a bit."

"Now see what you've done, fleas-for-brains?"

7

Lady Farnham returned to St. Cecilia's as promised, with a basket of food from the White Oaks kitchen for the needy. She managed to get Lord Whittendale to drive her, to carry the hamper inside, and to apologize for any insult he may inadvertently have given Mr. Merriweather.

Inadvertent? The man had nearly threatened to have Evan boiled in oil for merely speaking to this woman. Or to Alice. Still, the vicar graciously accepted the basket and the new opportunity to win the viscount to St. Cecilia's side. A reprieve, thank the Lord. He gladly shook the peer's hand, then felt a coin pressed into his own palm. The viscount might merely be trying to appease his conscience,

Evan thought, but St. Cecilia's would be grateful nevertheless. He put the coin in his pocket.

When his lordship left to wait outside while the beautiful young widow prayed, Evan softly vowed, "Never again will I doubt the power of prayers."

Lady Farnham smiled. "And never doubt the effect of a woman's weeping. When Randolph told me what he had said to you, I confess I turned into a watering pot again. I understand women become highly emotional at such times."

"He must love you very much, then, to care about your tears."

She shrugged in her fur-lined cloak as she sat in one of the far pews, indicating that Evan should sit with her. "I suppose he does, in his way."

"But not enough to . . . ?"

Bea dabbed at her eyes with a scrap of lace-edged linen. Evan reached for his own, more adequate, handkerchief, but Lady Farnham shook her head. "No, I have used up all my tears. In fact, I must return the handkerchief you so kindly lent me."

Evan took the freshly laundered square she held out, feeling the coins in its folds. "This is not necessary, my lady."

"No, but you and your little church need it far more than I do. A few shillings will not make a difference in my condition, but they might mean the difference between an empty larder and a full one for some of your parishioners."

"I thank you, madam, but surely you are going to need every groat for when—"

"No, Randy is being very generous. Shortly after Christmas he is going to purchase a little cottage not far from

London, so that he can come visit frequently. He will make sure I have the best of care and want for nothing. I . . . I have hopes that he will let me stay on there with the baby, although he says he will have his solicitor look for a likely family. Perhaps if I cry enough, he will relent. Who knows? I understand that such an unsanctioned arrangement cannot find acceptance in the eyes of the Church, but will you pray with me, Vicar?"

"Of course, my lady. Surely our Lord will hear your prayers, so close to Christmas and the birth of His own son."

While the vicar and the widow prayed, the mice eyed the wicker basket of food sitting so invitingly in the aisle.

"Got to be something better than paint chips in there, don't you think?"

Ed licked his lips. "And better than the pine needles from the decorations. I say we are as needy as anyone in the parish, and charity does begin at home."

"Let's go."

So the last remaining hopes of the Churchmouse clan took a break from their gnawing and scurried across St. Francis's niche, down the molding, under the loose floorboards, surfacing inches away from the basket.

The sexton's wife's cat was also speculating about the contents of Lady Farnham's basket, and his chances of helping himself to a chicken leg or a bit of cheese or an apple tart. He was deserving of a reward, wasn't he, keeping watch in this cold, drafty, dusty church, instead of sitting by Mrs. Cotter's nice warm cookstove? Fred cocked one scarred ear toward the praying pair and stealthily stalked toward supper. Instead he saw . . . dessert!

"Well, bless my soul if Christmas isn't coming a week early!" With a loud meow he leaped at the two mousekins.

Passeth-All-Understanding made it back to the gaping floorboard, with Dread Fred's fetid cat-breath on his shoulder, but elder Exultemus Domine was too slow. Now the marauding mouser was between him and the hole. The people were between him and the crumbling stone wall. Ed froze in place, as still and stiff as the statue of St. Francis.

"Run, Ed. Run for the roof! You'll be safe there."

So Ed fled, up the post that the vicar had propped in the corner to support one of the sagging roof beams. Dread Fred followed.

The pole collapsed under the weight of the well-fed Fred. With the sudden loss of the upright, the rotted roof beam groaned, shifted, and cracked. Cat, mouse, post, beam, and a good portion of the roof fell onto the floor of the church, scant feet away from Lady Farnham and Reverend Merriweather. She screamed, he screamed, and Mrs. Cotter, who was coming to fetch her precious puss for a spot of tea, screamed. Viscount Whittendale screamed from the outside, tearing into the church and shoving rubble out of his way as he raced to reach Beatrice's side.

Ed screamed, but no one heard him. He burrowed deeper in the debris.

Mrs. Cotter reached her pet first, not that anyone else was trying to rescue the feline.

A board had fallen on Dread Fred's head.

He bled, but he hung on by a thread, not quite dead.

Mrs. Potter scooped him up in her apron, sobbing that the church must truly be bedeviled, picking on innocent pusses now, instead of preachers. Still screaming, she carried him away to safety and his blanket-bed near the cook-stove.

Evan was choking on the cloud of disturbed dust, but he went to look at the damage as soon as he made sure Lady Farnham was uninjured. She was uninjured so far, but the way Lord Whittendale was clutching her to his chest, Evan worried that she'd soon have broken ribs.

"Are you all right, Bea?" the viscount was desperately asking. "Are you sure? God, when I heard that awful noise, I thought for a moment I had lost you."

Lady Farnham caught her breath and nodded. "I am fine, truly. Mr. Merriweather pushed me aside when he realized what was happening."

"And the baby? What about the baby?"

Lady Farnham reached up to wipe a smudge of dirt from his cheek, a smudge that had a suspiciously moist track through it. "We are both fine, I swear. But do you really care about the baby?"

"Lud, Bea, more than I thought possible. Losing the child now would have been the perfect solution, but I couldn't bear the idea of not seeing my son or daughter at your breast. Ah, Bea, I don't want any milk-and-water miss in my bed or sitting across the breakfast table or beside me at the Opera. I want you, none other. Perhaps I am a fool for needing such a near-tragedy to show me what I value most in this world, but will you marry me anyway, my dearest?"

"But what of Society?"

"Society be damned." The viscount noticed Merriweather standing nearby, the remnants of the wicker basket in his hands. "Sorry, Reverend." Then he turned back to Bea. "Say you will, darling, and make me the happiest of men."

"Oh, do, Lady Farnham," Evan put in, "before he changes his mind. That is, excuse me. The excitement, don't you know."

"You can give me your answer in the carriage, my love." The viscount scowled over her head. "As for you, Merriweather, rest assured I shall not change my mind. I owe you for protecting my lady, and for your plain speaking on Sunday, so I will raise your wages. That doesn't mean that I am willing to throw good money after bad, though. If no one will come to this church, cursed or not, I see no reason to repair it. I will make you a bargain, Merriweather. You fill this church for Christmas morning service, and I will make the repairs and endow your charities. Yes, and I'll make the vicarage more habitable, too. If the church is not used, especially on Christmas morning, it is not worth fixing, so I will let the living lapse. I'll ask the bishop to find you another post, and have Most Holy take over the parish duties.

"But Christmas is next week. I cannot—"

They were gone, their eyes only on each other.

"Watch out for the rotten stairs!" Evan called.

The viscount waved a casual acknowledgment with the hand that was not around Lady Farnham. "Next week."

As soon as word reached the Manor, Alice hurried to the church to assess the latest damage and disaster.

Evan was standing behind the lectern, using his handkerchief to wipe dirt from the ceiling off the large Bible there. A small collection of coins, two of them golden, rested beside the Book.

Alice picked her way over the debris, careful not to snag her cloak, and joined him at the front of the church. She looked up at the grayish-blue sky visible above and said, "At least it is not raining."

"Ah, my heart, trust you to find the silver lining in this cloud of dust." Then he went on to describe Lord Whittendale's ultimatum.

"How dare he make a game out of people's lives. That worm!"

"That worm is going to marry Lady Farnham after all, thank goodness, despite the censure of his friends and acquaintances."

"Then they will go back to London and not give another thought to St. Cecilia's or Lower Winfrey."

"No, I think he will keep his word about supporting the parish, if we meet his conditions."

Alice looked up, not to seek divine guidance, but to watch a passing cloud. "How can we satisfy him, Evan? The church has not been filled since the viscount's mother's funeral. There are not enough people in the village to fill the pews, even if no one goes to Most Holy instead."

Evan stacked the coins. "I've been thinking. I can use these contributions and the rest of my quarter's salary to fix the ceiling. Then our people might not be so anxious about attending St. Cecilia's."

Alice did not want to worry Evan further by reminding him that the villagers feared the bad luck of the previous vicars' deaths, not the bad roof. She nodded encouragingly.

"Or else," Evan reflected, "I could use the blunt to buy foodstuffs. If I promise the poor souls in the almshouse a Christmas dinner, maybe they will come to services. Unfortunately, I cannot do both. It's either the roof and the villagers, or the food and the unfortunate. Either way, the church will be half empty."

"No, it won't, for I have some pin money of my own put by. We can fix the church and have a feast to celebrate. And I can help with the repairs, and the baking, too."

He shook his head, sending dust from his hair back onto the Bible. "I cannot take your money, Alice."

Alice brushed a smudge from his cheek, her fingers lingering there. "It's not for you. It's for St. Cecilia's."

"But you know that without Lord Whittendale's money, we'll never have enough brass to make the church really safe for anyone to worship here, not even you. Especially you, my dear."

"I'll be here. And I will make sure everyone I know is here, to help save St. Cecilia's."

Evan kissed her fingers, so near his lips. "Poor Lord Whittendale."

"Poor, that makebait?"

"Aye. He doesn't get to marry the finest woman in the kingdom."

"I thought you liked Lady Farnham. She is certainly beautiful enough."

"She isn't you."

8

White Oaks had not opened its vast doors to the community in ages. Not since the viscount's mother's time had the huge ancient pile hosted what used to be an annual Christmas Eve ball. Tonight the party was twice as joyous, twice as lavish as any Lady Whittendale had ever thrown, for tonight the current titleholder was going to announce his engagement.

Money had flowed through village hands from the influx of travelers and traders. The restored fortress needed to be refurbished, restocked, and restaffed, and what could not be ordered in time from London was purchased nearby. Since everyone in the vicinity was also invited to the lively party in the barn if not the formal dance in the ballroom, spirits were high, and not just because spirits were flowing as well as Lord Whittendale's blunt.

One person was not enjoying himself. The Reverend Mr. Merriweather could not share in the joy of the occasion. Oh, he'd made a sincere blessing over the happy couple and, indeed, wished them well. He'd also blessed the meal, both at the long oak table and at the trestles set up for the common folk. He was pleased to see his neighbors so carefree, so happy in the moment, yet he could not join in their merriment. Here it was, Christmas Eve, perhaps his first, last, and only Christmas Eve as vicar of St. Cecilia's, and here he was, watching Alice dance with all the London bucks and blades. She was beautiful in her new gown of ivory lace over emerald-green satin, with holly twined in her upswept hair, and every man there knew it. All those wealthy, titled, landed gentlemen were waiting in line for her hand, to dazzle her with their diamond stickpins and polished manners, to shower her with flowery compliments and flirtatious conversation. Evan could no more turn a pretty phrase than he could turn into a Town Beau.

He'd had one dance with his beloved, a stately minuet as befitted his station, and their relationship as minister and congregant. Whittendale was getting to have nearly every dance with his affianced bride, the lucky dog. No one would think any the less of Lady Farnham, not in light of her betrothal, and the light of adoration in the viscount's eyes. No one would dare slight her, or bring up old gossip, not once the engagement was announced. Beatrice was going to be Lady Whittendale, a blanket of respectability that could ward off all but the chilliest of disapproval.

Envy sat heavily in Evan's heart, along with uncertainty over his own future.

Another gentleman was also less than delighted with the occasion. Mr. Prescott found Evan leaning against a pillar, half hidden by a potted palm tree. "Wretched thing, balls," Squire complained. "How they expect a fellow to cavort around on his toes after feeding him six courses, I'll never know." He accepted another glass of punch from a passing footman, and leaned on the other side of the pillar. "Much rather have a nap or a quiet game of cards. M'wife insists I stay right here, though, keeping an eye on Alice, what with all those randy, ramshackle rakes Whittendale calls friends around. As if one of those loose screws is going to drag the gal behind a drapery to steal a kiss when there's all this mistletoe in plain sight."

Botheration, Evan hadn't noticed the mistletoe. He could have— No, he could not have. He was the vicar—the impoverished vicar. He sighed.

Squire sighed louder, watching Alice float by in a cloud of lace, in the same set as Lord Whittendale and his radiant wife-to-be. Lady Farnham was wearing the Whittendale heirloom engagement ring, the enormous diamond reflecting the hundreds of candles around the room. "Deuce take it, I suppose now I'll have to take Alice back to London in the spring. I was hoping to be done with all those folderols and furbelows, especially at planting season."

Mr. Merriweather could only nod in commiseration. The thought of Alice going to London to find a *parti* to wed stuck in his throat like a piece of Mrs. Cotter's Christmas pudding.

"I don't suppose she mentioned an interest in any of these coxcombs when you were as close as inkle weavers all week, did she?" Squire asked hopefully. "I could get a ring on her finger by New Year's. Not the size of Lady Farnham's, of course. None of the popinjays can touch Whittendale's deep pockets. Not that I mean to sell my gal to the highest bidder or anything. Won't even hold out for a title if the chap is a decent sort."

The pain in Evan's chest grew with each of Squire's words. He swallowed and said, "No, she never mentioned any of Lord Whittendale's company by name, although I know she dined with them a time or two, and entertained some of the gentlemen at tea."

"Hmpf. She could have fixed any number of the toffs' attention if she'd set her mind to it and stayed home instead of spending every minute at St. Cecilia's. Her mother had to tie her down, nearly, to be at home in the afternoon."

"Miss Prescott was a great help this week. She lent her hand to mending the altar cloth and helping Mrs. Cotter prepare Christmas dinner for the needy. She taught the children their lines for the Nativity pageant, and she sewed their costumes. I don't know what I would have done without her." Yes, he did. He would have given up and handed in his resignation before Lord Whittendale could dismiss him from his post.

"Aye, she's a good girl, my Alice."

"There is none finer." Evan raised his own cup of wassail in a toast to the only woman he could ever love. Then he made his farewells, citing exhaustion and last-minute work on his sermon for the morning.

He was certainly tired from all the work he had done this week, and anxious about the morrow, but mostly he could not bear to wait for midnight and the lighting of the Yule log in White Oaks's cavernous hearth. All of the revelers would come into the Great Hall for the ceremony, where a sliver of last year's log would be used to start the new mammoth, thus ensuring the prosperity of the house and its inhabitants. Evan did not know what they would use as last year's kindling, since Lord Whittendale hadn't been in the county, but he did know that everyone would lift their glasses and cheer the viscount and his lady, toasting the health of his unborn sons, the continuance of his line, the hope of the community.

Evan was pleased for Lady Farnham, and more relieved that that firstborn child would bear his father's name. Still, he could not stay to watch.

Besides, he told himself, his sexton could not be trusted to leave the party in the barn in time to ring the church bell at midnight, or to be sober enough to pull the rope. If this was to be St. Cecilia's last Christmas, the bells had to ring.

He'd done his best to save the church, Evan reflected. He'd used his money to hire carpenters and buy lumber, and he'd been sawing and nailing alongside the workmen. The roof was secured, albeit temporarily. The new stairs would not collapse under the weight of the heaviest worshiper. A few broken pews were shored up, a few more stones were remortared. All the dust and dirt was swept out, fresh pine boughs, holly, and ivy were brought in.

Evan had not stopped there. He'd helped roll out the

gingerbread for the children, and found parts in the Nativity pageant for every child he could bribe, knowing their parents would then attend, if only to see their offspring as Magi and shepherds.

Now it was up to the Lord to see if His servant's best was good enough.

On his way home in the gig Alice had convinced the squire to put at his disposal, Evan counted. He did not count the miles back to the vicarage, nor the stars overhead, nor the number of smiles Alice had bestowed on her various dancing partners. No, he counted seats, empty seats.

The poor from the almshouse. The loyal villagers. The sheep farmers whose children were sheep in the pageant. Alice and her reluctant family. Those were all he could count on. And they were not enough. He doubted if any of the White Oaks guests would attend, not after the revelries of this evening. The rest of the gentry at the Christmas ball would undoubtedly go to Most Holy, with its gleaming stained glass windows and its choir's voices raised on high.

In despair, Evan knew the only thing to be raised at St. Cecilia's was more dust. He had too many seats, and too few sitters.

The mice had toiled mightily that week also. With Fred holding on to the last of his nine lives, and firmly intending to spend that one safely alongside Mrs. Cotter's nice warm stove, the desperate, determined duo worked all the harder, not having to look over their shoulders. They were invigorated by the crusts of bread and apple cores the carpenters left behind, too, as well as the vicar's efforts to save their home.

They had St. Francis polished to a fare-thee-well. His back side still had patches of paint and plaster, but his front shone as lustrous as soft fur and mouse spit could burnish it. His robes showed a few extra folds, and his face a few more wrinkles, where the gnawing had been a tad too enthusiastic, and one of his fingers was sadly missing altogether, but his smile seemed all the sweeter to the weary rodents. Surely now, after all of their work, one of the worshipers would notice the golden gleam.

Unfortunately, they realized St. Cecilia's had too many dark corners and not enough candles.

"What if no one sees the statue?" Pass fretted.

"They have to," Ed insisted. To a mouse's eyes, the gold was as unmistakable and beckoning as a ripening ear of corn.

"I don't know, Ed. These human people aren't all that bright. They forgot about hiding the golden statue when the bad men were coming, didn't they? We've got to do something."

So when Vicar Merriweather came to his church to pray for a miracle, he heard Cotter ring the bells for midnight. He heard the answering chorus of Most Holy's pair of bells chime back. And he heard another pair of tiny, tiny voices.

"Look to St. Francis," Evan thought he heard.

"Fine," he muttered. "Now I am hearing things. It is not enough that I shall lose my church and lose the woman I love; now I am to lose my mind as well."

"Look to St. Francis," floated again across the empty church.

Evan supposed it wouldn't hurt to pray to each and every one of the plaster saints in their niches, though he rather thought he'd do better starting with St. Jude, patron of lost causes. Still, he would not deny the little voice in his ear. Lifting his candle the better to pick out the correct niche, Evan walked to the side of the church.

There was St. Francis, one arm extended to an alighting sparrow, the other cradling a . . . bear? Another creature sat by his feet. Odd, Evan could not recall any such animals surrounding the saint when last he'd dusted the statue. He stepped closer, holding his candle higher.

"You see, you see!" Ed was hopping up and down, and Pass had to wrap his tail around St. Francis's neck to keep from falling off in his excitement.

"I see," Evan murmured, and he had eyes for nothing but the statue, gleaming golden in its niche, as bright as the Christmas star leading the Wise Men to Bethlehem, as bright as the love he had for Alice. "I see."

After the shortest prayer of thanks in Christendom, Evan ran for the door and shouted, "Ring that bell, Mr. Cotter. Keep ringing it. Tell everyone. We've got our miracle."

9

Most Holy Church was almost empty that Christmas morning. Everyone came to St. Cecilia's to see the golden statue, treasure lost since the times of Cromwell, found, by everything holy, on Christmas Eve.

The pews were filled, and the aisles, too. So many people crowded into the little building that the heat from their breaths warmed their bodies and their souls and the old stones of the church.

The collection plate was filled. Evan would not have to petition the bishop to sell the statue in order to finish the repairs, but would even have some money left to feed the hungry. There would not be so many needy mouths, not once Lord Whittendale kept his promise to better conditions for his dependents.

Alice's eyes were filled with tears of happiness.

Mr. Merriweather's heart was filled with joy and hope.

The mice's bellies were filled, too, with the slice of Christmas pudding the vicar had hidden behind the lectern where no one could see.

Never had there been a more glorious Christmas service. The children all remembered their parts, and so many voices joined in the hymns and carols that no choir could have sounded sweeter. Evan was so elated that his words, for once, flowed smoothly, movingly, in benediction. No souls burnt in eternal damnation in this sermon; he spoke only of the love of God for His children. Feeling the vicar's sincere spirituality, knowing he cared for their well-being as well as their redemption, the congregants vowed not to miss a single one of his Sunday services.

Evan knew that would take another miracle, but he smiled as he shook hands with everyone leaving the church. Some were on their way to the feast at the vicarage, while others were on their way home to share Christmas dinner with family and friends. Some were headed toward White Oaks and another elegant repast.

"My man of affairs will call on you in the morning, Merriweather, to see what's to be done and in what order," Lord Whittendale told him.

"I have some of the ready in the church funds now, my lord, so St. Cecilia's can get by on its own for a bit."

"Nonsense, the sooner the church is fully repaired, the better."

Lady Farnham, stunning in her white furs, laughed. "I told him I wanted to be wed in St. Cecilia's, that's why Randolph is in such a rush. A special license would only give rise to more talk, so we would prefer starting to call the banns this Sunday, if you will."

"I would be honored, my lady. And St. Cecilia's will be glistening for the wedding in three weeks, I swear it."

The viscount nodded. "And not a moment too soon, lest people start counting months. I'll come by later, after my guests have left, to discuss what changes we can bring to the parish. Perhaps we can establish a pottery or a brick-works, to employ some of our people, so they don't have to leave for positions in the factories and mines."

"Don't forget the school," Lady Farnham reminded him.

"That's right, we'll set up a proper school for the children, boys and girls, so they can better their lot in life. That's if you are willing to oversee its operation, at a raise in pay, of course, in addition to the increase I already promised."

"I . . . I . . ."

"Can't expect you to do more work without recompense. Yes, and I intend to recommend that the bishop consider you for rector of Most Holy, when old Bramblethorpe there retires. No reason you cannot hold two livings, earn a decent wage. That ought to make your days brighter, by Jupiter."

"You are too generous, my lord. That was never part of our bargain, nor a school nor a pottery."

"Nonsense, my son is going to be born here, isn't he? Can't have him living in some beggar's backwater."

"Your daughter Cecily will be born here," Lady Farnham corrected. "Then your son Francis."

"Francis?"

As the two left, arm in arm and bickering over the sex of their firstborn, Squire Prescott took their place, with his womenfolk behind him stopping to greet some of the neighbors.

The squire pumped Evan's hand. "Good show, lad, good show, I say. Didn't know you had it in you. Alice said you did, of course, but she always had a soft spot for this church. I heard what Lord Whittendale said about when Bramblethorpe retires, and I'll second his recommendation. Meantime you've got a respectable livelihood, eh?"

"More than respectable. In fact now I can—"

"And I suppose now that you've come into your own you'll be looking around you for a wife."

"Why no, I don't need to—"

The squire shook his head in regret. "You'll be off to London, I'd wager, before the cat can lick its ear."

Since the cat could barely lick its foot currently, Evan would not be leaving any time soon. He tried to tell Squire he had no intention of seeking a bride in London, or anywhere else, for that matter, but Prescott was bemoaning his fate. "Dash it, just when I find an eligible match for m'daughter, one that will keep her in style but close to home, he up and marries a dashing widow. Now you'll be looking over the crop of heiresses in Town, the devil take them, and I'll have to traipse off to Bath or some outlandish place to find puss a proper match."

"I am not going to London, Squire, and I am not looking for a bride. I already found one, if Alice will have me, and if we have your blessing. We do, don't we?"

"Love her, do you?"

"With all my heart, till my dying day."

"Good, for I fear she'll have no other. Just like her mother, she is, knows her own mind and won't settle for less. You're a lucky man, Vicar."

"She hasn't said yes yet."

Squire laughed. "She will."

She did, after the rest of the worshipers left the churchyard.

"You are sure, Alice? Life won't be all parties and pretty gowns and trips to Town."

"Such a life would be pointless, without you in it. But are you sure, Evan? You could find a woman with a larger dowry."

"But none I could love more. Will you marry me, my Alice, now that I am a man of means and can make you an honorable offer? I promise to fix the vicarage roof and windows first, of course, so you are not frozen by the drafts."

"I would marry you if we had to take up residence in the barn, my love. And I refuse to wait until all of the renovations are completed. You will just have to keep me warm until then."

As Alice and Evan went to help serve Christmas dinner in the vicarage, they made a detour around the back of the church, to seal their pledge with a kiss. They were out of sight of everyone but two very small observers.

"I told you they weren't very smart," said Pass, rubbing at his ear.

"How so? These two seem to be catching on to the really important business of life. I'd wager there's the patter of little feet in the nursery before next Christmas."

"What, are those barn mice moving in now that Dread Fred stays in the kitchen?"

"No, you dunderhead, a baby."

"Oh. Well, I might be a dunderhead, but how long do you figure before those human people think to look at the rest of the statues?"

The parishioners uncovered the rest of the gold before Twelfth Night. St. Cecilia's didn't need half as many candles, with all the gleaming. It just needed an extension, to hold everyone who came to see.

And Exultemus Domine was right: The Merriweathers had a daughter within the year, named Faith. She arrived not too many months after the somewhat premature birth of the viscount's heir, Randolph Francis Pemburton Whitmore.

Long before that, young Passeth-All-Understanding had a mate of his own, and her mother and sisters moved in, too, with a cousin or three, and an old auntie to keep Ed company. Together they managed to drag a new book behind the altar, for bedding and names for the next generation.

The firstborn, the biggest and strongest and smartest mousekin, was the cub chosen to be the leader, the one destined to guard the clan's perpetuation. They named him after the vicar who made sure they were well fed, and after the new book.

His name was Merriweather Christian Hymnal Churchmouse.

They called him Merry Christmouse, for short.

The Marriage Stakes

by Allison Lane

1

December 17, 1815

"Are you ready to talk about it?" Sophie asked her half sister as their hired carriage bounced across a rut. Caroline had said little since leaving London the previous afternoon.

Nor did she now. Hands cupped around her bulging stomach, she stared out the window as dusk faded toward full dark. Rocks rattled beneath the wheels.

Sophie ground her teeth. Every hour of silence increased her frustration. How could she ease Caroline's unhappiness if she didn't understand the problem? Where was the carefree sprite who had left with her new husband only a year ago?

A gust of wind knocked the carriage sideways. Sophie considered ordering the coachman to slow down, though she knew it was pointless. He had already ignored a dozen other requests in his determination to reach Bedworth tonight. But every jolt increased Caroline's discomfort.

"John died at Waterloo," murmured Caroline at last.

"I know." She'd seen his name on the casualty lists. "I also know he sent you to his aunt when he was posted to Brussels. You wrote that much from Vienna. What I don't know is why you never wrote again. Eight months without a word, Caroline. Mother is frantic. Her health has deteriorated badly, in part from concern over you."

Pain exploded through Caroline's eyes. "I wrote," she insisted. "When I didn't hear from you, I wrote again and yet again, assuming the other letters had gone astray so you no longer had my direction."

"For eight months?" Sophie snapped her mouth shut. Marriage hadn't changed Caroline's credulity. Her habits of air dreaming and accepting even ridiculous explanations so she needn't address problems had been points of contention since she'd been in the nursery.

"Maybe Aunt Agnes lost the letters," Caroline suggested wearily. "She handled the post, for I couldn't leave the house while I was increasing—or so she claimed; she never hid her contempt for my parentage, so she might have been hiding me. But what could I do? I was sick for weeks after reaching London. Then John died, and I lost interest in everything. I miss him so much." She burst into tears.

Sophie hugged her close even as she cursed herself for pressing. She had hoped that Caroline had repudiated her family to gain acceptance by society. That cause of her silence would have hurt, but at least their mother would have understood. Now her worst fears seemed true. Agnes Laiks sounded as arrogant and intolerant as her own father's family. John's elopement with the sixteen-year-old daughter of a land steward would have appalled the woman, for blood and connections were everything to the aristocracy. Lack of money could be overlooked. Breeding could not.

Poor Caroline. John had been a good man—kind, caring, and deeply in love. Not once had he decried Caroline's breeding, so when he'd received orders to return to his regiment, Sophie had approved an elopement. Now she wondered if he'd known his family would never accept his choice. Or had he also ignored reality?

"I don't think John understood his aunt," murmured Caroline, as if reading her mind. "He was always her favorite, so he expected her to rejoice over our marriage. But she'd wanted him to wed Lord Hadley's daughter. Richard is too ill to get an heir, so John would have inherited the viscountcy one day."

More complications, Sophie realized. She hadn't known that John expected the title. If Caroline's child was a boy, they would be plagued by the Laiks family forever. But she would address that problem later.

For now, she encouraged Caroline to talk about her months with Agnes Laiks. Every word validated her decision to flee with Caroline from London before Agnes returned from her morning calls.

John's aunt was obsessed with family and social position, and she decried the laxity with which her brother had raised his sons. Richard had turned into a dissipated wastrel who'd squandered years in brothels and opium dens before contracting consumption. Now he was dying. John had begun well by distinguishing himself in Spain, but in the end he'd disgraced his name by running off with Caroline. The various cousins weren't much better. To restore the family's reputation, Agnes hoped to raise the next viscount herself, avoiding the evils of tutors and schools so that he learned only her concept of duty. Once John wed a subservient bride, Agnes would join his household and take charge. His elopement had not changed her plans. If anything, it had provided another excuse to take over.

Sophie hid her fury with difficulty. The last thing Caroline needed was to realize that Agnes would have removed the baby from her keeping. Confining Caroline to the house prevented her from making friends who might object when she was packed off to the country after the child was born.

She should have checked on Caroline as soon as John died. Despite her own experiences with aristocratic cruelty, she should have known that Caroline would never repudiate her family.

Air dreams and childish excitement had filled Caroline's Vienna letters, but there had been no embarrassment over her origins. She could not have changed so quickly, especially knowing how much their mother had suffered from society's rejection. Nothing would have induced the girl to add to that pain.

Sophie prayed that her mistake would not cause worse trouble. The journey home would take nearly a week, even with good weather. She'd hired a job coach so Caroline wouldn't have to endure a crowded stage, but coaches were expensive. Money was scarce. It might take months to discover whether Agnes had lied when she claimed that John had made no provision for Caroline. They didn't have—

A loud crack rent the air. As the coach tilted crazily, Caroline screamed.

Sophie's head slammed into the side as she threw herself atop Caroline in protection. The carriage careened across the road, bouncing several times before coming to a stop.

Caroline whimpered.

"Are you all right?" Sophie asked, shakily sitting up.

"I think so."

The coachman cursed as he crawled from the ditch. Blood trickled down his temple.

"Anyone hurt?" he called.

"Just shaken. What happened?"

"Broken wheel." He kicked the remains. "Musta hit a rock."

Sophie snapped her mouth shut. Mentioning his speed served no purpose now.

"What can we do?" asked Caroline.

He wiped blood onto the sleeve of his greatcoat. "Coaching inn's about three miles up," he announced. "Can you ride?"

Sophie flinched. Caroline had feared horses since one had broken her leg in childhood. Judging from the size of her eyes, marriage to a cavalry officer had changed nothing. "No."

The coachman sighed. "Best stay here, then. You should be warm enough. I'll be back in an hour." Unbuckling the team, he mounted the leader and left.

Silence settled over the carriage—and darkness. The last of the sunset had faded from the western horizon.

"Does this mean we won't be home for Christmas?" asked Caroline in a small voice.

"Of course we will," Sophie hastened to assure her. "This delay should cost us no more than a day. Mother will be thrilled to see you and learn she will soon be a grandmother."

"It will be a relief to have her help," admitted Caroline. "I know little about babies."

She followed the admission with a spate of hopes and fears for her child. Sophie encouraged her to talk, for planning her future would help mitigate her grief. But even as Sophie listened, most of her mind fretted over what to do next. Despite her earlier assurances, she had no guarantee they would reach home by Christmas. This delay would cost her dearly. Every night on the road ate into her purse. Once the money ran out, they would be stranded.

She was wondering if transferring to the mail coach would harm the baby when Caroline clutched her stomach and screamed.

Damon glanced over his shoulder as the sky brightened behind him. Dawn was breaking, which meant he had been driving for two hours. But he was no closer to a decision than when he'd left home.

He should not have succumbed to impulse, but he had been desperate to escape the house. So many people had assembled that he'd had to open wings unused for years and force two and sometimes three people to share each room. Even the Elizabethan state rooms were in service, despite a century of disuse, and most of the villagers and tenants had been pressed into helping. People were everywhere, all of them making demands. After a month of unrelenting pressure, his head felt stuffed with lint. He needed to think, free of interruptions. So he'd gone for a drive.

The growing light revealed a signpost.

"How the devil did I get here?" he demanded in disgust. Bedworth was twenty miles from home, and a storm was rapidly swallowing the sky.

"Idiot." He was going to get wet, or worse. He started to turn, then remembered a track that could shave four miles from the journey if it didn't mire him in mud. He studied the clouds a moment, then pushed his team to a trot. He would try it.

Hunching his shoulders against a rising wind, he returned to his impending decision. He had to wed, and it had to be now. The crowd filling Westlake Abbey included two dozen eligible ladies. But despite a month of consideration, he still did not know which one to choose.

He shook his head. From the moment he left his rooms in the morning until he retired at night, he was surrounded. But even that didn't satisfy some. His mother had actually burst into his bedroom last night, urging him to accept Miss Fielding. His valet had routed his aunt from his wardrobe last week. He had to keep a gentleman at his side whenever he left his room to prevent compromises, for being mistress of Westlake Abbey was a coveted position even without the title and wealth that went with it.

As he slowed to turn down the track, he spotted a derelict Yellow Bounder in the distance—the job coach's color was unmistakable. He was thanking fate that he could afford his own vehicles when a scream rent the air. The Bounder was occupied.

Two minutes later, Damon jumped from his curricle. Another scream pierced his ears as he rapped sharply on the door.

"Are you badly injured?" he demanded.

"Thank God!" A woman emerged. "What took you so long?"

"I beg your pardon." He frowned.

Her shoulders sagged as she noted his curricle. "You didn't come from town?"

He shook his head. "I heard a scream."

"I can't imagine where that idiot coachman went," she muttered. "He promised to return in an hour."

"When was this?"

"Dusk." She nearly cursed, but changed it to, "Would you take my sister to Bedworth, sir? She is in labor."

He glanced at the narrow seat of his curricle.

"I can walk, but Caroline needs a bed and a midwife immediately."

Another scream faded into moans. "Sophie? Help me," sobbed a woman.

"We will try for that village," he decided, nodding toward a distant cluster of buildings along a narrow lane. "I doubt she can sit, so I must lead the horses."

"Thank you, sir." Relief smoothed the lines from her face. She was younger than he'd thought—mid-twenties perhaps. The dawn light revealed auburn hair, gray eyes, and cheeks turned rosy by the wind.

"Hold the team." He reached for the carriage door. "I'm Damon, by the way. Is this her first child?"

"Yes. Why?"

"First labors last longer—at least in horses."

"I hope so. I've no idea when this began. We thought yesterday's pain was caused by the bouncing carriage."

The words raised real fear, but he kept his face calm as a gust of wind tore the door from his hand. Inside, a pale blonde curled on the seat, clutching a rug round her shoulders. She barely looked fifteen. Blue eyes widened, and she tried to muffle her next scream.

Carrying her to the curricle, he tucked rugs around her to ward off the plummeting temperature. "Have you luggage, Sophie?" he asked.

"In the boot."

He was shoving two valises under the seat when the clouds opened, dousing them with freezing rain. "Damn." Raising the hood against the wind was a challenge, but even its limited protection would help Caroline.

"Easy, Max," he murmured as he led the team forward.

Sophie soothed his second horse. The storm and Caroline's agony were making the animals nervous.

"Why were you traveling so close to her confinement?" he asked, picking up speed after the first hundred yards. Sophie was sturdy enough that he needn't shorten his stride.

"Her husband is dead. I can't afford accommodations for more than a few nights, so we must return home."

"Where is home?"

"Cumberland, near the Scottish border." She glanced back as Caroline groaned. "Why couldn't this have waited until next week?"

"You really have nowhere to go?"

She shrugged. "John's family repudiated her—he is in line for a viscountcy, but she has only remote ties to the Quality."

"Which viscountcy?"

"Laiks."

He should not pry, but he couldn't help one last question. "The Laiks family is wealthy, so why can't you afford decent care?"

"Agnes Laiks swears John left Caroline nothing, though that does not sound like him. I will start inquiries when we reach home, but it will take time."

And in the meantime, she was penniless.

As they struggled through the deluge, Damon's mind fretted over the puzzle she presented. She was unlike anyone he knew, even others on the fringes of the gentry. To be here, she must have won a confrontation with Agnes Laiks—no mean feat, for the woman gave no quarter. Now she faced a host of problems—a sister in labor, a broken carriage, freezing rain, a lack of funds—with an equanimity he couldn't begin to match. How could she remain so calm?

Most women would be in hysterics by now. The rest would have swooned at the first sign of trouble. How refreshing to meet someone who could cope with disaster. She had more sense than any of the girls competing for his hand.

He ran down the list yet again, trying to guess how each candidate might face trouble. The images weren't pretty.

2

Sophie was frantic by the time they reached the buildings—which turned out to be a farm. But she took care to remain outwardly calm lest she communicate her fears to Caroline.

Wind slashed through her wet clothes. Only terror kept her feet moving. Without shelter, the baby would die. Without a midwife, Caroline might also die. And it would be her fault for forcing this journey. *You really have nowhere to go?* His question had plagued her every step of the way. Had she overreacted when she'd swept Caroline from Agnes's house? Perhaps Agnes wasn't the ogre instinct declared. Had she needlessly endangered her sister and the babe?

She might die even with shelter and help. That jostling did her no good.

Sophie thrust down the voice, though it spoke truly. Childbirth was perilous enough without this storm. Caroline's pains were coming faster and harder now. How could that frail body survive so much agony? She was barely seventeen.

"We're here." Damon's voice penetrated her stupor. "Hold the horses, Sophie. I'll—"

Caroline's scream drowned the rest of his words. This pain seemed endless, twisting Sophie's stomach into knots, but she could do nothing except hold the team steady and pray Damon could summon help.

It seemed an eternity before his pounding drew a response. The door opened, revealing a huge man who glared suspiciously at the curricle.

"We don't need no strangers round here," he growled.

"These ladies need help," insisted Damon, thrusting a booted foot over the threshold to keep the door open.

"Try Bedworth."

"There's no time. Mrs. Laiks is well advanced in her labor."

Another scream punctuated the statement.

" 'Tain't my fault you left it so long."

Sophie cringed. To the farmer, this looked like a gentleman taking his pregnant mistress to the country for her confinement, accompanied by a very bedraggled servant.

"Looks can be deceiving." Damon's voice sounded dangerous. "These ladies suffered an accident last night when their carriage lost a wheel. Instead of fetching help, their coachman disappeared."

"A nice stor—"

"Land sakes, George Parker." A diminutive woman shoved him aside. "You are the most suspicious man on the face of this earth. Let that poor woman in this instant, then fetch the midwife. She'll be at the Anderson's, but

Mary can do without her for an hour or so. She always takes days to birth a babe."

"But Martha—"

Caroline screamed.

"How can you leave anyone outside in this storm? You fetch that midwife right now or you'll be delivering her babe yourself," snapped Martha, routing George completely. "Peter! Come hold these horses!"

Damon scooped Caroline from the seat as a lad raced out to take the team. Sophie grabbed their valises. The scent of mince pies enveloped her as she stepped through the doorway, raising a tear, for they would not make it home for Christmas now. She would have to find a job if they were to make it home at all.

"Thank you, Mrs. Parker," she said as they followed her upstairs. Damon laid Caroline on a bed. "Words cannot convey our gratitude."

"Don't you worry, none," Martha said soothingly as she built up the fire. "We have the best midwife in the shire. Mrs. Laiks is in good hands." Her raised brows reminded Sophie that introductions were in order.

"I am Miss Sophie Landess, Caroline's sister. Her husband died at Waterloo." She'd hardly uttered the words before castigating herself. The claim sounded false even to her own ears. How many cast-off mistresses claimed to be war widows to give their children a respectable name?

"John Laiks was a hero of Waterloo," said Damon, smoothly continuing her explanation. "He was mentioned in dispatches and lauded by the regent himself. I am Westlake," he added, handing her a card.

Sophie glared when she glimpsed its inscription. Why was an earl soiling his hands with the likes of her? "Thank you for your assistance, my lord," she said stiffly. "I hope your journey contains no further surprises."

"I won't be leaving until this storm is over," he countered. "The roads would be impassable long before I could reach home. But I can find out what happened to your coachman. Would it be faster if I also fetched the midwife?" he asked Martha.

"No." She gestured out the window. George was striding across a field. "He can be back in a trice. A carriage would take an hour in this weather. I will stay with Mrs. Laiks. Perhaps Miss Landess could find the kitchen and tell Annie to send up hot water."

"Of course." She followed Westlake from the bedroom, still dizzy from discovering that he was a lord. He certainly didn't act like one.

Damon tried to catch his breath as they descended the stairs. Shock had pushed his own problems aside for a time, though fear was hardly an improvement. At least he wouldn't have to deliver a child on his curricle seat in a freezing rainstorm.

But he must remain here, and not only because of the roads. Martha seemed capable, but her husband was surly and suspicious. Sophie and Caroline might need protection.

"I will drive to Bedworth and inquire about your coachman," he said to prevent another expression of gratitude. She had turned wary the moment she'd learned his rank, but he would explore her reasons later. "You concentrate on Caroline."

Squeezing her arm, he let himself out the front door. The wind was even stronger than when he'd entered.

The coaching inn was on the near side of town. It didn't

take long to find the information he needed, but the tale made him furious. He hated incompetence.

Returning to the farm, he settled his horses in the barn, then found Sophie pacing the parlor.

"How is she?"

"I don't know. They won't let me in the room." Tears filmed her eyes.

"Hardly a surprise. You are neither married nor experienced in midwifery." He leaned against the mantel, letting the fire's warmth seep into his bones.

"I know, but I hate turning her over to strangers. I just found her again." She shook her head, then changed the subject. "Did you talk to our coachman?"

"No. He staggered into the stable yard on foot about midnight, but passed out before he could say a word. They think he suffered a blow to the head."

"His temple." She bit her lip. "He was thrown from the box when the wheel broke. I should have known the injury was worse than he claimed."

"What else could you have done?" he demanded. "You could hardly have left him with Caroline."

She took another turn about the room. "Will he recover?"

"I don't know," he said bluntly. "He remains unconscious. The innkeeper might have sent a groom to investigate, but a brawl had broken out in the taproom just before the coachman arrived. Two grooms carried him inside, but did not speak to the innkeeper, so when he found the body, he thought the man had been injured in the fight. He didn't question that conclusion until someone found a strange team in the meadow this morning. Barnes sent a man out then, but he found only an empty carriage."

"Poor man. He was so anxious to be rid of us that he

was trying to cover the same ground he could in high summer."

"He didn't like you?"

"Caroline's condition made him nervous."

"Ah." He returned to business. "I arranged to have the road cleared and canceled the remainder of your contract. Caroline won't be traveling for a while. You can hire another coach when necessary."

"I can't thank you enough."

"Then don't try." He gestured her to a couch. Did she know that he could not sit while she remained on her feet?

George paused in the doorway and glared. "You back again?"

"The roads are too muddy to go far, but I discovered why Miss Landess's coachman disappeared." He repeated the tale.

"Hmph!" George stalked away.

"You can't blame him for suspicion," said Sophie softly, taking a seat. "He thinks Caroline is your mistress."

"Perhaps, but he is suspicious of everyone," he murmured, joining her. "The innkeeper told me George was robbed twice by homeless soldiers. Then his favorite daughter ran off with a man he'd hired to help with the planting. He no longer trusts anyone."

"How awful for him."

"He won't appreciate your sympathy. Tell me how you routed Agnes Laiks. She allows no one to stand between her and a goal. I can't believe she wants John's heir born anywhere but under her roof."

"So Caroline claims. Actually, I never met her. We hadn't heard from Caroline in months, so I finally scraped together enough money to investigate—fretting over Caroline is worsening Mother's illness."

"Your father did nothing?"

"He's dead."

He flinched. "Why didn't you just write?"

She glared as if he were simpleminded. "I did write—often—but I hadn't heard a word since she left Vienna to join John's aunt. When I arrived at Laiks House, the butler refused me entrance, but Caroline was on the stairs, so I pushed past him. She was so shocked to see me—and so ecstatic—that I acted on instinct, packing her clothes and leaving. I wasn't sure I could make it past the butler again."

"Why?"

She shook her head. "From Caroline's description, I suspect Agnes planned to raise John's son herself so the boy would avoid the mistakes made by his father and uncle."

It made sense. And control of the Laiks heir would increase her own standing. But he had no interest in other people's squabbles. His own family provided enough of them.

He turned the conversation to neutral topics, but questions about Sophie teased his mind. Why was she unwed? She was far more attractive than her sister, and poverty was not an impossible obstacle to matrimony. Of course, her determination might put off some men. She would never be conformable, for she was far too confident in her own abilities. Only an equally confident man could handle her.

But that was not his concern, thank heaven.

Talking with her relaxed him for the first time in months. She was refreshingly different, with perceptions unlike anyone else's. And she was the first woman he'd ever met who seemed truly unselfish. She fretted over Caroline, the babe, her mother, even the coachman who had endangered her life, yet she made no complaint on her own account.

A new wail erupted upstairs, this one clearly from a child.

Sophie jumped up. "I must check—"

"Wait." He stopped her with a gesture. "The babe is clearly healthy. Let the midwife finish her work." He continued his description of how his cousin James had once startled his aunt by hiding a hedgehog in her sewing bag, spinning the story out for a quarter hour until Martha Parker arrived.

"Mrs. Laiks is fine," she announced. "She is safely delivered of a healthy son—John Stewart Laiks."

"After her husband and father," Sophie murmured. "May I see her now?"

"For a moment, but she is sleeping."

Once they left, Damon rose to pace. He would see that John Stewart was recognized as the Laiks heir and that Caroline and Sophie were allowed to raise the boy. Their good sense might restore respectability to the Laiks family. He had met John three years earlier and had been impressed with the man.

But the ladies' immediate problem was a place to stay. Whatever the weather, he must leave tomorrow. Christmas Eve was only six days away, and his guests would already be frantic over his absence. By tomorrow, half would be in hysterics. Yet he could not leave Sophie and Caroline at Parker's mercy. And he wanted to talk to Sophie again. Perhaps she could guide him to the right decision. She might see something he was missing.

Ideas circled his mind as his feet paced the room. When

the midwife clattered down the stairs, he paused in the doorway.

"How soon can Mrs. Laiks travel?" he asked.

"Not for a month," swore the midwife. "She's frail and suffered much during her pregnancy."

"But she cannot impose on the Parkers that long," he reminded her. "How long before she can remove from this house?"

"If her bleeding is normal, she could go as far as Bedworth tomorrow—provided you use a well-sprung carriage, move slowly, and keep her warm enough. But her home is far away. She can't manage that journey for a month."

"Thank you. I must leave tomorrow and wish to see them settled first."

The midwife nodded.

He added a sum to what Sophie had already paid, then resumed his pacing. If Caroline could manage the three miles to Bedworth in a well-sprung carriage, might she manage the twenty miles to Westlake Abbey? The shortcut would never do, but the main road was good. Sophie could not afford a month in an inn. She would refuse a loan, but accepting his hospitality was different.

He would do it, he decided, resuming his seat. Christmas would be dreary in a country inn. Caroline needed a comfortable place to recover. John Stewart needed safety and warmth. He needed Sophie's good sense. They would return to the abbey together.

The faces of his potential brides paraded through his mind. This time he tried to see them through Sophie's eyes, but they blurred together. No matter how hard he tried, he could not seem to shorten his list.

3

Cradling John Stewart in her arms, Sophie stared out the carriage window. She shouldn't have allowed Lord Westlake to run roughshod over her. Granted, Christmas in the sort of inn she could afford would be miserable, but forcing Caroline to travel so soon was insane.

Yet what else could she have done? Staying with the Parkers was impossible. George had begrudged them every morsel of food and breath of air. Martha and Westlake had kept him in line, but Sophie feared what would happen once Westlake left. Staying at even the cheapest inn would empty her purse, preventing them from going home even after Caroline recovered. She didn't like moving Caroline or placing them at the mercy of a family of aristocrats, but she had no choice. So here they were, trundling up the abbey drive.

Caroline shifted restlessly on the facing seat. At least she had managed to sleep for the last hour. And her condition did not seem any worse. Perhaps this visit would work.

But Sophie didn't believe it. Earls did not invite chance-met strangers into their homes out of the goodness of their hearts. Nor did they help commoners without ulterior motives. Westlake was unusually attractive with his dark hair and vivid green eyes, but that made his behavior even more puzzling.

She'd met handsome lords before. They always used their looks for venal purposes. Her uncle enticed women into his bed. Lord Tumfield, her stepfather's employer, lured lads into backing investment schemes that never prospered.

His neighbor hid brutality behind the façade of an angel. Others ingratiated themselves with more powerful men, always for personal gain. In her experience, handsome gentlemen expected pampering, exploding into anger if anyone thwarted their desires.

So Westlake confused her. He continued treating them like royalty, despite knowing their low status. What could he possibly want?

The Laiks heir.

It was so obvious that she nearly kicked herself for not seeing it earlier. She shivered, hugging John Stewart closer. She must remain alert. They had to accept his hospitality, but she could not allow him to use Caroline and the baby for his own purposes.

The drive curved, offering a glimpse of Westlake Abbey. Her mouth dropped open. It was the largest house she'd ever seen, sprawled across a rise in seemingly endless wings.

"My God," she murmured. "It's like a palace." How could she hope to protect Caroline against the owner of such magnificence? Merely snapping his fingers could summon a hundred footmen to do his bidding.

The carriage rocked to a halt behind Westlake's curricle. He was stepping down when the abbey doors flew open, disgorging dozens of people. Sophie gaped as they leaped down the steps, pushing and shoving to reach his side.

"Where have you been?" demanded a gentleman. "We've had search parties out for hours."

Westlake had no chance to respond, for others pressed close, all talking at once.

"We've been so worried?" cried a blonde. "We feared you'd been killed by highwaymen."

"Or suffered a fatal accident," said a brunette, gripping his arm.

"Or ran foul of a riot," added another.

Sophie's eyes widened as the ladies jostled for position, each flirting madly even as she tried to cut the others out. Gentlemen also crowded close. Some demanded explanations. Others chided him for leaving or related events that had occurred during his absence.

But not everyone in the crowd was concerned about Westlake's welfare.

"Move aside, Miss Lofton," hissed a young lady just outside Sophie's carriage. "You must know he repudiated fortune hunters last week. So go back in the house and give the rest of us a chance to speak with him."

"I've a better chance of winning than you do, Miss Travis," Miss Lofton countered, shifting to block her rival from penetrating the crowd around Westlake. "Not only do you lack a dowry, but your family rarely produces sons."

"That is a lie," swore Miss Travis. She tried to push past Miss Lofton, but was again blocked. Grabbing the girl's arm, she dragged her behind the carriage, out of Westlake's sight. Their argument continued in hisses and whispers, but Sophie quit listening once it was clear they would not disturb Caroline. At least their personal animosity had not dimmed their sense. Westlake was too close to risk shouting.

"Shocking manners!" snapped a dowager, pulling Sophie's attention back to Westlake. The blonde had squeezed so close that she was practically inside his greatcoat. "I always suspected Miss Payne was low-class."

"At least she would introduce spirit into this family," claimed another "Miss Fielding has all the animation of a corpse."

"He should ignore the lot of them and consider Miss Conway. That girl is all that is proper. If she were here, she would condemn these hoydens—and rightly so."

"Hah! She was caught embracing Wigby last month. And her sister is no better than she should be."

Protests greeted the statement—and insults. Tempers flared. One lady cut another, only to be cut by two matrons and a gentleman in turn.

Sophie shuddered, wondering how to get Caroline and John Stewart safely to the house. Nothing had prepared her for this. Why didn't Westlake stop it? The argument behind the carriage was growing louder. Two men marched their daughters into the abbey, but a dozen others emerged, enlarging the crowd. A matron swooned. Another fell into hysterics. She could no longer see Westlake through the press. The shoving to reach his side grew more violent.

"What is that noise?" murmured Caroline, trying to sit up.

"Nothing to fret about."

But her words proved woefully wrong. The carriage rocked sharply as someone slammed against it. A horse screamed. John Stewart awoke with lusty cries.

Trembling, Sophie pulled the curtains shut, then slipped John under Caroline's cloak so she could nurse him. She could only pray that nothing worse would happen.

Voices swirled outside the door.

"Every earl will rise from his grave in protest if Miss Lofton becomes Lady Westlake. She's worse than the fourth countess."

"At least no one in her family is insane. How can you support Miss Travis after seeing her aunt?"

Miss Travis hissed from behind the carriage. "Your mother's lies are even more audacious than yours." A slap echoed through the thin wall, followed by another.

Sophie cringed. How could an earl allow girls as low-class as these two into his home?

"Her aunt is more sensible than your Aunt Emeline," snapped Miss Travis's champion.

"There is nothing wrong with Emeline but a touch of rheumatism."

"Then why has no one seen her in two years?"

"Clear the drive before the horses kick someone!" ordered a man.

Caroline's eyes were too wide. Sophie listened to the mob outside, fearing that tempers would explode into violence. She clutched a half-boot in case someone burst through the door. It was the closest thing she had to a weapon.

But weapons proved unnecessary. The voices gradually waned as the drive emptied. A footman arrived to carry Caroline into the house. John Stewart had finished nursing and was again fast asleep.

But little else had changed. Westlake was still surrounded, Sophie noted as they passed a drawing room on the way to the stairs. The girls were still flirting, and the matrons still arguing. The dispute had merely moved indoors.

Damon groaned as people burst from the house. He had expected concern over his two-day absence, but nothing like this. A glance showed that Sophie remained in the carriage. He had time only to bless her sense before he was surrounded.

"Move away from the horses," he shouted, fearing a serious injury. The slow pace had left his team with plenty of spirit.

Girls pressed against his sides, desperately trying to garner his attention. Others approached from front and rear. Only one of them remained on his list, but now he scratched her. He despised forward behavior.

"Let us go inside," he begged. "I am cold from the long drive." But his words made no impact. Tempers flared. He caught a glimpse of Miss Travis hauling Miss Lofton behind Sophie's carriage. One of his aunts was making a spectacle of herself by cutting everyone in sight. How could they behave so badly with Christmas only a week away?

It took him half an hour to reach the hall. As he ordered Dobbs to put Sophie and Caroline in his bookroom—no other space was empty—his face heated. What must they think? He owed them an apology for exposing them to such uncivilized behavior.

An hour later, the last maid left the bookroom. Sophie couldn't believe how quickly they had converted it into a comfortable bedchamber. But if this was the only empty room in the entire abbey, then the mob outside represented only some of the guests.

"What is going on?" asked Caroline weakly, exhausted by a day of travel.

"I believe Lord Westlake is supposed to choose a bride from among the ladies gathered here."

"Ah. Daisy called it the marriage stakes." Caroline's eyes shifted to John as she named the maid assigned to care for him. "Lord Westlake has reached the age of twenty-nine. Unless he announces a betrothal this week, the family will be cursed."

Sophie laughed. No wonder he would rather roam the countryside, helping strangers. "Who can believe such nonsense?"

"His family. This house party began more than a month ago. Even the servants are betting on who will win. Daisy asked if you were in contention."

"I hope you set her straight. My position will be awkward enough without having people think I wish to rise above my station."

"You would make him an excellent wife," insisted Caroline. "Far better than those horrid girls outside."

Sophie stifled an unexpected longing for a family of her own, though the desire sharpened her tone. "Did those months with Agnes Laiks teach you nothing?" she demanded. "The aristocracy abhors bad blood. You know very well what they think of mine. And how could I expose Mother to more of their spite? She has suffered too much already."

She headed downstairs for dinner, cursing Caroline for baring dreams she had never acknowledged. And rightly so, she reminded herself. She was far happier living as Miss Sophie Landess, beloved spinster of Fronash Corners, than as Lady Sophie, despised daughter of the Earl of Sheldon.

The house party was even larger than she'd deduced. People filled four large drawing rooms to capacity. But that was a blessing, she decided, slipping into a corner. Her clothes marked her as insignificant, allowing her to blend in with the companions and poor relations. The important guests would pay her no heed.

Westlake was again surrounded. Two gentlemen kept tempers under control by deflecting those whose emotions threatened the peace. Watching girls primp before moving in to flirt with him had Sophie smiling. They were all so serious, so dedicated to winning, so determined to catch his eye. Yet no one was making the slightest progress. Westlake's expression was the same one he'd worn at dinner last night—a thin veneer of civility covering a simmering temper. Yesterday George Parker had been responsible. Today, it was the unrelenting pressure.

Because the dining room could not seat a crowd this large, dinner was served in the great hall, which formed the oldest portion of the house, dating to the original abbey. It could easily have contained her mother's spacious cottage several times over. Wainscoting and paintings filled its stone walls. Centuries of smoke blackened the beams of the open timber roof. But even heat from hundreds of people and four roaring fires could not dispel the chill. Thankful for her wool gown's long sleeves and high neck, she wondered how the contenders tolerated low-cut muslins.

Westlake presided from a table raised on the dais at one end—a table at which no females were seated, eligible or otherwise, she noted. An elaborate tapestry hung behind him. She sat near the foot of one of three long tables, amidst a group of aging dowagers and cousins.

"Who did you say you were?" asked Lady Montrose from her right.

"Miss Sophie Landess."

"Landess . . . Where do I know that name?"

"I can't imagine," she lied. "I live in a Cumberland cottage with my ailing mother. Lord Westlake offered us shelter while my widowed sister recovers from childbirth."

"How did that come about?" demanded Mr. Whitlaw from her left.

"I was fetching her home for Christmas when our hired carriage broke a wheel, stranding us after dark. Caroline was in desperate need of a midwife by the time Westlake happened along. When he discovered that I could not afford an inn, he brought us here."

Heads nodded as if that was usual. Several ladies asked about the baby, but conversation soon returned to Westlake's impending marriage—the topic engrossing every table in the hall.

"What is this talk about a curse?" Sophie asked Lady Montrose half an hour later.

"It is not a formal curse," she admitted. "But unless Westlake announces his betrothal on Christmas Eve of his twenty-ninth year, strife and misfortune will plague the family for a generation."

"That sounds odd."

"Perhaps, but it has been true since the first earl began the tradition in 1500. Those who ignore it die young, and disasters plague the rest of us—accidents, disease, waning fortunes, family rifts . . ."

Sophie stifled hilarity at such absurdity. The urge grew even stronger as she listened to the supposed evidence. They seemed to think that a simple announcement would bring them peace, prosperity, and eternal happiness.

Deluded fools. Even if it was possible, she doubted this crowd would benefit. Everyone in the room was arguing the merits of this girl or that. None agreed. No choice could please even a fraction of them. But she found their antics entertaining. Two gentlemen earnestly debated whether blue eyes or brown were best in a wife. Others disagreed on whether graceful dancers produced sturdier sons.

When their assertions became too ridiculous—she nearly burst into whoops of laughter when Mr. Graveston swore that Westlake's long-dead father was responsible for his gout—she asked Mr. Whitlaw to tell her about the house.

Westlake Abbey had been deconsecrated and turned into a residence two centuries before Henry VIII broke from Rome, so it lacked the monkish ghosts reputed to haunt other abbeys. But the earls' escapades offered a wealth of stories just as compelling. Her dinner companions threw themselves into this new competition, vying to top one another's tales, their efforts raising chuckles instead of ire. Sophie relaxed. At least this group accepted her as harmless. And as long as she avoided the subject of Westlake's marriage, they were quite congenial.

Retiring to the drawing room with the other ladies offered more insight into Westlake's predicament. She did not envy him this decision. With no gentlemen nearby, girls abandoned propriety, hurling insults at one another and arguing over his preferences. Mothers instructed their daughters in tactics. Grandmothers mourned that young men no longer wed where they were bid. Tension was mounting, for Christmas Eve was only five days away.

Sophie smiled as a girl joined her on the couch. Her blue gown was covered with the most beautiful embroidery Sophie had ever seen, but her face was wary. "Did Lord Westlake house you at a neighboring estate to spare you Miss Lofton's spite?" she asked.

"Of course not." Sophie sipped coffee. "He rescued my sister and me from a carriage accident yesterday."

"Oh." She sounded disappointed. "I had hoped that he'd chosen you."

"Why?"

"Mother insists that I catch his eye," she confided. "Even though I cannot like him, she is adamant, hoping this connection will improve our fortunes. We can't go to London next spring because Papa lost at cards again."

"You aren't the only one under pressure," said a girl dressed in yellow silk, joining them. White ruching and red roses echoed its scalloped hem and framed the low-cut bodice. "Papa refuses to accept that my heart belongs to Sir Percival Vance. Poor Percy has only a modest fortune." She sighed. "Papa forces me to approach Westlake at least once a day. If he offers for me, I'll die. Papa won't allow me to refuse."

"Why not tell Westlake you are not interested?"

"I couldn't do that," gasped the first girl. "Mama would scold me for weeks."

"I would be locked in my room on bread and water for a month," swore the other. "He is the best catch on the Marriage Mart."

Sophie blessed her uncle for disowning her. She would never have succumbed to such pressure. Every new fact she learned about the aristocracy made her thankful that she was no longer part of it.

"But you could tell him," suggested the first.

"Yes, he would listen to you."

"I doubt I can get near enough in this press, but if I manage it, I will try," she agreed, taking their names.

The girls left after heaping her with gratitude. Within minutes, another arrived, bearing a similar tale. How had she come to be Westlake's messenger?

Privately, she suspected that they were overreacting. Only half a dozen names had been mentioned as serious contenders for his hand. Since three of these were protégés of close relatives, she doubted the others had a chance.

Within the hour, she gave up trying to approach him. People mobbed him the moment he entered the room. If she did not see him at breakfast, she would send him a note. But for now, she would check on Caroline and John Stewart.

4

Sophie crept down Westlake's secret staircase and hesitantly rapped on the door.

John had awakened at dawn. To give Caroline privacy, Sophie had slipped through the connecting door into a sitting room she'd discovered last night. Westlake had been disappearing through a hidden door on the other side. Curious—and anxious to be rid of her messages—she had followed.

The bookroom must be part of Westlake's suite, she decided—which explained the Italian plaster ceiling and linenfold paneling in both it and the sitting room. She had been overwhelmed to find herself in so grand a place.

"What is it, Ortley?" he demanded now.

"It is not Ortley, my lord." She pushed the door open. Westlake was seated at a desk in a small study.

"How did you get here?"

"I followed you." Her face heated at the admission.

"Damnation," he muttered under his breath.

She squared her shoulders. "Forgive me, my lord, but I wished to thank you for your hospitality."

"No need. If anything, I should apologize for that appalling welcome yesterday. If I'd expected such a thing, I would have pushed ahead so you would not be offended by my unruly family."

"It wasn't your fault." She sighed. "But since we arrived together, most of your guests suspect a connection. Several ladies have charged me with messages."

"Not here, for God's sake." His eyes flashed in irritation. "This is my last refuge. Even my bedchamber is no longer safe."

"I suspect you might want these, but I won't intrude." She turned to leave.

"Come in." Rising, he gestured her toward the fire. "Forgive me, Sophie. I know you are not like the others."

She hesitated, but took the chair he indicated.

He relaxed into the other. "What are these messages?"

"Three girls wish to inform you that despite parental pressure, they are not interested in becoming your wife."

"How novel." He sighed. "Who are these paragons?"

"You don't believe me?"

"Of course I believe you, but I cannot say the same for the others. This could be a new approach to pique my interest."

A hint of pain threaded the words. How could he tolerate having to suspect every word and deed? "Yes, I gathered that you are the most sought-after gentleman in England at the moment. But I doubt these claims would pique interest, so they are probably true. Miss Smythe-Adams begs you to ignore her. She is enamored of Sir Percival Vance, but her father refuses to consider his suit because Sir Percival is merely comfortable rather than wealthy. Lady Andrea Simmons is under pressure to wed wealth, for her father recently lost a fortune gaming, but she is a romantic at heart and still hopes to find love—she finds you intimidating and cannot bring herself to like you."

"Good God, an honest woman," he murmured.

"The world is full of honest women," she countered. "You merely have to look for them. And Miss Dodson is overwhelmed by the size of the abbey and terrified of the responsibilities it would demand of her."

"They needn't fret." He shrugged. "I had already dropped them from consideration. Their lack of interest was obvious."

"So I thought, for they were not on Lady Forsythe's list of finalists in your competition." She could not keep censure from her tone.

"You condemn me for carrying out my duties as head of the family?" he asked softly.

"I would never condemn duty, but marriage should not be the prize in a contest."

"Yet how else would you describe the Marriage Mart?" he asked.

"It is a marketplace. Participants look for merchandise that will meet their needs, but if none is found, they wait until next market day." She caught his eye. "You seem too intelligent to be ruled by superstition. If your ancestors had resolved their troubles by killing the transgressors, would you feel obligated to do that, too?"

"Of course not!"

She already regretted her outburst. His marriage was none of her business. Yet she owed him a debt, which made it impossible to sit quietly while he participated in such craziness.

He ran his fingers through his hair, revealing his frustration. "I agree that superstition is ridiculous. And this one is not even true. The family history contains as much strife and misfortune in generations that followed its demands as in those that didn't."

"Then why do this?" She kept her voice merely puzzled this time.

"Because they believe it. And I am responsible for them."

"So you will sacrifice your own happiness, knowing it will change nothing."

"It is not that simple, Sophie."

"Why?"

"Perception can be very powerful." He rose to pace the room. "Did anyone tell you how this started?"

She shook her head.

"It had its roots in the War of the Roses. The Westbridge barons passionately supported the Yorks, branding the Lancasters as usurpers of the throne. They led the Yorks in every battle and were instrumental in wresting control into York hands on more than one occasion. Even after Elizabeth and Henry united the two houses to end the conflict, the Westbridges still hated the Lancasters and their supporters—all except the baron's second son, Edward. He had not only supported the Lancastrian Henry before he took the throne—that support earned him the earldom and the abbey, by the way—but he'd fallen deeply in love with a Lancaster lass. Unable to convince his father to condone a betrothal, he finally stood up during the Christmas Eve feast at his father's castle and reminded the family that his new title gave him more power than his father wielded.

After declaring an end to ancient hatreds, he introduced the girl he would wed and vowed that their union would unite their houses in peace for the next generation."

"Not unlike *Romeo and Juliet*," she murmured, though Westlake's tale predated Shakespeare by nearly a century.

"Perhaps, though our story has a better ending. Edward was a seasoned warrior, who enforced his edicts in ways we would frown on, but his wife was a genuine peacemaker. She soon won the family's admiration and loyalty. Only Edward's father refused to welcome her. By the time one of his tirades triggered a lethal apoplexy, most considered it justice. Edward and Ellen's love remained steadfast through sixty years of marriage. Their son announced his own betrothal on Christmas Eve in tribute to them, as did their grandson."

"But none believed that doing so actually brought peace to the family," she objected.

"True." He fingered a book on the desk before resuming his pacing. "That connection began with the fourth earl. He was a Puritan who considered Christmas revelry to be an invention of the devil that seduced Christians into paganism—considering the drunken orgies typical of Old Christmas, he may have been right." His eyes twinkled, making her blush. "So he abolished everything but a simple church service. He wed quietly in June without an official betrothal. No one objected until they realized that his marriage marked the beginning of the family's troubles—failed crops, lost fortunes, bad health. The countess was a shrew who sowed endless contention. Arguments arose between those who blamed the betrothal's timing and those who scoffed at such nonsense. The fights led to rifts that tore the family apart. Is it any wonder that most came to believe the idea of a curse?"

"Perhaps not, though I suspect that the earl and countess would have caused trouble regardless of their wedding date."

He shrugged. "It matters not. Their son sealed our fate. He announced his betrothal on Christmas Eve of his twenty-ninth year, just as the first earl had done. Two days later, cholera struck down his parents, though no one else caught the disease. The following year produced bumper crops. Fortunes revived. People smiled again. They laughed. The contrast was too startling to miss. For the next five generations, the heirs were careful to follow the custom. Their betrothals were arranged, often years in advance, so it made little difference when or where they were formalized."

"Did nothing bad happen all those years?"

"Of course, but the victims believed their problems would have been worse without the first earl's protection—perception again." He shook his head. "Which brings me to my own problem. My father fell in love during the Season of his twenty-first year. He was an impetuous man who could not wait even seven months, let alone eight and a half years, so he eloped on a sunny day in June."

"Shocking the family, I suppose." She had to squint against the sunlight, for he'd stopped by the window.

"Shock doesn't begin to describe it. Their condemnation drove him from the country. Mother was already with child, so he left her here and went on an extended Grand Tour. By the time he returned, he no longer cared for her—I doubt I saw him half a dozen times in my life. Ironically, she is beloved by the family."

"But they blame him for every little problem," she put in.

"Exactly." He resumed his pacing. "Every misfortune in the last thirty years has been laid at his doorstep. And his dying in a freak accident at age thirty-two adds to their belief."

"How serious are the misfortunes?"

"The world has not been bountiful in recent years. We were at war for most of that time. Several cousins were killed fighting Napoleon. Prices have risen steadily. Another cousin was injured in the Luddite riots. Bad weather has affected the crops. Lightning started a fire that destroyed years' worth of timber harvests. That hoof fungus ten years ago hit Westbridge flocks particularly hard."

"Everyone in England has suffered similar problems."

"That is not the point. The Westbridges firmly believe that my father's actions cursed them. Thus they dwell on any misfortune. They make no effort to settle arguments. Since even hard work won't affect the outcome, they've grown lazy. They ignore illness, for my father has cursed them to suffering. They—"

"I understand. Instead of helping themselves, they wait for you to announce the betrothal that will magically make everything right. But it won't happen."

"It will, though magic has nothing to do with it. By adhering to this tradition, I can eliminate their excuses. Once those are gone, they must sink or swim on their own, just as everyone else does. But unless I remove this crutch, they will do nothing."

"Which brings us back where we started. You are sacrificing your life to help a bunch of people who don't deserve it."

He resumed his chair. "I am not *that* altruistic. I was going to send for you today. And not just to apologize."

She frowned. "Why? I can't convince them that superstition is silly."

"I know, but I have to announce a betrothal in four days. You were right that this house party is nothing like the Marriage Mart. In London I would have ample opportunity to talk to candidates without raising expectations. That isn't true here. Not a person in the house is behaving normally. Conversations are short, superficial, and always in groups. Friends remain with me at all times, making it even more difficult to learn anything useful. As a result, I don't really know any of the candidates. Can you find the information I need to choose wisely?"

"You want me to spy on your guests?" She was appalled.

"Of course not! But I am under pressure from so many quarters that I can't even tell which girls are interested."

Her heart wept at the agony in his voice. He was the one who was cursed. And he would remain cursed for the rest of his life.

He shook his head. "All I want you to do is talk to them, Sophie, as you talked to Miss Smythe-Adams and the others. I don't want a wife who prefers another or who finds me unappealing or who will cause greater rifts than already exist in this family. I don't want someone who will become a shrew or bleed my coffers dry or present me with a questionable heir. I need to know that an offer is welcome, for too many fathers would force acceptance for their own purposes."

Sophie had never thought she could admire a lord, but she couldn't help admiring Westlake. He truly cared about his impossible family. He would sacrifice anything, even his own happiness, to give them a chance at peace. The contrast to her own relatives was stark. They were selfish, arrogant monsters who would gladly crush anyone who annoyed them.

"Surely your friends could gather that information," she suggested.

His head shook. "Friends or family won't work. No one lets down their guard for fear their words will get back to me. That is why I need you. No one knows you. You are a stranger from a different class, thus you pose no threat."

He was right, and she could understand his concerns. She owed him too much to refuse this request. "I will do what I can," she vowed, offering her hand to seal their bargain. "But I won't make the decision for you. I will not be responsible for dooming you to a life you can't enjoy."

"Thank you." He shocked her by raising her fingers to his lips. "I've pared the list to four, but I don't know where to go from there. My mother is championing Lord Fielding's daughter Margaret. Lady Fielding has been Mother's closest friend since her marriage, so the choice is no surprise."

"What is your objection to Miss Fielding?" She clasped her hands in her lap to reduce the tingling raised by his touch.

He raised a brow as if surprised by the question. Perhaps he'd not thought beyond the advantages each candidate offered. "I find her boring," he admitted, "but I cannot decide if she is truly without conversation or if she is so intimidated by this house party that she has become tongue-tied. She has little experience with large gatherings."

"Surely you met her long before this house party."

"True, but I paid her little heed until Mother began pressing. She just turned eighteen, and I was in London until recently."

"Last fling?" she asked.

He started to object, then turned rueful. "That is as good a description as any. I've known all my life that I could not wed until age twenty-nine, thus I was free to enjoy myself until now." He sighed. "The second candidate is my aunt's choice."

"Lady Payne?"

He nodded. "Anne Payne is her husband's niece and ward and has been living with them since her parents died two years ago. She seems nice enough, but I have a niggling feeling that something odd is going on with Lord Payne. Until I understand his situation, I can't consider strengthening ties with his family."

"Miss Fielding and Miss Payne. Who else are you considering?"

"My cousin James is pressing Miss Portland's case, though I've no idea why. There is no connection between the Portlands and Westbridges, and James is not even their neighbor." He shrugged. "It doesn't matter. Jane is intelligent, which I consider a benefit, but she seems overwhelmed by the tense atmosphere of this party. And I know little about her family beyond the fact that her father is a baron. No one but James has heard of them, but I cannot trust his word when he is pressing her case so diligently."

"And the last candidate?"

"Lady Chloe Houghton. She has no official sponsor, which is why she remains on the list. Choosing one of the others might cause the very trouble I hope to avoid. Mother and Lady Payne have never been close, for example."

"I see. Lady Chloe is the best of the rest."

"Exactly. Her breeding is quite good. She is well-read and can converse reasonably—a godsend in this crowd—but she rarely seeks me out, making me question her interest. I'll not offer for someone who doesn't care."

She stood. "I will do what I can, but don't expect too much. There is no guarantee that these people will even speak with me."

"You undervalue yourself. Just as I seek an impartial eye, others will also enjoy escaping the competition for a time—your description was unfortunately all too accurate. I doubt we can meet again today, as I will be surrounded the moment I leave my rooms—and it would defeat the purpose to disclose that we are working together. Perhaps you can join me here before breakfast tomorrow."

"Very well."

Damon watched her leave, then filled the room with curses. Why couldn't he have been born into a normal family? *Peace for a generation.* What the devil did his marriage have to do with peace? By the time he made a decision, the rifts would be so deep, no one could repair them. He still couldn't believe that appalling welcome yesterday. Fighting, for God's sake! Miss Lofton and Miss Travis had actually struck each other, thinking they were out of view.

Mortified, he had nearly turned tail and run. Sophie had passed it off with her usual serenity, but if she had not been at her wit's end and Caroline so weak, he doubted they would have stayed.

His eyes had turned often to Sophie during dinner last evening, though he'd tried to mask it lest it create new strife. Those seated near her had been the only ones enjoying the meal. Their animated discussion had lacked the contention prevalent elsewhere. Of course, he had placed her with people who had little personal stake in his decision, hoping to spare her another scene like the one in the drive. But their relaxed demeanor had still been a surprise.

The clock struck nine, reminding him that his private interlude was over. It was Robert's turn to accompany him to breakfast. His friend would be waiting in the hall.

But he wasn't.

"There you are, my lord," exclaimed Miss Lofton, helping herself to his arm and pressing far too close to his side.

He stifled a sigh. Where the devil was Robert?

"You must break your fast with me," she continued brightly. "Then you can show me the pavilion you were describing last evening."

"You must have confused our conversation with someone else's, Miss Lofton. The pavilion is closed for the winter."

"But surely you have the key. It sounds a fascinating place." She pressed closer, eyes gleaming with excitement as they took in the empty hallway.

"No." He stepped back, pulling his arm from her grasp. Robert would hear about this. Whatever stratagem she'd used to draw him away could not work again. "The pavilion is closed. Good day, Miss Lofton."

Her voice hardened. "You will accompany me to breakfast, my lord. Else I will describe this interlude to others. And it won't sound benign."

He met her greedy gaze with a look that made her gasp. "I do not recommend that strategy, Miss Lofton," he said softly. "I will send my entire family to perdition before accepting a schemer to wife. If you wish to protect your own reputation, you will turn your eyes elsewhere. I know about your fight with Miss Travis yesterday. Such appalling manners will bar you from every genteel drawing room in England if they become known."

"But—"

"Protest changes nothing. I regret to inform you that you are not among the contenders in this race. You would be happier directing your efforts toward a new goal."

She locked gazes with him, but it was she who finally withdrew. "I must seek breakfast, my lord, if you will excuse me."

"Of course." He watched her leave, then breathed a sigh of relief. One danger averted. Too bad so many remained. Miss Travis would doubtless be next . . .

Sophie paused outside the morning room, shocked by the contrast between the Christmas baking aromas permeating the house and the sound of angry voices escaping the closed door. Was she the only guest anticipating Christmas? That alone proved that she was an outsider. The staff was scurrying about trying to prepare for the holidays, while the guests spent every waking moment arguing about Westlake's betrothal. Perhaps it had been a mistake to bring John Stewart downstairs.

Several ladies at dinner had wished to see Caroline's baby, so she had promised this visit to the morning room. Now she wondered. At least two of the voices inside belonged to dinner companions—ladies who hadn't seemed to care about the marriage stakes.

"You cannot believe that Miss Travis would make an acceptable countess," snapped Lady Martin. "She is the most selfish girl of my acquaintance."

"Hardly," countered the piercing tones of Lady Montrose. She is under the same pressure as every girl in the house, but she seeks more than a title and fortune—which alone makes her better than Miss Payne."

Sophie shrugged. These arguments would only get worse. As Christmas Eve approached, tempers would grow even shorter. Pushing the door open, she entered.

"Is this the babe?" demanded Lady Montrose, her voice surprisingly soft. "What a sweet boy."

"He has a strong chin," commented Lady Martin.

"The chin came from his father," said Sophie, handing John to Lady Montrose.

"He died?"

"At Waterloo. He was a captain in the Queen's Hussars."

"A wonderful legacy," said an elderly dowager with a sigh. "He must have had good connections to join so prestigious a unit."

"John Laiks, second son of Lord Laiks." Sophie said the name proudly, wondering if these women might counter Agnes's determination to raise John.

"I hadn't heard that he married," said Lady Martin.

"A year ago. Caroline accompanied him to Vienna, but after Napoleon escaped, he sent her to London to stay with his aunt, Agnes Laiks. Unfortunately, he died."

"I knew he'd died, but Agnes said nothing about a wife when we spoke only two months ago." Lady Montrose looked puzzled.

"I believe she found Caroline's breeding unacceptable," Sophie said. "Her connection to the aristocracy is slight."

"Others can say the same," murmured Lady Simmons, stroking John's cheek. "Wrexham's wife has limited breeding, but she is a delightful lady. What is Caroline's background?"

"Her father was Stewart Villiers, steward to Lord Tumfield and great-grandson to Lord Stratford on his mother's side. The Villiers family has a very distant connection to the dukes of Whitfield."

"Honorable names," decided Lady Martin. "Laiks should be relieved to find someone in the succession ahead of that dissipated cousin. His own health is so bad that he has no chance to get an heir."

"So I understand." She tried to keep her voice steady, but her heart was soaring. Their words made it more likely that she could establish John Stewart's place in the succession and obtain Caroline's portion—John would have provided for her; he knew too well the dangers inherent in his career.

They discussed the Laiks family, the ladies offering ideas for how best to present the claims. John Stewart helped by captivating everyone in the room.

Once she'd accepted the last suggestion, Sophie turned the talk to Christmas, asking about the abbey's customs. By the time she returned John to his cradle, the ladies were busily planning how to decorate the abbey now that all the rooms were in use. Lady Westlake had seemed overwhelmed at the prospect, but the others overruled her, each choosing a section of the house to supervise.

5

Damon relaxed when Sophie joined him the next morning. Anticipating this hour of conversation had kept him going through another evening of craziness.

Even this very private study no longer provided the peace he needed, though he blessed his ancestors every day for creating it. He suspected that the room had originally housed someone's mistress, for the only other door opened into the servants' hall. Later a priest's hole had been added. At the moment, the public door was firmly bolted. Even if someone explored belowstairs, they could not enter.

Yesterday had been the most harrowing yet. Miss Lofton was not the only girl becoming desperate or even the only one willing to abandon honor to win. Finally, to keep his sanity, he had sought refuge with Miss Smythe-Adams and Lady Andrea, alluding to Sophie's message so they would know they were safe. In return for that quarter hour of peace, he would speak with Smythe-Adams about considering Sir Percival's suit.

"Are Caroline and the baby well?" he asked as Sophie closed the secret door and joined him by the fire.

"Quite. John is already becoming a charmer. His appearance in the morning room yesterday quelled another argument."

"I heard about that." He smiled. "Anyone who can captivate both Lady Montrose and Lady Martin deserves praise."

"I have not yet spoken to everyone on your list," she said, turning to business. "But I saw your mother—she came up to welcome Caroline shortly after breakfast."

"Mother undoubtedly informed you that Miss Fielding has won."

"Of course. How else could she warn me not to overstep my place? Besides, she expects you to follow her advice—apparently you have a history of relying on her judgment."

It was true, at least for minor decisions. He had spent much time away from the abbey in recent years, so he'd asked her to keep an eye on the staff and tenants.

Sophie hadn't noted his distraction. "Your mother believes Miss Fielding is perfect, for the girl strongly resembles Lady Fielding. But she doesn't realize that the traits she reveres in her friend would bore you to tears in a wife."

"I had not thought of that," he said, relieved that he had not misjudged Margaret after all. Lady Fielding was a subdued woman who agreed with everything his voluble mother said and rarely entertained original thoughts. Both she and Margaret were dominated by Lord Fielding, who dictated every aspect of their lives. Thirty years ago, the man had encouraged his wife's friendship with the new countess, hoping it would produce closer ties to the earl. Now he was using his daughter for the same purpose.

Sophie continued. "I next spoke with Margaret. She is enamored of her vicar, though I doubt he is interested. His living is too small to support a wife, and her father would never approve."

"Fielding has visions of grandeur, but she is his only daughter."

She nodded. "I cannot tell whether she seriously wants the vicar or uses her infatuation to mentally escape a dreary life. Her mother believes that marriage will put an end to her fantasies."

"But not with me. I'll take no one who prefers another." Especially a girl who already bored him. Sophie's willingness to argue made him admit that he didn't want a reticent wife. "Did you see anyone else?"

"Your aunt and Miss Payne. Your aunt does not care who Anne marries. Her husband is the one pushing this match. She agreed to plead his case because it irritates your mother."

"They have always been at odds," he admitted. And his aunt would enjoy tying him to a penniless girl of minimal breeding. She thought he deserved no better. In the chaos of this house party, he had forgotten her usual disdain.

"Lord Payne is pressing hard for this match. From conversations with others, I deduce two reasons. He never wanted to raise his brother's brat, as he calls Anne, so marrying her off will relieve him of the burden. You offer the first opportunity to be rid of her, for she just turned seventeen. Why do you think you have anything in common with someone twelve years your junior?" she asked in an aside.

He opened his mouth, then snapped it shut when he realized he had no answer. She was right. Anne was childish, with no conversation to speak of. And she needed help to perform even simple tasks. He'd been so afraid to raise expectations in the candidates that he'd learned almost nothing about any of them. Conversations had been wary and superficial, with most of his information coming from sponsors.

She continued. "I also suspect that Lord Payne's finances

are not as good as he claims—or so Anne hinted. He seeks a connection that will benefit him in the future."

"So accepting her will guarantee endless requests for money, financial backing in outlandish schemes, and who knows what else," he concluded bitterly.

"That is my impression."

"No. Payne is not my responsibility, thank heaven. I have enough others without adding to them."

"A fair assessment." She rose. "I will try to find Miss Portland and Lady Chloe today."

He remained in the study after she left, mulling over her report. She was even more helpful than he had hoped. Neither Margaret nor Anne would do, which was a relief. Choosing one over the other would have increased the antagonism between his mother and Aunt Payne.

Sophie was a remarkable woman—intelligent, comfortable, desirab—

He cut off the thought, for he could not afford to fantasize about someone not in contention. He must find a way to keep her out of his dreams. She would not do, alas. Recalling his aunt's antagonism had reminded him that he owed his family a wife of impeccable breeding to make up for his own shortcomings. His thinking had become too fuzzy.

Not that he wanted to lose Sophie. She was special. Perhaps they could remain friends. He needed to keep her in his life.

Suppressing the thought that friendship was not all that he wanted, he cast a last glance around his haven and headed upstairs to begin another contentious day.

His friend Henry was waiting to escort him, but Henry wasn't alone. James also lay in wait, praising Miss Portland all the way to the dining room, where breakfast was laid out. Damon wanted to ask why he was so interested, but experience had shown that he would get no credible response. Perhaps Sophie could turn up the information. James was not the sort to let superstition rule his life. Nor did he need to play matchmaker. He had his own fortune, a profitable estate, influential friends, and no problems.

Damon listened, but he refused to divulge his inclinations, even though Sophie's report left Miss Jane Portland firmly atop his rapidly dwindling list.

6

Sophie didn't find Miss Portland or Lady Chloe until the next day. Too many guests filled the abbey, with even more servants scurrying about to wait on them. Because helping Damon required hiding her purpose, she could not inquire about their whereabouts or request an introduction. So she had to explore the house on her own, speaking to everyone she encountered and hoping to find the ones she sought.

John Stewart helped in this endeavor, even when he remained upstairs. Everyone recognized her and knew she posed no threat to their ambitions. Damon never spoke to her in public. Her awe at the service and the elegant furnishings placed her firmly in the lower classes. But that helped her now. The other guests could take pleasure in her pleasure. They could coo over John and discuss his progress, then pat themselves on the back for their display of seasonal kindness. And because she was not part of their world, the marriage stakes contestants could say things they wouldn't tell their peers.

She learned much about Damon's guests that she kept to herself—Mr. Conklin's wish to emulate Davy's chemical experimentation; Miss Leaburgh's fear that her aborted elopement with a smooth-talking dancing master would ruin her chances of marriage; Miss Washburn's infatuation with Damon's friend Henry; Robert's yearning to start an import business if only it wouldn't disgrace his family.

Other facts she shared with Damon. Like rumors that a cousin was being abused by her husband. And another cousin's dream to stand for Parliament; in the meantime, he sought a post as secretary to a politician, though his father refused to help, demanding that he buy colors.

"It is a worthy ambition," Damon had agreed when they'd met that morning. "I will see to it. Hamilton is seeking a new secretary."

"He will be pleased." She was pleased herself, for she had feared that he would be angry over her lack of progress.

"I should have known you would have trouble finding the others," he'd continued, his rueful expression making him look ten years younger. "They are less forward than the rest. I believe Lady Chloe spends mornings in the Venetian room. And Miss Portland is often in the music room."

"I will find them today," she'd promised, rising to leave. But he had begged her to remain in the study.

"Each day is more wearisome than the last," he'd confessed. "I need rational conversation if I am to face it."

So she had stayed another hour, talking about his hopes for the future and her trip to London. His admiration of her search for Caroline surprised her, for she had done nothing that wasn't necessary. Caroline's silence contributed to their mother's ill health. How could she not have investigated? But her mother's fretting would soon end.

Damon had franked a letter announcing John Stewart's birth.

Now, as she greeted more guests, chatted with Lady Chloe, and answered questions about Caroline and John Stewart, the warmth of Damon's admiration remained. Her heart grew heavier every day—from sadness over his future, she assured herself. He deserved the best, yet he was arranging a marriage that would bring him no joy.

She understood his need to wed, for she saw ample evidence that his family used the curse to excuse laziness. But surely there was someone in this crowd who wanted him rather than his title, who could converse rationally, appreciate his integrity, and share his dreams. She refused to recommend a wife, but she could not help considering everyone she met in light of his needs.

Nothing. Damon was too different from the others. Somehow he had grown up without the arrogance and selfishness so many lords displayed, almost as if he'd been raised in the lower classes. He would never abuse his position or run roughshod over people as he pursued his own desires. She blushed to recall her fear that he had brought her here so he could control John Stewart.

And that wasn't the only misconception she had corrected since her arrival. Few of these people exhibited the qualities she hated in her own family. The guests were a diverse group, their only similarity being tension and the short temper tension created. Some were intelligent, some silly, and others dissipated. Yet even the worst showed no sign of the cruelty she'd expected.

Instead, they entertained her. She chuckled often as she explored the house—at the two aging dandies prancing like fighting cocks as they argued whether Miss Fielding's gown would have looked better in blue or green; at the dowagers sniffing disapproval over Miss Travis's flirtation, when she'd seen every one of them encouraging more blatant behavior in their own protégés; at Miss Barstow's false swoon that landed her in a thorny plant. Her instant revival and inelegant squawk had raised chuckles in half of her audience.

Damon frowned at the butler. "Those were her exact words?"

"Of course, my lord." Dobbs managed to appear affronted without moving a muscle. "Miss Landess requests a private word with you."

She must have found the other candidates, he decided as he slipped upstairs to his rooms. But it was ominous that she could not wait until morning to report her findings.

Yet even fear of her report did not prevent him from relaxing the moment he entered the study. This unexpected respite was more welcome than he would have guessed. With only two days left, the pressure was mounting. This marriage was supposed to bring peace to the family, but it seemed more likely to ignite a war.

Desire gripped him at the sight of Sophie. The fire had burned out some time ago, chilling the room, which tightened her nipples. Pulling his eyes from the evidence, he thrust lust aside. The last thing she needed was to find him leering at her. That was no way to treat a friend.

"Is something wrong?" he asked, shutting the door.

"You must judge that for yourself," she said solemnly. "I spoke with Lady Chloe this morning and Miss Portland this afternoon."

"And?" he asked when she paused.

"Lady Chloe seems all that is proper," she began, shaking her head. "She is witty and intelligent, but something about her does not ring true, if you know what I mean."

"Instinct is often more observant than the eyes."

"Exactly. She is very smart. Of all the people I have met, she is the only one who suspects that I am gathering information for you. Even your closest friends do not know."

"You still find helping me distasteful?" he asked, noting the line that had deepened across her forehead.

"I hadn't, but Lady Chloe made me feel like a spy, though she was both friendly and proper on the surface."

He frowned. "Why would she mind?" She had seemed flattered by his attention the few times they'd spoken, but never forward like so many others. That alone had attracted him. Some girls had shunned him—several had no interest in wedding him, but were here because they were part of the family or because someone thought they might suit. But Lady Chloe had welcomed his attentions with quiet serenity.

"She is very intelligent, as I said. Miss Barstow is not, though they are friends. She believes that Lady Chloe is desperate to attach you. Her father refuses to take her to London, insisting that she accept the offer he already has from a neighbor. But she has wider ambitions than ruling a corner of Shropshire—such as becoming London's leading hostess. She talked her father into giving her a chance to attach you and hopes to draw your attention by avoiding the pressure other candidates are applying."

It had nearly worked, he admitted in chagrin. His conversations with Lady Chloe stood out because she exuded tranquility rather than pressure. But now that he compared her behavior to Sophie's honesty, he could see the careful calculation underlying Lady Chloe's words.

"I do not want a wife whose ambition is to lead London society," he admitted.

"So I thought." She sighed. "But the real reason I needed to see you today was Miss Portland."

"Is she ineligible?"

"No, but I found out why James is so desperate to see her wed."

He raised his brows.

"She has many of the qualities you admire, especially education and intelligence. But her father distrusts bluestockings and abhors a woman smart enough to question his pronouncements. Deeming her a freak, he despairs of settling her. She shows little interest in the gentlemen he brings home—or they in her."

"His own taste runs to horses and hounds from what I hear," he admitted.

She nodded. "A year ago, he abandoned persuasion in favor of threats. Her sisters cannot enter society until she weds. Charlotte is barely seventeen, but Cecily is already nineteen and furious at the edict. To enforce the vow, Lord Portland refuses entrance to anyone except suitors for Jane's hand. Her sisters are effectively locked away even from female friends."

"So James—"

"—is in love with Cecily," she finished for him. "Lord Portland understands his interest, but he won't allow him in the house, hoping Cecily's pressure will force Jane to accept one of the offers he has coerced. James is now singing her charms to every man he knows."

"Why?"

"Jane believes that love is driving him, but that does not explain his urgency. He has been meeting Cecily on the sly for months, and I fear—"

"Dear Lord." He closed his eyes. "If they don't wed soon, she will be ruined and James will lose an heir."

"Exactly, but Lord Portland is adamant."

"That explains James's motives, but what about Jane herself."

Sophie's eyes darkened. "That I cannot say. She is extremely reticent—which is another of her father's complaints; he cannot abide her somber manner. My own impression is that she will make a quiet, conformable wife, but you will never know what she is thinking. She has much experience in remaining aloof. Her father's demands drive her into herself."

"So what should I do?" he murmured, half to himself.

"That is your decision, my lord," she reminded him.

"Damon, please. You are the closest friend I have at the moment."

"Very well—Damon. I think you should wait until you find someone you truly care for—next Christmas Eve will satisfy tradition as well as this one."

"But by next year I'll be thirty. The others wed at twenty-nine."

She shrugged. "Even the most adamant can't produce evidence that your age makes a whit of difference—or so I gathered from talking to your Uncle Harry last evening. The first earl was twenty-nine when he wed, but his son was nineteen and his grandson thirty-two."

"That may be true, but everyone since the fifth earl was twenty-nine. And I never want to go through this again.

Besides, as head of this family, I am responsible for its welfare. However silly this superstition might be, it has acquired the force of divine command. Ignoring custom gives everyone an excuse to fail. I can see no other way to help them."

"I know." Her eyes filled with sadness and pain. "But I fear you will sacrifice our own happiness in the process. And that could lead to the very strife you seek to avoid. Make sure you can live with your decision. It will be with you for the rest of your life."

There was nothing else to say, but the look in her eyes haunted him for the remainder of the day, then invaded his dreams that night. Yet what could he do?

After leaving Damon, Sophie donned a cloak and wandered the abbey grounds for an hour. Damn the man! How could he ignore his own needs to help a band of lazy leeches? It wasn't right.

She knew what he would do. Jane Portland was the best of a bad lot, so he would wed her. But Jane lacked passion. She would never argue when he was wrong or praise when he was right. He would be bored to tears in a week, for Jane had little conversation. She might be intelligent and well-read, but that counted for nothing in the aristocracy, so she could not even bring him prestige.

Tears escaped when she imagined Damon chained to a woman he could never love. In shock, she finally admitted what she should have known days ago. She wanted him for herself.

"I can't," she whispered, horrified at the idea. She was even less suited to be his wife. Usually she could ignore the gulf between her and marriageable females, but her sojourn at Westlake Abbey made that impossible. She lacked the training even the youngest guest took for granted. Her family had disowned her, so she could offer no connections. She had no dowry and the additional burden of an ailing mother, whose presence would be a constant reminder of her bad blood.

"What have I done?"

She quickly reviewed the reports she had made, terrified that she'd skewed the facts to make his candidates sound worse than they really were.

But at least she could absolve herself of that mistake. Her words had been more than fair. If anything, she had left out her worst impressions because only her instincts supported them.

She must forget this attraction immediately, for it would do them no good. He sought friendship. Nothing more. She must supply it without burdening him with emotions he did not want and could not use.

7

Sophie halted in shock when she reached the dining room for breakfast. This was the last day before Christmas Eve, the last day before Damon must announce his decision.

It showed. Today's gathering raised no hint of humor. Explosive tempers made the previous week seem idyllic. Already a dozen arguments drowned rational conversation. Girls pushed their way to Damon's side. Even Lady Chloe hovered nearby. Every girl believed that she could still win his hand if only she caught his eye.

And it wasn't just the candidates who jostled for his attention. Sponsors shouted their protégé's attributes. Relatives lectured him on duty, reminding him of the disasters they'd suffered because of his father's neglect. His friends wrestled the most brazen aside, trying to protect him.

Sophie bit her lip. Manners were disintegrating before her eyes. Fists pounded on tables. Chairs crashed into walls as people surged to their feet. If she didn't do something, the room would erupt in warfare. Tempers were so high, a fight could cause serious injuries and open permanent rifts.

"Has anyone noticed the snow that fell last night?" she asked loudly, distracting a dozen guests nearby. "I haven't seen a white Christmas in years. Let's take advantage of it. Who wants to join a snowman-building contest?"

The clouds parted with her words, sending shafts of sunlight into the dining room. All eyes turned to the windows.

"Wonderful idea," said one of Damon's cousins.

"What kind of snowmen?" asked another. "Tall? Massive? Artistic?"

"We can choose a winner for each," suggested someone.

"You'd win on height," said a lady, smiling. "Remember that snowman you built at Warrington Park last year? It must have been six feet tall. I felt the veriest dwarf standing at its side."

"It was at least seven," he swore. "I could barely reach high enough to place its head."

"We'll meet on the terrace in half an hour," announced Damon.

Sophie met his eyes, sharing his relief. "Send for the children," she murmured when they passed in the hall on their way to fetch wraps. "It is time people remembered that it's Christmas."

That's what had been missing, she realized. Though the nurseries were bursting, only John Stewart had appeared downstairs.

Damon gazed in awe across the abbey's south lawn. In the two hours since Sophie had drawn attention to the snow, the lawn had sprouted an army of snowmen, four forts, and a dragon. The atmosphere had changed completely. Instead of arguing, his guests were laughing. Laughing, for God's sake! Inviting the children had been a stroke of genius. Their enthusiasm was infectious, as was the innocence of their competitive efforts.

He had declined to judge, fearing that it would invoke images of that other competition. Instead, he suggested Uncle Peter, one of the few gentlemen who remained friendly with every guest. Thus he was free to lend a hand here and there and to participate in the inevitable snowball fight.

He was still grinning when he slipped into his study half an hour later. He should have thought of using the snow himself, for a resounding snowball fight relieved tension. The rest of his guests would be drinking chocolate in the dining room by now.

Except Sophie, who was already in the study. His blood stirred as he joined her. Several people had been tossed into the mound of snow that had been cleared from the terrace, including him. He had landed atop Sophie, his apology cut short when he realized how perfectly her body fit against his. The last thing he needed was to lust after his best friend, but he couldn't seem to help it—which explained why friendships between men and women rarely worked for long.

But he was determined to avoid that pitfall. Stifling another surge of desire, he set down his tray and shut the door.

"You are a goddess," he said, surprising himself.

"The cold must have affected your mind," she countered.

"Hardly, but words cannot express my appreciation for quelling tempers this morning. I was ready to throw James out the window."

"People are so focused on your contest that they've forgotten why Christmas Eve is special. They should be thinking about peace and good will rather than money and position—or family curses."

"If someone had told me as a child that I would dread Christmas, I would not have believed it." He handed her a cup of chocolate. "But it is true. For ten years, it has grown increasingly burdensome. This year surpasses my worst nightmares."

"I am not surprised. Placing a deadline on marriage prevents you from choosing wisely and ruins the season for all of you. How can that scene in the dining room bring prosperity to this family? Who can expect peace when every discussion triggers tempers?"

"But thanks to you, it did not." He sighed, for the decision weighed heavily on him. Her reports had answered many of his questions, but he could not take the final step.

And why not, demanded his conscience. *You know that only one name remains on your list.*

True, and it was the same name that had sat atop it for a week now, yet he could not summon her father. Jane's reticence loomed larger every day. He needed a wife who could share conversation.

"I won't tell you what to do," Sophie said softly, reading his mind. "It would be unfair to you and destroy this friendship you claim to value."

"You think I will blame you if it doesn't work out?"

"Not deliberately, but it would be natural. I won't risk it."

The words raised a treacherous glow, but again he suppressed it. "Why are you so concerned about my making a mistake?" he asked instead.

She set her cup aside and stared into the fire. "Marriage is the most important decision you will make in your life," she said finally. "It will affect everything you do from now on. If you choose someone you don't like or don't respect, you will be miserable, and every year will add to your loneliness and isolation."

"How do you know so much about an institution you have never tried?" he dared, refilling their cups before taking the other chair.

"Observation. I am unmarriageable, but that does not make me blind."

"Unmarr—"

She interrupted. "Do not pretend surprise. You understand the world as well as I do. Even the lower classes expect certain standards of their wives. I am a managing female with no dowry and no connections. My looks are passable, but not good enough to overcome those handicaps. It is something I accepted long ago." She shrugged.

He disagreed, but he could see that the subject saddened her, so he let it be. "I am aware that choosing a wife is serious business. Why else would I agonize so long over balancing my wishes with the needs of my family?"

"But you are not giving adequate weight to your own

needs," she countered, relaxing. "Nor have you considered the effect your decision might have on your bride. It is not enough to know that she is eager to accept your offer. There are many things that can turn that eagerness sour, like discovering too late that you disagree on important issues, such as how often you will visit London. And you must plan for unexpected tragedies. Take my mother, for example. Her first marriage was a love match. Her husband doted on her and assumed that everyone else felt the same."

"I take it he was wrong."

She nodded. "His family pretended acceptance so he would continue financing their idleness. But in truth they despised Mother. Her breeding was unacceptable, she lacked a fortune and family they could exploit, and she recognized the evil lurking beneath their fawning. The day he died, they threw her out. She had no marriage contract to protect her."

He stared, but she was serious. "How could that happen?"

"It doesn't matter. I only mentioned it so you won't make the same mistake. People often smile to cover hatred or fear. No matter what your family superstition claims, this contest has created too much animosity for everyone to support the winner. It's up to you to protect her."

"I will. Did your mother return to her family?" he asked, shocked that anyone could toss a woman out on the very day her husband died.

"No. Her parents were gone. She couldn't impose on her brother, who could barely support his own family. So we headed north. She hoped a cousin in Cumberland would take us in."

"How old were you?" He hadn't realized the marriage

had been fruitful. Throwing out the daughter was even more appalling.

"Six. I remember that period quite well. Starvation stays in the mind." She frowned as if she had said too much. "The cousin was gone. Fortunately, we met Stewart Villiers. He wanted a wife and thought Mother would do. She was desperate enough to accept, even though Father had died barely a month earlier. But it worked out. Stewart was a good man. Caroline inherited his coloring."

"So why are you so concerned about me? Your mother proved that even the oddest alliance can bring contentment in the end."

"Only if you choose wisely. Stewart and Mother had much in common, so they made good partners. But though they become close, they never found the passion she had shared with Father. And without their basic compatibility, they might have come to hate each other—which is my point. If anything annoys you about the girl you choose, you can be sure that your irritation will grow after marriage. Think about her habits. Can you stand facing them every day, even when you are in a temper over other matters? If not, you will be miserable and have to retreat to your club to avoid contact. Or hide in here."

She gestured to the room, then left him to his thoughts. And annoying ones they were. Miss Portland offered no conversation, as he'd known all along. He had assumed that she would relax after marriage, but now he wondered. These daily talks with Sophie filled a need he hadn't previously recognized. Could Jane fill it?

8

The faintest hint of dawn appeared on the eastern horizon as Damon stared out the study window. Christmas Eve. His day of decision. His day of doom.

He had been sitting at his desk for hours, but nothing had changed. Yesterday's talk with Sophie had clarified his needs, but that made little difference.

Dipping pen in ink, he trailed aimless swirls across a sheet of paper. Designs nearly obliterated the writing, not that it mattered. Only one word was inscribed there—Jane. Very small, centered precisely on the page. Shrinking the list to this one name should have relieved his mind. Yet he could not rise, could not walk to the library, could not summon Lord Portland.

Again he reviewed the candidates he had dropped. Even if marriage turned Miss Fielding's eyes from her vicar, it would not relieve the boredom she promised. Sophie was right. If Margaret bored him now, how could he tolerate fifty years with her?

Anne Payne wouldn't bore him, though her childish behavior already annoyed him. Time might remedy that, but he was tired of pressure. This house party made him long for tranquility. How could he choose a wife whose guardian was a gamester? He already faced endless demands from his own family.

Lady Chloe might be intelligent, but she was little different from a fortune hunter. He had no desire to spend every Season in London. Choosing her would lead to a lifetime of arguments over parties and clothes and jewelry. She would be happier wed to that neighbor in Shropshire.

Which left only Jane. Plain Jane. A silent intellectual who needed a husband to save her sister from scandal.

Get it over with, urged his conscience. *Nothing will change now. This agonizing is going nowhere. Do it.*

He was rising when Ortley burst in.

"The ice just broke, dropping a man into the lake," the valet panted.

"Does Dobbs know?"

"I don't know. Miss Landess saw the accident from her window. She sent me to fetch you, then rushed downstairs."

"Find Dobbs and make sure hot baths are ready." He might need one himself before this was over. The footmen would still be abed, so getting other help would take time. Throwing the bolt, he raced toward the servants' entrance.

Sophie was already at the lake, as was Jane—she must have been in the hall when Sophie rushed out. They were wrestling with a heavy branch, trying to maneuver it across the ice to where a man floundered in the water. Though most of the lake was shallow, a stream entered at this point, deepening the water and keeping the ice thin. Weighed down by soaking clothes, the victim was in danger of drowning—or freezing.

"Give me that," he ordered, grabbing the unwieldy branch from Sophie's hands. She had been the only one making any progress. Jane was clearly out of her depth in a crisis, pushing ineffectively on the branch while tears streamed down her face. At his nod, Sophie turned her attention to quelling Jane's hysteria.

He shifted left, where the ice was thick enough that he wouldn't fall into the water himself. Then he lay down and slid the branch toward the hole.

"Can you grab it?" he called, hoping the victim was

conscious. The thrashing had abated while he maneuvered into position.

"Y-yes-s."

"Make your fingers grip tightly," he advised, forcing calm into his voice. This would be the only chance for rescue. If those hands slipped, cold would claim him before more help arrived.

"P-p-pull."

At least the victim was male. The added weight of a sodden dress would make this nearly impossible.

He was trying to gain enough purchase on the ice to move the branch when someone grabbed his ankles.

"Hang on," called Sophie.

Glancing over his shoulder, he saw that she held one foot while Jane tugged on the other.

"Good." They had better footing than he did, and she'd somehow calmed Jane enough that the girl was actually helping. With both of them pulling, they dragged the man from the lake.

"Thank God!" Jane cried, throwing herself into the victim's arms the moment he staggered to his feet. "I feared you would die."

Damon stared, stunned, as the growing light revealed Jane Portland in a desperate embrace with Harold Westbridge, a second cousin he barely knew. Tears streaked both faces. She must have been with him when he fell. If Sophie hadn't seen them, he would have drowned. Jane was nearly useless.

"Help them inside," he told Sophie. "Dobbs should have baths ready. Then find out why no one knows of this attachment. Harold is hardly ineligible. I will be in the study."

Lightheaded from lack of sleep, shock, and cold, he headed for the house.

"They want to marry," Sophie announced bluntly half an hour later. "But Jane is terrified of her father. She fears he'll forbid it."

"What the devil is wrong with Harold?" He jumped up to pace the room.

"He is barely twenty, still in school, and has limited prospects. She is twenty-one. What father would condone such a match? Harold tried to speak with Lord Portland last month, but Portland refused permission to call, concluding that Harold was trying to see Cecily. He cannot believe anyone wants Jane."

Damon swore under his breath. "Why didn't Harold just ask for her hand?"

She shook her head. "He is more timid than Jane, and her fears clearly affected him. They are in love, but neither possesses a backbone."

"I will speak to Portland." Damon sighed. "If he is desperate to get Jane off his hands, he can hardly object to the age difference. I can offer Harold a position that will support them well enough."

"So I thought, but Jane is so accustomed to hiding her thoughts, she could not bring herself to approach him." She laid a hand on his arm, stopping his restless motion. "What will you do now?"

"I don't know."

"I suppose you could stir all the names into a Christmas pudding and see who turned up in your slice," she said, shaking her head. The smell of boiling puddings wafted from the huge fires the cook had built in the kitchen courtyard, permeating closed doors and sealed windows.

"It's too late to make a pudding." He tried to match her light tone, but his voice caught. "Damnation, Sophie, my guts are tied in knots," he admitted on a sob, pulling her close to share her warmth. "I don't have a clue what to do."

Her hands circled his waist. Compassion wrapped him in a warm cocoon. And comfort. He stifled the urge to kiss her or even to bury his face in her hair, unwilling to abuse her friendship. But he couldn't let go. He needed her too badly, so he let his cheek rest atop her head while tears slid down to soak her hair.

A quarter hour passed in silence before she finally loosened her arms, caressing his back in one long stroke as she pulled away. "Wait a year," she advised before slipping upstairs.

Sophie set Damon's problems aside, determined to enjoy the day. She had not celebrated a real Christmas in twenty years—Lord Tumfield didn't believe in the traditional festivities, so he'd banned them from the estate. Thus she looked forward to this one. The snow made the occasion even more special.

The atmosphere was lighter than yesterday. Damon had made it clear that he would not join the company until dinner, so the contest was over, leaving everyone free to celebrate.

That didn't stop them from speculating about who would win, of course, but the antagonism was gone. As they headed out to collect greenery, children raced in and out of the crowd, tossing snow at one another. Their excitement was contagious.

Sophie had volunteered to cut holly, in part because she remembered her father lifting her high in the air to clip branches from the holly trees at Sheldon Park. His thick gloves had swallowed her hands, protecting her from the sharp points. Other guests collected ivy, evergreen boughs, and clumps of mistletoe. Servants piled the spoils into wagons and passed out chocolate heated over a roaring fire.

Several people noted Jane's absence. Rumor claimed that her father was meeting with Damon. More than one frown greeted the talk, but most of the attention was on Christmas. By the time they returned to the abbey, holiday spirits had eliminated the last tension.

"I'll make the kissing bough for the great hall," Miss Smythe-Adams volunteered, laughing.

"We'll need another in the morning room."

"And every drawing room."

"The hall."

"Will that be enough?"

"Shouldn't we have one for each public room?" asked Sophie, remembering her father and mother cavorting under the kissing boughs a month before he died.

"Wonderful idea," agreed Henry, leering laughingly at a dozen ladies in turn. "And one above Westlake's table. He'll need it tonight."

"Why not?" agreed Lady Westlake. "We've enough hands and enough greens."

Henry grinned before leading the gentlemen off on another expedition.

"I'll start a garland for the stairs," said Sophie.

"I can tie bows," offered Miss Fielding shyly. Miss Travis and Miss Lofton rushed to help her.

The servants had unloaded three towering wagonloads of greens, but so many hands set to work that the piles dwindled rapidly. Sophie hummed while she worked. Others joined in, their voices filling the air with music. Children laughed, their unskilled fingers hampering as much as helping, but no one cared.

Before the last of the greenery was in position, the men returned with the Yule log. It took twenty of them to wrestle it into position, ready for lighting after church. When the guests gathered to admire it, another song burst forth. Footmen passed punch. It was Christmas, the season of good cheer.

Sophie treasured every moment of the day, storing away memories to sustain her through tomorrow's sorrow. Damon would announce his decision at dinner, breaking her heart, though she must never let him suspect.

What would he do? She had felt his pain during those exquisite moments of communion as he'd held her that morning. He cared too deeply and took his responsibilities too seriously. No matter how strongly she protested, he would choose a wife this day, though she had no idea who. The rest of his life would pass in loneliness, for there wasn't a lady here who was worthy of him.

But she thrust the thought aside. Christmas Eve was a time of rejoicing. They were preparing to celebrate the birth that promised peace and salvation to anyone willing to accept the gifts.

Damon paced the study, idly wondering if he would wear holes in the carpet before this day was over. He could not sit still. At least the constant motion excused his dizziness.

He had been running in circles mentally as well as physically since the moment Sophie had left. The same arguments, the same obligations, the same uncomfortable facts. How many times had his thoughts trod the same tired ground?

Music and laughter vibrated the wall the study shared with the great hall, startling him from his preoccupation. There had been no celebration in the abbey since the June day when his father had introduced his unexpected bride. For thirty years the family had walked through Christmases, christenings, marriages, and births. But the closest anyone had come to gaiety was a polite titter.

Now he listened to the strains of a Christmas song and marveled. Climbing to his sitting room, he summoned Dobbs, then stared out the window. A dozen laughing children were adding new creations to the snow army on the lawn, assisted by their governesses. Smoke from the courtyard and kitchen fires now mixed the tantalizing aromas of mince pies and roasting meats with the earlier whiffs of Christmas puddings. The original abbey kitchen was also in use, its chimneys belching smoke for the first time in a century.

"What is going on?" he asked Dobbs when the butler arrived.

"Decorating the abbey, my lord."

"But that has never been more than an obligatory chore. Why is everyone so enthusiastic this year?"

"I believe Miss Landess is responsible," ventured the butler. "Her enjoyment is catching, if I might be so bold.

And she suggested that the children help. Their wonder at joining the adults has proved beneficial."

Sophie. He should have known. She cared little about what others thought, enjoying herself openly if the situation called for it. And her excitement was contagious. He must thank her for making this week more bearable than he'd expected. She saw the world through different eyes than most. Whenever tempers flared, she had been there to defuse anger and remind everyone that life could hold pleasure as well as strife.

But he digressed. Thinking about Sophie was so much easier than making this decision.

"No more procrastinating," he murmured, thanking Dobbs and returning to the study. Reviewing the candidates was useless. He had been over that ground too many times. It held nothing new. Perhaps he should take a page from Sophie's book and try a different approach. He had assumed that her suggestion was a joke, but maybe not. Heaven knew nothing else was working. It was too late for a pudding, but he could put the names in a bowl.

He spent the next hour listing every unattached female in the house past the age of sixteen. His great-aunt Abigail. His cousin's companion. Caroline Laiks. That governess who'd designed the snow dragon. Every girl he'd rejected. . . .

Cutting the paper into strips, he crumpled each one into a ball. Then he shook the bowl, shut his eyes, and took a deep breath.

He needed a wife. Whom would fate choose? Rummaging through the scraps of paper, he pulled out a name—

Hope leaped in his breast as a face shimmered against his closed lids.

Shock froze him for only a moment before he relaxed into peace. It was right. If years of planning for this gathering had not locked him so thoroughly into the process, he would have seen it sooner.

Dropping the unread scrap back in the bowl, he emptied it into the fire and summoned Dobbs.

Sophie's heart sank when Dobbs sent her to Damon's study. She would not choose for him, but perhaps he would finally agree to postpone the choice for another year. He clearly did not want to marry any of the ladies gathered here.

Or was he expecting her to approve his choice? That would be nearly as bad, she decided. It would be little better than choosing for him, for it would allow him to put the onus of the decision on her shoulders.

"What now?" she demanded belligerently the moment she jerked open the door.

"Is this the woman who has been charming my family all day?" he wondered lightly.

"I won't help you decide, nor will I approve your choice," she stated firmly, her glare drawing an answering frown.

"I don't want your approval," he snapped. "I want your hand in marriage."

She stared, certain her ears were betraying her.

"I said, I want your hand in marriage, Sophie," he repeated, nearly shouting.

"You can't be serious."

"I am very serious." He followed as she retreated behind a chair. "You are the perfect wife, the only woman I know who can bring peace to this fractured family. You need look no further than today. It has been thirty years since this house rang with laughter or song."

"I cannot believe you would offer marriage because I enjoy music. Stop this dithering, Damon. Either choose someone or tell your family that you will choose next year."

"I have chosen," he swore, grabbing her shoulders so she had to face him. "I want you. No one else. Not now, not next year, not in fifty years. Only you."

She closed her eyes, shutting out the truth shining from his face. Allowing him to befriend her had been a mistake. Somehow she had led him astray, but this would not last. It couldn't. His family would never accept her. The moment they discovered her breeding, the rifts would widen into gulfs that might never heal.

"Damon, think. I know from bitter experience how people view my breeding. Your family would be no different. They accept me now because I pose no threat to them—and because they know nothing about me. But that would end the moment you offered me the prize."

"You are wrong. There are many guests who pose no threat, but not one of them is beloved by all. I spoke true just now. It has been thirty years since people sang in this house. Or laughed—truly laughed, not a polite chuckle that means nothing. You quelled a brawl yesterday with a word. I watched you leave with Aunt Rose and Cousin Maggie this morning. They were both smiling."

"So? I asked whether mistletoe grew here—it is uncommon in Cumberland, for the winters are too cold. Naturally they smiled. They were remembering the kissing boughs of their youths and the bucks who had lingered there."

"They haven't spoken to each other in thirty years, Sophie. Not since the June day my father announced his elopement to a woman Aunt Rose had introduced to him."

She frowned.

"And they aren't the only ones. The abbey hasn't seen good cheer since that day, yet you managed it in less than a week. Peace. The point of this silly superstition is that marriage should bring peace to the family. Only you can do that, Sophie. But beyond that, you've given me a greater gift than you know, for I love you with all my heart."

"Don't do this to me, Damon." She turned away to hide the tears shimmering in her eyes. "I never meant to hurt you, though it seems I must, at least for now. This infatuation will die the moment I leave. You only think you care because we've spent too much time together."

"You can't see inside my heart, so don't tell me what I feel," he snapped. "I love you. I want to marry you. That is all that matters."

"How can you say that when every conversation since we met has been about duty and this idiotic curse? I can never bring peace to your family. The moment you disclose my breeding—and there is no way to hide it—your family will rise against me."

"You don't know that."

"I do know that. I've seen it happen. My father's family threw us out in a snowstorm rather than endure us another day."

"My family would never stoop so low."

"Thus speaks ignorance." There was no hope of escaping with his friendship intact, she realized. Just once she had hoped for acceptance. "My mother was the bastard daughter a baronet got on his mistress. When Grandmother succumbed to the pox, he took Mother in, but he never acknowledged her. After all, he had only Grandmother's word the girl was his. He'd dismissed her before she learned she was pregnant, and the babe looked nothing like him."

"Yet he took her in."

"He would have done better to foster her elsewhere." She drew a breath to steady her nerves. "His wife despised her. His real children abused her. He rued his impetuous decision for the next ten years, for he had no idea what to do with her. She spared him the decision by eloping when she was barely sixteen. He washed his hands of her, thankful that it was over."

"No wonder she couldn't return after your father died." He rested a hand on her shoulder.

"He was dead by then. His heir had always despised her, so there was little point in throwing ourselves on his mercy." She pulled away from his touch, moving to the window to stare at the lake.

"Why did your father reveal her background?" he asked, joining her, though he kept his hands to himself this time. "Even if it didn't matter to him, he must have known his family was intolerant."

Her heart cracked at the words, though she had known how he would react. "He didn't. I was born barely seven months later, obviously full term, prompting his brother to investigate. Mother and Father swore the child was his, but Mother's lack of breeding made it easy to believe otherwise. If I had been a boy, my uncle might well have killed me to avoid tainting the line. As it was, he bided his time. I've often wondered if he had something put in Mother's food to make sure there was no heir—she had no trouble conceiving Caroline once we left. Not that it matters now.

To put the sordid incident behind him, he got rid of us the moment Father died."

"He must have been mean-spirited beyond comprehension," Damon said, turning her so she again faced him. "This family would never do something so base. I love you, Sophie. Please marry me."

"I would have to bring Mother here," she warned him. "She is too ill to manage by herself. People would demand to know her background. They won't like learning that her mother grew up in a St. Giles rookery and worked as a common prostitute before Grandfather took her under his protection."

"She is welcome." He placed a finger across her lips to prevent another protest. "I don't care what her background is. She produced the most wonderful woman in the world. And no one else will care, either, as long as we announce our betrothal today."

She gazed into those green eyes that had become so dear so quickly, and finally nodded. "I love you, Damon."

"You are the most stubborn lady I've ever met," he murmured before drawing her into a kiss to seal the bargain. But he wouldn't have it any other way. She made him feel alive.

He had meant the kiss to be a formality, for time was growing short, but her response awed him. His hands pulled her closer as he savored the pleasure. He forgot the time, forgot the guests waiting in the great hall, forgot everything in his need for just one more touch, one more taste, one more moan of passion.

She blossomed under his touch. Innocent, yes, but her hunger was as great as his own. Only a rap on the door kept him from stripping off her dress to discover what else they could share.

"Dinner, my lord," said Dobbs through the locked portal.

"Is everyone seated?" he asked, trying to sound normal as he smoothed his hair and fought for breath.

"They will be by the time you arrive."

Straightening his coat, he smiled at Sophie. "Ready to make our grand entrance? It's—"

"—traditional," she finished as he unbolted the door. "I hope you are right. Just promise me that we can call this off if the family turns on me."

"They won't." He was already leading her through a maze of servants' corridors. "By the way, who was your father?"

"The Earl of Sheldon."

He stopped, his mouth hanging open, then threw his head back and laughed until he could hardly stand.

"What is so funny?" But his laughter was so contagious, she couldn't help chuckling.

"Dear Lord, Sophie. I thought your mother eloped with a merchant or something. No wonder everyone loves you. You inherited that knack from your father. I've heard tales of the man. There wasn't a soul in England who didn't adore him, save his vicious brothers. No one will blame you for the way your mother was treated."

"I am glad to know my memories weren't skewed, but I hardly call that funny."

"No, but you will have to forget all that talk about bad breeding. Yours is better than mine. You are Lady Sophie Landess."

She stared as if he had grown two heads. "I hate that title."

"I can understand, but that wasn't my point. Not only was your father an earl, but your mother was the daughter of a baronet, whether he recognized her or not. Mine was an opera dancer."

"Which explains why the family decried his marriage."

"No!" He glared. "The only—*only*—reason they criticized his marriage was because he refused to wait until Christmas Eve. They don't care who the earls marry as long as the betrothal is announced properly. And you must have seen how beloved she is. No one blamed her for Father's actions."

She had to agree. Perhaps this would work after all.

"We'll make it work, my love," he said, reading her mind. "Now pin on that smile and let's go."

Sophie floated through the next two hours in a daze. Only three images stayed in her mind afterward: the sight of four hundred eyes widening in surprise as she and Damon emerged from behind the tapestry in the great hall; two hundred glasses raised to toast the peace and prosperity the Westbridges would now share; and the cheers that greeted Damon's use of the kissing bough hovering overhead.

As they led the procession into the abbey church to celebrate that very first Christmas, tears tickled the backs of her eyes—tears of happiness, of gratitude, and of love.

"Behold! I bring you tidings of great joy," intoned the vicar as the last guest entered. "Tonight we celebrate peace and the promise of a better tomorrow. But before we remember that first Christmas, I take great pleasure in publishing the Banns of Marriage between—"

Sophie lost track of the ritual as Damon caressed her arm. She hadn't expected the process to move so quickly, yet with his warmth burning into her side, she suddenly couldn't wait for it to finish.

"Peace be yours until the end of time," he murmured softly as he slid his arm around her waist. "I love you."

"Amen."

The Gift of the Spoons

by Nancy Butler

1

Pippa Spoon . . .

Not a name calculated to inspire confidence, Christopher Herne mused as he poked at his overdone mutton chop. The name brought to mind a cackling crone or a gibbering village idiot of the female variety. Certainly not someone he wanted to entrust with his son's life.

He looked up abruptly as a group of drovers came rollicking into the tavern taproom, making a jolly commotion as they were greeted all around. Four days before Christmas, Herne thought, and already the air of festivity and bonhomie was rife. For a moment, he pretended he was a normal traveler, on his way home to spend a warm, cozy holiday with his family. Then he scowled at the truth of his situation—the house he'd left behind was a place of despair. And it was this cursed season that was the cause of his troubles.

The boy's health had been improving since summer; everyone agreed on that. But then in early December it had snowed. The dusting of white outside his bedroom windows had cast the child into a deep melancholy. He began to cry in the night, pitiful cries that upset the whole household. Even his old nurse, the redoubtable Elsie Gain, had been unable to comfort him. Herne had dismissed his son's illness at first—it was nothing more than a bout of the grippe, he assured himself. But a vicious wasting fever followed, as though the boy's troubled spirit had somehow infected his frail body.

The doctors had been called in then, including several noted physicians from London. But none of them had an answer. They had poked and prodded the boy's limbs, examined his teeth and the shape of his head; they had spoken of water cures, hot tongs, and belladonna potions.

"It's no better than witchery," Herne pronounced after the last of the doctors had taken his leave. Mrs. Gain had given him an odd look then, and later that evening she came tiptoeing into his study.

"Perhaps it's true witchery you need, sir," she said.

If she hadn't been with his family for thirty-odd years, if she hadn't been his own devoted nurse once upon a time, he'd have shouted her from the room for her foolishness. But instead, he listened. He had no other course. The doctors had disagreed to a man over what ailed his son, but they had been in accord on one thing—unless some cure was found for the child, he would not live to see the new year.

Mrs. Gain told him of a young woman she'd known in her youth, one who possessed a healing touch. She thrust away Herne's protests over such humdudgeon, claiming that she herself had been the beneficiary of this woman's special skills.

"Took a mortal fever, I did, sir, just before I was to wed my Joe. My parents scratched together enough money for the local doctor, but he could do nothing. My father gave up on me then, and wanted to call in the village priest, but my mother would not quit. She went off by herself into

Chatham Wood, which lay beyond the village. She went there to find the wisewoman, Pippa Spoon."

Herne recalled the chill that rippled through him when he'd first heard that name. He had immediately shaken it off.

"She returned with my mother that same night . . . through a dreadful storm, it was. She came right to my bedside, drenched to the skin, and set her hands upon my head. I thought she was the angel of death, standing there in her long black cloak."

Mrs. Gain clutched his hand then, her narrow fingers biting into his skin. "But mark my words, sir, she was the angel of life." She paused to let this sink in. "I was sitting up and eating breakfast with the appetite of a field hand the very next morning. My parents still send her a basket of food at Christmastide."

Herne protested this melodramatic tale, pointing out that fevers often seemed most severe just before they broke, but Mrs. Gain remained adamant.

"If the doctors have no answers," she said forthrightly, "then where is the harm in seeking out this woman? I know she was still alive this summer past—my mother wrote that she had cured the local squire's son of smallpox."

Herne had refused to consider the idea for weeks, watching helplessly as the boy's condition worsened. He grew too weak to be wheeled around the house in his bath chair. He stopped playing with his tin soldiers, barely spoke to anyone, and three days earlier, he had stopped eating. Herne's cook prepared the boy's favorite meals, but they were returned to the kitchen untouched. Mrs. Gain had been keeping him alive by feeding him porridge and watered wine.

Last night, Herne had saddled his most brutish horse and ridden out onto the moors. He screamed into the black night, railing at this strange sickness, railing at the fates that had taken his wife in a senseless accident last winter, one that had also injured his child. He swore then, by everything he believed in, that they would not have the boy.

Mrs. Gain tried not to look smug when he asked her for directions to Pippa Spoon's cottage. She had dutifully written down the quickest route to her village, an ancient place called Riddley, and told him he must ask at the local tavern for the exact route to the wisewoman's home.

Before he set out that morning, he'd spent an hour in the boy's room, watching his uneasy sleep. The child opened his eyes once, his gaze unfocused.

"I'm bringing someone here to help you," Herne had said, gently brushing the hair back from his forehead. "I'll be home before Christmas. I promise."

The boy nodded in understanding. Then he leaned forward slightly, reaching out to grasp his father's hand. "I'm sorry," he rasped before his head fell back to the pillow.

"You have nothing to be sorry for," Herne responded softly. "You are ill. But very soon you will be well again."

"I am sorry, Father," the child repeated.

He had lapsed back into sleep before Herne left his room, but there was no expression of relaxed ease on his face. Even in slumber, the boy's face was twisted with pain, as if the devils that beset him never released their hold for an instant.

Herne now forced himself to finish the dry chop; he would need sustenance to get him through the next few hours. It was tempting to linger here in the tavern, with its roaring fireplace and gathering of merry patrons. Though the place was rude by most standards, a scattering of lit tapers gave it a mellow glow. The dark beams over his head were hung with pine garlands, and near the bar, a sprig of mistletoe dangled, beckoning the farm lads to steal a kiss from the rosy-cheeked barmaid.

It was a bright, cheerful place, holding fast against the dense black of the wood that lay beyond it. But Herne's business was in that wood, and the night would not keep him from his course. The sooner he spoke to this wise-woman, the sooner he could return home. If Pippa Spoon refused to aid him or if her aid did no good, he wanted to be beside his son for whatever time was left him.

He threw down a few coins on the table and rose. When Mr. Trumble, the landlord, saw him gather up his cape, he came hurrying over.

"I have drawn a map for you, Mr. Herne." He held out a sheet of paper. "But surely you do not intend to go into the wood tonight."

"Tonight's as good as any time." Before the landlord could continue his protest, Herne added, "In the war I did a bit of reconnoitering at night. Finding a woman's cottage should be less arduous than locating French pickets."

"As you will," the landlord muttered. "The main thing to look out for is this lightning-struck tree." His finger jabbed at the paper. "If you miss the left-hand turning, you will end up in an abandoned quarry. It's treacherous terrain, sir. If you find yourself in a clearing, you'd best go forward on foot."

"Thank you for the warning." The landlord looked as though he was about to say something more. "What is it?" Herne coaxed. "What else should I know?"

The man led him out of the taproom into the narrow hallway. "'Tis the night, sir. The solstice is upon us."

"I am aware of what day it is," Herne said gruffly.

The landlord rubbed a hand over his mouth, then his eyes met Herne's. "The old ways are mostly lost now. But there was a time when this night held great meaning. My gran'dad always warned us to stay inside and keep all the candles lit, because the spirits were about in the land."

Herne tried not to roll his eyes. Though he'd been brought up in the country, he had no patience with these rural superstitions. Still, he himself was on his way to find a purported wisewoman, so perhaps he had no right to scoff.

"I will go cautiously, Mr. Trumble."

"You do that, Mr. Herne. You look to be a man who can take care of himself, but they do say there are things in Chatham Wood that are not of this earth."

"You mean like Pippa Spoon?" he drawled.

"Not Pippa. She isn't like other people, there's no arguing that. And some do call her a witch. But if she is one, well, she's *our* witch, and we look after our own here in Riddley. No, there's other things . . . it's whispered that unholy creatures come out after dark. And the woodchoppers who make their living in the forest are now all gone home to their beds. It's a lonely road you are taking, sir."

Herne swung his cape over his shoulders. "If Pippa Spoon is not afraid to live in the wood, why should I be afraid to ride through it?"

He was gone out the front door and missed Mr. Trumble's reply. "Because Pippa Spoon is armed against such things," he said softly, "as you or I shall never be."

* * *

The kettle was finally boiling. It seemed as if it had taken an age. Pippa shifted it from the hob to the sideboard and gingerly tossed in a mixture of herbs, stirring them with a long wooden spoon. Within seconds the tangy odor of mint and the sweet scent of chamomile blended in the room.

It was a comforting smell, one that reminded Pippa of her mother—though her mother had always carried with her a cornucopia of rich, lovely scents. Lavender and thyme, rosemary and verbena. The light herbs, Pippa had been taught to call them. As opposed to the dark ones, the henbane and mandrake, the nightshade and foxglove. Though they, too, had their uses—noxious weeds and poisonous plants put to good use for healing. There was little that grew up from the ground, her mother often said, that did not have some practical application.

Pippa stirred the pot once more before she put the lid on the kettle. The tea would need to steep for another ten minutes. Brushing back her long hair, she went to the kitchen table. Both her cats were sleeping upon it; one of them, a ragged gray tom, was stretched out over a large, open book. She hefted him off it and set him gently down on a chair cushion. He didn't even open his eyes.

She scanned the pages of the old book, squinting to read the places where the ink had faded. If only her mother were here to help decipher them; *she* knew the pages of this book by heart. But that was an idle wish. Pippa had to make her way alone now.

Christmas would be a bleak, lonely time without her mother bustling about in a frenzy of baking and decorating. Pippa hadn't been able to muster any enthusiasm for making gingerbread cakes or hanging pine boughs. The wall over the parlor mantel, which should have boasted a fine holly wreath, still wore a spray of corn husks and oak leaves. She knew it was wrong to let her sadness overwhelm her, especially since her last words to her mother had been a reassurance that she would stay in good spirits.

Ah, but she missed her dreadfully, especially tonight, this darkest of nights, when she felt the fingers of real fear gripping her for the first time in her young life.

Something was out there in the wood.

She'd been uneasy and restless all day, but had attributed it to the solstice. All the Spoon women were attuned to the astronomical calendar, the solstices and equinoxes. Their powers increased with the waxing of the moon and were most potent when it was full. Though Pippa bridled at the notion of witches, at least the unholy ones who purportedly made pacts with the devil, she had an abiding belief in the tradition of wisewomen—healers, herbalists, and midwives. A pity few people made a distinction between the two.

Her grandmother, another Pippa Spoon, had been accused of witchcraft in her village in Dorset and had barely gotten away with her life. She had settled here in Chatham Wood because it was ancient ground and such places were welcoming to wisewomen. The forest had indeed been a haven for the Spoons. Every manner of local plant grew within its bounds and some that were unusual for this part of the country. It was rare that her mother had to send away for her herbs, though when she did, it was to exotic places like Morocco and Greece, and once, even to distant China. Pippa still had the amber bottle with the strange, beautiful calligraphy on its label.

She finally located the section of the book marked *Portents.* These were very old entries, written before the age of reason had made such notions obsolete. But Pippa was grasping at straws, trying to convince herself that her fears were groundless, that there was not something dangerous coming toward her through the forest.

Scanning down the parchment page, she stopped at one entry. *Be warned when owls fly by day.* She grimaced. She'd seen a barn owl lofting over the wood that very afternoon. Below it she read, *Pay heed to the kettle that will not boil.* This was getting worse and worse. *Mark the milk that curdles before its time.* Beside the hearth lay the cats' dishes, where she had poured out a pot of cream that had gone sour, even though she had milked the cow only that morning.

She slammed the book closed and paced away from the table in agitation, again wishing her mother were here to advise her, not this book full of archaic beliefs.

We do not fear the night, her mother had told her as a child. *The night is our time of harvest and our time of worship. Darkness is our sanctuary . . . and our cloak of safety.*

Pippa never feared the coming of night. She never slid the heavy bar across the cottage door or sealed up the shutters on the windows. Until tonight.

There was a distant howling deep in the wood. Her gaze flew to the door. If there was trouble in the forest, it was her duty to be out there. She couldn't shirk that responsibility—the wild creatures were in her charge as much as the villagers.

The howling rose to a keening pitch, and then was abruptly cut off.

Her heart in her throat, Pippa crossed the room, took up

her oak staff, and plucked her thick woolen shawl off its peg by the door. If there was danger for her tonight in Chatham Wood, she would face it head-on, not cowering in her cottage.

Let the night be her cloak and her sanctuary.

Herne's gray gelding was rattled by very little. Merlin had been battle tested in Spain, where he had learned to stand calmly in the face of enemy fire. But as he and his master made their way deeper into Chatham Wood, the gelding broke out in a frothy sweat. Herne stroked his neck and uttered a few soothing words. This was the most stout-hearted beast he had ever known, and it troubled him that the horse was showing such unease. For himself, his chief regret was that he hadn't worn a warmer cloak. It seemed the tightly spaced trees did little to block the force of the icy wind.

To his relief the path they rode along had been clear-cut, the road bed wide enough for a small cart. The moon was nearly full, offering more than enough light for him to see the landmarks Mr. Trumble had pointed out—the three boulders near the entry to the path, the stand of alders that marked his first turning. When he reached the lightning-struck tree, he realized it would have been hard to miss, even in the full dark—it was a massive, majestic oak that would have been an object of worship in the days of the Druids.

As he approached the cloven tree, something large and hairy shambled out from behind it, onto the left-hand trail. The gelding snorted and danced in alarm. Herne fumbled for his pistol in his greatcoat pocket, but could not get his cold-stiffened fingers around the butt.

The creature kept coming toward them, snuffling the air with its snout. Herne had never seen a bear up close, and he didn't intend to rectify that omission any time soon. As the bear reared up onto its hind legs and let out a series of low grunts, Herne set his heels against the horse's side and aimed him toward the right-hand fork.

The gelding tore along the narrow track, his fear almost palpable. Herne tried to restrain him, but Merlin fought the bit and refused to slow down. Finally, they reached a clearing where Herne was able to turn the gelding in a wide circle. Once he'd stopped the horse, he leapt immediately from the saddle, mindful of Mr. Trumble's warning. This had to be the outskirts of the old quarry.

He led the horse cautiously around the scattered trailings of stone that littered the ground. The woman's cottage lay somewhere off to his left; he should be able to cut through the wood and regain the original trail. His horse, it seemed, had other ideas.

"Settle down," he said gently when Merlin refused to enter the trees. "Whatever that was on the trail back there, we've left it far behind. Now be a good fellow and—"

A sustained howling suddenly erupted from somewhere beyond them, echoing up into the treetops. It skirled eerily around man and horse, rising up as though it came from the very pits of Hell. The gelding threw himself back on his haunches, nearly wrenching the reins from Herne's hands. He knotted them around one fist, and with his free hand he drew the pistol from his pocket.

"Steady," he whispered as he took a step forward. The horse locked his legs, refusing to budge. Herne discarded the notion of tying Merlin to a tree; a panicked horse could snap a pair of reins as though they were made of twine.

So he stood where he was, his eyes narrowing as he surveyed the barren clearing. Some distance beyond him, the ground fell away into blackness, marking the edge of the quarry pit.

His breath caught as something came over the lip, a swift shadow the size of a large dog, moving low to the ground. Herne raised his pistol, following the progress of the creature as it skirted the edge of the clearing. It was coming toward him, but in the roundabout manner of a cautious predator.

He was loathe to shoot at it; after all, it might only be a farm dog out for a night of hunting. But then, when it was ten yards away, the creature stopped and looked directly at him. Its eyes blazed with an unearthly light, the shimmering green of foxfire.

There was a noise in the wood behind him, of something rapidly approaching through the underbrush. There were animals that hunted in pairs, he knew, one distracting the prey, while its mate attacked from ambush. He was debating whether he should dispatch the visible animal now, when the second creature broke from the wood with a loud cry. Merlin jerked back violently, dragging Herne with him. A pistol shot echoed sharply in the still night.

The animal across the clearing yelped, leaping into the air as the ball hit its mark.

The next instant Herne felt a jarring blow on his wrist. The pistol went flying from his grasp. As he spun to face his attacker, a wooden staff whooshed hard into his middle. He doubled over, grunting in pain.

"You've shot my wolf, damn you!" a woman's voice cried raggedly.

Herne watched in disbelief as the woman raced across

the clearing and threw herself down beside the still figure. "I knew you would bring trouble to this place," she snarled over her shoulder.

"I was . . . s-seeking Pippa S-p-poon . . ." he managed to gasp out as he straightened up. Lord, the shrew had knocked the wind right out of him.

But she was not paying him any heed. "Oh, my poor Ranulf," she murmured as her fingers danced over the animal's rough coat.

"He was stalking me," Herne called out to her. He was dashed if he was going to feel guilty over shooting a wild animal, especially since it had been an accident.

"Wolves don't stalk humans," she muttered darkly as she got to her feet. "Even when they are starving." Her voice rose a notch. "Here, bring your horse over to me. I need to get Ranulf home, and I'm not strong enough to carry him."

"Can't you just leave him here? I'll help you bury him—"

"He's not dead. But he's losing blood. I need to get him properly bandaged."

Herne shook his head. "You may know wolves, but you don't know much about horses if you think Merlin will let that animal anywhere near him."

She was still muttering imprecations as she recrossed the clearing and tugged the horse's reins away from him. "He will do what I ask him to do." She was halfway to the fallen wolf, Merlin walking docilely behind her, when she turned back to Herne. "You'd better come, too. I don't think I can lift him myself."

"Yes, General," Herne said as he started after her.

She didn't acknowledge his sarcasm as she knelt to bind

up the wolf's shoulder with her apron. Herne noted the tender way she ministered to the animal, her touch both gentle and sure. "Perhaps," he said softly, "we can take him to Pippa Spoon, the healer."

She turned to look up at him; he caught a glint of silver-green light in her eyes and was reminded of the wolf's eerie stare. For the first time that night, his hackles stood up. The denizens of the forest held little fear for him, but he had been to war and he knew the evils men could inflict on one another. And so he was wise enough to be wary of his own kind, even a stripling country girl. But then her gaze softened and one side of her mouth twitched up. "What if I told you *I* was the woman you sought?"

He frowned and rubbed his still-tender stomach. "I am not in the mood for jests."

She shrugged. "As you like. I don't have time to argue. I must get Ranulf home. Lift him over the saddle, and I'll climb up and hold him steady."

Herne did as she asked, amazed at the way she had commandeered his horse. He hefted the wolf into his arms, feeling the soft fur against his face as he raised the animal and draped it over the saddle. Merlin danced a little when the limp weight was placed across his withers, but the woman calmed him with a word. She groped for the stirrup, managed to get her foot into it, and sprang up into the saddle.

"That way is the quickest," she said to Herne, pointing to a nearby stand of trees. "Oh, and don't forget my staff."

"Yes, General." He leaned down and plucked the length of oak from the ground. "But perhaps you'd better go first since you know the way."

"You have to lead me. I need both hands to hold Ranulf." She then added a bit hesitantly, "Plus, I've rarely been on a horse before."

He looked up at her, sitting astride and relaxed on his high-bred gelding. She looked like she could lead an army, if confidence counted for anything. He took up the dangling reins and started toward the woods. They were almost to the first trees when he paused. "I should warn you . . . we came across a bear on the trail."

He heard the catch of fear in her voice. "You didn't shoot him, too, did you?"

"No, but . . . Good God, don't tell me he's another of your pets."

"He was my mother's pet. She rescued him from a troupe of traveling players."

"You are lucky," he said as he resumed walking, brushing aside branches and vines as they went deeper into the trees. Her shortcut was not a forgiving path. "Lucky that no one has shot at your menagerie before now. Most people wouldn't think twice about killing a bear or a wolf."

"You mean people like you?" she drawled.

"I mean," he said between his teeth, "that a stray traveler meeting up with either of them wouldn't wait to discover whether the animal was a threat or not."

"The few villagers who come into the wood leave the bear alone—they know he is not dangerous. And no one enters the wood at night, which is the only time Ranulf is allowed to roam. He comes home at dawn."

Herne shook his head. He was dealing with a madwoman, one who thought she was the healer, Pippa Spoon. The real Pippa Spoon would be closer in age to Mrs. Gain, who was well over fifty, not the twenty-odd years this woman boasted. But Herne decided not to tax her with that; it never paid to argue with the addled.

The wolf whimpered once as they climbed over a fallen log, but the woman calmed him with a stroke of her hand.

"Aren't you afraid he'll snap at you? Dogs in pain will often bite their masters."

"He knows my touch," she said. "I got him from a tinker when he was a pup. The man claimed his father was a wolf, but he just looked like a snippet of black fur to me. Then he grew up, and it occurred to me that both his parents were wolves."

"And that didn't frighten you, bringing a wild animal into your home?"

She reached forward and patted Merlin's neck. "They were all wild once . . . we *all* were. But we take to the warmth of the hearth and the stable, and then we bide."

"We bide," he echoed under his breath.

His whole life long he'd wanted nothing more than to bide. But he'd been sent away to school as a young boy after his mother's death and went off to university after that, where he'd lost himself in the study of science and mathematics. He'd returned home briefly when his father died, but almost immediately had been recruited to work at the Home Office in London. It seemed someone in Whitehall had learned, through an acquaintance at Oxford, of Herne's passion for ciphers and codes and all things mechanical. That talent had kept him out of combat, but not away from France, where he went on occasion to spy out any new developments in French artillery.

While he was returning home from one such mission, a storm had forced him to stop off at a friend's home in Sussex. He'd met a young woman there, a planter's daughter from Barbados, who was visiting his friend's wife. She had enchanted him with her pale beauty and charming manner. In a matter of days, he'd fallen headlong in love.

After resigning his post with the Home Office, he had carried his new wife off to his estate near Glastonbury, prepared to enjoy the pleasures of wedded life. Unfortunately, he quickly learned that his wife detested the countryside—it was the excitement of London she craved. And, eventually, after the birth of his son, the attentions of other men. When he fled from his home three years later, betrayed and disillusioned, it was with the sure knowledge that she had married him only to escape her narrow, colonial life.

He had enlisted in the army then, the real army, not the dusty corridors of Whitehall. The deprivations of camp life had distracted him from his pain, but had also enlightened him as to the wretched nature of humankind in general. There was no glory in war, save the small, bright spark of camaraderie that sometimes flared in the midst of battle. Yet even in battle, a man had a sense of cause and effect. When he returned to England, to the tattered remnants of the life he'd fled, nothing any longer made sense. His whole world had gone topsy-turvy.

Perhaps he was the one who was addled, he thought grimly, and not this strange young woman.

They finally came to a clearing where several outbuildings were arranged around a snug, slate-roofed cottage. Splinters of light escaped from the shuttered windows, and a curl of smoke wafted up from the wattled chimney.

"If you would just carry Ranulf inside for me," the woman said as she slid from the saddle, "before you go on your way."

Herne lifted the wolf down and carried him through the

arched doorway. The shadowed interior of the kitchen smelled of chamomile and spice, and he had a fleeting impression of rich colors and exotic fabrics. As he laid the animal on a rug beside the hearth, he couldn't resist running his hand along its side, below the crude bandage. The dark pelt was thick, crisp on the surface, soft as goosedown closer to the skin. The wolf raised his head and drew his lips away from his teeth. Herne snatched his hand back.

"Don't be afraid," she said. "He's grinning at you. He knows you helped him."

"Then he also knows I shot him," Herne said. "I'd better see to my horse."

2

Pippa watched the door close behind him and gave an audible sigh of relief. It was one thing to know danger was out there in the woods . . . it was quite another to invite it into your home. And this tall, harsh-faced man *was* a danger to her. The instant she'd run into the clearing, she had a clear vision of him looming over her in anger. The premonition she'd been feeling all day had not been false. Ranulf had been shot, but that was not nearly the end of the threat this man represented.

"Poppycock," she said aloud. It was her mother's favorite expletive. Ranulf's tail thumped against the hearth rug. "No, she's not here any longer, as you very well know. I did sound just like her, though, didn't I?"

She gathered her medicines together, and set to work on him. Wetting a cloth in the still warm kettle of tea, she used it to soften the bandage where the blood had clotted.

Fortunately, the pistol ball had merely grazed the wolf's shoulder, leaving behind a ten-inch furrow. She first dabbed on a paste made from the root of Solomon's Seal, which would stop any bleeding, followed by a drawing salve made of comfrey and mullein. Ranulf lay still while she tended him, whining only slightly when she rebandaged his shoulder.

"You've a nice touch, General."

Pippa nearly yelped in surprise. She'd been so engrossed in her doctoring, she hadn't heard the stranger come back into the cottage. He was sitting at the table now, the book of arcana open before him.

"Why are you still here?" she said without an ounce of cordiality.

He disregarded her question and merely tapped the pages of the book with one long finger. "I see you have been studying your spells. Are these woods full of witches, then? Have I stumbled into a . . . a coven?"

She moved to the table and shut the book with a thud. A thin veil of dust rose up from its cover. "I am no witch. And since you are in my home, you'd best take care what you say."

"I have no desire to bide here." He nearly started at that particular choice of words. "But I need to find Pippa Spoon, and since your pet bear made me lose my way, I think the least you can do is give me her direction."

"What business do you have with her in the middle of the night?"

He scowled slightly. "That is my own affair."

She shrugged and turned away from him. After filling a shallow bowl from the hand pump beside the soapstone sink, she carried it to the wolf and set it down near his snout.

"I am not leaving until you answer my question." He rose from his chair, filling up the small room, his wide shoulders and broad chest accentuated by the voluminous black cape he wore. His eyes bored into hers, quiet anger simmering in their depths.

"I answered you at the quarry."

His jaw set. "I insist that you tell me how to find that blasted woman's cottage . . ."

"Pippa Spoon wants nothing to do with you," she declared.

Herne leaned toward her. "I have a son," he said slowly, "who is racked with fever. It is a strange, wasting malady the doctors cannot name. His nursemaid lived in Riddley as a girl, and she told me she was cured of a fever by Pippa Spoon. Now, I doubt you were even born yet when Elsie Darrow lived here."

"It was my mother who helped Elsie. She and I have the same name—Phillipa."

"Then, for the love of God, tell me where can I find your mother."

Pippa shook her head sadly. "She is . . . gone."

"Gone?" Herne refused to believe he'd made this wretched journey for nothing. "Where has she gone?" His voice lowered. "I *must* find her."

"She is gone where no man can find her."

He sank back into his chair, his head in his hands. He would not be defeated; it was not an option. If the woman he sought was dead, then he would find another healer. The doctors had failed him, science had failed him . . . so he had no choice but to explore any remote possibilities that might help the boy.

He raised his head. "Then *you* must come in her stead." He spoke the words with an authority that bordered on arrogance.

"Me?" Pippa drew back. "It is out of the question. First of all, you shot my wolf. Even if I forgave you for that, which is unlikely, I need to stay here and nurse him."

He rose again from his chair, his hands gripping the table edge. "You would place the life of an animal before the life of a child?"

She disregarded his sneer. "Furthermore, I cannot leave my livestock untended."

"I will not be thwarted in this. I can pay whatever you ask. Anything."

Pippa went to the tall dresser that sat against the far wall. She lifted a wooden coffer from its top and opened it. "See? It's full of gold. I do not need your money."

His hands curled at his sides as his brow knit in frustration.

It was a noble brow, Pippa had to concede, high and intelligent. The eyes beneath it were a dark pewter gray, deep set and thickly lashed. The hair above it was also dark, the windblown nut brown locks curling slightly above his collar. His clothing—the fine wool cape, seamless buckskin breeches, and gleaming top boots—would not have shamed him in London. His refined attire, however, did not match his face, which was too tanned and weathered for any elegance. Yet there was something about his face that was familiar to her. And not in a reassuring way.

The stranger caught her examining him. It did not faze him, but merely provoked a wry, humorless smile. "Everyone has a price, Miss Spoon," he uttered. "It just takes time to discover what it is. Unfortunately, time is the one thing I do not have. So I throw myself on your mercy . . . come home with me . . . attend my son. You will find yourself in the rare position of having Christopher Herne in your debt."

Her eyes widened. "Herne?" she echoed. Her head began to shake back and forth. "No," she said in a faint, faraway voice. "No, please . . ."

"What is it?" He took a step toward her, his hands outstretched.

"You must leave here," she said, crossing to the door and flinging it open. "Now."

"But—"

"I am not a healer," she said forthrightly, clutching her hands to her chest. "My mother was the healer. I am sorry, but I can do nothing for you. Nothing."

Muttering an oath, the stranger swept out into the frigid night, his cape brushing her gown as he went past. She slammed the door and slid the bar home, her pulse racing, her fingers unconsciously brushing at her skirt where his cape had touched it.

She stood unmoving for several minutes, waiting for her heartbeat to steady. Maybe she was starting at shadows. Maybe the man's name was nothing more than a coincidence.

She stumbled to the table, urgently leafing through the ancient book until she found the page she sought, a page she had purposely avoided for many years. On it was a crude but detailed sketch of a man's head, eyes deep set beneath the high brow, wide antlers sprouting from the mass of wildly curling hair. It could have easily been the stranger's face that looked out at her from beneath those pagan horns. The words below the drawing read *Herne the Hunter.*

Herne . . . The great horned lord of the forest. She trembled at the notion that the most feared god in ancient Britain had been here in her cottage.

Poppycock.

She'd heard the word inside her head, but it was as if her mother had spoken it over her shoulder. Her dear mother, who had taught Pippa the old lore, but who had professed little belief in those stories. However, they had lodged in Pippa's imagination with a vengeance. The mystery and magic of those tales had thrilled her, but they had also frightened her. They still did.

No wonder the stranger had seemed ominously familiar to her—Herne had been the chief denizen of her worst childhood nightmares, pursuing her through the forests of her dreams, giving chase among the shadowed trees of night. Those dreams had haunted her youth. As she grew older, the dreams altered—Herne still pursued her, but there was no blood lust in his pursuit, but another sort of hunger, one that frightened her even more.

She'd never mentioned those dreams to her mother, who, in spite of being a wisewoman and a healer, had far less imagination than her daughter. She would have called Pippa a ninny and prescribed a nice, brisk tonic for her.

Fortunately, Pippa was perceptive enough to know, even as a child, that the forest that rose around their cottage was not the terrible landscape of her dreams, and so she never feared going out into Chatham Wood. Well, not before tonight.

She sat beside Ranulf for a time, talking to him in a low voice, refusing to give in to her fears. Christopher

Herne was an English gentleman, not a pagan god. He meant her no harm, merely sought her aid. So what if he had tried to bully her? His son was ill, maybe dying, and she could excuse the worst behavior in such circumstances.

A trickle of regret ran in an icy rivulet over her heart. She had promised her mother to carry on their good work, but Pippa knew her own limitations—knew them and chafed at them. It would have done no good getting the man's hopes up. She was not blessed with the healing powers her mother had possessed. What powers she did have were more of a befuddlement than a blessing.

Eventually, Ranulf fell asleep, with the two cats tucked against his belly. Pippa put on her nightgown and crawled into bed. Just before she nodded off, she touched the tiny gold cross she wore on a chain around her throat. The old gods and spirits of Britain had long ago been subdued by the followers of the carpenter from Galilee. But a wise-woman, even one who had been a faithful Christian her entire life, knew that they sometimes stirred.

When Herne went to retrieve Merlin from the barn, he realized he was too worn down, emotionally and physically, to ride back to Riddley. The barn was warm; the sweet scent of dry clover blending with the pungent odors of horse and cow lulled him into a state of inertia. After removing Merlin's tack, he lay down wearily on a pile of hay in a vacant stall, thinking he'd had far worse bivouacs in the war.

He shrugged the collar of his cape around his chin and stared up at the raftered ceiling. In the morning he would convince Pippa Spoon to help him. He didn't believe for an instant that she wasn't a healer; he'd seen how she doctored the wolf. There had to be something he could offer her that would tempt her to leave home for a few days. Surely a woman who lived alone in the woods must lack for something.

Alone . . . The word struck a lingering chord. Christmas was but four days off, and he would bet his entire fortune that Pippa Spoon would be spending it alone—alone and grieving. He hadn't missed her bleak expression when she'd spoken of her mother.

Christmas was no time for anyone to be alone. Whenever he'd been away from home over the holiday season, he made sure to surround himself with lively people. After his marriage, when he still cherished the hope of a happy life, he'd hosted parties and sleigh rides for his neighbors. The house had brimmed with gaiety.

But not this year. There were no decorations in the house, no holly sprigs or pine garlands, no beribboned gifts set upon the landing. This year his home held its breath, awaiting not the merry anticipation of Christmas morning, but the grim finale of his son's illness.

Still, even if he couldn't offer Pippa Spoon a cheerful Christmas, he could tempt her with the company of others to pass the holiday. And who knew, perhaps the task of ministering to his son might even distract her from her own loss.

Herne awoke with a start and lay there shivering in the hay. The barn was still deep in shadow, the first faint light of dawn barely peeping in through the opened stable door. He was puzzled by the sight; he knew he'd closed the door before he fell asleep.

He tried to get up, then realized there was something

sitting on his feet. Not at his feet, *on* them—something large and hairy.

"Go away," he whispered fiercely. The animal shifted slightly, but did not remove its weight. Herne shot a look at Merlin, who was dozing calmly in the next stall. The horse had clearly been beguiled by this place. The nervous creature of last night had vanished.

"Get!" Herne said forcefully, wondering how one reasoned with a bear. The animal began licking Herne's boot tops, his tongue rasping audibly on the fine leather.

"Good Lord, he's going to eat me," he muttered.

The bear woofed once, and then rose to all fours. He trundled up next to Herne and lay down with a heavy sigh, nestling into the bedding. Herne cursed under his breath when he felt the wide backside nudge against him. There was no way he was going to share his berth with a bear, pet or no pet. He sidled away from the beast, got cautiously to his feet, then fled through the open door. The air was bitter cold, and he was shivering violently by the time he reached the cottage.

He banged several times on the stout door, praying the woman would show him a little charity. After a minute had passed, he banged again. "Please," he whispered, his face against the wood.

The door swung open, and he nearly fell into the room.

Pippa Spoon skittered back from him. "You're *still* here?" Her voice was thick with sleep, her eyes glassy in the light of the taper she held.

"Your b-bear . . ." he said through chattering teeth. "H-he came into the barn . . . he was trying to eat my boots."

"Rolly sleeps in the barn." Her voice held a hint of

amusement as she added, "And he eats fish and berries . . . not gentlemen's boots."

He glowered at her for a moment; then the humor of his ridiculous situation struck him as well, and he began to chuckle softly. "Good Lord, I must be dreaming this. Wolves and bears and . . ." He looked at her keenly. "What other surprises do you have in store for me, Miss Spoon? A lurking unicorn . . . a recalcitrant griffin?"

"No, just a cat or two." Her eyes danced as she reached forward and plucked a piece of straw from his hair.

She was laughing back at him openly now, this wraith in a long white gown. Well, not a wraith, precisely. Where her dress and shawl had earlier obscured her figure, her plain cambric nightgown now revealed it. She was nicely rounded at breast and hip, he observed approvingly, and then thought himself moonstruck to be noting such things.

He shifted away from her to the hearth—where Ranulf had raised his head in sleepy curiosity—and tried to rub some circulation back into his arms. "I thought you wouldn't mind if I borrowed your barn. I was too weary to ride back to the village. And I believe I still have business with you. I'm not a man who gives up easily."

She leaned back against the door. "I am not a woman who is used to taking orders, Mr. Herne."

"Was I so overbearing?" he asked.

"I believe autocratic is the term."

There it was again, that trace of dry amusement in her voice. She looked away for a moment, as if thinking through a problem. When she turned back to him, there was guarded acceptance on her face. "Would you like some cocoa?"

He nodded. He watched while she filled the kettle at the pump. Her hair was unconfined and fell to the middle of her back in a rich cascade of chestnut waves, sparking red and gold in the firelight. As she came up beside him and bent over the hob, a thick lock of it tumbled over one shoulder. Before she could brush it back, Herne caught it up in his hand and drew it slowly behind her ear, letting his fingers sift through the silky strands.

"Thank you," she murmured, looking up at him with a tiny, fleeting smile.

As he retreated to the table, something inside him clenched. A need that had been dormant for far too long stirred and stretched. It flexed insistently now, undeniably awakened by the woman before him, who was young and well-favored. And ripe—if the soft rise of her breast against the embroidered bodice of her nightgown was any indication.

But there was more tugging on him than mere physical attraction—there was the intelligence in her angular face and the sweet generosity of her mouth. Most compelling of all, there was that expression of infinite tenderness he'd seen in her eyes as she cared for the fallen wolf; he wondered now how it might make a man feel to have such a look bestowed on him.

When she handed him the steaming mug, he wrapped his fingers tightly around it, grateful for the heat.

"It will warm you better inside you," she chided gently as she sat down opposite him and raised her own mug to her lips. As she sipped it delicately, her silvery green eyes observed him cautiously from over the rim. Herne was surprised by that caution.

"You have nothing to fear from me, you know," he said quietly after a long swallow of the blessedly hot liquid. He reached across the table to reassure her, but she quickly pulled her hand back with an indrawn breath.

"What is it?" he cried softly. "You're looking at me as though you've seen a ghost."

"Perhaps I have." She set down her mug and opened the book, pointing to the page with the picture of Herne the Hunter. "Look . . . He could be your twin."

He studied the drawing, wondering how she could mistake him for this wild-eyed pagan god. Then he noticed the set of the jaw and the fierce brow, the long mouth and deep-set eyes. Certainly not a true likeness of the face he saw each morning in his mirror, but close enough to send a little shiver up his spine.

"Must be a long-lost Herne ancestor," he said with a twisted grin. "Though we seem to have given up the antlers over time."

"You think I am daft."

"I think you are making up ways to scare yourself. It comes from being alone too much." She started to object, and he raised one hand. "No, hear me out. I believe I can offer you something, after all. Christmas is soon upon us, and I suspect you will be spending it alone." Her eyes flashed at him warily. "I have a comfortable manor house a day's ride from here—it is open to you for the season. Though we will not be making merry, there are kindly people there who would welcome you. More so if you were there to attend my son."

"And my animals, what of them if I leave?"

"I've given this some thought. My son's nurse still has family nearby. I will pay them to look after your livestock. As for your wild charges, you said yourself that the bear wanders in the wood unmolested. We can take the wolf with us. I . . ." His voice caught, and he steeled himself to speak again. "I was wrong to suggest you could go off and leave an injured animal."

She set down her cocoa. "You have planned this out very neatly, I see. Except for one problem. I am not a healer."

"Nonsense," he said briskly. "I saw your skill with the wolf."

"That was mere doctoring," she stated flatly. "I do not have my mother's special gift, Mr. Herne. To my everlasting regret, I do not."

He cocked his head slightly. "But you have . . . ah . . . other gifts?"

She closed her eyes for a moment and sighed. "Yes, I suppose that's what you might call them. But they are troublesome things . . ."

"I've seen the power you have over animals, the way you calmed Merlin with just a word." He thought a moment. "And I suspect you have the 'sight,' as well. You knew I was coming here last night, didn't you?"

She flushed slightly. "Yes, I did. I knew it since morning. But I am frankly surprised that a . . . a rational man like yourself would even credit such things."

He shrugged. "I have studied the natural sciences. I know there are many forces that can't be explained, but which exist, nevertheless. I'm willing to concede that your skills might fall into that realm."

"But, Mr. Herne, those 'skills' can't cure your son. Not if he is really ill."

"What do you mean? Of course he is ill. The physicians tell me he's dying."

"Then go home and be with him," she pronounced. "Stop

wasting your time with a woman who is a pale shadow of her mother. There is nothing I can do for him."

This time he managed to capture her hand. He held it firm against the worn tabletop, his fingers curled around her wrist. "You can tell me," he said in a ragged whisper, "what his fate will be. I cannot stand this waiting; it is a torment to me."

"And knowing will make it better?"

He nodded. "Yes. Up till now I have refused to let him go. I've damned the doctors and their prosing diagnoses. I swear there are times when I think the strength of my will alone is keeping him alive. But if you tell me there is no hope, I will stand away."

Pippa felt her tears gather. This man might seem cold-hearted and harsh, but he had a terrible, fierce love for his child. She felt it emanating from the hand that held hers in its firm grip. That was another of her gifts, one he did *not* suspect—an ability to intuit things about people merely by touching them.

"There is always *hope*, Mr. Herne," she said gently, turning her hand up to twine her fingers with his. They sat there, hands clasped for several heartbeats, gazing into each other's eyes. Silvery green met deepest gray, and she watched Herne's face pale. She knew that he, too, was feeling the ripple of energy that was passing between them.

He released her hand abruptly and stood up, an expression of victory on his face. "You *will* come. I don't understand these gifts you possess—perhaps you don't even fully understand them yourself—but you have strength and compassion. That is what my son requires right now."

"Surely his mother—"

"His mother is dead," Herne snapped. "And she nearly took the boy with her to perdition."

Pippa blinked at his tone. "I think I need to hear this—"

"There is no time now. We must be off if we are to reach my home by nightfall."

She rose to face him. "But I have not said I will come with you."

He circled the table and took up both her hands. Her body hummed with the power of the connection. This was new, this tangible energy that flowed between her and the stranger. It was unlike any touch she had ever experienced—vivid, exciting, potent. She wanted to prolong it, to examine it.

She saw his pupils dilate slightly and knew that he felt it, too. But this time he did not try to break free. Instead, he tugged her closer.

"Well?" He was looking down at her from his great height, the sides of his cape folded back like the furled wings of a dark angel. She felt a brief ripple of yesterday's fear pass through her, and then it was instantly supplanted by a shivering, intense premonition of joy. For good or bad, Christopher Herne had come into her life. She had no choice but to let things play out.

"Yes," she said with a halting smile. "I will come with you."

3

Farmer Darrow made no objection to Herne's plan. He also made no objection to the generous purse Herne passed to him behind Pippa's back. Darrow promised to fetch her cow and goats from the cottage and to feed her cats until she returned.

They drove off then—Pippa seated on her pony cart, Herne riding ahead of her—with the well-wishes of Farmer Darrow ringing in their ears.

"He is a very kind man," Pippa said as they entered the winding lane that led away from the farm. "He would have done as you asked without your gold, you know."

"For you, perhaps. But I never ask favors of strangers. Gold ensures a good outcome. And speaking of gold," he said over his shoulder, "how did you come by your little hoard? I would think the people hereabouts dealt mostly in barter."

"My great-grandmother healed the son of a wealthy earl. He gave her the coffer. Though we rarely touch the gold; Mother's patients were always generous."

"And what sort of work did your father do? I assume you had a father, unless you just appeared, like Athena, fully grown and ready for battle."

Pippa grinned at his nonsense. "My father was a merchant ship captain."

"And where is he now?"

She frowned and bit her lip. "With my mother," she said after a long pause.

"Oh," he said and let the subject drop. He'd had enough of death and loss.

They took a brief luncheon in a small inn, where Herne convinced Pippa to leave behind her weary pony. He oversaw the hitching of a stout bay cob to the cart while she hand-fed some meat scraps to the wolf.

"How's he doing? Does he need to . . . ?" He nodded toward some distant bushes.

"Yes, if you don't mind helping him again."

That morning, before they left the cottage, he had carried the wolf to the edge of the yard, where the animal had quickly found an appropriate bush for his business. Herne now carried the wolf to a patch of shrubbery. Ranulf limped into the bushes and reappeared several minutes later, an expression of doglike glee on his lean face.

"Found something interesting, did you?" Herne muttered as he hefted the animal into his arms. "Something rather dead, by the smell of you." The wolf twisted his head up and licked Herne's ear.

They were both grinning when they returned to the cart. Pippa was able to get most of the offensive smell off Ranulf's pelt with a wet rag, chiding him fondly the whole time. She was secretly delighted by the bond that was growing between Herne and her wolf. She was less thrilled with the feelings the man stirred in her.

It wasn't as if she were a greenling around men. She'd had suitors in the past, mostly young men she'd met while working with her mother. But since none of them, not farmer or tutor or squire's son, had ever stirred any strong emotions in her breast, she'd become convinced that she was immune to romantic feelings. Her mother witnessed these one-sided courtships with bemusement, and had finally told Pippa to stop fretting. When the right man came along, she'd said, Pippa would know. And she would respond.

Pippa looked at Christopher Herne, who at the moment was teasing her wolf with a bit of straw, and her heart sank. She wasn't feeling any of the things she thought she should be feeling—she wasn't elated or giddy. Mostly, she felt out of patience with him. She only knew that he'd made her breath catch when he stroked her hair beside the fire. And that the air hummed whenever he touched her. The truth was, even if he wasn't the right man, she wanted very much to respond to him.

Herne insisted on driving the cart during the next leg of their journey. Pippa welcomed the warmth of his body on the wooden seat and wondered, each time his knee grazed hers, whether it was purely accidental. Midway through the afternoon, she fell into a light doze and let her head loll against his shoulder. He made no protest; some minutes later, he slipped one arm around her to hold her steady.

This, she thought as she tucked her nose into his throat, *is not a bad start.*

Herne tried to focus on his driving, not that the placid cob needed much minding. But anything was better than thinking about the woman who was nestled against him. She smelled like an autumn garden and fit perfectly beneath his arm. He was reminded of the briar roses that sometimes twined around a hedgerow—country blossoms, to be sure, but a treat to the eye. Once, the wind danced a rippling strand of her hair across his cheek, and he nearly groaned in frustration.

For twelve months his only thoughts had been for his injured son. It seemed a betrayal, somehow, that now, when the boy lingered so close to death, Herne's body should be clamoring for a woman. Such a hunger seemed profane and, yet, he knew it was also an affirmation of life. And it was not just any woman he craved, but this slim, green-eyed girl, with her strong will and her unusual gifts.

He'd played the fool for love once in his life, and it was not a role he ever intended to repeat. Right now his attraction to her was purely physical—an appetite he was sure he could curb—and he'd see that it never went beyond that. He merely desired her, which was a perfectly normal response, since he had not bedded a woman in over a year. The dark-eyed courtesans in Lisbon, had they known it, had offered him his last taste of pleasure before his world crashed down upon his ears.

He began to sing softly, a relatively tame barracks ballad, and Pippa stirred. She drew away from him and stretched her arms.

"Mmm . . . not very seasonal," she remarked with a yawn.

Herne looked away from her. With her sleepy eyes and tousled hair, she might have just awakened from a man's bed. From his bed. *Damn.*

"Would you mind driving?" He pulled up the cob. "I think Merlin's rested enough."

Before she could respond, he jumped down from the cart and mounted his horse, then rode past without looking at her.

He shared only the most cursory conversation with her after that. At one point, when the silence between them grew pronounced, Pippa asked him for more details of his son's ailment.

"You'll see them for yourself, soon enough," he said dismissively.

"Please, Mr. Herne . . . you have told me only that it is a mysterious, wasting fever."

"If you insist." He drew his horse up beside the cart. "It started in early December with endless bouts of crying. Which was followed by weeks of fever and delirium. Now he hasn't even the strength to eat."

"Is there a cough present? Any vomiting or spasms of the stomach? A rash or inflammation anywhere?"

"I've been through this a dozen times," he muttered.

"Not with me, you haven't."

"No," he said, after a long breath. "Only the fever . . . no other symptoms."

She began to feel more hopeful. Among her pharmacopoeia of herbs were several cures for fever—basil and balm, borage and meadowsweet. If this was all that ailed the child, she might indeed be able to help him.

"And what of his mother? Does he still mourn her? You see, there is often more to illness than the state of the body. There is a malaise of the soul that can lead to—"

"There is nothing wrong with my son's soul," he said curtly. "He merely suffered a bit of melancholy with the onset of the winter weather. It's possible, I suppose, that it reminded him of his mother's death—she died two weeks before Christmas. And now I hope you are done raking me over the coals." He dug his heels into Merlin's side and cantered off.

She raised her eyebrows at his show of temper, wondering, as she clucked to the cob, about the state of Christopher Herne's soul. She'd never met anyone who was so reluctant to talk about his past; in her experience, once you got a person going on that topic, they nattered on forever. But he was so guarded. Still, she had a strong suspicion that his son's illness and his wife's death were deeply entwined.

Herne insisted they push on through dinner, and Pippa was glad she'd packed some scones. She purposely did not offer any to her aloof companion, but managed to sneak one to Ranulf. By the time they reached Herne's estate, darkness had fallen. Pippa got only a fleeting impression of a sprawling Tudor manor.

As they entered the stable yard, a groom ran out and went to Merlin's head.

"The boy, Tom?" Herne asked quickly. "How is he faring?"

The bandy-legged groom shook his head. "No better, sir, I'm sorry to say."

Herne dismounted and came up beside the cart; he laid one hand on the wolf's side. "Tom Bailey can put Ranulf in the hay barn for the night. Now, if you will follow me—"

"But it will be freezing in there. He's still recovering—"

Herne's expression was regretful but firm. "I can't allow a wild animal under the same roof as my son, Miss Spoon. You must understand that."

The groom motioned for a stable lad to take Merlin. He then approached the cart and squinted at Ranulf. "I'll take him to my quarters behind the stable if you like, miss. I think I can manage him. I raised a fox kit as a boy."

"Thank you," she said as she lowered herself from the seat. Her legs wobbled under her as she touched down on the cobblestones. Herne reached for her at once, steadying her with his hands. She tugged back from him. "Don't," she said. "I am fine."

The groom lifted Ranulf from the cart, and Pippa started after him.

"Miss Spoon," Herne called out, "the house is this way."

"I'm sorry, but Ranulf is my first responsibility. I'll be in shortly."

He started to protest, but she had already turned away.

She followed the groom to his one-room cottage, where she helped make up a bed for the wolf.

"He's very tame," she assured the man. "I'll have the kitchen send over some scraps for him. And he'll need a bowl of water close by. He still isn't walking very well."

"What happened to him, miss? Poachers?"

"Your master shot him."

The groom started back. "And yet you've come here to help his son?"

"I have a very forgiving nature," she said dryly. "And your master is not one to give up easily."

"No," he agreed. "He's not given up on the boy, in spite of what the doctors say."

Pippa was at the door, when she had a sudden inspiration. "Could you tell me something, Mr. Bailey? What happened to your master's wife? He would not speak of it to me. Closed up like a clam, in fact. I'm not asking you to gossip, mind. I would just like to know, in case it has some bearing on the boy's illness."

"Poor mite," he murmured. "Before the accident, he was always underfoot in the stable. Loves horses, he does. But his mama refused to let him ride, no matter how he pleaded. And now he will never ride, even if he does recover."

Seeing Pippa's perplexed expression, he exclaimed, "Why, didn't Master Kit tell you? The boy is crippled. The coach accident left him with two broken legs. They were badly set and never mended properly."

Silently cursing all cow-handed physicians, Pippa sat down on a hassock and motioned Tom to a chair. "Start at the beginning, if you please. I fear there is a great deal your master didn't tell me."

* * *

Half an hour later, Pippa entered the house through the kitchen door. The cook looked up from her breadboard, her arms white with flour up to the elbows.

"Miss Spoon, is it?" she said with an Irish lilt. "Himself is up in the library, pacing about and scaring the posies off the wallpaper. You'd best go up quick now."

After requesting some food for Ranulf, Pippa looked longingly at the leftover roast that sat on the sideboard. The cook grinned at her. "I'll send a tray to your room when you are done with the boy."

Pippa thanked her and made her way up the servants' staircase. She emerged into a dark hall, where a tall wall clock was ringing the hour of nine. She didn't want to see Christopher Herne just then—she was far too vexed with him for one thing. For another, she didn't want him hovering over her while she examined his son. That was the cardinal rule of medicine she had learned from her mother—keep the family members away during treatment.

She went up two flights of stairs to the nursery level. After peeking into several empty rooms, she came to one that was lit by a lone candle. A thin woman with gray-brown hair was nodding in a chair beside a wide bed. The bedclothes were rumpled, and it took her several seconds to detect that a child lay in their midst.

Pippa crouched before the woman and took up her hand. "Mrs. Gain?"

The woman stirred and opened her eyes. They widened in shock for an instant.

"Miss Spoon . . . dear me, is it you? You have not changed in thirty years . . ."

Pippa grinned. "I'm her daughter, Mrs. Gain. She cannot help the child, I'm afraid, so I am here in her stead."

"The master told me he'd brought you. I was so sorry to hear about your mother, but, sakes alive, if you don't look just like her. As pretty as a songbird, she was."

Pippa fought down a blush. "How is he doing tonight?"

"I got him to eat a little porridge, but most of it came right back up. It's a fearful wasting illness he has, miss. We all pray there is something you can do for him."

I pray it, as well, Pippa murmured to herself. She saw that her carpetbag of medicines had been brought up; it lay on the floor beside the bed.

"Will you leave me now?" she asked gently. "I need to do this part by myself."

Mrs. Gain looked hesitant. "The master should be here."

"Indeed he should not," Pippa responded. "Your master and I see eye to eye on very little, I'm afraid. If I am to help the boy, then I must do things my own way."

The older woman sighed. "Mr. Herne is hardly himself these days. When things became . . . er, difficult . . . with his wife, he turned away from her. But since the accident, he's closed himself off from everyone. Ah, but it's not my place to speak of it. You just tend to my boy there and never mind about Mr. Herne. What ails him is beyond the reach of doctoring, I'm afraid."

She left the room, and Pippa knelt down beside the bed. She was about to speak the child's name, when she realized she didn't know it. Herne had never referred to his son by name; neither had the groom nor Mrs. Gain. How very strange, she mused.

Well, she would just make do. She took one of the limp hands from under the coverlet and held it between her own two. She felt his pulse, weak and fluttering, beneath her fingers. "Wake up, my poppet," she coaxed softly.

The boy sighed restlessly, but did not awaken. She reached up and brushed a stray tendril back from his forehead. His hair was straight and as dark as his father's, a startling contrast to his pale face. There was nothing of Herne's harsh features there, save perhaps a hint of stubbornness in the chin. Healthy and fleshed out, he would have been an attractive child; now he was little more than a wraith, the shape of his skull showing clearly beneath the dry, stretched skin.

Closing her eyes, she tightened her hold on the thin hand and forced her mind to go blank. Minutes passed while she waited.

The gift would not come . . . not now, when she needed it, when this child needed it so desperately. Again she made herself relax. *You are the vessel*, she intoned silently, *the open book, the uninscribed page.* Still nothing.

Pippa laid her head against the edge of the mattress in frustration. What did it serve her that she could commune with horses and cats and wild creatures, when she could not muster up an ounce of skill to aid one of her own kind? Her gift felt like more of a mockery than anything else at that moment.

Then her own words came back to her, the words she had spoken to Christopher Herne in the woods. *We were all wild once.* Humans and animals . . . indelibly linked by nature, not nearly so separate or disparate as the former liked to believe. This child was no different from any ailing creature she had been called upon to aid.

Again she clasped his hand, murmuring softly . . . *Fly to me, little sparrow. I will not hurt you.* She prayed that the strong bond she had felt with the father in her cottage could be replicated with the son.

Slowly, tentatively, a series of images and emotions began crossing the barrier of flesh, moving from the boy's inert hand to her warm palm. With a swift, satisfied smile she closed her eyes again and gave herself over to the gift.

The sounds of carnage flashed through her brain—screaming horses, a woman's wail cut off abruptly . . . and then the solitary keening of a child. She delved deeper, and felt fear wash over her, stronger even than the fear she had felt yesterday. There was a monster in the shadows, an ogre . . . large and dark and threatening.

The boy stirred, plucking at the covers with his free hand. Pippa felt his consciousness returning. Something slipped toward her from the edges of the child's mind—the heavy, suffocating coils of guilt. They were coupled with a feeling of remorse that nearly shredded her with its intensity.

Pippa released his hand and fell back against the padded chair, needing to regroup. The complexity of what she'd just experienced shook her. It was wrong, so wrong, for a child to feel such things. The memory of the accident she understood. Even the fear of the dark bogeyman was not unusual—except that the boy's ogre bore a striking resemblance to his own father. She'd have to ponder that notion awhile. Her chief concern, however, was that crushing sensation of guilt.

The reading had knocked the stuffing out of her, but she was also feeling a glimmering of relief. She knew now what ailed the boy. The fevers and delirium were only the symptoms. He was being eaten up, consumed, by his own imagined guilt.

When she leaned forward again, the boy was looking at her. His eyes were the clear, pale gray of a winter pond.

"My name is Pippa Spoon," she whispered. "I've come here to help you."

"Hello," he mouthed. He weakly raised up one small hand.

"I am going to give you something to drink that will ease you while you sleep. It will taste very nasty, but you must swallow it all."

He watched with solemn eyes as she drew several small flasks from her bag and unstoppered them. "Meadowsweet for fever," she recited under her breath as she measured out each tissane into a wide-mouthed, dark bottle. "Horehound to restore appetite and lady's slipper to aid sleep."

She poured out a dram of the tonic into a tin cup and held it to his mouth. After he had drained it, he wrinkled his nose. "Nasty," he croaked.

"Mmm, but good for you all the same. Rather like brussels sprouts."

She saw the hesitant beginnings of a grin and smiled back at him. Within minutes he was asleep again.

She sat beside him for a time, letting her gaze wander over the room. The draperies were shut tight, and a fierce fire burned in the hearth. There were no toys or any other signs that a child dwelled there. The dark, paneled walls were bare, save for a still life over the mantel, a morbid painting of dead game birds.

When Mrs. Gain came in to relieve her, Pippa immediately went down to the library. She found Herne pacing before the hearth. He was nursing a glass of brandy and looked at her askance when she went to the sideboard and poured one for herself.

"I see, General, that you have placed my entire household under your orders," he said sourly. "Tom Bailey has never countered my authority in fifteen years. And Mrs. Gain all but cast herself in front of me to prevent me from entering the boy's room."

She walked right up to him. "The boy's room . . ." she said, mimicking his tone. "The *boy's* room. You've mentioned your son over and over, and have never once spoken his name. Yet I know the names of your servants and even that of your horse. Does your son even have a name? Have you forgotten it? Or is it just one more item you have neglected to tell me?"

His face darkened. "I will not be spoken to in this manner."

"Oh, fiddle. Don't come all over pompous with me, Christopher Herne. You have a great deal to answer for, and I am in no mood for your . . . moods."

"Colin," he said quietly. "The boy's name is Colin. I thought surely you'd have learned it by now."

"None of your servants use his name either." Her voice lowered an octave. "It's as though he were already gone from this house, as though all were forbidden to speak the name of the dead. You might just as well hang the black crepe on every doorway."

He ran both hands wearily over his face, trying vainly to erase the lines of worry that had been etched there. "Have we really been treating him that way?"

"I wager every time he awakens he sees an anxious servant hovering over him, checking to see if he still breathes. There is a deathwatch going on in that bedroom, Mr. Herne, and I'm sure Colin is aware of it."

"But he needs constant care. He is failing. Surely you saw that for yourself?" His voice faltered. "Ah, but it is for you to tell me what you saw, Miss Spoon."

"He *is* failing." He flinched as if she had struck him. She added quickly, "Because he thinks he deserves to die. That 'bit of melancholy' you said he was suffering is, in fact, a serious case of misplaced guilt."

His face darkened. "I brought you half across the county to hear this foolishness?"

She was not surprised by his response. "You brought me here because I am your son's last hope. I am sure you did not belittle the doctors when they made their diagnoses. I expect the same courtesy."

"What of the other . . . your ability to glimpse the future? Did you see what will become of him?"

She shook her head. "I saw enough, though. Now, I've given him a tonic to bring down the fever and restore his appetite. Tomorrow will be critical. If he responds, then there is a chance for recovery." She hesitated for a heartbeat. "There is one other thing—I do not want you visiting him."

"What? Look here, I won't be ordered about in my own—"

"He is afraid of you," she said flatly. "Terrified, even. Understandable, perhaps, since you were off in Spain for a good part of his young life."

"I have been here with him this past year. This is preposterous . . . he is my son."

She looked longingly toward the door. Her limbs were trembling from exhaustion, and the expression of barely contained anger on his face was not helping. She took a long swallow of the fiery liquid, hoping it would act as a restorative. She had a bag full of potions upstairs, but had yet to find anything as effective as brandy for easing rattled nerves.

"You have put him in my care, Mr. Herne. But I can't help him if my methods are questioned or undermined."

With a soft growl he sank into a chair. "I wish you would tell me how you came to know these things. The child barely speaks to anyone."

"It's another of my gifts." She crouched down before him, her fingertips angled on the carpet. "I can sometimes decipher a person's emotional state merely by touching them. It doesn't always work . . . but it worked almost too well with Colin."

He leaned forward so they were nearly eye to eye. "I don't believe you."

"Very well . . . I will prove it. I will tell you what *your* state of mind was last night when you touched my hand." She paused to take a breath. "You were feeling alone and friendless. And full of cynicism because the things that once brought you pleasure have no meaning any longer. You trust no one, it appears, and have lost your faith in the goodness of humanity."

There, that was truthful and relatively benign. She could have said a deal more. Still, she must have touched a nerve—his eyes hooded over, and he rose abruptly to his feet, nearly knocking her back onto the hearth.

"You have shown me nothing," he snarled. "Any two-penny fortune-teller could hazard such a guess, knowing my situation here. Still, I do not care for your parlor games. I trust you will do no harm to my son, but for myself, I want no further contact with you."

She watched with a tiny smile as he strode out of the library. "Oh, and Mr. Herne," she said softly to the closing door, "there is one other thing. I believe you like me very much. It's a pity you keep fighting it."

She moved to the chair he'd vacated and finished her brandy. The child was probably going to survive. She wasn't so sure about the father, however. She imagined men like Christopher Herne, the proud ones who resisted any efforts on their behalf, were the very devil to help. Not that he had asked for her help. But she was here in the house, at his insistence, and it would serve him right if she plied some of her wisewoman skills on him.

It was nearly eight when Pippa awoke. She dragged herself from the warm haven of her bed, rallying her heart to face a difficult truth if the child had not improved. She found Mrs. Scofield, the birdlike housekeeper, sitting beside Colin's bed.

The woman yawned delicately before she rose from her chair. "He spent a quiet night. And managed to keep down a coddled egg this morning."

Pippa crossed to the draperies and drew them back. Watery sunlight spilled into the room. "He needs the light," she said to the housekeeper, then motioned to the grim painting over the mantel. "And are there any pictures in this house that are cheerful, something a child would enjoy?"

Mrs. Scofield bit her lip. "This is not the child's own room. It's where the master's tutor stayed years ago. We moved the boy in here because the fireplace draws better."

"Yes, well, we don't need to keep such a roaring fire going. There is barely enough air to breathe. And no round-the-clock vigils any longer. Checking in on him every hour should suffice."

"As you wish, miss," she said with a quick nod of her head.

This time the boy stirred to wakefulness immediately when Pippa took his hand. His eyes brightened when he recognized her. "I thought I had dreamed you," he said, his voice stronger now. "Are you truly going to make me well again?"

She shook her head. "No, you are going to make yourself well, Colin. That's the way it works, you see. It's all in your own power."

His face fell. "I have no power," he rasped. "I cannot even walk . . . did you know that?" He eyed her intently.

"Yes, I did know that." *No thanks to your father*, she added silently. "Do you think that should matter to me?"

"What is the use of making me better. I will never run and play like other boys. I will never have a pony or a dog."

"I have a pony," she said thoughtfully, "but I had to leave her behind. I do however have something like a dog."

He scrunched up his small, pointed nose. "What is *like* a dog?"

"A wolf." She was gratified by the look of astonishment on his pale face. "But you are probably afraid of wolves and such," she commented in an offhand manner.

"Oh, no, I'm not!" he protested, trying to rise up from the bed.

She soothed him back down to the pillow. "I could bring him in to visit you. He is a bit under the weather, too. You could convalesce together. That means to get well."

He turned his face from her. "I will not ever get well. I heard what the doctors said. They talked about me like I wasn't here. I am dying." He said it baldly, almost proudly.

"Eventually," she said flippantly. "I fear we all go that

way." She leaned in close. "Any particular reason you need to do it now?"

His brows knit at her cavalier tone. She was sure he was used to everyone creeping about him and speaking in hushed, deferential whispers.

"You are making fun of me," he said with a small pout.

"I am teasing you, Colin. That's a different kettle of fish. You only tease people you like."

"You don't know me. How can you know if you like me?"

She shrugged. "Good instincts. And you like wolves. That puts you rather high on my list. Now I'm going to give you another glass of your tonic. And this time you can have a peppermint to chase away the nasty taste."

He swallowed the medicine dutifully, grimacing all the while. She popped a peppermint into his mouth.

"They never let me eat sweets," he complained as he crunched on the mint.

"I'll see that you have a plum pudding for Christmas. How's that?"

He shook his head slowly. It pained her to see how the skin was stretched over his thin neck. "There is no Christmas in this house. Not this year. I can tell. No one comes to visit, there are no carolers. When I asked Mrs. Gain if there were presents on the landing, she got all red. She only does that when she is upset."

"They are worried about you. It's hard to make Christmas when you are worried."

"Were you making a Christmas in your house?"

It was Pippa's turn to blush. "No," she said softly. "I missed my mother, and was not feeling the Christmas spirit at all."

A small hand crept into hers and squeezed it. *I know*, his eyes said.

"Tell you what . . . sleep now, and I will see about making a Christmas for you."

"And the pony? I would very much like a pony. Even if I can never ride, he could be my friend."

She held a finger to her lips. "Who can say what Christmas morning will bring?"

She sat with him till he slept, and then for another hour, just to make sure the tonic was keeping his fever at bay. As for the other demons that troubled him, it was as she had told the boy—that cure lay completely within his own power.

Pippa conferred with Mrs. Gain and Mrs. Scofield over lunch in the housekeeper's parlor. Both women heartily endorsed her plan of action. Then she sought out Tom Bailey and enlisted him as co-conspirator in Colin's cure. He assured her he wouldn't suffer Master Kit's anger if they were found out.

Colin's eyes widened when Pippa came into his room and set her armload of toys on the bed. He sat up and immediately shook out the box of lead soldiers.

"I also brought a book of fairy stories. I can read one to you, if you like."

"I can almost read my own stories, you know," he stated proudly. "Mrs. Gain was teaching me. But my father had all my storybooks taken away."

Pippa made no comment as she made up Colin's tonic, but her expression boded no good for his father. Once the medicine was swallowed, she handed him a peppermint.

"And now I have a surprise for you."

Tom Bailey came into the room, carrying Ranulf and wearing a wide grin. As he set him down on the carpet, he winked at the boy. The wolf shook himself, his stance still a little wobbly, and then moved closer to the bed.

Colin's eyes grew to saucer size. "He doesn't bite, does he? My mother said dogs bite and tear up the carpet."

"I don't know about the carpet, but he doesn't bite. I promise."

Colin reached out one hand tentatively; Ranulf sniffed it, and then licked it slowly.

"He tastes the peppermint," the boy crowed. As he reached out farther to stroke the wolf's head, the bedclothes fell away from his frail body. Pippa saw the scars that marked his legs below the hem of his nightshirt.

"Here, roll over," she said, coaxing him onto his stomach. "I want to look at these pipe stems of yours. You just keep tickling Ranulf between his eyes."

Pippa wished again for her mother's skill as she ran her hands down the boy's damaged legs, her fingers tracing the hardened knobs where the broken bones had healed. She ran one finger along the sole of his foot and heard him giggle.

"You felt that?"

He nodded and turned to her. "Is that good?"

"Mmm, it means your back was not damaged."

She pulled the covers over him again and sat up with a satisfied smile.

Tom was carrying Ranulf from the room an hour later when he came face-to-face with his master. Pippa winced when she heard Herne's voice. She immediately went out into the hall, closing the door behind her so that Colin would not be disturbed.

"It was my idea," she said at once. "Colin wanted to meet my wolf."

Herne scowled. "And my orders that he was not to be allowed in the house?"

Pippa motioned Tom away with her chin. He shot her a look of gratitude and faded back into the shadows. "It appears you give a great many orders that are unwarranted. Taking away your son's books, for instance."

"I don't have to defend my actions to you."

"And when will you give them back to him? When he's at Oxford?"

"Sarcasm does not become a woman," he said bluntly.

"Pigheadedness does not become anyone," she shot back.

"It's a moot point. He will never see the halls of Oxford."

"A little louder, Mr. Herne. I don't think Colin heard you."

He swung away from her, his hands fisted. "You are a trial to me, Miss Spoon. Subverting my servants, disregarding my direct orders. You are supposed to be ministering to my son, not inciting my household to rebellion."

"Hardly rebellion," she said, with a tiny jut of her chin.

He pointed to the stairwell. "The grooms have left a pile of holly branches in the front hall, and the maids are making pine garlands in the parlor. My cook is preparing plum puddings by the dozen, and Mrs. Scofield is half buried in tissue paper and ribbons. They all look at me with the blandest of expressions when I ask them what they are doing. 'Christmas,' they say. 'It's Christmas, Mr. Herne.' "

She could hear his teeth grinding clear across the hall.

"And you had ordered that there was to be no Christmas this year."

"My son is dying," he cried. "How could there be any Christmas in this house?"

"Oh, he heard you that time, I wager." She opened the door behind her and ducked her head in. "Don't pay him any mind," she said with a grin to Colin. "He's had a bit too much eggnog."

"Give him a tonic," the boy said, grinning back at her.

She shut the door and turned around to face the stupefied man. "See, he's making jokes. Hardly dying, Mr. Herne."

"Then it's time I went in to visit him," he said in a challenging voice.

She sniffed once. "You are the master here. Anyway, *I* have to oversee the hanging of the garlands."

She was gone before he could utter another word. He watched the chestnut curls dance over her shoulders as she headed down the stairs. She was smug, flippant, and odiously managing. Three things he couldn't abide in a woman. It was his own cursed luck that his pulse raced out of control anytime he got near her.

Herne went into the room and drew a chair up close to the bed. "Hello, Colin. Mrs. Gain told me you ate a coddled egg and a bowl of soup."

"Yes, Father."

They sat in silence then, the boy purposely looking away, the man twisting his fingers on his knee. After several minutes had passed, Herne asked Colin if he was feeling better. "Yes, Father," he said and lapsed back into his silent study of the ceiling.

Herne gave up and left the room. The child who had

bantered with Pippa Spoon, a virtual stranger, would not even meet his own father's eyes. Somewhere the fates were laughing. The coaching accident might not have taken his son's life, and his current illness was obviously not going to prove fatal, but Herne felt as if Colin was lost to him, just the same.

After taking supper in her bedroom, Pippa went in search of something entertaining to read—her solitary thoughts were proving poor company tonight. Mrs. Scofield intercepted her on the staircase and informed her that Mr. Herne wanted to see her in his study.

She knocked once and entered the small room. He looked up from his ledger and quickly whisked off a pair of reading glasses. Her heart tightened at that small vanity—he couldn't know it, but his frailties drew her to him far more than his strengths.

"You can gloat if you like. Colin wouldn't speak to me at all." He gave her a sullen, resentful frown. "But he is looking much better. There's color in his cheeks now and alertness in his eyes. I wanted to wrap my arms around him."

"Then why didn't you? Everyone hovers over him, but no one touches him. He's not made of porcelain."

"The doctors feared his ailment might be contagious."

"That's poppycock," she muttered. "You and your doctors. Colin was convinced he was going to die, mainly because your learned doctors offered *their* diagnoses within earshot of the boy. Lord, don't you know that children absorb everything they hear?"

Herne winced. "The doctors were imprudent. And worthless, in the end."

She moved beside the desk and touched his shoulder. "Why do you think he fears you? He was not one bit afraid of my wolf."

"I have no answer to that." He rose from his chair and paced to the leaded window. "I used to know the answers," he said with a weary sigh. "I used to know how to take action, how to solve problems and get things done. But this . . . this has confounded me."

"Sometimes," she said slowly, "it is better not to take action. Sometimes just sitting down and paying attention works."

"I give him all my attention. Even when he's asleep, I go into his room and whisper to him—so that he knows he is not alone. Damn it, I never stop talking to him."

"Then perhaps it is time you started listening." Her voice held a hint of accusation.

"He won't talk to me. He's barely said five full sentences to me since I came back from Spain. It's been 'Yes, Father,' and 'No, Father.' He squirms and fidgets . . . if he had the use of his legs, I swear he would run away whenever he saw me approaching. It got to the point where I felt like I was talking to a captive prisoner."

His dark eyes met hers for an instant. "I am sorry I was so abrupt with you last night. I . . . I was ashamed that you had discovered his fear of me."

"You will not like this, but now would be a good time for you to tell me about your wife." Pippa settled on the arm of the small sofa and gazed at him expectantly.

"You mean, did she poison the child against me?" He gave a dry laugh. "I wouldn't put it past her. We did not part on good terms. I . . . I discovered she had never cared a groat for me, and that knowledge destroyed any feelings I still had for her."

"Then why did you come back from Spain? I understand you were in London when the accident occurred." She was relieved when he didn't ask her how she'd learned that.

His fingers gripped the windowsill until they were white against the dark wood. "After three years, I was sick to death of war, Miss Spoon. I missed my home and my son. When I arrived in London, I wrote my wife that I would be coming home in a day or two. She left with the boy the same morning she got my note. Went running off to her latest lover, I expect, since she had no family in England.

"Ice and sleet were coming down like the furies when they drove off. Not five miles from here, the coach skidded on a turn and broke loose from the team of horses. It pitched over into a ravine. The coachmen managed to jump clear, but . . ." His face was full of anguish when he looked at her. "Do you understand now, Pippa? She was fleeing from me that morning. I was the cause of her death. And of the crippling of my son. I am so afraid that if he dies now . . ." His voice broke. "If Colin dies . . ."

She moved rapidly across to him and wrapped her hands tightly around his arm. "Hush, Kit. He's not going to die." She held him for a moment, her face pressed to his back.

"Still, I know he blames me for his mother's death. What can I do, Pippa, to make him forgive me? God, he must feel so alone. I have had him to sustain me this past year . . . but if he truly fears me, then he has no one."

"I don't know what you can do," she said truthfully. "But you're wrong about one thing. He blames himself for her death more than he does you, and his guilt has doubtless magnified over the past year. That first snowfall you spoke of must have torn something loose inside him . . . and then the guilt began to affect him physically."

"How is that possible?"

"You mean those forces we can't explain, but which exist, nevertheless?"

His mouth twisted wryly. "Throwing my own words back at me, hmm?"

"There has to be some way to convince Colin that neither of you were to blame." Her eyes held his intently. "Because it was *her* fault, Kit. Whatever your wife's reasons for leaving, she had no right to take a child out into an ice storm." She cocked her head. "Do you have any idea why she was so afraid to see you again?"

Herne hitched his shoulders. "I never even raised my voice to her when we lived together. Back then, my habit was retreat. Perhaps she ran off because she thought I would put a stop to her . . . liaisons. I imagine she'd gotten used to going her own way and couldn't stand the thought of anyone interfering in her life. Or maybe she feared I would divorce her and take Colin away from her. For all her self-indulgent behavior, I believe she truly loved him."

Pippa had some doubts on that score, but kept her own counsel.

"Whatever made her run off, you and Colin have been bearing the guilt for far too long. There won't be any resolution until one of you gets past that. And since you're the adult"—she shook his arm for emphasis—"I suggest you go first."

He offered her a weak grin. "You make it all sound so

reasonable. If you'd ever met my wife, you would understand how good she was at twisting everything."

"She still is, Kit," she murmured. "As long as she has power over you and Colin, your lives will be twisted out of shape."

He raised his hand and touched the side of her face. She drew in a swift breath as the air began to vibrate around them.

"I like it when you call me Kit," he said, almost to himself. "No one's called me that since I was a boy." His fingers drifted over her cheek. "And what is this curious thing that happens whenever I touch you, Pippa Spoon, this strange humming in the air? Is it more witchery?"

She could barely speak; the sensation of his warm fingers stroking over her skin was making her brain go all hazy. She was not reading his thoughts, not even trying to, yet the sense of connection was incredibly strong.

"I don't know," she managed to rasp out. "It's only ever happened with you . . . and only when we touch, skin on skin." Pippa nearly groaned when she realized what she'd just said.

But he hadn't missed her inference. His eyes burned now, like ebony coals, and the hunger in them nearly scorched her. She drew back from his touch, and the humming ceased. He frowned slightly and set his hands tentatively on her shoulders. Nothing happened.

"Skin on skin?" he purred. "I'll have to keep that in mind."

Pippa made a little noise of distress deep in her throat, and then muttered something about needing to look in on Ranulf.

Herne tightened his hold on her and shook his head. "Not just yet."

He wanted to savor this moment. He'd finally succeeded in breaking her composure, and fine payback it was, too, after she'd prodded him into revealing his own weaknesses. They were even now. Well, not precisely. She was keeping his son alive, which put him eternally in her debt.

She was glaring at him, her green eyes frosty. "I think I'd better leave."

He dropped his hands. "Yes, perhaps that would be wise."

She made it to the safety of the door before she turned around. "Before I go, I need to ask a favor of you. I . . . I told Colin he would be getting a pony for Christmas."

Herne cocked his head as if he hadn't heard her correctly. "You told him what?"

"He's wanted one for so long. It might even get him up and about. You know, he still has some feeling in his legs; I think that one day he might walk again."

"And have you told him that? Is this your idea of a cure, Pippa? Telling him lies? Getting his hopes up so that they can be dashed to pieces. He will never walk again . . . the doctors all agreed on that."

"The same doctors who told you he was dying?" she shot back.

He spun away from her. "Lord, you are a trial to me. You've done what I brought you here to do. Can't you leave it at that? I don't need you meddling in his life . . . or mine. Do you understand me?"

Her eyes widened in shock at his tone. "I thought I did," she said with barely contained anger. "I thought you wanted me to help your son. To help him get better. But I want him to *live* better, as well. Curing his fever was only the beginning. He is bright and clever . . . and if you would stop being such an obstacle, there is nothing he cannot do."

"He cannot walk!" Herne practically roared the words. "He will never—"

She flung the door open and ran out, needing to be gone from him before her tears of frustration overwhelmed her.

Herne paused to look in on Colin on his way to bed. To his surprise, the boy was sitting up, marching his leaded knights over a battlefield of rumpled bedding.

Colin looked up at him with a guilty frown. "I couldn't sleep."

"Didn't you have your tonic tonight?"

He nodded, and then said in a strained voice, "But I was still upset." His eyes darted anxiously to his father's face. "I heard you shouting at Miss Spoon this afternoon."

That was nothing, Herne remarked ruefully to himself. *You should have heard me shouting at her just now.*

"Sometimes she can be . . . irritating," he said, sitting on the bed. "But that doesn't mean I don't appreciate what she's done for you."

"Well, I like her." The knights recommenced their sortie across the comforter.

Herne reclined on the bed, curling his upper body around the boy's legs. "That's good, because I like her, too. Very much." He picked up one of the leaded figures and danced it over his son's knee. The boy giggled. Herne's gaze flashed to his face.

"Colin," he said haltingly, "I have not spoken of this before . . . but your mother and I . . . we did not get along very well. That is why I went off to the war."

"Was *she* irritating?"

"She was difficult. We had different notions of what made us happy, very different notions. You were, perhaps, the only thing we agreed on. You made us both extremely happy. But in spite of that, she needed more than a life in the country. . . ."

"She went to London a lot," the boy said with a sigh, "for months and months."

"And did you miss her?"

"Mmm. I used to wish I had a dog or a pony for company."

Herne heard the wistful longing in the boy's voice and twice cursed the woman who had left her son alone in this rambling house for months at a time. But, still, she had been Colin's mother, so Herne knew he had to go cautiously.

"She was concerned," he began slowly, "that when I came back from Spain, I would not let her go to London any longer. That is why she took you away with her, Colin. She thought she was going to lose her freedom."

The boy's eyes lowered. "No," he said in a thin, flat voice. "That is not why she left."

"Tell me, then. Why did she run off in the storm?"

There was no answer for nearly a minute. Finally, Herne took up the boy's hands. "Colin, I do want to hear this. But whatever you say, it will not change how I feel about you. Do you understand that?"

"You will be angry with me." His mouth had formed into a tight little knot.

"Indeed, I will not."

"I didn't mean to do it, truly. It was that teetery old statue in the front hall. I was playing inside because it was so icy in the drive. My ball hit into it. It crashed down into a hundred pieces. Mama said it was very valuable . . . and that you'd be furious with me when you found out."

Herne recalled wondering what had become of the badly rendered plaster statue of Hermes that had adorned the hall table since his childhood. "That wasn't true, Colin. I wouldn't have been angry."

"Well," he said with a sniffle, "she *always* said you were going to punish me when you came back home, whenever I did something I shouldn't. But this time she told me you were coming home the very next day. I started to cry. Oh, I cried and cried. So Mama said we would run away together, and then she bundled me up and carried me out to the coach. Y-you know what happened after that. . . ." His voice drifted off.

Herne wrapped his arms around the boy's shoulders and hugged him tight. "That's not why she left, Colin. Not because you broke the statue. She had other reasons, reasons you will understand one day. Please believe me, it wasn't your fault. None of it was your fault."

The boy was trembling under his hands. "And you're not angry about the statue? I've been waiting and waiting for you to notice it was missing."

"I hated that statue," he said without thinking. "And it wasn't valuable. Practically worthless, in fact."

The boy processed this information for several minutes.

Herne watched him with his heart in his throat. He feared that through the intemperate words he'd just spoken, Colin would realize his mother had purposely made him afraid, so that she would have no trouble getting him to leave with her.

But when Colin spoke at last, his face was calm. "I expect she didn't know it was worthless."

"I expect she didn't," Herne said gently, relief rolling over him.

Herne walked through the house and gazed around in wonder, as if noticing his surroundings for the first time. Lush pine garlands hung above the doorways and along the mantelpieces. Holly wreaths adorned the walls, and the smell of bayberry candles pervaded every room. There was a tidy pile of gifts stacked on the landing, and even in Colin's room, the mantel had been festooned with pine boughs.

He was amazed by the transformation Pippa had wrought in his home. His own transformation was clearly still in the early stages, however, since he'd been cow-handed enough to make her angry after she'd offered such support to him. But he'd remedy that. His heart was feeling green and festive.

He found her curled up in the library, poring over a tattered book with a faded leather cover. When she looked up, her expression was not welcoming.

"I just spoke with Colin," he said. "Spoke with him *and* listened to him. It was rough going . . . for both of us. But I think he is beginning to understand."

She folded her hands over the book. "I am very pleased to hear that, Mr. Herne."

"Kit," he said in a rough whisper. "You can't go back to calling me Mr. Herne, Pippa. I won't allow it."

She set the book down and rose from the couch. "I'd better go up now—it's late."

"Pippa! Don't do this. Don't shut me out. Not when I am feeling so relieved about Colin."

She shook her head. "You can't have it both ways. Seeking my approval one minute and then browbeating me the next. Anyway, I really must go."

"No," he said, placing himself between the couch and the door. "Not until I have thanked you." He reached for her hands, but she spun away.

"Very well. Go then. I can wait until tomorrow to tell you what it's meant to me having you here, how glad I am that I braved Chatham Wood to find you. How much my son cares for you . . . how highly I regard you. To let you know how wonderful it is to walk through this house and feel Christmas all around me." He smiled inwardly when she turned to face him with an expression of amazement. "It will all be just as true tomorrow as it is today."

"Oh, Kit, it already *is* tomorrow." Her gaze flitted to the mantel clock, which showed quarter past twelve.

"So it is." He walked up to her and laid his hands on her shoulders. "Then I must wish you a happy Christmas Eve." He set a chaste salute high on her cheek.

It was enough—enough to set the air humming and both their hearts racing.

Skin on skin, he thought with a shivery jolt of anticipation. That was all it took to make this woman quicken. Not expensive baubles, or promises of devotion. Just the whisper of his flesh against hers.

He fought the temptation to succumb. Told himself that she was a passing fancy, a momentary lapse. That he could never muster the feelings a woman like Pippa Spoon required. But when she tipped her head back, naked yearning in her eyes, he was lost. He drew her closer, until her body was nearly up against his.

He was staring down at her, his eyes dark and intent, and Pippa could not look away. For the first time since she had met him, it occurred to her that Christopher Herne might know something about the natural world that she did not—something quite good.

I mustn't, she warned herself. *This is wrong. He is not the right man. I would know it if he were. Oh, but I do want him to touch me. . . .*

As if he'd read the conflicted desire in her face, he bent his head and whispered, "Touch me, Pippa. Please. Make the air hum again."

The urgent need in his voice decided her. She raised her trembling hands and set them on his lean cheeks. Her eyes held his as her fingers traced over the planes of his face. Her touch eased the lines of worry at his brow and the weathered creases beside his eyes. It softened the gaunt hollows below his cheekbones. When her fingertips moved over his long, sculpted mouth, she felt, more than heard, his ragged groan.

"Phillipa," he said raggedly. "I'm not . . . I can't . . ."

She dropped her hands immediately and felt the blush rise up from the tips of her slippers. "Kit, I'm sorry. I thought . . ." She pushed away in confusion, turning to flee. His hands closed hard around her waist.

"Don't think," he growled softly, just before he set his mouth on the side of her throat. He pulled her straight back into the cradle of his arms, molding her spine to his chest until she was flush against him. And still he kissed her, sliding his mouth slowly along her throat, from the edge of her gown to the sensitive patch of flesh behind her ear.

"Don't think, sweeting," he crooned against her skin. "Don't speak, don't breathe . . . just feel." He lifted her hair away from her nape, knotting it in his fist, before he lowered his head and set his teeth there.

Pippa's ragged moan brought his hand to her breast. He pressed his palm against her until she cried out. As she did, he swung her to face him and took her openmouthed, slanting his mouth over hers, his hunger palpable and fierce.

She clung to him as he bent her back, her fingers curled into his wide shoulders. Nothing in her lifetime had ever felt like this . . . no wild dream, no flight of fancy. Herne the Hunter was finally closing in for the kill, and all she could think of was surrender.

And then she *knew* . . . knew why she had been so frightened of the stranger who had come into the woods. Herne and his son were to be the test of her powers and of her willingness to surrender herself to them. She'd been brought here to find her future.

"Ah, Kit," she cried softly, raking her hands through his hair. She surged up to meet his kisses now, returning them with mindless hunger.

Herne felt the last of his caution evaporate the instant she began to respond. The desire he had been holding in check—practically from the moment he'd met her—had free rein now. Her kisses tasted like spring meadows, honeyed and sweet. Her body was a bright torch, burning him, branding him, everywhere she touched him. He felt engulfed by the sweetness and the light that had been missing for so long from the bleak reaches of his bitter, dark soul. He wanted to hold onto them forever.

His heart jolted erratically at that thought. *Forever.* There *was* no forever.

"Pippa," he rasped out. He raised his head, trying to catch his breath. "This wasn't supposed to happen. *You* weren't supposed to happen."

Her mouth, rosy and swollen now, curved into a tremulous pout. "I . . . I don't know what you mean."

The expression of regret in his eyes was all the explanation she required. She pushed away from him.

He let her go, then quickly reached one hand out to her. "Pippa?"

"No, you don't have to apologize. We've both been under a strain these past days. You needed someone to hold you and touch you. Perhaps I did, as well."

She was amazed at how quickly her equilibrium was returning, considering how her heart ached. One minute ago she'd have sworn he'd never let her go. But then he'd pulled back from her. Rejected her. *Dear Lord, how could she have misread him so badly?*

"That's not what just happened here," he sputtered angrily. "I wasn't looking for comfort."

"Sport, then?" Her eyes had gone a glacial green. "I'm sorry to disappoint you, but my services don't extend to that area."

"Dammit, Phillipa, you are the most contrary, infuriating woman I've ever met. I was not trying to seduce you. I only wanted . . ." His voice faltered. "I only wanted to know what it felt like to kiss you. Because you are lovely and warm. And because the blasted air sizzles when you touch me."

"Oh," she said. A sad smile traced across her mouth. At least he was being honest with her. "And have you satisfied your curiosity?"

"It would take a thousand years," he growled. "Now go

up to bed before I lose my resolve. We'll talk in the morning."

Pippa slipped in to see Colin early the next morning. She hadn't much time, since she wanted to be away from the house before anyone else was up. She didn't have the heart to tell him she was leaving, but she hugged him extra tightly before she left his room.

She asked one of the stable lads to hitch the cob to her cart. Tom Bailey looked puzzled when she told him she'd be back directly to fetch Ranulf, but he made no comment as he turned and walked away.

This is it. It was Christmas Eve, and she was going home. She'd succeeded with Colin, but had been a miserable failure with his father.

Last night she had realized Christopher Herne was the right man. She finally *knew*. Not that it did her a lick of good. It was a pity her mother hadn't cautioned her that sometimes the woman knew and the man didn't.

This wasn't supposed to happen. Kit's words of regret had hounded her to sleep and had been pounding in her head ever since she woke up. He may have wanted to kiss her for a thousand years—which was a very gratifying notion—but that was clearly all he wanted from her. What did it matter if the way he made her body throb and set her senses spinning was everything the pagan part of her nature cried out for? Those feelings meant nothing if he only held her in his arms and never held her in his heart.

"Tom Bailey warned me something was afoot." Herne was leaning against one of the stalls, his arms crossed over his chest. His neckcloth looked like he had tied it in the dark. "Where the devil are you going?"

"Home." She set her carpetbag on the seat.

"You can't leave . . . it's Christmas Eve. Colin is expecting you to be here until the New Year, at least."

"Colin will be fine. I left a bottle of his tonic for Mrs. Gain—"

"Damn your blasted tonic."

She shrugged off his show of temper. "You told me yourself that my work here was done . . . well, except for one thing. I intend to get a present for Colin before I leave. Put my mother's gold to good use."

She climbed into the cart without looking at him and was nearly out of the stable yard when he came running up beside her.

"Move over and let me drive."

"But you don't know where I'm going."

"I know full well where you're going," he bit out as he climbed onto the seat. "To the farm we passed on our way here. The one with all the ponies in the field."

She grinned smugly to herself. *Well, well, well.*

"You know," she said musingly, "there's a great deal too much of this mind-reading business going on lately."

The farmer brought out several likely looking ponies and trotted them around his stable yard. Herne was taken with a fat piebald, but Pippa kept looking at a ribby dun who stood in the pasture, craning his bony head over the rail fence.

"That one," she said to Herne, pointing to the dun.

His face fell. "Honestly, Pippa. What you know about horses could be lodged in a thimble."

She blew out a breath of impatience. "Listen to me. Colin needs something to take his mind off his infirmity. Caring for another creature is the best distraction in the world. The fat pony doesn't need him. But that little dun looks starved for affection. He and Colin will be a perfect match."

"I don't want an old pony. The boy will grow attached to him, and then have to watch him die."

"Oh, pish, that pony's not yet turned fifteen. I wager Colin will be off at university by the time the little fellow gives up the ghost."

The farmer nodded sagely. "Got Dartmoor bloodlines, that one. Those moor ponies often live past thirty. I had him off a Spanish Gypsy last week—he'll fatten up nicely once the spring grass comes in."

Herne looked disgusted. "That is not the sort of pony my son should have."

Pippa shrugged. "Get him the piebald then. You can afford the finest pony in the kingdom . . . just as you were able to afford the finest doctors."

His mouth tightened. "Tie the dun pony to the cart," he muttered to the farmer. "Pray God, he makes it back to my home."

"Does he have a name?" Pippa asked the farmer.

"The Gypsy called him Amigo."

"That's Spanish for 'friend,' " Herne explained, his frown starting to relax.

"Perfect," she said.

"I wish you wouldn't turn everything into a battle of wills," he said once they were on their way home. "I gave in on this pony matter—the boy can drive him in a cart, I suppose—but now you've got to stop thinking that Colin will walk again. There are some things, Pippa, that you can't mend."

"Mmm, but my mother can."

He tugged the cob to a halt. "What did you just say?"

"You're going to be cross with me." She took a deep breath and blurted out, "My mother is not dead. She is in Bristol."

"Bristol?" he sputtered. "What in blazes is she doing in Bristol?"

"My father had a two-month layover. He stayed with us through November and then took my mother off to Bristol on holiday. I didn't want you haring off there and bothering her. She was ill herself this past autumn; it left her in very low spirits. She needed this time with my father, so I lied to protect her."

He mulled this over. "Still, I can't believe they left you alone for Christmas."

"It was her gift to me. She said I would never come into my powers if I felt as if I was always in her shadow."

"Well, I have to agree with that. I don't think you really understood the scope of your abilities until you came here."

"You believed in me before you even knew what my powers were." She leaned her head on his shoulder for an instant. "Anyway, I've written to her. I'm sure she will come here to see Colin once my father is back at sea."

"Ah, so you are planning on staying then?"

"If you want me to."

Herne stroked the back of his hand along her cheek. From that brief, electrifying touch of skin on skin, Pippa got the answer she'd prayed for, even before he spoke.

"I want you," he said gruffly.

Herne found Colin deep in slumber when he came in to say good night. Ranulf was snuggled tight under the boy's arm. Herne had relaxed his edict on allowing wild things in the house. He reckoned if he could handle the untamed Miss Spoon, a pet wolf was small challenge.

Pippa turned from the tall window where she was standing and held out her hand. "I fear the story of the Nativity put him right to sleep."

Herne clasped her hand and moved beside her. "The pagan wisewoman spinning Bible stories?" His eyes teased her gently.

She cocked her head. "They are my stories, too. And I am not a pagan, just a tiny bit influenced by the old ways. Not a bad thing, having a foot in both camps."

She gave him a saucy grin, and then leaned back against him, gazing up at the clear night sky. There was a tracing of whispery white clouds high overhead. It would snow on Christmas Day, but she knew Colin would not mind so much this time.

"What do you see out there?" Herne whispered, his mouth against her hair. "Your pagan spirits?"

"They're *all* out there, Kit. And inside here with us, as well . . . the Roman ones who gave us the winter feast, the Hebrew ones who gave us the light in the darkness. The ancient Britons who gave us the greenery . . . but the spirit of the day, of the season, comes from the Christians. All those bright feelings of renewal and hope."

He looked at the bed where his son was sleeping peacefully, his restless dreams fled away. "Renewal and hope . . . yes, I like that a lot."

"Too bad he fell asleep. I was going to tell him about the three wisewomen."

He tugged one of her curls. "You mean the three Wise Men, don't you?"

"There were also three wisewomen who visited the baby

Jesus in Bethlehem, after the Wise Men went home. Now, it was typical of men to bring material gifts—gold and frankincense and myrrh. Valuable, yes, but hardly useful to a child who had such great tasks to perform. So the wise-women brought other gifts. They blessed Him with courage and compassion and, the most important one of all for what lay before Him, the gift of persuasion."

"That's not anywhere in the Bible."

Her chin tipped up as she turned to face him. "There are many stories that never made it into the Bible. But I choose to believe this one. After all, it is what women have done best all through time, knowing just what the best gifts are."

He touched his nose to hers. "You mean like Eve and the apple?"

She laughed outright. "I gather I am supposed to say 'touché.' But I don't blame Eve. It was the serpent who gave *her* the apple. As I said, males never give the right gift."

"I am not going to discuss the Bible with you. You have the most unorthodox beliefs of anyone I have ever met."

"Afraid of a little healthy debate?"

"Not if you'd stick to facts and absolutes. But you go off into feelings and instincts."

"That is because I am a woman."

"Which is another of your gifts," he said as his arms drew around her. "And though you might not be a healer like your mother, you have so many other gifts. Courage, compassion, and such sweet persuasion." His hold tightened perceptibly. "Ah, Pippa Spoon, why has no man carried you off from Chatham Wood?"

"It takes a rare man to court a Spoon woman, Kit."

"I am not a rare man, sweetheart. I am not a man who can make pretty speeches or spout romantic lines. I can't tell you how lovely you are with the moonlight on your hair or how I look forward to the sound of your voice each morning."

Her eyes danced up at him. "Then tell me again how much I infuriate you."

"Incredibly," he murmured, lowering his head to nuzzle the side of her throat. "Profoundly." His lips moved to the sensitive lobe of her ear. "Endlessly." Then his mouth settled over hers, and there was no sound in the darkened room, save an occasional shuddering sigh.

After a time, Herne raised his head and took her face between his hands. The tenderness in his expression made her breath catch. There was no misreading the emotions in his dark eyes—love and hope brimmed there in equal measure.

"Bring your wolf and your bear . . ." he said hoarsely, "your griffin and your unicorn. Bring all your gifts and bide here with me, Pippa Spoon."

"Yes, Kit," she said with a low throb of joy. "I will bide with you."

He kissed her again, a slow, languid kiss that, as the air began to hum and quiver, quickly surged into passion. "Soon," he murmured urgently into her throat.

Yes, very soon, she thought with a giddy rush. Even a wisewoman couldn't keep Herne the Hunter at bay for long. Not that she wanted to try.

When he drew her toward the bed where the child lay sleeping, Pippa laid her palm against Colin's cheek in gentle benediction. Herne covered it with his own hand.

"A *family*," he whispered. He made the word sound like a prayer.

She shifted her hand and twined her fingers with his. "You asked me once what I foresaw for the future . . . I think I can answer you now."

He leaned his head closer. "Yes?"

"Happiness," she said. "Great happiness."

He was smiling as they went from the room—she could feel it shimmering in the darkness.

Colin grinned into his pillow. Earlier that day, he'd been gazing out his window and had seen his father and Miss Spoon returning in the cart with the little dun pony tied up behind. But the words he'd just now heard them say to each other delighted him even more than the sight of the pony. Knowing that Pippa Spoon was going to stay here with them was the very best gift of all.

And wonder of wonders—she had a bear!

He reached out and stroked Ranulf's head. "It looks like we're making a Christmas after all," he whispered glee-fully.

The wolf's tail thumped three times on the coverlet.

The Reckless Miss Ripley
by Diane Farr

It wasn't the best dinner he had ever had. On the other hand, he had not been forced to wolf down the over-done mutton and underdone potatoes in four minutes as the unfortunate passengers on the Royal Mail had been obliged to do.

Fred Bates clicked his tongue sympathetically as the young couple with the whining toddler were harried mercilessly back onto the coach. "Should have eaten in London," he murmured. Experienced travelers set aside their normal mealtimes and consumed a substantial repast prior to the mail's departure, even if that meant dining at the unholy hour of six or seven o'clock. The London mail would, at all costs, arrive promptly in Bath. If the weather hindered its progress, the time must be made up by shortening the stops along the way. And the weather tonight was ferocious.

Mr. Bates, seated comfortably before the fire in the tap-room at the Coach and Horses, stretched his long legs out before him and congratulated himself on his independence. It would be a cold and miserable experience, of course, to drive a gig through weather like this. But he was young and strong, and not the sort of chuff who quailed at a bit of cold and damp. Better by far to set one's own hours, and not be subject to a coachman's brutal timetable. He could eat his nasty dinner at his leisure, he reflected, grinning. And travel in daylight. Not for him the uneasy doze that was the best one could achieve in a jolting carriage. No matter how bad the beds at the Coach and Horses might prove to be, they would, at the very least, be stationary. All in all, driving oneself had much to recommend it.

The mail had not been gone three minutes when a slight commotion, as of someone struggling with the heavy door and finally banging it shut, sounded in the entrance hall. Fred could see a portion of the hall from his vantage point, and looked up to see a huddled figure in a wet cloak, covered with snow, stumble into view. The girl was shivering and out of breath. She gasped gratefully as the comparative warmth of the inn's interior smote her icy cheeks.

"S-s-s-Stourbridge!" she cried through chattering teeth. The small valise she was carrying slipped from her frozen grasp and hit the wooden floor with a thump. "Stourbridge!"

Fred dimly recalled that Stourbridge was the name of the inn's proprietor. Since the taproom was empty except for Mr. Bates, Stourbridge had understandably vanished to parts unknown once the mail coach departed.

No one was coming to the girl's aid, however, and she appeared quite distressed. Well, anyone in her condition would be. She had the unmistakable appearance of one who had arrived on foot. No one could become as wet and breathless as she was, merely alighting from a carriage and crossing the stable yard.

Fred rose and approached. "I beg your pardon," he said pleasantly, "but may I be of assistance? This inn seems a bit understaffed. Stourbridge is the only person I've seen on the premises, apart from a couple of greasy underlings."

He retrieved the girl's valise and moved to hand it to her, but thought better of the impulse and set it on the counter for her instead. She was shivering violently, and it went very much against the grain with him to hand a fairly heavy box to a female. Why the deuce was she carrying it in the first place? "I believe he may have gone to the back of the house. Shall I roust him out?"

The girl raised wet eyes to his, sniffling. Her nose and cheeks were bright red, and for one startled moment he thought she was weeping. Then he realized she was simply chilled to the marrow. She was also distraught. Her pupils were dilated with anxiety. She neither thanked him nor replied to his offer, but simply blurted, "Has the m-mail b-been through yet?"

"Come and gone, not three minutes hence. Why, what's the matter? I say!" exclaimed Fred, catching her as she staggered. The girl moaned, and covered her face with her hands.

"The devil fly away with George!" she exclaimed passionately. "Oh, I knew it! I knew it! Merciful heavens, what am I to do now?"

"The first thing to do is to come nearer the fire," said Fred firmly, briskly knocking the snow from her shoulders and the top of her hood. He then pulled the resistless girl gently into the taproom and seated her on a wooden settle. She mumbled her thanks and slumped onto the bench, gazing dejectedly at the leaping flames.

Fred cleared his throat delicately. "Shall I go and find Stourbridge for you? I think you should bespeak a bowl of gruel, or a cup of tea, or . . . or something. Something hot."

She gave a listless shrug. "Thank you," she said. The words came out in a bitter little whisper. It was clear that the absent George had somehow blighted her life, and that a bowl of gruel would do little to mend matters. Still, Fred thought it politic to summon Stourbridge. If the girl perished of cold, it wouldn't be because Fred Bates had abandoned her to her fate.

Fred went back to the entrance hall and set up a shout. Stourbridge soon appeared, wiping his hands on his apron and looking much harassed.

"A young lady has arrived," Fred told him.

The gleam in Stourbridge's eyes and the eager way he headed toward the outside door told Fred that he had given the man a mistaken impression. "There's no carriage to be seen to," he informed the innkeeper hastily. "She's come on foot."

The host stopped in his tracks. His gaze traveled in surprise and suspicion to the valise Fred had placed on the counter. It was secured with two leather straps, rather worn, and its top bore a light dusting of snow. It looked soggy, battered, and disreputable. Stourbridge's cheeks puffed with disapproval.

"What's this? What's this?" he exclaimed, bustling into the taproom.

When he saw the bedraggled figure dripping melted snow onto his hearth, some of the air went out of the innkeeper's sails. He set his arms akimbo. "Miss Ripley," he said grimly. To Fred's surprise, the gaze he bent on the shivering girl mixed sternness with affection in a manner that was almost parental. "I might ha' known it would be you."

Miss Ripley sneezed. "Yes, you certainly might," she uttered when she had recovered. "For I booked a space on the mail from you only two days ago! How could you let it leave without me?"

"Come now, miss, you know better than that! There's no stopping the mail."

"Yes, but I was on time! I *know* I was."

"You was late," retorted Stourbridge. "And there's never any knowing what maggot you might have in your brain! I thought mayhap you had come to your senses. For you hadn't ought to be traveling alone, as you know well! Where's Master George?"

"At home," sniffed the girl, struggling to pull off her wet gloves. "He wouldn't bring me."

"Ha! Never thought I'd see the day I'd be grateful to that rapscallion. I'm glad someone down at the Hall was having a care to your reputation."

The girl's chin began to jut alarmingly. "If you are suggesting that any harm could have come to me on the Royal Mail—"

"No, now, I'm not suggesting nothing, one way or t'other!" interposed Stourbridge hastily. "I'm only telling you what anyone would tell you, and that's that young ladies don't jaunt about the countryside unprotected. But there was never any use in telling you a blessed thing, no way, nohow! You've gone your own way since you was born."

The girl must have seen the amazement and disapproval on Mr. Bates's face, for a deep chuckle escaped her. "Stourbridge was in service with my family," she explained. "His wife was my nurse." She shot the man a darkling glance. "And now that she's gone to her reward, Stourbridge thinks *he's* my nurse!"

"Well, if ever a young lady wanted looking after, it's

you!" retorted Stourbridge. "If my good wife was here this minute, she'd bring you a posset." He looked the girl over critically. "And a dry blanket, I dessay."

Miss Ripley would have replied indignantly, but another sneeze prevented her. Stourbridge bustled off, frowning and blessing himself.

"Well, if he's gone to brew you a posset, you have my sympathy," remarked Fred. "He served me the most shocking dinner an hour or so ago. I say, he's right about the dry blanket, though. May I help you to remove that cloak? It can't be doing you any good."

Miss Ripley's face was slowly returning to its natural hue, but she still bore a strong resemblance to a half-drowned kitten. Her hair, escaping from her ruined bonnet, clung to her forehead and dripped down her cheeks. She reached up now and tugged fruitlessly at the tangled strings. Her fingers were stiff with cold.

"Allow me," said Fred politely. She looked a little doubtful, but stood and permitted him to struggle for a moment with the tangle. She had tied the hood of her cloak on top of a close bonnet, and the strings of the hood and the bonnet had worked themselves together into a hopeless snarl. The fact that the strings were also soaking wet made untying the mess even more challenging.

Miss Ripley was a lady of medium height, but had to tilt her chin very high to permit tall Mr. Bates a view of the knots. He thought he spied a speculative gleam in her eyes as she regarded him from under her lashes. This, coupled with her rather unnerving proximity, caused Fred to feel the color come into his face. He had been living a decidedly Spartan existence for the past twelvemonth, and Miss Ripley was the first female he had touched since—

"Sorry!" he said hastily, stepping back. "I'm afraid we'll have to take a knife to it."

"Never mind. I can untie it once it's dry," said Miss Ripley prosaically. She seized the strings and yanked them unceremoniously over her head. The bonnet and cloak fell, together, in a heap on the floor. She kicked them aside and sat back on the settle, raking her fingers through her damp hair.

Miss Ripley appeared to have a resilient nature. Her despair had melted away like the snow on her cloak, and she now looked merely thoughtful. One could almost see the wheels turning in her brain as she tried to determine what her next move should be. It was impossible to say whether she was pretty or plain, since she was still sniffling and watery-eyed from the cold, but Mr. Bates observed that her hair, cut short, was a pleasing shade of brown, and that it boasted just the right amount of natural curl. Her figure was attractive, too. Then he turned his eyes away, embarrassed. A man in his position had no business thinking such thoughts.

Stourbridge hurried back into the room, bringing with him a woolen blanket and a steaming kettle. He draped the blanket round Miss Ripley's shoulders and picked her discarded cloak up off the floor. "Come along, then, miss," he said. "I'll put you in the blue bedchamber and pour you a nice hot footbath."

"Blue bedchamber?" Miss Ripley's eyes widened with alarm. "But, Stourbridge, I cannot *stop* here!"

Stourbridge looked severely at her. "You should ha' thought of that afore you went traipsing off alone! Joe's gone home, and so has Dick. With the snow setting in, and only Mr. Bates here to see to, I sent them off an hour ago.

I can't send word to the Hall until the morrow. They'll be worried to death, but there's no help for it; here you are, and here you'll stay. You'll be safe enough, and I'll give you a key to lock your door."

"No, you misunderstand," said Miss Ripley earnestly. "I'm not worried about the proprieties."

"Well, I ought to have known that, I do declare!"

"I'm worried that I shan't make it to Bath in time. I must wait in the taproom for the next coach. What time does the stage come through?"

Stourbridge set the teakettle down on the scarred surface of a nearby wooden table, with the air of a man who moves deliberately for fear he will otherwise explode. "Let me understand you, miss," he said, slowly and carefully. "You have not given up this crazy scheme? You still mean to travel to Bath, all in a quack, and without your maid to bear you company?"

"Pooh! You know I don't have a maid. And it would be cruel to ask anyone at the Hall to come away the day before Christmas, just to play propriety. Come, now, Stourbridge—I *must* go to Bath, and you must help me! Have you a drying rack I might borrow? No? Never mind; I daresay my cloak will dry nicely if we spread it over a chair. Just bring that high-backed one a little nearer the fire, would you? Thanks *very* much."

Miss Ripley was the lucky possessor of a singularly winning smile. She bent it coaxingly upon Stourbridge, and it won for her his grudging cooperation. He moved the chair to the fireside for her, grumbling under his breath, and spread her cloak across it to catch the warmth.

"I don't mind drying your cloak for you, miss, but I won't help you run away to Bath, and I'll be hanged if I let you sit up all night in a taproom. I'll light a fire for you in the coffee room, and there you'll sit—if you must! There's only one more stage comes through here tonight. It might get you to Bath tomorrow, but as you're not on the waybill, you're wasting your time. They won't take you up."

Miss Ripley's smile was confident. "We'll see about that."

Stourbridge snorted, then glanced at Mr. Bates as if seeking corroboration of his unspoken thoughts. Mr. Bates, in fact, understood what they must be. His eyes twinkled with empathy.

"The stage comes through here between three and four o'clock," announced Stourbridge. "After which, miss, you'll be put in the blue bedchamber—for you *won't* cozen a place on the coach, I'll be bound—and home you'll go at first light!"

Miss Ripley's eyes widened in dismay. "Three or four in the *morning*? Oh, Stourbridge, pray do not banish me to the coffee room! That's a dreadful period to sit all alone, and what if I fall asleep?"

He eyed her sourly. "Then you'll miss the coach, I suppose. And a good thing, too! Trying to wheedle your way onto the stage at dead o' night—chasing after Mr. Harry like the veriest hoyden—" He seemed to recall that he and his former charge were not alone, and broke off short. "Well, I'll say no more on that head. I'm off to light the fire in the coffee room."

"But what is there to *do* in the coffee room? I can't sit there for hours on end with no one to talk to! Can't Mr. . . ." She turned helplessly to Fred.

"Bates," he supplied promptly.

"Can't Mr. Bates bear me company?"

Fred started to laugh, and had to turn it into a cough. It no more occurred to Miss Ripley that he might have other plans for his evening than it occurred to her that her suggestion was improper. She turned to him, her eyes filled with innocent surprise. He smiled kindly at her. "I've no ambition to scandalize the neighborhood," he explained.

She looked relieved. "Oh, if *that's* all—"

"That's a great deal!" interrupted Stourbridge. He favored Mr. Bates with an approving nod. "You won't go behind closed doors with a total stranger, and that's that."

Miss Ripley appeared momentarily deflated. "I hadn't thought of that," she admitted. "I suppose it wouldn't do. Well, I shall have to stay in the taproom, then, for there are no doors here to close. Come now, Stourbridge, don't puff up! You know you are too busy to ready the coffee room just for me. It is absurd; why should I put you to so much trouble? I am perfectly safe and comfortable here. And I daresay Mr. Bates will not mind talking to me for a while."

She turned her brilliant smile upon Mr. Bates. Fred, dazzled, returned it. "Not at all," he said politely.

It was a foregone conclusion, he mused later, that Miss Ripley would prevail. Stourbridge, after issuing a few weak threats and dire warnings, was forced by the exigencies of his rigorous schedule and Miss Ripley's invincible smile to let her have her way. He lumbered off, presumably to catch a few winks of sleep before the arrival of the stage, and left her alone with Mr. Bates and a bowl of steaming broth.

Victory did not make Miss Ripley giddy—in fact, she

seemed to take it completely for granted. She was clearly the sort of female who generally achieved her ends. After Stourbridge's exit, she sipped her broth serenely and inquired, in a friendly way, whither Mr. Bates was bound.

"Lacock," he told her. "My mother and sisters are expecting me for Christmas."

Her eyes brightened. "Oh, you have sisters? I am so glad! Then you won't mind, will you, if I remove my boots? They are wet through, and my feet have gone quite numb."

Fred blinked. "Why, I . . . why, no," he stammered. "No, I don't mind." He glanced nervously at the door, thinking that Stourbridge would likely evict him from the premises if he came back in to find Miss Ripley, of whom he seemed quite fond, taking off portions of her clothing. This harrowing thought certainly did not occur to trusting Miss Ripley, for she immediately bent to her bootlaces, prattling cheerfully.

"There is something so comfortable about a man with sisters," she confided. "One feels *instinctively* that he can be trusted. Or, at the very least, that he cannot be easily shocked! But you have such a pleasant, open face, you know, that I was nearly sure I could trust you even if it turned out that you did not have sisters." She peeped up at him, her smile appearing even more charming from the peculiar angle afforded it by bending over her boots.

"Thank you," said Fred gravely.

Her smile brightened for an instant, but then was hidden from view as she turned to the laces on her other boot. "Have you come from London?"

"Yes, I live there."

"How lovely! I have only visited the metropolis three times in my life, if you can believe that. Only an hour or two away, yet we scarcely ever go there! I had to pay full fare from London, by the by, or the wretched mail would not agree to let me board in Brentford. I suppose they could have sold my place to someone in London for full fare, so they charged me full fare, even though one would *think* that very few people would be willing to pay the shocking price they charge. I was astonished when Stourbridge told me the cost. Had it been any other innkeeper I should have thought he was keeping part of it for himself. But of course I know dear old Stourbridge would never cheat me."

Her boots, which really were completely wet, finally came off. She set them neatly beside her to dry. "And now the others on that coach—if there *were* any others, at that price—will have the extra space to themselves. Really, it hardly seems fair. And to think that the driver would not wait for me, nor even inquire where I was! I could not have been more than a few hundred yards from the inn when they left; had they turned round they might very well have seen me!"

"Did you see them?"

"Well, no," admitted Miss Ripley, stretching her stockinged toes toward the fire and wiggling them appreciatively. Her feet were small and shapely, with short toes and a high, curved arch. "But I was *walking*. That is an entirely different matter, you know. I had my hood all round my face, and was looking at the ground to keep from stumbling."

"Ah."

"A *driver*—a driver of the Royal Mail!—ought to keep a sharper lookout," she said severely. "Why, he has travelers in his care! And think of the guard sitting up behind, with his feet on the mailbox! The more I think on it, the more I think he should have seen me, even if the driver did not. What is a guard *for*, if not to look about? What is the point of hiring a guard who does not look about?"

"Very true."

"I think they ought to refund my money." She flung the remark out as if daring him to disagree.

"Well, don't work yourself into a passion over it," advised Fred, deciding that his best course was to treat her as he would one of his sisters. He was finding her artless chatter and her pretty feet disconcertingly attractive. "They'll say you ought to have arrived in time to meet the coach."

Miss Ripley took no offense at his blighting reply. She sighed, then twinkled up at him. "I have the most lowering feeling that you are right." Her face abruptly clouded. "It was all George's fault."

"Your brother?" guessed Fred.

She nodded glumly. "He was to drive me here in time to catch the mail. I could have driven myself, you know, if only he had hitched up the wretched horses for me, but he refused to do so—at the last minute! I never dreamed he would use me so."

This all sounded a little strange to Fred. Miss Ripley had the appearance of a young lady who had grown up in affluent circumstances. Had not Stourbridge referred to her residence as "the Hall," and had there not been mention of servants in her family's employ? He wondered if her family had suffered some reversal of fortune that had forced them to dismiss their staff. He hoped, he thought bitterly, that Miss Ripley did not have—as his own sisters had—a profligate fool for a brother, who had made such catastrophic inroads on the family's estate that—

His torturous train of thought was interrupted by Miss Ripley uttering a clarifying remark. "I could have asked the stable boy to help me, of course, but it might have cost him his situation when Papa found out."

Fred perceived that Miss Ripley's journey was of a clandestine nature. "Miss Ripley, have you been forbidden to go to Bath?" he inquired sternly.

"Certainly not," declared Miss Ripley indignantly. But then she ruined the effect by biting her lip and peeping roguishly up at him. "I simply didn't tell them I was going."

Fred choked. "Except for George."

"Except for George," she agreed. "For I did think I might trust George. I was never more deceived!"

"How old is George?"

"Sixteen."

"You know, I can find it in my heart to feel sorry for George," remarked Fred. "An action that would cost your stable boy his situation might very well cost your sixteen-year-old brother a caning."

"Well, that is exactly what George thought. Not a caning, of course, for Papa never does *that*, but he did think Papa would rake him over the coals, and very likely stop his allowance or some such thing."

"Unhappy George! He still will, once he discovers that George kept your secret—which he undoubtedly did, or your papa would be here by now."

Miss Ripley brightened. "Why, you are right! So George must have said nothing after all. I am glad to learn he was not *completely* faithless."

"May I ask why you are traveling to Bath?"

Her natural color had recovered to the point where he could now tell when she was blushing. She pushed her bowl of broth away and began tracing patterns on the tabletop with the edge of her spoon. "Well, I . . . it's a rather long story. I don't believe it would interest you."

"On the contrary. Who is Mr. Harry?"

She looked up at that, her eyes wide with startled dismay. "H-how did you know . . . ?" she stammered.

He grinned apologetically. "Stourbridge mentioned the name. Said you were *chasing after* him—but I'm sure, of course, that Stourbridge quite mistakes the matter."

Miss Ripley was pink from her neck to her hairline. "Yes, he does," she said with dignity. "Mr. Harry—*Harry*, I mean—is the man I am going to marry."

Mr. Bates was already sufficiently acquainted with Miss Ripley to take this statement with a grain of salt. "Is Harry aware of his impending nuptials?" he inquired politely.

Miss Ripley spluttered indignantly. Fred kindly recommended that she finish her broth.

"I shan't; it's horrid," said Miss Ripley crossly, flinging down her spoon with an air of finality. "There are bits of something burned floating in it. And you, sir, are mistrustful and rude."

"I beg your pardon," he said, grinning. "I daresay you would like to tell me that Harry's intentions—or lack of intentions—are none of my business."

"Well, of course they are not! And besides, he always agrees to anything I propose. That is—oh! There is no point in discussing it with you, after all!"

She had turned quite scarlet. Fred burst out laughing, and she bent upon him a look of deep reproach. "Oh, I *am* sorry!" gasped Fred at last. "No, really—it's disgraceful of me to laugh. I daresay you feel your situation is desperate, whatever it is, or you would not be running off to Bath without a chaperone."

She appeared only slightly mollified. "Well, I would not characterize it as *desperate*," she said stiffly. "Hardly that. But it is . . . it is certainly an emergency, for I must arrive in Bath no later than tomorrow evening."

"Christmas Eve?" Fred shook his head. "My dear girl, you will never make it. The mail was your last hope. Bath is nearly a hundred miles from here, and the coaches will not run from noon tomorrow until Boxing Day."

Miss Ripley paled. "Oh, no! Are you certain?"

"No, of course I am not certain," he hedged, not liking to inflict further distress on her. "But I fear you will find it so. Why must you arrive in Bath tomorrow, of all days?"

Miss Ripley did not appear to have heard him. She stared straight ahead, her eyes wide and her hands pressed to her cheeks. Then she rose and began pacing the room, careless of her stocking feet. "I could do it in a post chaise," she said under her breath, as if thinking aloud. "But Stourbridge will never, never let me hire one here. And there is not another coaching inn for miles."

She halted, looking intently at Mr. Bates. "Stourbridge seemed to think the stage coming through tonight would reach Bath tomorrow."

"Yes, but you are not on the waybill."

She nodded absently. "And ten to one Stourbridge forgot that tomorrow will be Christmas Eve." She raked her hand distractedly through her hair, causing her curls to spring riotously forth, and began pacing again. "I feel quite sure that you are right," she said anxiously. "I feel it in my bones. I dare not place my dependence on the stage."

Miss Ripley abruptly returned to her place on the settle and began working one foot back into its wet boot.

"I say! What are you doing?" asked Fred, alarmed.

"I must walk to Hounslow. It is only a matter of two or three miles. I will be able to hire a chaise there."

"You cannot walk all the way to Hounslow! In this weather? At this hour? And all alone? It is madness!"

Miss Ripley's chin had assumed a very determined tilt. "I can, and I will," she replied firmly.

The wet boot was giving her some difficulty, and she winced as her foot finally slid home. She must have blistered it in her earlier walk, from her home to the inn. Fred snatched the other boot up and held it away from her, shaking his head. "I can't let you do this. You will do yourself an injury. Miss Ripley, pray consider! If you make it as far as Hounslow, which is by no means certain, you will arrive in the middle of the night, quite alone, at an inn where no one knows you. It isn't safe."

She rose and glared at him. "I shall walk to Hounslow. I shall hire a chaise. I shall leave *immediately* for Bath. And if you do not hand me my boot, I shall do it barefooted."

She looked capable of it. "But why?" demanded Fred, harassed.

"Because if I do not arrive in Bath tomorrow, my entire life will be ruined! Pray hand me that boot." She held out an imperious hand.

Fred tried to look stern. "I can be mulish, too," he promised her. "I'll not allow you to run such a heedless, foolish risk. Walk to Hounslow, my eye! What will become of you if you sprain your ankle on the road? Or if you arrive, but cannot hire a chaise? You will be stranded—and very likely ill, after walking all that way in the snow with no rest! You may not be aware of this, my good girl, but a respectable inn will not put you up."

Her eyes narrowed, and she tilted her head like a baffled kitten. "You're bamming me," she said accusingly, revealing the fact that her brothers did not guard their tongues in her presence.

"I'm not," Fred retorted. "Females don't travel alone. You should have seen the way Stourbridge hopped in here, before he realized it was you. He was ready to throw you back out in the snow."

Uncertainty flickered in Miss Ripley's eyes. Fred pressed his advantage. "Your best course, I believe, is to take Stourbridge's advice and go to bed."

"But he will send me back to the Hall in the morning!" Her eyes were huge and tragic. Then a sort of wild hope suddenly ignited in their depths. She put out her hand and placed it on Fred's sleeve. "Oh, sir—did you not say you were traveling to Lacock? Oh, pray, *pray* take me as far as Hounslow!"

Fred was appalled. "No! That is, I . . . I shan't leave until after breakfast. Mid-morning! By the time you reach Hounslow, it will be too late for a post chaise to take you as far as Bath tomorrow."

Her face fell. "Very well," she said sadly. Then, quick as thought, she reached up and snatched her boot from Fred's hand while his guard was down.

"Why, you little minx!" he began, then stopped, chagrined, as Miss Ripley danced neatly away from him. It was her boot, after all. Still, he had to fight a very strong urge to wrestle it away from her again. Had they been ten years younger, by George, he would have. "You definitely have brothers," he said grimly.

"Six of them," she informed him serenely. She sat back down and began stuffing her left foot into the newly regained boot.

A new insight occurred to him. "And I'd bet a monkey you are the only girl among the lot."

She glanced up, surprised. "Why, yes, that's right. How did you know?"

Fred dropped onto the chair across from her, a wry smile twisting his features. "You, Miss Ripley, have all the earmarks of a chit who has been shamelessly indulged by her parents, and frequently pounded by her brothers."

Her mischievous look returned. "You mean I am a spoiled tomboy."

"Meaning no offense, of course," said Fred politely.

"None taken," she assured him. "It is a masterly reading of my character, actually. And on such short acquaintance! Quite impressive." She finished tying her bootlaces and rose, picking up her still-damp cloak. "It has been a pleasure meeting you, Mr. Bates. I wish you a pleasant journey to Lacock. Farewell."

He regarded her sourly from beneath his brows. "Sit down," he growled. "You win."

Her eyes dilated in what seemed to be genuine surprise. Fred had to bite his lip to keep his countenance. "Save that dewy-eyed look for another chap; you'll not hoax *me* with it!" he informed her austerely. "The instant I told you I could not let you walk to Hounslow, you knew I would eventually agree to drive you there."

Miss Ripley was instantly transfigured. She favored him with a smile so radiant that, despite his ruffled sense of propriety and his deep misgivings about assisting this unknown girl in what was probably an elopement, he found himself smiling back. She clasped her pretty hands before her. "Thank you!" she exclaimed fervently. "Oh, thank you! And—we will leave now?"

"No, we will not leave now! We shall fortify ourselves with a few hours' sleep before beginning. Why do you think I stopped in Brentford rather than Hounslow?"

"Well, I don't know. And I have been wondering about that, you know, ever since you told me you lived in London," said Miss Ripley frankly. Having won her point, she returned to practicality and busied herself in returning her cloak to the chair back. "It seems a bit odd to leave London for Lacock and come only as far as Brentford." The brilliant smile was turned on him again. "Although I am very glad you did."

"Well, I was detained rather longer than I expected, and got a late start," explained Fred, reminding himself that she would smile that way at anyone who helped her. It was idiotic for him to feel so much pleasure at being the recipient of that smile. "But I stopped in Brentford because too many travelers change horses in Hounslow. The inns there are busy, noisy, and high-priced. The Coach and Horses, on the other hand, is comparatively quiet and inexpensive. And since I am driving myself, I require a bit of rest. Of which, it now appears, I shall receive a limited quantity." He pointed at her, in the manner of a schoolmaster singling out a naughty student. "You, my girl, may consider yourself fortunate that I shan't keep to my intended timetable, and make you wait for breakfast! Can you be ready to leave here by six o'clock?"

"Oh, yes! Yes!" she cried, the picture of eagerness. She

turned up to his a face that was glowing with gratitude. "Indeed, I am so much obliged to you, sir! I only wish there were some kindness I could perform for *you.*"

It was a fortunate thing, reflected Mr. Bates, that innocent Miss Ripley had not fallen into unprincipled hands. Her ardent desire to repay his kindness with an unselfish feat of her own might, had he been another sort of chap, have landed her in treacherous waters.

Mr. Bates was one of those lucky individuals who can quickly fall into a deep sleep and awaken at the hour he chooses, but despite her protestations he had no serious expectation of finding Miss Ripley ready to depart by six o'clock. He was startled, therefore, when, some several minutes before that hour, he walked smack into her in the dark passage that led from his chamber to the public rooms.

"Ssh!" she warned him, placing a small hand over his mouth to stifle his yelp. "Do not trip over my valise; it is directly at your feet. Dick Harvey is rattling about in the kitchen, but I believe he is the only person up as yet. There's an ostler or something in the yard, but I do not know him—thank goodness. Oh—good morning," she added, removing her hand.

"Good morning. Why are we whispering?"

His eyes were adjusting to the dimness, and he could tell that she was fully dressed and thoroughly bundled up, with her cloak tied on over a thick pelisse. "Well, I have been thinking, and I believe it will be better if no one sees me go with you," she explained. "Stourbridge will assume that I am still asleep in the blue bedchamber, and I daresay he will not think of disturbing me until eight or nine o'clock. And by then, you know, it will be too late to catch us. Can you pay your shot and leave directly? I shall slip out the back and start walking, then meet you round the first bend in the road."

Fred felt the hair rise up on his neck. "Good God, they will think I have abducted you!"

"Pooh! They will not think it for long," she assured him blithely. "Everything will be made right in a trice, once I reach Bath."

However, it was only the firm knowledge of his own good intentions that prevented Mr. Bates from feeling profoundly guilty as he paid his shot and called for his carriage. The ostler seemed to take an unconscionably long time to bring the gig round, and Mr. Bates fretted, picturing Miss Ripley struggling down the cold, dark road alone.

He drove off as quickly as he could and, as she had promised, soon saw a cloaked and hooded figure slip out of the shadows beside the road and wave as he rounded the first bend. He immediately pulled up and reached for her valise, but Miss Ripley was frowning critically at his vehicle. There was just enough light reflecting off the snow to give her a fair idea of what she was seeing.

"Why are you driving a gig?" she demanded, without preamble.

Fred felt himself color up. "Hand me that valise, Impertinence! I dare not get down for fear this beast will trot off without us."

She did so, but still looked dubious. Fred stuffed the valise beneath the seat and reached his hand to her. She clambered up without comment, but as soon as he had given his horse the office to start he became aware that she was regarding him fixedly. "Well? What is it?" he asked testily.

"A London gentleman should drive a curricle," she informed him unnecessarily. "Or perhaps a whiskey. This is a cab-fronted gig."

"There is nothing wrong with a gig. It's practical."

"Practical it may be, but it is not fashionable." She glanced critically at the cut of his driving coat and, in the brief silence that ensued, he sensed that she was mentally calculating what he must have paid for his clothing—which *was* fashionable—and his boots, which had been made especially for him by Hoby. "I had thought you would drive a curricle."

"I did, at one time," said Fred, nettled. "But I sold it."

"Really? Why?"

"To buy a cab-fronted gig, of course! Allow me to recommend that you tuck that rug round you. It's cold."

"Thank you," she said absently, complying. "Do you mean this gig is actually yours?"

"Yes."

"How odd. Oh—I know! Are you economizing?"

"Yes!"

"Well, don't bite my nose off. I daresay it's very commendable."

Fred was too mortified to reply. Eventually she added, in a pious voice, "Thrift is a virtue."

"I am astonished to hear you say so," said Fred acidly. "You do not strike me as the sort of girl who admires caution in any form, however virtuous."

Another of her deep chuckles shook her. "You are right, of course. And not for the first time! Really, it's wonderful how you hit unerringly on every defect in my character. You seem to see them all at a glance."

Fred snorted. "If you would not parade your flaws before

me, one after the other, I daresay I would remain as ignorant of them as any other man."

"On the contrary! I feel sure you have a remarkable degree of insight." She dimpled. "There are any number of persons who have known me for years without tumbling to the awful truth about me."

"The awful truth about you, Miss Ripley," Fred told her austerely, "is that you have somehow managed to take optimism to such an extreme that you have turned a virtue into a vice."

She opened her eyes at him and gave a startled little laugh. "No! How is that possible?"

He shook his head, trying to look glum. "I don't know. I have never encountered anything quite like it."

She immediately bestowed another of her brilliant smiles upon him. It took more than a few withering remarks to wither the likes of Miss Ripley. "Well! If you ever find yourself at *point nonplus*, which I'm sure I hope you never may, you can run off with the gypsies and tell fortunes. I never met anyone with a greater gift! What is your Christian name, Mr. Bates?"

He blinked at her. "It is Fred. Why?"

Her smile sweetened. "Fred. I like that. Mine is Claudia. I was just thinking that we ought, perhaps, to pose as brother and sister when we reach Hounslow. Just to avoid the appearance of impropriety, you know."

"But we look nothing alike!" He looked askance at Claudia Ripley in the growing light. She was not diminutive, but she appeared so next to his tall, lanky frame. Her hair was decidedly curly, and his was straight as straw. Her face was round and rosy, and his was lean and dusted with freckles. "No one will believe for a moment that we are nearly related."

"Well, we cannot pretend to be *distantly* related! It isn't respectable. I can't run round the countryside in the company of just anyone."

Fred stared at her in wild exasperation. "Miss Ripley, that is exactly what you are doing!"

"That is neither here nor there. I can't be *seen* to be doing it." She tapped one gloved fingertip thoughtfully against her teeth while Fred choked helplessly beside her. "I have it," she announced. "You will be my stepbrother. There is nothing scandalous about traveling to Bath in the company of one's stepbrother."

"Now, look here!" said Fred, alarmed. "You are not traveling to Bath in my company! I am taking you only as far as Hounslow, where you will hire a post chaise and go on your merry way—while I recruit my strength with a hearty breakfast and try to recover from the effects of having met you!"

But when they arrived at Hounslow, it proved more difficult than Fred had foreseen to hire a post chaise for a single female. They stopped at the largest of the coaching inns, which was so busy and full of rough-looking men that Miss Ripley grew apprehensive and clung to him like a shadow. There was no question, from the moment they alighted in the bustling yard, that she could be allowed to enter into the transaction on her own behalf. So Fred stepped forward to make the arrangements for her. Even at that early hour, the place was crowded with travelers anxious to reach their various destinations before Christmas, and eager to depart before the weather closed in again.

They finally were able to secure the hire of what seemed

to be the last available chaise, a pair of horses, and a postilion. But then Fred saw that postilion, lounging against the wall with a straw between his teeth and leering at Miss Ripley. He felt his hackles rise. The thought of pretty little Claudia all alone in the carriage, mile after mile, with that insolent-looking blackguard her sole protector and companion, was insupportable.

He drew her aside and spoke to her in an urgent, low voice. "Miss Ripley, I cannot let you do this."

For the first time, as they huddled in the entrance hall, jostled and buffeted by the busy staff and trying to hear each other above the din of shouts, whistles, neighs, and the clatter of plates and silverware from the nearby coffee room, she appeared a little daunted. "I own, I mislike the look of that postboy. But what am I to do? I cannot fly to Bath."

"You ought not to go to Bath at all, and well you know it! Miss Ripley, I urge you to reconsider. Stourbridge is right, you know. This is a mad scheme, and it is not at all the thing for you to be traveling alone."

"I am not such a poor creature, to turn tail at the first setback," she said staunchly. "Besides, whether I go on or whether I go home, I must hire that chaise. I had rather go forward than go back."

Fred gritted his teeth. "Very well. If I'm in for a penny, I may as well be in for a pound. I shall take you on to Colnbrook."

Her relief was palpable, but she seemed to feel a certain crisis of conscience. "Oh, thank you! But you need not take me as far as Colnbrook. Indeed, I am grateful for your help, but I do not wish to impose upon you more than I need. There is an inn at Sipson Green—"

"Yes, the Magpies! I shan't entrust you to that lot. Colnbrook it is. We'll do no more than break our fast here, and then go on."

They did so. The weather held clear and cold, although the clouds hovered thickly overhead and there was snow on the road. At times the roadway was rendered invisible by the snow covering it, but the sturdy animal Fred had hired at the Coach and Horses trotted on, so familiar with the route that it could probably have followed the track blindfolded.

Miss Ripley fell into a pensive mood. She sat silently beside him until they were halfway to Cranford. At that point, Fred had to pull off the crown of the road to allow a swan-necked traveling coach to overtake them. It was being driven at a spanking pace behind four strong horses, and the wheels sprayed snow in every direction as it passed. Miss Ripley's pensive expression deepened. When they had returned to the crown of the road, she peered up at her companion and ventured to ask, "Is it possible to hitch two horses to this gig?"

"A gig is a one-horse vehicle."

"Yes, everyone knows that. But is it possible?"

He looked down at her with misgiving. "Why?"

"I was just thinking that we could travel a little faster behind two horses."

"Do you know," said Fred pleasantly, "I have come to dread those words."

"What words?"

" 'I was just thinking.' Your thought processes, Miss Ripley, tend to result in mayhem."

She beamed. "How well you know me already! Mr. Bates, you are a marvel."

"Yes, it is uncanny, isn't it? By the simple process of observation, and prompted solely by some faint instinct for self-preservation, I have deduced that your company is dangerous."

She chuckled. "Not my company, Mr. Bates. Merely my ideas."

"Since one invariably accompanies the other, Miss Ripley, you have failed to comfort me."

"Yes, but this time I have hit upon a really nacky notion," she told him earnestly. "No, no, only listen! You have already confessed that you are trying to economize. Well, I have no desire whatsoever to economize—my whole purpose is to reach Bath as speedily as I may. I ought not to travel alone; you have said so yourself. And indeed, now that I have seen what these posting inns are like, I own I am not quite comfortable with the prospect. So I was just thinking—"

Fred groaned and covered his eyes with his hand.

"No, really! I was just thinking that I could hire you—as my courier."

"What!"

She plunged hurriedly on. "If you were my courier, I could pay all the expenses of the journey—and if we cannot hitch two horses to the gig, we could hire a post chaise—and since I would bear the cost, just think of the money you might save! And we could travel much faster, and not be out in all this wind and cold."

She must have seen the thunderclouds gathering on Fred's face, for she placed her hand urgently on his sleeve and said in a different tone of voice, "And I would have your protection. Which, I must say, I would be very glad to have."

Fred paused, the words of denial dying on his lips. He considered the face turned up to his. She had said the one thing that might be calculated to win his cooperation, but he did not think it was calculation on her part. Miss Ripley's speaking eyes—which, he was now able to discern, were gray—held a sort of desperate anxiety. They were also watering a bit from the cold breeze spanking her face.

His conscience smote him. She really ought not to be out in the wind and the cold, but it seemed impossible to explain to such an innocent all the reasons why her "nacky notion" was wholly ineligible. Still, her plan to post all the way to Bath by herself was downright dangerous. And there was no particular reason to believe that the kind landlady at the Ostrich would take better care of her than he himself could.

Stourbridge's words echoed in his memory: *If ever a young lady wanted looking after, it's you!* Despite her firm belief to the contrary, it seemed to Fred that Miss Ripley did need looking after. She was entirely too trusting. If he abandoned her in Colnbrook because he was too fastidious to ride in a closed carriage with her, she would probably climb into a closed carriage with some other gentleman who offered—and, since Miss Ripley was a pretty girl, someone would surely offer.

It would be, he realized, a heroic act to swallow his pride, abandon all hope of reaching Lacock today, and allow her to "hire" him. It would inconvenience him, it would probably compromise him, it would surely compromise her—but since his intentions were honorable, it would be truly chivalrous to shield her from those whose intentions might not be. The more so, he supposed, since the idea galled him.

Fred realized he was still frowning down at Miss Ripley, whose face was growing more hopeful the longer he paused. "If ever I met a more troublesome chit!" he exclaimed, goaded. "You seem to fly from one reckless idea to the next—and now you are dragging me with you on this crazy excursion! How have you survived to reach your majority? Someone should have strangled you by now. I've half a mind to pull up right here, set you down at the side of the road, and drive off as quickly as this slug of a horse will allow."

Miss Ripley bestowed a blinding smile upon her reluctant cavalier. "How good you are!" she said gratefully, correctly divining that he would do no such thing. "I am fortunate indeed to have met you."

With the most pressing of her concerns alleviated, Miss Ripley's natural high spirits returned. She beguiled the tedium of the remaining few miles to Colnbrook with cheerful reminiscences of the many occasions when one or another of her brothers had been ready to strangle her, just as Mr. Bates had guessed, and congratulating him on his intuition which, she assured him, was quite out of the common way.

When they reached the Ostrich, Mr. Bates, after a short, but heated, argument, accepted Miss Ripley's purse and used a portion of the funds it contained to hire a chaise and—following another brief argument, this one conducted in agitated whispers outside the hearing of the landlady—four horses. The rapidity with which that swan-necked traveling coach had passed them had taken strong possession of Miss Ripley's mind, and she refused to allow any consideration of expense, comfort, or safety to weigh with her. Four horses she must have.

The suspicions which the landlady harbored regarding the nature of the young couple's journey were deepened by Miss Ripley's anxiety regarding the speed at which they ought to travel. Fred had to endure a severe scold from the motherly soul who ran the Ostrich, and his scarlet-faced protestations failed to move her. She did not believe for a moment that Claudia was his stepsister. In the end, Fred had to pay nearly twice what the hire of the chaise was worth and ignore the sniggering of the ostlers as he climbed in beside Miss Ripley and pulled the door to.

Fuming, he mopped his red face with his handkerchief. "If nothing else has served to show you the error of your ways, I hope this has done so!" he told his companion reprovingly. "I have not suffered through such humiliation since I was a boy! Now I shall have to find another inn at which to change my horses, for I'll be da—I'll be hanged if I ever come back to the Ostrich!"

"You must come back for your gig," Miss Ripley reminded him. She smiled kindly at Fred's harassed expression and patted his arm to soothe him. "Now, Mr. Bates, you mustn't allow what the landlady said to upset you."

"Alas, I do not share your extraordinary ability to ignore the disapproval of others!"

Her eyes twinkled reprehensibly. "I recommend you cultivate it. It makes life so much more comfortable! Besides, everything she said was rubbish."

"It wasn't *all* rubbish," grumbled Fred. "Four horses, indeed! On a snowy road! If the postboy springs 'em, we shall be overturned—and if he doesn't, we'd have done as well with two!"

"If it saves an hour—if it saves a quarter of an hour!—it shall have been worth every penny."

Fred looked down at her determined little face and some of his exasperation left him. In a milder tone he asked, "May I inquire exactly what your business is in Bath, and why it must be conducted on Christmas Eve? Now that you have embroiled me in this scheme, whatever it is, I hope it is not criminal."

As he had hoped, his query made her chuckle. "It is not criminal, but I do think that the less you know about it the sounder you will sleep tonight."

"Miss Ripley, you horrify me! Pray give me a round tale at once."

She looked mischievous, but shook her head. "You must be content to know that you are saving my life. Or, at the very least, my future happiness."

It was an elopement, then. He had suspected as much, but for some reason a stab of disappointment went through him that had nothing to do with his general disapproval of elopements.

"Your future happiness lies with Harry, no doubt." He tried to smile and speak archly, but did not quite succeed. She looked quickly up at him, and he had to look away. Out of the corner of his eye, he saw her nod.

"You startled me. I forgot that you had already stumbled upon that fact," she confessed. When he did not immediately reply, she seemed to hesitate. "I suppose you are guessing the rest."

He shrugged apologetically. "I can't help it, you know. I am such an intuitive chap."

She agreed to it, but seemed preoccupied. She was frowning at the passing trees as if trying to estimate their rate of speed. The postilion was urging the horses to the fastest speed possible, as Miss Ripley had requested, and the resultant rocking and bouncing required both passengers to steady themselves by clinging to the leather straps provided for that purpose.

"How long do you think it will take us to reach Bath?" she asked.

"If the weather holds, and if the postboy is able to keep us rattling along at this infernal pace, I daresay we could arrive in ten hours."

Miss Ripley paled. "Ten hours! But . . . it will be dark long before then! Can we travel this quickly after dark?"

He had to hide a grin; the prospect of jolting along in a Yellow Bounder for ten hours seemed to cause her no dismay. "I don't know," he admitted. "But the mail travels very fast, and they travel all night. I suppose a post chaise could do the same if you insist upon it. The chancy thing is the weather."

She leaned anxiously forward to study the sky through the window. What she saw apparently did not reassure her. "If we do not arrive in time, I shall murder George when next I see him!" she exclaimed. "If only I had caught the mail as I had planned, I would be in Bath this very minute!"

Fred looked sideways at her. "Do you know, if it is so all-fired important for you to reach Bath today of all days, it strikes me as peculiar that your precious Harry did not come himself to escort you," he said with asperity. "What the deuce is he about, letting you come all this way by yourself?"

He was expecting her to tell him that Harry was ill, or injured, or perhaps that Harry shared her sanguine belief that nothing particularly bad could happen to her. He did not expect her to say what she did say, which was: "Oh, Harry does not know I am coming."

Fred stared. Miss Ripley looked so calm that he decided he must have misunderstood. "I can't have heard you aright," he said. "I thought you just said that Harry does not know you are coming to Bath."

Her lips parted in surprise. "Yes! I thought you knew that."

Words failed Mr. Bates. As she saw his dumbfounded expression, a slow blush crept up Miss Ripley's throat and bathed her face in pink. "You needn't look so astonished," she said stiffly. "You seem to know so many things without being told, how am I to know what you have deduced and what you have not?"

He continued to stare wordlessly at her. She dropped her eyes, very pink indeed. "I s-suppose you think it wrong of me," she said in a small voice.

"Well," said Fred carefully, "let me be sure I understand you. I do not wish to jump to erroneous conclusions. But it seems to me that you have run away from home, without a word to anyone—except, of course, the unfortunate George, for whom I feel more compassion every moment—in order to join a man named Harry in Bath. A man who has no idea that you are about to descend upon him, on Christmas Eve, unaccompanied and unexpected—and for what purpose I shudder to conjecture."

Miss Ripley, scarlet-faced, hung her head. Fred did not know which he wanted to do more—to laugh out loud, or to shake her. "Good God! So it's true, then?"

She drew herself up with as much dignity as she could. "Yes, I suppose it is. But it is not nearly as bad as you have made it sound! For if Harry would but *think* for a moment, he might very well expect that I would come hotfoot to Bath."

Fred choked. "You seem to place little dependence on the likelihood that he will think."

"No," admitted Miss Ripley, "for he rarely does. Now, what have I said to cast you into whoops?"

"Oh, nothing in the world!" gasped Fred. "Just the idea that your *future happiness* lies with a man who rarely thinks!"

Miss Ripley's dimples reappeared. "Well, that is why we are so well suited," she said mischievously. "I do the thinking for both of us. And really, he has the best and sweetest nature!"

"He would have to have that," Fred agreed. "Any man who allowed you, of all women, to do the thinking for him must be touched in his upper works! Is that why he offered you marriage? To spare himself the trouble of thinking? Or did you simply wear him down until he agreed to anything just to be rid of you and escape to Bath?"

She looked injured. "Neither, of course! Harry and I have had an understanding all our lives. And you needn't sneer at poor Harry's intellect," she added indignantly. "For although he is not needle-witted, he is not a *complete* slowtop. And I believe that a mild disposition and a readiness to please are rare and valuable traits in a young man."

"Oh, no doubt. If you have found a man meek enough to allow you to lead him round by the nose, I congratulate you! I daresay it was difficult to locate such a biddable chap. Most men are unwilling to live beneath the cat's paw—"

Miss Ripley gasped.

"—and now that you have found him, I can easily understand your eagerness to join him, willy-nilly, wherever he may be."

"I know you are joking," she said severely, "but really, it is shabby of you to imply that I would henpeck poor Harry! Or, indeed, anyone!"

"I beg your pardon. Pray explain to me, if you can, why Harry should realize—if he would but think—that you are rushing down to Bath, entirely by yourself, on Christmas Eve. For you have credited me with an uncanny insight into your nature, and yet I would never have expected such a thing from you. Or from any other young lady of breeding."

His words must have stung, for the face she turned to him was filled with reproach. "You *do* have an uncanny insight into my nature. And, to speak truth, I feel I have a certain insight into yours—which is the reason why I refuse to pull caps with you! However uncivil you are on the outside, I know perfectly well that you are laughing on the inside."

Since this was true, Fred could not suppress a grin. "Very well, Miss Ripley! I am in your corner, come what may. Now tell me the whole."

She looked very pleased at that, and instantly relaxed her defensive posture. "All right, I will. For I do trust you, Mr. Bates."

Her smile was even more blinding in the close quarters of the post chaise. It made a chap almost dizzy, as if someone had landed him a facer. But the sunny smile soon faded as Claudia cast about, frowning a little, for a way to explain her adventure.

"You see, Harry and I have been friends forever. And we always planned to marry, because we both decided simply ages ago that we would never like anyone else half as well as we like each other."

"I see."

"But we were never in any particular hurry, you know, because . . . well, we just weren't. And our parents were always rather unenthusiastic about the match, so we thought we'd wait until they came round a bit. And then . . ." She paused, seeming at a loss.

"And then?" prompted Fred.

She glanced uncertainly at him. "Well, for the past five winters Harry has always escorted his mother to Bath. She takes the waters there, you know. And the past two years, he has gone to London for the Season as well. So I haven't seen him quite as often as I would like, except in summer. And somehow, last summer . . ."

She broke off again, frowning. "I am not sure how it happened, but somehow I began to think that we ought not to marry after all. Or at least not until we had had an opportunity to meet other young persons. So I . . . I told him as much."

She raised anxious eyes to Fred's face. "It was a mad thing to do; I can't imagine why I said it! For I never go anywhere, and I daresay I shall never meet anyone." Then light seemed to dawn, and Claudia caught her breath, apparently cudgeling her brain in an effort of memory. "Why, do you suppose—it seems incredible! But—oh! Do you suppose Harry led me to say that?"

She seemed stunned by the very idea that her guileless Harry might have succeeded in tricking her. Fred shook his head. "Impossible!" he averred. "No man who had the felicity of securing your hand would ever attempt to relinquish it." He spoke jocularly, but the words sent a strange little pang through him. He gave himself a mental shake and tried to concentrate on her problem; he ought not to joke when Miss Ripley's face was so troubled. "Why do you suspect a subterfuge?"

Claudia looked mournful. "Because, a few days ago, I received a letter from Bath." Her lower lip trembled. "Harry thought he should inform me before telling anyone else, because of the . . . the special relationship in which we have always stood. But since I had so generously released him from his promise, he said, he is going to offer marriage to some dreadful female he has met in Bath. And he is going to do it on Christmas Day."

Her face was so woebegone, Fred had to resist an impulse to put his arms around her. "Did Harry actually say she was a dreadful female?" he asked, appalled.

Claudia blushed. "Well, no. I added that part."

"Oh. But why did you not write back to him and ask him to wait? Surely it would have been simpler to send a letter than to go yourself."

"I couldn't! There wasn't time." Fred must have looked puzzled, for she hastened to add, "You don't know Harry's mother. She's very fond of me, but she has always thought me a . . . a bad influence on Harry. When we were children, you know, I did lead him into scrapes. Fairly regularly, I am afraid! But that was *years* ago. Everything is quite different, now we are grown up, but she still maintains that I am not a proper bride for her darling boy. And although Harry would never credit it—for Harry never thinks ill of anyone!—I am certain that she would have hidden from him any message I sent. She would simply have intercepted it, waited until Harry was safely betrothed, then pretend after the fact that my letter had just arrived."

Fred was disgusted. "Good God, doesn't Harry have enough gumption to intercept the post?"

Miss Ripley shook her head dolefully. "Harry has no gumption at all."

Fred could not help thinking that Harry's mother was probably a woman of great good sense, since it was difficult for him to picture Claudia Ripley happily wed to a man with no gumption. But he could not say so, of course. Neither could he bring himself to ask the question burning in his brain: Was this a love match, or was it not?

It was none of his business, he told himself fiercely. Even if he were interested in courting Miss Ripley himself—which, of course, he was not, since his own heart was irretrievably broken—he was in no position to do so. Why, Bella had left him virtually penniless. He was only now, after more than a year of severe penance and privation, beginning to make a recovery. And every farthing that he managed to save he had sent home, so that Mother and Susan and Fanny might be comfortable.

He had vowed that they, at least, would not suffer for his sins, and they had not. This had been his only solace during this year of desolation and misery. But it was just as well that his heart had been stolen along with his fortune. Until the day when he could support a wife, it was useless to think about looking for one.

But it would always be useless to think of that, he reminded himself. He could never feel for anyone what he had felt for Bella.

Had felt? He meant, of course, felt. *Felt* for Bella. *What the deuce was wrong with him this morning?* His passion for Bella was immutable— Unchanged, unchanging, and unchangeable. In fact—

"What's wrong?"

Fred blinked. "Nothing."

Miss Ripley's gray eyes were soft with concern. "You looked so . . . bleak, for a moment."

He had felt bleak for many months, actually. Fred gave her a twisted smile. "Claudia," he asked abruptly, "have you ever been in love?"

"No. I love Harry, of course, but—" Her eyes rounded with awe. "Have you?"

He nodded, his features drawn into a stern and haunted expression. Claudia appeared enthralled. "What was it like?" she asked eagerly.

He cast her a scornful glance. "It was ghastly," he informed her scathingly. "If you ever begin to feel the slightest tug on your heartstrings, take my advice and run for your life."

She looked skeptical. "I don't believe you were truly in love. My parents made a love match, and they are the happiest of mortals."

"Perhaps they chose more wisely than I," said Fred hollowly.

She opened her eyes at him. "Well, obviously they did."

It was clear that she failed to appreciate the depth of his wound, or the seriousness of his warning. Fred felt a little annoyed. "I hope you never know what it is to suffer a broken heart," he told her darkly.

She smiled. "Thank you. It's not likely that I shall, however, since I am going to marry Harry."

Fred lapsed into offended silence.

It was not possible to nurse a grievance, however, in Miss Ripley's bracing company. She was the most entertaining creature he had ever met. Maddeningly cheerful, innocent and wise by turns, and completely trusting, she inspired affection as easily as a baby. He laughed at her, argued with her, listened to her artless confidences, entered into her feelings and opinions, and, to his own surprise, shared his own with her. He almost told her about Bella, but thought better of it. It was not a tale for a young lady's ears.

Despite the bone-jarring motion of the coach, it seemed to Fred the easiest and most enjoyable trip to Bath he had ever taken. Deep in conversation with Claudia, the miles fairly flew by. At nearly every town, they both exclaimed that they could scarcely believe they had come so far already.

The road was straight and level for the most part all the way from Reading to Speenhamland, and Claudia was thrilled by the rapid progress they were making. She and Mr. Bates had completely dispensed with formality by the time they reached Theale, since Claudia was afraid if she did not practice calling him by his Christian name she would blurt out "Mr. Bates" in front of some stranger and give the lie to their pretended relationship. Really, mused Fred, as he helped his supposed stepsister out of the post chaise for a quick bite of ham and a mouthful of tea, it was amazing how quickly an intimate friendship could grow between two people. He supposed it was because they had been thrown entirely together and forced by circumstances to call each other by their first names. She seemed to feel the same, for when they climbed back into the chaise, refreshed and ready for another hour or two of discomfort, she flashed her radiant smile at Fred and confided that she felt as if she had known him all her life.

It began to seem that they might reach Bath earlier than Fred had predicted, since they were making such excellent time. However, as they neared Marlborough, the sky took on a distinctly leaden look. Soon the postboy was forced by the condition of the road and the failing light to slow the horses considerably.

And then the snow began to fall.

The postboy would not take them past Silbury Hill. All Miss Ripley's impassioned pleading and scolding were entirely in vain, and even an offer of largesse failed to interest him in traveling on. The sun had gone down long ago—it was dark as pitch on the road—the snow was falling steadily—a nasty wind was coming up—and it was Christmas Eve. It had taken all his skill to bring them safely this far, he averred, and he wouldn't go no farther, not for a king's ransom. When Miss Ripley showed signs of wishing to prolong the discussion, he simply stumped off to the taproom, leaving her fuming in his wake.

She turned to Fred, bristling with determination. "It may not be possible to go on in a post chaise—well, if that insolent postboy refuses to take us, I suppose there is nothing more to be said about that. But I was just thinking—"

"Oh, no!"

"—that when coaches are stranded in foul weather, the passengers often continue on horseback."

"My dear girl, we've seen no other travelers on the road for well over an hour! I am very sorry to disappoint you, but the postboy is surely the best judge of what can, and cannot, be done. We must stop here until the weather clears."

A cheer went up in the taproom, and a dangerous sparkle lit Claudia's eyes. "Did you hear that?" she exclaimed. "That was for our postboy! Everyone knows him here! I believe he lives in this neighborhood, and only refuses to go on because he wishes to spend Christmas at home."

"Claudia, it is snowing," said Fred patiently. "It is dark. It is cold. I know you wish to reach Bath—"

"I will reach Bath!"

"—but it is useless to rail against Mother Nature. We must own ourselves defeated, and make the best of it."

"Pooh! Defeated by a few paltry snowflakes? Not I! I am sure I have ridden in worse weather than this. I believe it was as bad as this last night, and I walked in it!" She placed an urgent hand on his sleeve. "Oh, Fred, pray—! I cannot bear to stop here. We are so close to Bath!"

Fred saw the brave jut of her chin and the unquenchable spirit in her weary little face, and did not have the heart to argue further. He had to admit, the storm did not look so severe that horses would refuse to carry them in it. So Fred hired two saddle horses and a pack horse, and out into the dark whiteness they went.

It was madness, of course. He ought to have known better than to fall in with Claudia Ripley's heedless optimism. To her, all things were possible. In Fred's experience, however, some things were not. And this turned out to be one of them.

Once had they left the light and warmth of the inn well behind them, he quickly discovered that he had underestimated the difficulty—and the discomfort—of riding through a snowstorm in full dark, on a road he did not know well. Simply following the Bath Road sounded easy enough, but it turned out to be impossible. Eventually, he was forced to trust the horses. The weather was coming in from the west and driving the snow into their faces, and even the animals walked with their heads down. He said nothing, hoping that Claudia would not realize he had given his horse its head. He did not wish to frighten her with the knowledge that her "courier" had no earthly idea where they were, or where they were headed.

At the end of this very long day, to find oneself huddled on the back of a strange horse, gritting one's teeth against the cold and wet, and—not to put too fine a face on it—*lost*, was not Fred's idea of the best way to spend Christmas Eve. Even the pleasure of scolding Miss Ripley was denied him, since the horses were walking single file and she was bobbing along between his horse and the pack animal.

The horses plodded on for a timeless time. The most likely end to this demented adventure now seemed, to Fred, that they would be found on Christmas morning frozen to death at the side of the road. He had long ago stopped wondering whether they were likely to reach Bath before midnight, and had begun wondering whether they would reach Bath at all, when a wordless, terrified wail startled him out of his misery. He gasped and pulled his horse sharply up, his heart hammering.

"Miss Ripley! Claudia!" he shouted, half falling out of his saddle and stumbling blindly back toward her. "Are you all right?"

"Oh! Oh! Oh! What is it?" Her voice was breathless with horror.

When he reached her horse, patting its flank and her knee like a blind man, she immediately slid all the way out of her saddle and into his arms, almost knocking him backward into the snow. Alarmed, he braced himself and closed his arms around her shuddering form. She clung to him, shaking with mingled cold and fright.

It was then his eyes fell on what had startled Claudia, and he instinctively recoiled. A massive and menacing shape loomed out of the whirling snowflakes beside them—but, the instant after he jumped, he realized what it was.

"Ssh, Claudia—there, then! It's nothing," he assured her, hugging her tightly. "It's a stone. There are standing stones all over this part of the country."

"I . . . I thought I saw it move!" She pressed her face against his greatcoat, choking on an embarrassed laugh. "I'm s-s-s-sorry. It came up out of the darkness so suddenly . . . wh-what an idiot you must think me!"

"Not at all. I don't like them, myself," he muttered under his breath. It was absurd to lower one's voice, but even in daylight the eerie stones appeared sentient to him. They had always made the back of his neck prickle as if he were being watched. In the darkness, he now discovered, the sensation was even stronger. "Can you get back up on your horse?"

"I can if you boost me," she replied confidently.

Her confidence, however, was misplaced. On the first attempt, she merely fell back into Fred's arms. On the second, more vigorous, attempt, she slid all the way across the saddle and fell off the other side of the horse. She was unhurt, but when Fred pulled her to her feet and tried unavailingly to brush the snow off her cloak, she admitted, through chattering teeth, that she was not much of a horsewoman.

"Thanks. I can see that," Fred said. By now they were both wet to the skin and shivering. "You know, I hate to put a damper on the evening, but I think we should get to the nearest inn without delay. Would you mind terribly sharing my horse? I think it might be warmer."

She did not mind, and even seemed relieved at the suggestion. This seemed to indicate that she had, for the moment, relinquished her mania for speed. And not a moment too soon, thought Fred grimly. He hoped she would not ask him where the nearest inn was, because he hadn't a clue.

He mounted his own horse and reached down to Claudia. He half lifted her until she was able to step on his foot, and then managed, somehow, to drag her across the saddle bow. She perched precariously there and plastered herself to his chest. Despite everything, he actually smiled a bit as he reached his arms round her and urged the horse into a walk. Wet and cold and wretched as they were, there was something about holding Claudia in his arms that took the edge off his despondency.

He gave the horse its head again and they rode on. The snow was letting up a bit, but it did not get any warmer. More stones loomed around them, some very near and some almost invisible at a distance of perhaps ten yards. Fred wondered uneasily where they were. Surely the standing stones did not approach so closely to the Bath Road? He racked his brain, but could not remember. A deep sense of foreboding held him silent as they moved like ghosts through the snow-covered fields. It seemed that they were traveling up and down hillocks. He was very much afraid that they were on no road at all.

Then the horse's head lifted, and its long-suffering gait quickened beneath him. He looked up, squinting into the darkness, and saw what appeared to be lamplight ahead. If he hadn't been half frozen, he would have heaved an enormous sigh of relief. Soon they had made their way into the yard of an inn, and people were pulling Claudia out of his stiff arms, helping him off his horse, and ushering them, stumbling, into the blessed warmth of a firelit interior.

The innkeeper's wife met them, blessing and exclaiming, and issued a series of brisk orders. Various members of the staff bustled round them, divesting Claudia of her wet cloak and Fred of his greatcoat, muffler, and hat.

"Where are we?" Fred managed to ask.

The landlady clucked her tongue at this evidence of the travelers' bewilderment. "Lord ha' mercy, sir, were you lost? It's a mercy you've landed here, then! You're safe and sound at the Red Lion, in Avebury."

"Avebury!" cried Claudia in dismay.

"Thank God," said Fred fervently. He was glad to hear that they were safe and sound anywhere.

"But—"

"Oh, bless me, miss, you'll go no farther this night!" interrupted the landlady. "Why, it's Christmas Eve! And you're half dead with cold as it is."

Through the fog of unthawing, Fred became aware that they were conversing in very loud voices. A riotous sound of singing and banging, as of pewter mugs thumping vigorously against wooden tables, was issuing from somewhere nearby. The landlady indicated the noise with an apologetic shrug. "It's Christmas," she shouted above the din, then favored the two newcomers with a gap-toothed grin.

Fred and Claudia were able to do no more than blink painfully at her. She correctly interpreted their expressions as indicating physical discomfort rather than disapproval, and clucked and shooed them into a small private parlor across the passage. Her sharp eyes had assessed the quality and cut of the young couple's clothing and determined that, whoever they were, they would be able to pay their shot.

"You'll be wanting rooms for the night, and p'raps a hot bath," she announced, arms akimbo.

"And a bowl of rum punch," added Fred. "The hotter the better."

She nodded, chuckling, and scurried off. Fred opened his mouth to tell her to leave the door open on her way out, but she was already gone, and had closed it behind her. He and Claudia were left alone, behind closed doors, in a cozy little room with a fire crackling on the hearth. Holly and mistletoe were hung from every possible place, including the ceiling beams. Evergreen bedecked the mantlepiece, its fragrance filling the air. Carols still sounded from the taproom, muffled by the closed door.

It all struck Fred as uncomfortably intimate—romantic even. For the first time since he had met Claudia Ripley, he suffered an acute attack of shyness. He felt his tongue cleave to the roof of his suddenly dry mouth and realized, unhappily, that even though his heart would, naturally, always belong to Bella, it was still possible for him to feel attracted to another.

Strongly attracted.

Attracted to the point where he wished his heart didn't belong to Bella. Bella had brought him nothing but grief and humiliation. Now, if a chap were to fall for a girl like Miss Ripley, the outcome might be entirely different.

If, of course, the chap in question hadn't fallen for Bella first, like a prime idiot, and beggared himself as a result. Fred's heart sank into his shoes. What a dolt he was, he thought bitterly.

Claudia was busy pulling off her gloves with her teeth.

Fred found this uncouth but efficient gesture oddly endearing. Watching her stretch her chilled hands toward the fire, seeing her lean gratefully into the warmth beating up into her face, even hearing her prosaic little sniffles as her face thawed, he felt a deep longing rise up and form a lump in his throat. If only he had met Claudia before he met Bella. He would have had a comfortable life to offer her, a whole and unbruised heart, and a husband with his honor intact. She might very well have chosen him over Harry.

Well. No sense thinking of that.

Claudia looked up, hearing Fred's heartfelt sigh, and tried to smile. "Do not sigh, dear sir," she said softly. "Indeed, indeed, you did your best. I cannot imagine anyone doing more—and for a stranger, too! I am very grateful." Ignoring her own advice, Claudia herself sighed and dropped into one of the wing chairs flanking the hearth. "I suppose it was not meant to be. I ought to have known that before I began."

She looked dispirited. It was most unlike her. Fred walked forward and sat across from her, wincing a bit as his stiff muscles protested. "Do not despair, Miss Ripley," he said gently. "Perhaps your Harry will not propose to the lady after all. Or perhaps he will be delayed, and you will still reach him before he takes the fatal step."

"Perhaps," she agreed, but listlessly. "I don't know what would stop him, however." She looked a little shamefaced. "It has occurred to me now—which, I promise you, never crossed my mind before I left on this mad journey—that even had I reached Harry in time, I might not have succeeded in preventing him."

Fred's eyebrows flew up in surprise. "No! What do you

mean? Surely all you had to do was remind him of his prior promise and assure him that you still desired the match."

"Well, that is what I thought when I booked passage on the mail," admitted Claudia. "But I did not know . . . that is, I never realized how strongly . . . I failed to take into account . . ." Her voice had trailed off in embarrassment. Fred, astonished, saw a slow blush staining her cheeks. Her eyes lifted to his briefly, then fell. She squared her shoulders and bravely finished her sentence. "Harry may *love* the lady in Bath. In which case, I could not—must not—force him to give her up."

Fred cocked his head, puzzled. "Had you not thought of that before? You suggested that he might have led you, somehow, to release him from his promise. It seems to me that his only reason for doing so would be that he had fallen in love."

"Oh, yes! I see that now," said Claudia quickly. "I daresay it would have occurred to me earlier, had such a thing ever happened to me. But I had no experience of such emotions, you know. I did not realize how powerful an affinity between two persons can be. It would be wrong, very wrong of me, to ask poor Harry to wed me if his heart lies elsewhere."

It hit Fred like a thunderclap that she was speaking in the past tense. The silence that fell between them suddenly sounded very loud indeed. What did she mean by saying that she had not understood such emotions when she booked passage for Bath? Did she mean that she understood them *now*? And if so, what—or who—had enlightened her?

He dared not speculate. A wild hope leaped in his soul. He sternly repressed it. Even if—even *if*—she felt drawn to him, he liked her too well to wish her such a fate. He was penniless. Penniless, he reminded himself harshly. Or as near to it as made no odds.

Claudia was folding her snow-sodden gloves into tiny pleats, her eyes concentrating on this foolish task as if she could not look away. "To speak truth," she said softly, "I am no longer certain that I ought to wed Harry, whatever his feelings may be."

Fred swallowed hard. He cleared his throat. "I . . . I think I shall ask the landlady what became of that punch," he said faintly, and almost bolted from the room. He knew he would do something rash if he stayed.

As soon as he left the parlor, reality hit. The quiet crackling of the fire was replaced by caroling and laughter from the taproom. The heady fragrance of evergreen was replaced by the reek of pipe smoke and strong spirits. He came back to earth with a jolt, leaned his back against the wall in the passage, and expelled his breath in a long, slow sigh. His heart was pounding. A kind of madness must have seized him; surely it was not possible for one's life to change course in the span of twenty-four hours. And yet he felt such a strong presentiment—perhaps he had contracted some sort of fever.

He had definitely contracted a fever. Leaning against the wall, struggling to gather his wits, he stared numbly at a strange woman standing near the taproom door. Her profile looked, to his delirious brain, exactly like Bella's—the same retroussé nose, the same flaxen ringlets. She was about the right height, and had the same plump, enticing little form. She was even dressed like Bella would be, he thought cynically. That blue velvet pelisse must have cost a small fortune. And the matching bonnet and ermine muff had probably tripled the price of the pelisse. Bella had taught him more than he had ever cared to know about the cost of female fashions.

An elderly gentleman stepped round the corner of the passage behind the woman in blue velvet and touched her elbow possessively. She turned and smiled prettily up at the besotted old codger. Fred was sure, now, that he had stumbled into nightmare. He dazedly recalled the days, not so long ago, when he had thought that particular smile the loveliest he had ever seen, the sweetest smile this side of heaven. It now struck him as sickeningly false.

"Bella," he croaked. If the wall had not held firm at his back, he was sure he would have slumped to the floor.

They were not ghosts, or visions, after all. The old man looked up when Fred spoke. Bella flinched as if she had been slapped. Her round blue eyes, dilated with horror, fixed on Fred's stricken face. She made a swift recovery, however. By the time her companion turned his suspicious eyes back to her, her expression was one of polite puzzlement.

"Sir?" she uttered in her tinkling little voice. "You mistake me for someone else."

Fred's jaw dropped. Bella placed one fragile hand on her protector's sleeve and peeped beseechingly up at him. "Edgar, pray take me out of this draft," she murmured. "May we not step into the taproom?"

Although still plastered against the wall, too stunned to move, Fred found his tongue. "Do you pretend you do not know me? It needed only that!" He gave a crack of mirthless laughter. "Perfect. This is perfect. Thank you. You have removed your last remaining talon from my heart." He shook his head in wonder. Anger he felt, and shame, and wounded pride, but where was the desire that had driven him mad for this creature? Gone—not a trace of it left in any corner of his being.

The old man glanced distractedly from Fred to Bella, then back to Fred, his brows beetling. When he opened his mouth to speak, however, Bella tugged on his sleeve again. "Edgar, pray! Take me away. I don't know this man. I fear he is mad, or ill. And it is cold in the passage." Her voice, although still sweetly coaxing, had taken on a sharper edge.

Her protector frowned down at her. "The taproom is no place for you," he said gruffly. "Bunch o'rough customers, more n'likely."

When he heard the man speak, disgust coiled in Fred's belly. This wasn't even a gentleman; it was just a wealthy Cit. He had to remind himself that there was nothing surprising about that. If Bella did not cavil at the man's age, why should she cavil at his lack of breeding? It was the money she cared for, not the man. It had always been the money.

Bella flashed her practiced smile again. "You take such care of me," she cooed, leaning adoringly on the Cit's scrawny arm. "But, oh, Edgar, they are singing carols! I am terribly fond of Christmas."

The elderly roué patted her hand and gave an indulgent chuckle. "Well, if it would please you, my pet, in we'll go. Just for a little while, mind!" He gave a last, glowering glance at Fred, and seemed as if he might say something. Then Bella's insistent little hand pulled the old man into the taproom.

They had vanished, and Fred felt as if he were awakening from a bad dream. He scrubbed his face with his hands, groaning. What had he ever seen in that disgusting little tart? How could he ever have believed he loved her? There had never been such foolishness in the world as the foolishness of Frederick Bates!

A boy in an apron came round the corner of the passage, carefully bearing a steaming bowl of punch. "Are you all right, sir?" he piped when he saw Fred leaning weakly against the wall. "Oh, thank you, miss."

This last was to Claudia. She was standing gravely in the door to the private parlor.

How long had she been there? Fred straightened up and regarded her blearily as she stepped aside to let the waiter through. Her clear gray eyes met his, and they stood, their gazes locked, until the waiter bowed himself out. Then they returned wordlessly to the parlor.

This time, Fred himself closed the door behind them, and they sat facing each other in the firelight. The intimacy of the firelight and evergreen stole across his senses as the two of them, Claudia and Fred, were wrapped in the beckoning warmth of Christmastide. Fred had to close his eyes for a moment against the pain of so much sweetness.

"That was she," said Claudia at last. "The woman you loved."

Fred nodded tiredly. "The woman I *thought* I loved."

Claudia looked wistful. "She's very pretty."

Fred gave a derisive snort and ladled punch into two glasses, handing one to Claudia. "She's a mercenary, heartless little mantrap. She's not a respectable female, Claudia."

"Oh." Claudia sipped her punch reflectively, while Fred stared into the fire and wrestled with the harshest wave of regret and self-condemnation he had yet weathered. She leaned forward hesitantly, trying in vain to catch his eye. "Why did she pretend she did not know you?"

He replied with an effort. "She must be feigning virtue to her present protector. Some men care a great deal for that, you know. She may have been afraid I would give her game away—let *Edgar* know she has a past." Fred shook his head bitterly. "If he's half the nincompoop I was, however, he'll turn a blind eye to any evidence that offers. She has a knack for that—bats those long eyelashes and weeps, tells you tales of all her nasty, nasty enemies, twists you round her dainty little finger until you swear you won't listen to anything anyone may say of her. And you don't. Lord knows, enough people tried to warn me! I wouldn't heed them."

He looked at her now, his heart aching with loss—not, he realized, for the girl he had thought he loved, the girl who had bled him dry and cast him off, but for *this* girl, this vibrant, wonderful girl who would never be his. Claudia's eyes were enormous with grief. By telling her of Bella's sordid past, of course, he had told her of his. This was a severe penance indeed. It was terrible to show innocent Claudia this side of the world.

"Is she . . . is she the reason you are . . . economizing?"

Fred closed his eyes again, shame coursing through him. "Yes, I'm afraid so. I was a fool." His mouth twisted wryly. "That is an understatement, of course."

Claudia shook her head in swift denial. "No. You cared for her, and she broke your heart."

Her words stabbed him to the heart. "Do not romanticize this," he warned. "There was no excuse for my conduct."

He saw that she was about to fire up in his defense and,

impulsively, he reached out to cover her hand with his own. "Claudia, I beg you. Do not give Bella another thought. Put her from your mind. She is not worth your notice."

Claudia looked down at his hand on hers. "I will not think of her again," she promised softly, "if you will not."

Fred felt himself stop breathing. Slowly, she raised her eyes to his. She was blushing again, but met his gaze levelly. How dared she say anything so bold? A smile wavered across his face. Claudia dared. It was one of the things one loved about her.

"Very well. It's a bargain," he told her. His voice sounded a bit unsteady, but her smile burst forth like sunshine, warming him to his toes.

Good God, what was he thinking? Fred hastily removed his hand and looked away. He tossed back the rest of his punch, hoping it would steady his nerves. Get a grip, old man, he told himself sternly. She is not for you.

Someone needed to make this clear to Claudia, however. She showed every sign of believing that she was, in fact, for him. He steeled himself to meet her adoring gaze and then turned to face her, clutching his empty cup tightly. "Miss Ripley," he said firmly, "I—"

He got no further. Claudia suddenly hurled herself into his arms, pressing her body against his and lifting her face for his kiss. The noble speech Fred had been preparing to say dwindled into an inarticulate sort of strangling sound. Then he threw caution to the winds and his punch glass to the carpet and fastened his lips to hers.

She kissed him with enthusiasm—but very inexpertly, he noted with delight. He could not help rejoicing at the knowledge that he must be the first man at whom she had launched herself. One hated to think one was merely the last in a long line of tackled beaux. And she was a quick learner; within seconds the kiss had relaxed and softened into the tenderest kiss Fred had ever experienced, and all hope of maintaining a detached analysis fled.

Where was all this emotion coming from? Inwardly reeling, he clutched her and gave himself over to it. Somewhere in the back of his mind, the bittersweet voice of reason whispered sadly that this would be his only chance to savor this particular sweetness. Soon, he would have to give her up.

It was the last thing he wanted to do, but eventually he broke the kiss and held her away from him, his hands tightening on her upper arms. "Claudia," he said hoarsely. "Claudia. Stop. We can't do this."

She looked dazed and rumpled and rosy and—well-kissed. It was an enticing sight, and it made him smile. Which was probably a good thing, because his smile staved off the hurt she might have felt at his rejection. She looked confused, but not wounded,

Good God, they were lying on the carpet. What if the waiter came in? Fred took a deep breath and ran his hands through his hair. "Sit with me," he invited, moving to pull Claudia to her feet. She came willingly enough and would have sat beside him on the sofa, but after he seated her there he pulled over a footstool and sat at her feet, holding her hands in his. He had to face her.

"Claudia, you don't know me—" he began stoically, but she immediately interrupted.

"Oh, I *do* know you! I do," she urged. Her face glowed with tender happiness. "Only think, if we had met socially we might have been acquainted for months—years!—and done nothing but dance with each other once or twice a week, and talk about the weather. We wouldn't have known each other at all. People fall in love all the time with people they don't know. But I know you."

Fred had to clear his throat and look away. "Even if you do know me, you don't know my circumstances."

"Well, I'm not a complete ninny," asserted Claudia with spirit. "You can't be married, or you wouldn't be driving off to Lacock alone to have Christmas with your mother and sisters."

A tiny smile flitted across Fred's features. "That wasn't what I meant, but I'm glad to see you thought of that much, at any rate."

"I thought as much as I could, under the circumstances," admitted Claudia, blushing. Her voice had gone shy and rather breathless. "For I thought I was falling in love with you by the time we left Theale, and by the time you lifted me up on your horse I was sure of it."

Fred groaned and dropped her hands so he could bury his face in his own. There was nothing to do but come out with it. "Claudia, I'm a pauper."

"No, you're not," she said comfortably.

He lifted his face from his hands to stare at her in bemused exasperation. "Of all the outrageous females I have ever met, you bear the palm!" he exclaimed, his voice quivering with laughter. "Will you listen to *nothing* that contradicts your views? What possible reason could I have for confessing such a humiliating secret if it wasn't true? Or nearly true, at any rate! That witch stole everything from me. She took my heart—or so I thought!—and with it she took my bankbook. I had horses. I had three carriages. I had a modest, but adequate, inheritance. Now I have nothing. Do you hear me? Nothing at all."

She smiled fondly at him. "You have an excellent wardrobe, a mother and sisters who apparently love you, a home in London and one in Lacock, and a cab-fronted gig. And now you have me."

It wasn't possible to resist kissing her again, after a statement like that. Fred abandoned his pointless attempt at self-restraint, seized her in his arms, and kissed her ardently. Claudia seemed to approve of this course of action, so it was again Fred who had to call a halt. This time, at least, he had not dragged her onto the floor. When he came to his senses, he discovered that they were seated together on the sofa. He buried his nose in her hair. She clung to him, pressing her face to his shoulder.

"Claudia, of all the rash, impulsive things I have seen you do, this is the worst," he told her ruefully.

"Well, you haven't known me very long," she reminded him. "I've done much worse than this."

Fred choked. "Deplorable girl! You'll turn my hair gray within a week."

She gave a delighted little chuckle and nestled closer. "Nonsense. You are the only man on earth whom I can neither frighten nor astonish."

"Claudia, believe me, you have already done both in abundance!" he said firmly, although his lips twitched with suppressed laughter. "Just look at you! You have thrown yourself at a man whom you barely know! This is the most dangerous thing a young lady can do."

She looked dreamily up at him. "Yes, but I have always been an excellent judge of character."

His laughter died away as he gazed down at her upturned face. Aching, he pushed a wayward curl off her forehead. "You deserve a better man than I," he whispered.

"I cannot support a wife. Not at present. But if you will wait, my darling heart—"

"Oh, no! I don't wish to wait." She pulled back against the circle of his arms and busied herself in straightening his cravat. "I was just thinking, Fred—"

"Not again! What now?"

"—that if you should want to marry me—"

"My love!"

She blushed furiously. "Well, I didn't wish to *assume*," she said with dignity.

At this, Fred burst out laughing. "I am amazed that you waited for me to say the word 'wife.' It would have been entirely consistent with your character for you to propose the marriage."

"But that is exactly what I am doing," she said, her eyes twinkling. "I have been thinking, as I said, and I think we need not depend wholly upon your circumstances improving. You see, I am an heiress."

He paled and pulled back from her. "No!"

"What is amiss?" Claudia looked anxiously at him. "I thought you would be pleased."

It was another mark of her innocence. Fred closed his eyes again for a moment and took a deep breath. "If you are an heiress, Claudia, it puts our wedding day further out of reach, not closer. It will take me that much longer to recoup my losses. Do you not see? I cannot approach your father until I am at least halfway worthy of you."

She chuckled. "If we wait until you are halfway worthy of me, Fred, we will never marry at all. Now, let us be serious! I did not say I was a *great* heiress. But I am the only daughter, you know, and my grandmother left me three thousand pounds to be paid when I turned sixteen."

"And have you turned sixteen?"

She pummeled him with her fist. "Beast! Of course I have. And, as it happens, last week I calculated what my dowry would be—because, you know, I was expecting to marry soon; isn't that fortunate? And because the principal has been sitting safely in the three percents since my sixteenth birthday, it has grown to the point where it will now give us £100 per annum."

She ended on a triumphant note. Fred grinned. "A princely sum," he agreed, relieved to learn that she was not, after all, too far out of reach. "Let's marry at once, and make an offer on Blenheim Palace."

She laughed delightedly. "I shall make you a present of it," she promised mendaciously. "For Twelfth Night."

Happiness swelled Fred's heart. "Whatever the future holds, this will be the best Christmas of my life. I am sure I will come about within two or three years, and then I will marry you, and we will share many happy Christmases—but none will surpass this."

He meant to kiss her again, but Claudia did not look as happy at his announcement as he had thought she would. She held him off, pressing her palms to his chest, and frowned a little. "Two or three years?"

"I'm afraid so, sweetheart. But that won't be so very long. I'll ride out from London every week to see you, I promise."

Now she looked pensive. She toyed with his lapels, not meeting his eyes. "Well," she said slowly, "that would be very pleasant, of course. But I think I should like to be married to you a little sooner than that."

"So would I. But, dear heart, your father will not allow

it," he told her gently. "No parent wishes his only daughter to marry a poor man."

"Yes, but I have been thinking . . ."

Fred groaned, and Claudia laughed, tugging on his lapels. "No, you will like this idea, for it means we will be able to marry much, much sooner than you thought! Attend, if you please—it puts me out when you laugh at me."

Fred assured her that he hung upon her lips. Claudia blushed, but looked pleased. "Well, pray recall that you met me only last night, and spent untold hours alone with me in poor old Stourbridge's taproom. Do you remember what you told me this morning, when I met you in the passage?"

"My word! How long ago that seems."

"Yes, a lifetime! But do you recall?"

He cast his mind back, frowning a little. Then light dawned. He gazed at his newfound love in respectful wonder. "By Jove! You've hit it. Everyone thinks I've abducted you."

She nodded, her eyes shining but her mouth very prim. "Mr. Bates, you have compromised me," she told him piously. "My father will *insist* that you marry me."

Fred leaped from the sofa with a shout, snatched Claudia up, and whirled round the room with her. "I'm a villain, begad! But he'll have to make the best of it! Oh, Claudia, you diabolical, adorable, clever little wretch!"

"Yes, I thought you'd be pleased." She beamed up at him as he brought their impromptu waltz to a halt before the fireplace.

Solemnly, Fred plucked a sprig of mistletoe from the arrangement that adorned the mantelpiece and held it over

Claudia's head. "Merry Christmas, Miss Ripley," he whispered.

She gave him that wonderful, invincible, blinding smile. "Merry Christmas, Mr. Bates," she said, and went up on her tiptoes to kiss him.

The author wishes to acknowledge the advice and assistance of Anne Woodley, whose encyclopedic knowledge of Regency England, and particularly the old Bath Coaching Road, far surpasses her own.

The Christmas Thief

by Edith Layton

On the day before Christmas, Lt. Major Maxwell Evers rose early, as was his habit, washed, dressed with care, and went out to steal a Christmas present.

He'd never stolen anything before, but he reasoned it couldn't be very difficult. Thieves were ill-educated, ill-bred, and immoral, everyone knew that. He was none of those things. In fact, he was the exact opposite. *Therefore*, he thought with the kind of logic that had enabled him to survive many a campaign, *he'd be better at it than most.* Except for that damned inconvenient conscience of his, of course.

His conscience had kept him from actually going out and doing the thing he had no choice but to do. Now Christmas was coming as fast as the snow was falling, and there was no time left to struggle with his morals. He had to either do it, or forget it. And he couldn't afford to forget it anymore than he could afford to buy a present.

He straightened his shoulders and strode out into the snowy streets. The snow had started as rain, but now it was growing colder, and the pavements were slick. The roads were covered with sleet, snow, and straw that had been thrown down to make the cobbles safer for the horses, and so were also full of the stuff horses let down as they safely passed. It was all holiday for the street sweepers. They were ready with their brooms at every intersection. One smiled and bowed as she saw Maxwell approaching.

Maxwell scowled, sidestepped the fellow, and marched straight into the street. He grimaced as he felt the ground squelch under his feet. His boots would be ruined. But he didn't have a ha'penny to spare for a sweeper. It had taken him the better part of an hour to shine his boots that morning. He plodded on. Hard work cost nothing but his time. He frowned. That was running out, too.

Tomorrow was Christmas. He could give a gift on Boxing Day, but the girl was arriving tomorrow. And they'd be leaving London immediately after she got here. This, then, was the last chance he had to get an appropriate present. *Why couldn't his niece have been a nephew?* he thought with exasperated sorrow. He had all sorts of things a lad might like. Or at least, he corrected himself, he had some things he hadn't pawned that a boy might fancy. Like all those useless medals he'd won in the service of his country. They didn't fetch enough at the pawnbrokers to bother leaving there with the rest of his kit. There were too many medals in their shops already. England was filled with penniless soldiers looking for money so they could eat—now that they'd won the war and weren't needed any more than their medals were.

So—a gift for a motherless, fatherless girl who was coming to stay with him. A girl from the countryside, alone and doubtless anxious about it. *Not alone*, he remembered. Another problem with having a niece. Her governess. She had one, and he needed one for her, what did he know about girl children? But that would cost him the last of his money.

That last, he thought, wincing as he shifted his wide shoulders and flexed his callused fingers in their worn gloves, *was very little, and even so it meant working laying brick on the outskirts of town all last week to get it.* Because Lt. Major Maxwell Evers, late of His Majesty's Heavy Hussars, couldn't be seen working. And certainly not with his hands and back. So he ruined his gloves trying to preserve his hands, and turned his back on London so his face wasn't seen as he went about the menial work he could find.

He had no other money. No man was paid just for breathing unless he was lucky enough to have had someone rich and sensible enough to leave a fortune for him. He had not. His elder brother had, but he'd squandered most of the money he'd inherited, and lost the rest. All he'd managed to hang on to in his short life were the things he couldn't sell, gamble with, or pawn—the name, the manor house and estate, his wife and little girl.

Maxwell had his career. He'd gone into the service of his country, as second sons do if the church wasn't for them. It hadn't been. He liked action. So, unfortunately, did his brother. But his brother liked the kind he found in fast horses, roulette wheels, and turning cards. Maxwell tried not to think of all the turned-up skirts his sister-in-law also claimed his brother fancied.

Because of his brother's many fancies, Maxwell stayed in service longer than he'd planned—long after he'd been wounded at St. Pierre, even after he'd taken a lance in his shoulder at Toulouse. Every penny earned in the king's service that he could spare went back to his brother, in response to fervent pleas.

"Max!" his brother wrote, *"It won't happen again. But*

think! The estate can't be lost. The name can't be disgraced. Our ancestors were counselors to kings. An Evers can't go to debtor's prison. For the love of God, Max, Help!"

Max sent money. It happened again. And again.

Pampered since birth, orphaned young and given power too early, his brother never managed to understand his responsibilities. Max did. Perhaps because he was an onlooker he saw it clearer. Or because, as his brother laughed, Max was such a serious chap, and had been since birth. His brother took nothing seriously. The estate ran through his fingers. Max didn't earn enough to support it and himself. He finally hit upon the idea of investing what little he could.

He wrote a letter to an old comrade in arms he'd once done a favor for. Ex-Captain Daniel Merrick was clever, taking advantage of the opportunities this new century was offering as the classes began shifting with the tides and times of war. He was eager to help. Soon Max was part owner in sugar plantations and rum distilleries in the Caribes, fur trading companies in Canada, and enterprises in the East that provided perfumes and spices. By the time the war ended and Max was ready to sell out, he was, he reckoned, a rich man, even with all his brother's expenses.

He'd enough money to go home and live like a wealthy man. More important, he'd every reason to hope he'd be able to live like the luckiest man on earth, too. He'd been gone from England for five years. But he'd written to his lady every day of those years. And she'd written back to him.

Now, at last, he had the funds to ask Lisabeth to marry him.

She'd been seventeen when they'd last met. *Lord! that*

was a long time ago, he thought miserably. Almost a lifetime, a lifetime for too many friends who wouldn't be coming home, so he knew he couldn't complain too much. But he ached for her, and had since the night he'd left her.

Slender but shapely, with a heart-shaped face so sweet it stopped his breath in his chest. Feathery, arched eyebrows—how odd that he remembered those brows now, when it was her plush lips he yearned for. Her hair was all the shades of honey, like her eyes, her scent like amber, too. Her skin was white and clear; she had just one little mark near her lips, such lips . . .

He loved her wit, her compassion, and the intelligence she shared with him in every letter. But it was her kiss that kept him celibate all these years. Because if she could pass up other suitors, if she could live with hope and quell those same desires that had racked them during those stolen hours they'd shared, he could do no less. He remembered how he'd left her the last time they'd met. And why.

Her gown was so thin he could feel her breasts growing tight against his chest, her round little bottom cupped in his hands so he could pull her close to his own body as his mouth sought all the incredibly sweet fire in hers . . .

He'd pulled away because if he hadn't then he didn't know if he'd have been able to later. But he'd no intention of taking her in her own parlor, in his best friend's house, against the express wishes of her father.

"No more, not now," he told her, looking down at the question in her eyes. "You *are* very young. Your father's right. He turned down my offer of marriage . . . and I don't blame him. I won't presume on your youth and trust."

Her eyes glowed with anger, and she opened her lips. He put a finger over them. "When I sell out—when I come home again to England—then and only then he said he'd hear my suit again. He's right, my love."

"No, he's not!" she said, stamping her foot. "You're young, too. Only two-and-twenty, and who knows . . ." She faltered, and then tears replaced the fury in her eyes. ". . . when you'll be home again."

"You mean *if,*" he said softly. "Exactly. So, much as I want you, I don't want you coming to me because of fear or pity. When I return, that won't be a factor. I will return. You'll see. And Lisabeth? If you change your mind, if you meet a likelier lad—well, I have to give you that opportunity, too. You need some more years. We'll have them and then we'll see."

What her father had actually said was he'd consider Max's suit when Max came home and could keep Lisabeth there, too.

He couldn't keep a mouse now. Much less the love of his life, the woman who was the reason he'd fought so hard to keep that life during all those years of war.

Celibacy hadn't been as painful as the wounds he'd gotten in battle. But it was a close thing. Nights lying on a bed of pain in the field hospital were bad, but her letters made them bearable. Nights alone in his bed racked by desire were no treat either, and her letters made them worse. But one sacrifice was for his country, the other for the woman with whom he wanted to spend the rest of his life. They'd promised to be true to each other, and he had the notion that if he betrayed that promise and sought his ease elsewhere, then so would she. They were that close in spirit. He had opportunities to buy relief, sometimes to flirt and dally for it. She had the omnipresent chance to marry for it. He waited.

He should have known how impermanent life was. Everything changed in the blink of an eye.

His brother died in a drunken accident, and his sister-in-law ran away with a dissolute friend, abandoning her daughter to her uncle's care. Max left his unit and headed home. He'd shoulder the responsibility. He always had. Now he had the funds to do it better. He wrote Lisabeth hoping she wouldn't mind that he'd acquired a girl to raise. She replied that she was hurt he thought she would mind. He was sure of few things in this life, but her word was one of them. He wrote to his friend Dan, asking him to send staff and new furnishings to the family estate, sparing no expense, and to send the same to his town house in London, to get all in readiness for his return.

First, though, he planned to hire a horse as soon as he landed and ride like the wind to Lisabeth, take her in his arms and . . .

But on the packet he took home across the Channel he chanced to pick up a newspaper someone had left behind on the trip out. And saw his friend Dan Merrick's name writ large. His blood froze as he read that Dan was the victim of an embezzler and had been brought to his knees—bankrupted. A pauper, with creditors and investors fighting one another on his doorstep to the point that the Watch had called the Runners to restore order. They were looking for Dan. He was rumored to have fled the country. They were raging for their money . . . and Maxwell's, of course.

Max had sat stunned. He'd nothing but an empty title, a pile of debts, no occupation, and no prospects. And a niece to shelter. How could he ask Lisabeth to share that?

* * *

He'd headed straight from Dover to London, then on to the family town house, to see a crowd of pushing, clamoring men on the front step.

They didn't recognize him. London hadn't seen his face in years, and he was dressed as any gentleman now. Women weren't the only ones who didn't look beyond the uniform.

"What's this then?" he asked one of the men.

"Wait yer turn in line, boyo!" the man snarled.

"For what?" Max asked.

"As if you didn't know! We're here to get our money, o'course."

"Money?" Max asked, carefully ignorant.

"Aye! Word is the new baron's back from the wars, and we need what he owes. Christmas is comin', and it's our last chance to get fat afore it does!"

Max nodded and strolled away, his legs shaky.

He couldn't go to the moneylenders. He'd nothing to offer in return. The estate was entailed, and probably bled dry by now. He owned nothing of value except the clothes in his cases and those he stood up in. So he sold most of them and took a room by the docks.

He couldn't pay his creditors, couldn't borrow. He'd too much pride to go to his friends . . . or the one he loved. All he had was a strong back and a plan of action.

After he'd been in London a week—or was it ten days?, he'd lost track of time—he wrote a carefully worded note to Lisabeth. He said good-bye and set her free. It was the only decent thing to do. He left no return address. She'd try to reach him if she could, she'd stand by his side, she'd work for him if she had to. He wouldn't have it. Then he turned his back on the past, leaving it to his dreams.

His niece was arriving on a late stage the next day,

Christmas Day. It was too late to stop that. He'd thought he'd have some money by the time she arrived, but he'd been wrong. So he'd watch for her at the coach stop and intercept her before she reached his besieged town house. He'd take her right back to the countryside. They'd live at the old estate and survive by the sweat of his brow. But he needed a gift for her at Christmas.

Every penny was counted. It was just enough for his lodgings, the trip back, and food for their first days at the estate. There was no more to sell except the blood in his veins, and there was no way to do that. Even a penny for a cheap trinket or shoddy toy the strolling peddlers sold on the streets was too much—which was as well. Something in him rankled at the thought of giving his brother's child anything cheap or tawdry.

There was absolutely no way to get her a decent gift unless he stole it. It went against his upbringing and his every conviction. But he saw no other option.

Maybe because deep in his heart, where he refused to look now, there was the small angry notion that he was owed something for all his pain.

Snow stung his cheeks, reminding him of present plans. Max strode on. No sense in regrets. All they gave a man was an ache in his heart and gut. Better a pain in his back than that. At least his conscience was clear on this. He'd done all he could, and had not an extra penny piece. The gift for his niece would be a little thing, a small theft, little missed, worth more to the recipient than to the merchant he got it from. He turned his thoughts to what he had to do now. No army could go forth without a battle plan. He had one, of course.

First, he'd go to the busiest toy shop in Town. He'd

walked half the city in the last days, and not just because he couldn't afford the price of a hackney carriage. He'd been mapping out the lay of the land since the night he'd dreamed up his desperate plan. No question the busiest toy shop would be Markham's. The place was an absolute palace of toys. Expensive, but that didn't signify; he wouldn't be paying. The important thing was that it was a prosperous place that could well afford a small loss. And big and confusing enough in the last flurry of Christmas buying so that a man with fast hands could make away with a doll.

A doll! He stifled a groan. Again, he wished his brother had left him a son to care for. *A top or a ball or a tin soldier would be easy to slip into a pocket. But girls liked dolls.* He hadn't had a sister and couldn't think of what else a girl would delight in. *So a doll it must be. A small one that could fit under his greatcoat. But a nice one. No sense stealing something inferior. If he was caught he'd be disgraced. Even more so than he was now. So if that was going to be his fate, it would have to be for something worthwhile.* He wore a bitter smile of satisfaction. *Good. He was already thinking like a criminal.* He marched on.

The crowded sidewalks cleared in front of him, in spite of the snow and the difficult footing. He was a formidable sight even in his civilian clothes. He had the face and form of a gladiator, and now the expression of a warrior to match. Tall, lean, and muscular, he was in prime fighting condition. His inky black hair was cropped close as a shorn lamb's, but there was nothing mild in his appearance. If his hair wasn't cropped, it would have curled; if his expression was sweeter, he would have been startlingly handsome—intense black eyes, cream-colored skin that seemed to glow from within, a strong chin, and a white smile that hadn't been seen in a long while. He looked a cut above the ordinary and a slice on the dangerous side. Men called him "devilish good-looking."

The truth was there was nothing devilish about him. He wasn't violent or bad-tempered. But he could be aggressive if he had to be, which was what made him such a fine soldier.

Women said he had the face of an angel—an avenging angel, or at least a fallen one. They couldn't resist trying to catch him. He didn't place much stock in his appearance, though. It had never gotten him much that he could see. He'd always been a favorite of the ladies, true, and that had been amusing. But he had a constant heart, and couldn't have the one woman he wanted.

And so what use were looks to him now? If anything, a hindrance, because people tended to remember his face. He'd have to keep his head down and leave fast. A thief didn't need good looks.

He needed money. He needed luck. He needed a doll.

He needed to step inside the shop whose window he was staring into now, steal a doll, and be done with it. He pushed open the door and went inside.

It was warm and bright and noisy—and huge. Not so much a shop as a cathedral devoted to playthings, big as a produce market, dignified as a bank. The ceiling was high and gilded, the main room marble-floored and vast, and the place was filled with expensive toys. And crowded with jolly shoppers.

Perfect.

Max strolled in, looking at the walls and counters, the tables and shelves filled with an array of toys and games:

wooden soldiers and tin ones, model coaches and horses and castles, iron knights and chargers, and an intricate model of opposing armies. *By God!* Tin dragoons facing the emperor's men on a tiny battlefield, to the life! And wasn't that a Hessian contingent . . . ?

"May I help you, sir?" a thin young man dressed like a clerk asked.

Max blinked. "I'm just looking, thank you," he said, turning his head aside, "trying to get an idea of what to buy."

"Is it a lad or a lass? And what age, if I might inquire?"

"A lad," Max said quickly, because when the doll went missing he didn't want to be remembered for having asked about one.

"I see. That's why you were interested in these soldiers. They *are* our finest. Or perhaps this Roman horde? We have a colorful set of His Majesty's Home Guard with their regimental band. Ah, no. We sold the last. You've left it late, sir," he said sadly.

"So I have. Still, I thought I'd just look for a while."

"Yes, indeed. Please do. Call when you find something to your liking. If you'll excuse me?" the salesman said, spotting a couple cooing over a intricately wrought model of a fairy-tale castle.

Max nodded, glad to be left alone to find his target. He stood still, looking over the heads of the crowd for the doll display. It was on the other side of the room. *Good.* Max looked through the spaces between the other shoppers, trying to see what was closest to hand. *Ah.* There was a low shelf. It had small dolls on it. Miniatures, no higher than his hand. He could take one when the time was right. He'd have to wait. He'd also have to fight back the sense of shame that was clamoring to be heard now that the final moment for his crime neared.

He waited, watched for an opening, and told himself not to be a fool.

A stout, gray-haired old lady stood nearby, fascinated by a display of wooden puppets. She looked like the grandmama of a child's fondest dreams. Handsome for her years, she was well dressed and seemed to wear a perpetual smile. She also wore her ermine-trimmed cape opened to show the impressive ruby necklace she wore around her neck—as well as the puppet she hastily stuffed inside her cape before she quickly pulled it closed.

Max drew in a breath, shocked at her audacity and his own misreading of her character. He felt a hand on his arm. A pickpocket would find only vengeance for his troubles. Max wheeled around, murder in his eyes.

"No, sir," the salesman whispered, hastily removing his hand, "pray do not cause a stir. I wasn't attempting to pick your pocket. Only to ask you to remain still. We're aware of the circumstances, you see."

Max frowned.

"The lady," the salesman explained, lifting a narrow shoulder in the old lady's direction. "That makes two puppets, which added to the three jack-in-the-boxes and the stuffed bunnies, comes to quite a sum. Which her children will pay, of course. We keep a running tally. The lady has her . . . oddities. Her family is aware, as are we. We merely think of it as shopping in a rather peculiar way. You do understand?"

Max did. He relaxed and smiled. *Well, well, then. Easier than he thought.* He could talk his way out of it if he were caught. But he wouldn't be. He rocked back on his boot heels.

"Clever business policy," he told the clerk as he saw the old lady meander away from the counter she'd just pilfered from. His gaze sharpened. Hours of watching forests and fields for the merest hint of something out of the ordinary had sharpened his perceptions. He smiled again. "Lord! You must be famous for it," he commented as he saw a well-dressed gent discreetly pocket a toy pistol.

The salesman frowned in confusion.

"I mean, the fellow over there that just took the pistol and slipped it into his trousers." Max chuckled. "Another old customer?"

The salesman's eyes flew wide. He fumbled in his waistcoat, drew out a whistle on a chain, and blew a shrill note. The gentleman looked up, saw the direction of the salesman's gaze, and paled. He ran. Two men erupted from the crowd and were hot on his heels as he charged out the door.

"We'll nab him, never fear," the salesman said, breathing hard. "It's the rope for him!"

Max blinked. "The rope?"

"Aye, he'll swing for it. The pistol cost over ten shillings. Five's a hanging offense. We usually nab that sort before an item gets halfway to their pocket, but today's been so hectic. We had to lay on extra help—Runners, without their red vests, dressed as customers. They patrol the store for us at this time of year. We pay well. They serve well. They'd have caught him on their own, they were that close they must have seen him acting suspiciously. But thank you for alerting me. Now. May I be of some help?"

"Uhm, no. Thank you. I think I'd better go talk to my niece's mother, at that."

"But I thought it was nephews you were buying for."

"Yes. Good day," Max said, and turning, quickly left him.

Hanged for a toy? Max was shocked. Looters on battlefields were summarily shot. But that was in wartime, to protect the living and honor the dead, a time when discipline had to be firmly maintained. He'd forgotten how easily men were hanged for lesser crimes here. He'd seen death dealt too often not to value life, and was disgusted at the thought he might have done something to cause another one. A life in exchange for a plaything was too cruel, especially at this season. Maybe the fellow also had a child he couldn't afford to buy a gift for. Maybe he needed the money to eat. It seemed too harsh a penalty for such a trivial crime.

"Sir?" a man's voice said close to his ear.

Max spun round.

"'Scuse me," the man, panting from exertion, said. "But you be the gent what made the clerk blow the whistle, 'e said. We lost 'im, the villain what pinched the pistol, that is. Only saw the back of 'im. But you seen 'im. What did 'e look like?"

Max remembered the pale-eyed, light-haired thin gentleman.

"Certainly," Max said. "A dark fellow. Jowls to here. Mostly bald, I believe. Well, go about your job, man. And Godspeed."

The man touched his hat and ran off to share the information with his fellow Runner. When Max reached the snow-covered pavements, he didn't see them or the unlucky thief anywhere. Hoping he wouldn't, he quickly walked in the other direction. He still didn't have a present. But he had another plan to fall back on, of course.

So it couldn't be anything over five shillings, Max mused as he approached the outdoor market. Not the sort of present he wanted to give. But prison was one thing, death another. This was the place for a smaller theft. A collection of peddlers huddled together under the bridge to sell their wares cheap, fast, and easily. *For them, and for me*, Max thought as he walked the makeshift aisles between the assembled tables and carts, barrows and pushcarts.

He was glad the snow was falling heavily. He hoped it wouldn't melt now that he'd gone under the bridge, because it covered his greatcoat and his high beaver hat so no one could see how well made they were. Rich men didn't shop here, and he didn't want to look conspicuous. Then again, he realized, his boots were filthy and he'd been washing his own linen, so he didn't need any disguise. He supposed he looked like a gentleman down on his luck, searching for bargains. It was what he was. Except he was really looking to steal one.

Now, to find the merchant who had least cause to regret a loss.

There was clothing, new and used, shoes and boots and cheap jewelry. Barrows filled with everything a person might want to give another for Christmas, from blankets to lamps, turkeys to sweets. There was soap, there were sewing materials, and . . . toys. He passed gaily decorated wooden nutcrackers, iron banks, china dolls too big to cart off without paying for, too expensive to risk his neck for, too.

Then he saw a pushcart with a jumble of rag dolls—floppy dolls with black button eyes and grinning painted faces. He stopped nearby. *Charming.* Old-fashioned, yet now he thought about it he remembered how many girls he'd seen lugging them about when he'd been a child. *Cheap.* One could be folded and stuffed inside his great-coat. *Perfect.*

The bearded fellow behind the cart had a paunch as big as Saint Nicholas and a pyramid of the things on his barrow. There was no way one could cost over three shillings. So if worse came to worst, Max reasoned, he'd sit in a prison for his sin, not swing from the sky. He strolled over toward the barrow, his heartbeat accelerating.

He stopped and gazed at the dolls with disinterest, as though thinking of something else entirely. *The one with the red dress, to the left. It was practically falling off the cart as it was.*

He reached out a hand . . .

"Hold! Thief!" the fat fellow roared.

Max thought his heart stopped. His blood certainly stopped flowing. *But he hadn't touched the damned thing! It was still there, lying on its side, blindly goggling at him.*

"Got you, you rogue, you villain, you wretch!" the merchant bellowed. "You'll look like what you stole when Jack Ketch is done with you, you young demon. Aye, with your neck broke you'll dance just as limp as a rag doll, I promise you," he shouted in triumph.

The boy dangling by his collar from the end of one of the merchant's beefy arms looked like that now, Max thought. He was a rail of a boy, thin as a wraith, none too clean, and dressed shabbily. His shoes were too big for his feet, his cap for his head, and his eyes were too big and filled with fear for any boy. Max had seen faces like that in war-torn towns. He saw them in his nightmares still. A rag doll with yellow yarn hair hung from the boy's clenched fist, just as he hung from the merchant's. The boy saw the direction of Max's gaze and remembered to drop the doll.

Max bent and picked it up.

"Stealing?" he asked the merchant. "I think not! Put my nephew down, if you please, sir.

The merchant and the boy looked at him dumbly. The crowd that had assembled when the merchant roared waited breathlessly, fascinated by this bit of street theater.

"Come, Jack, is this the one you picked for Cecily?" Max asked the boy. He huffed in exasperation as the boy, the merchant, and the crowd all looked at him stupidly. "Unhand my nephew," he demanded. "He wasn't stealing. We were shopping. He was about to show me the thing. I said," Max added in a terse, clipped voice that had sent men into battle, "put the lad down on his feet. *Now!*"

His voice and his face were enough to make the crowd move back a step and the merchant falter. But the merchant had sold goods on London streets too many years to let mere appearance overcome his judgment.

"Aye, I will, if you fork up my twelve shillings, sir," he said.

Max swallowed hard. "*Twelve?* For a rag doll? Are you mad? That's almost a pound!"

"Not mad. It's half what they ask in the fine stores for the same. Sentiment. Every lass's Ma had one. And these are the best. Never mind that, a rag's a rag. But these, they got imported hankies in their pockets, fine linen. That's what makes the price, you could ask anyone. I sell them for half the going rate, or at least, three quarters of it. Sell more if I charged less, but I know what I got."

"Aye, that's so," another barrow monger agreed.

"Too right," an onlooker agreed as the crowd murmured agreement.

"So," the merchant said, "you'll pardon me, sir, but I cut my teeth awhile back. The money, and you get the lad, and the doll."

Max hesitated. The money was for his dinner tonight, and the coach fare back to the countryside, and a bite to eat on the way. But if he didn't pay it, the boy would certainly hang. Max thought quickly. He could perhaps find work later today to make up some of the difference. He could pawn his hat. He hated to do it, but with that and the amount he had left, he'd have enough to go back to the countryside—just.

He dug into his pocket, counted out coins, and handed them to the merchant. The man released the boy and handed him back the doll.

The boy gained his feet. He shifted his thin shoulders to adjust his threadbare jacket and tugged his cap down again.

"Thankee," the merchant said with a shrewd look at Max. "It's a pleasure to do business with you. Next time, sir, be sure and tell your nevvy to keep hands off until you pay out. Oh," he added with a wicked grin, as Max turned to go, "and next time you go shopping with your nevvy, be sure to tell him to wait for you, too. These streets are dangerous for a lad on his own."

"What?" Max asked.

And looked down to see the boy gone.

And the doll with him.

* * *

There was no work to be done in London on Christmas Eve. No construction going on, no ships to be downloaded, no deliveries entrusted to a new man at this crucial time. The snow had stopped, so they didn't need more men to shovel or spread straw.

Max was cold and hungry and angry at himself.

He went back to his rented room. It was time to call the last plan into play. The scheme he liked least, but the only one left to him. Time was of the essence, no time for faint heart.

He'd failed with strangers. He'd have to steal from people he knew.

It was only noon. He had the rest of the day to do it in—time to quash the sick feeling he got whenever he thought of his last-ditch plan.

But now he had to eat. He'd skipped breakfast. He couldn't afford to eat, but he also couldn't afford to miss luncheon. A hungry man made mistakes. He had to be fed so his nerves were steady, so he could do the thing so suavely no one would ever know it was done.

He washed his face and looked at his reflection in the tiny mirror set in the lid of his traveling case. It was a fine leather case, with razor, brush, and comb in it. He'd have sold it days ago, but he needed it. He had to see his face to shave it. His batman had retired when the war ended, and Max had planned to hire a valet when he got to England again. Lucky thing he hadn't, he thought. It was hard enough trying to steal for one.

He ran his hand over his chin and found it sufficiently smooth. *Well, the face looked clean. The boots were polished again. Coat brushed. Last good shirt on. You'll do—*

enough to get you entree anywhere. So you can exit with your stolen goods. With your gift, he ruthlessly corrected himself.

First, he stopped at a pie seller's barrow and bought a small but steaming hot meat pie. He stood in the street, shifting from foot to foot, trying to eat it quickly before the cold wind chilled it, while also being careful to see it didn't drip on his clothes or face. Handkerchiefs were hard to launder, and he'd only two left—one to use, and one to keep clean in case anyone else needed the use of it. A foolish luxury, he knew. Old habits died hard.

It left him thirsty, but he decided he could drink later. He wiped his hands and raised his head. Time to begin. He strode onward.

Those who could afford the most and deserved the least were the ones to attempt, Max decided. That brought one person immediately to mind. He hated even visiting there. But he could pretend there were questions to ask. With any luck at all, he'd come away with more than answers. It was only fitting. She'd robbed his niece as surely as if she'd taken more than a father from her. Max decided to visit his brother's last mistress and see what he could steal back.

His sister-in-law had written to tell him the name, Eloise Wiggins. She included it with the usual complaints and pleas for more money. He found the Wiggins woman's town house easily enough. It was in a decent part of town. He was received by a footman, who referred him to a butler. *A butler*! A respectable-looking one, at that. Max gave his name and had the sour pleasure of seeing it make the old man's brow rise. A few moments later, he was shown into the house. She received him in her parlor. It surprised him.

The thought of dolls had brought her to mind. He had the notion such women kept them strewn everywhere. The whore he'd visited when he'd been at school had her room filled with them, along with tiny glass and porcelain boxes and figures of little clowns. He'd expected cheap gimcracks, perfume bottles on all the tabletops, frills on all the cloths, and a preponderance of red everywhere. But the place was furnished as properly as a maiden aunt's—a rich maiden aunt's.

The furniture was from the last century—dark, comfortable, and polished to a high sheen. A cheery fire bloomed in the hearth. She rose from a chair and greeted him with a radiant smile. It did wonders for her. She wasn't beautiful; her nose and the fact that her eyes were too small put paid to any notions of that. She was clearly accommodating; her smile and the cut of her gown certainly showed that. She had a small bosom and wide hips, and her hair was brown and done in ringlets. Not his idea of a seductress, Max thought as he bowed. God might know what she did to earn her money, but he certainly didn't care to find out. He was too busy wondering how much of that money had been his.

"Yes, you're his brother, all right," she said, eyeing him appreciatively from top to toe. "The same eyes. Such eyes! But his were always smiling."

As mine would if someone else earned my bread, Max thought. A dozen other bitter answers flew to his lips. He merely nodded.

"What can I do for you, sir?" she asked, and remembering, added, with more coquetry than sympathy, "Apart from offering my condolences on your brother's demise, of course."

"Thank you," he said curtly, remembering his rehearsed excuse for this visit, "It's been six months. But that's exactly what's on my mind. I've just returned to London, and my niece is coming to live with me tomorrow. I thought it would be best if I knew just how much she might know about you."

"Oh. Do have a seat," she said, indicating a chair by the fire.

He sat, waiting while she also sat. He took that opportunity to look around. There was nothing in the room he could pocket. It didn't matter. Suddenly, the thought of taking anything from this creature revolted him. He didn't want his niece to have a thing she'd touched. He'd hear her out and leave for someplace with richer pickings, and more palatable ones. But the way she was eyeing him made him realize she was definitely thinking of touching him. He sat on the edge of his chair, sorry he'd ever called here.

"You got my name from his wife?" she asked.

He nodded.

"He and I were together awhile," she said. "I wasn't the first of his fancies, I assure you—nor the last. We had fun, but we parted over a year ago. Whatever she told you, it wasn't any more than that. Well, what was the poor fellow to do? She had her diversions. He had his. I doubt his daughter even knows my name. Why should she? Unless her mama told her. Lud! I never budged from this place with him. He didn't pay me to dance."

Max's nostrils flared.

"You don't like to hear that?" she asked. "Well, but there it is. His wife wouldn't. I would. I didn't love him. He didn't love me. But it's my occupation. I make it easy and fun, and don't nag or complain. I know what to do and make a gentleman feel I enjoy doing it. Well, I do. Better than sewing my fingers to the bone, or doing laundry, or standing behind a shop counter or a barrow. You were an officer in charge of men. You must know what a valuable service an accommodating female can provide," she added with a conspiratorial smile.

His eyebrow went up.

"I know all about you, Lieutenant Major," she said. "That's what he bragged about. Not his wife or kiddy. Not his estate or his winnings. He didn't have any, poor fellow. But his brother, the great and gallant Lieutenant Major Maxwell. He was that proud of you. He said you'd the brains and the spirit in the family, and when you made your fortune, he rejoiced for you."

She saw the suggestion of a sneer on his dark face.

"And for himself, too, of course," she went on. "I can sympathize, believe me. I have a sister, too. . . . Any rate," she added, rising, "I expect you came to see what he gave me more than what you could tell his daughter about me. Come, sir. Who would tell a child about such as me, anyway?" She laughed, and he was surprised to hear that it was an infectious, silvery laugh. *That*, he thought, *yes*, that *a man might pay to hear.*

"I didn't cost him much," she added. "My price isn't high. I've never been lucky enough to have one gentleman exclusively. At least not since the year I started, and that was too long ago to mention, or remember. But I do all right as it is. Though it's clear you wouldn't have me for free, would you?"

Now there was defiance in her stance as well as invitation in her eyes. She probably didn't read the papers. She either thought he still had a fortune, or was willing to take him for tuppence. She'd already said she was cheap. So she was, in every way. He suddenly felt weary, as sorry for her and himself as he was for a world that made her occupation necessary. "No," he said, "but then, you see, I already have a lady in my heart, and can accept no substitute."

She nodded. "Nicely said. Everything he said about you is true. Including the fact that you have the looks as well as the morals in the family."

He didn't answer.

She laughed again. "Well," she said, "no sense fishing when the river's dry, is there? Pity, that. Down to the business at hand then. You think he gave me treasures from the estate? Nothing like, I promise you. He paid my going rate. But sometimes he did bring a present—flowers, sweets, odd things he'd won from other gents when his luck was running. The best was this."

She reached over, picked a small snuffbox off a nearby table, and flipped open its lid. A tinkling tune began to play. It was a sweet, lilting, intricate waltz. Max found himself enchanted.

She saw his rapt expression. "Not worth a fortune—he got it on a turn of the cards and complained it wasn't enough. But charming, isn't it?"

He nodded. His eyes glowed with sudden inspiration. It was exactly what to give a girl for Christmas! Not some trumpery doll. It mightn't be worth a fortune, but in his present circumstances he'd have to pawn his teeth to get anything like it. That made him smile. Until he realized it *had* been his money that bought it, even if it was winnings from gambling, because it was *his* money that had been gambled, and so should have been his niece's to begin with.

Then the grief and anger he felt threatened to overwhelm him.

"Thank you," he said. "I'm sorry to have troubled you." He rose and walked toward the door, then turned abruptly. "Why not marry?" he asked her suddenly. "I can understand not wanting weary work. But why not make a new life where love is not work?"

She'd been listening to the waltz. Her head came up. "You *are* everything he said, and no mistake," she breathed. Then she smiled sadly. "Because it's too late for me. Who'd wed me now? Only a man who wanted me to work for him, one way or another. But thank you," she said, her head to the side, "for even thinking it possible."

"It might be possible if you looked for it. You won't know unless you do. You can't have a victory unless you risk defeat—and God knows defeat can come even if you don't risk anything. It's worth considering. Give you good day, madam."

"To you as well. More's the pity that you won't share it with me," she said. "Happy Christmas, sir."

It would have been a happier one if he'd the music box in his pocket. But he nodded, took his hat from the butler, and went out into the afternoon again.

Max's next visit was made because of a lapse of courage, though he refused to look at it as such. *A respite*, he reasoned, a way to get out of the cold and get some heart back in him. He had two elderly aunts in London. He'd meant to visit, bringing extravagant gifts. That notion died when he learned he'd lost everything. Now he wished he could bring them something, because little as he had, they had less. So he wasted another precious shilling and bought a spray of mistletoe and holly tied with a bright red ribbon, but felt paltry giving it to them.

However, they received it and him with joy.

They looked just as they had when he'd been a boy, when Aunt DeWitt had lost her husband and her spinster sister, Araminta, came to live with her. Even their gowns looked the same. Perhaps they were, Max thought. Their clothes were always drab, with no claim to fashion. But they were tidy as a pair of pins, mismatched ones, because Aunt Araminta was as thin as her sister was plump. Their flat hadn't changed either, not by so much as a stick of furniture. At least they hadn't had to sell any off. They still lived in a good part of town, and their pensions were probably sufficient to pay the rent. Or else their neighbor, the dashing Duke of Blackburn, was helping with the rent as a charity; an excellent fellow, he was known as such.

The place was tidy, filled with memories and the delicious scent of gingerbread. It made Max feel homesick and happy at the same time. His aunts clearly didn't have much, but they knew how to use it.

They bustled around the parlor, bringing him hot cider and warm gingerbread, standing over him to be sure he finished both. They had dozens of questions, but the answer they liked most was the news that their great niece was coming to town.

"How wonderful!" Aunt Araminta crowed. "We need a child around here again."

"Gammon!" Max laughed. "I'll wager you bake these gingerbread men for all your neighbors' children. Which is as well. We won't be here at Christmas. I'll be taking Gwenn back home to Fair Oaks as soon as she arrives."

"No!" the sisters chorused.

"Yes, I'm afraid. I'm sorry to make her travel again," he said a little gruffly, "but as you may have heard, my fortunes have changed." He cleared his throat and went on, "And so I think Fair Oaks the best place for her now."

They grew still, and their faces fell.

"I suppose it is," Aunt Araminta said sadly. "The clean country air and so forth."

"I've a capital idea!" her sister suddenly said, "one that mends all. May we come, too? Oh tush, Araminta! How is he to know what we want if we don't ask? *Men*, after all." She turned her attention to Max again. "We love Fair Oaks at this season. What better place for Christmas? We were just talking about it the other day. How many years has it been since we were there?" she asked her sister.

"Since before Max left for the wars." Aunt Araminta sighed. "We weren't invited. Your brother had a care for us," she told him, "but it was clear his wife only tolerated us."

"I think it's because she knew we disapproved of the way they lived," her sister said shrewdly.

"Oh, do let us help with little Gwenn," his other aunt begged. "We can bring more than a gingerbread boy for the child. We can cook and bake, just as you always said you liked us to do!"

Max's spirits plummeted. They'd be a great help. But how could he feed two more souls, however small, old, and gentle they were? Besides, some old people ate like wolves. Maybe they were hungry, too. Gingerbread was hardly the stuff of a steady diet.

Very well, he thought with resignation, *the boots as well as the hat can be pawned* . . . No. Sold.

"You'd have to be ready to leave tomorrow," he warned them, "on Christmas Day."

Aunt Araminta clapped her hands, and her sister laughed.

He scrawled his new address on a bit of paper. He didn't want them realizing what a low district he was staying in. But he had to give them a chance to see how hard things were with him now, so they could make the decision, free of illusion. "Well, here's my direction if you change your mind," he said in embarrassment, handing the paper to them.

He still heard their delighted laughter ringing in his ears as he strode down the street into the afternoon again, fuller, but poorer in pocket—and spirits.

Max turned the corner and approached his club. He'd joined years before he'd come into his money and lost it again. He'd kept up his dues out of sentiment's sake, a way of showing faith he'd be back one day. He was glad he had. Now he could use all the services it had to offer—especially the food. There was always an assortment of free food set out for the gentlemen. Not a lot, but enough to take the edge off hunger. Stuffed eggs, little pasties, bits of cheese and biscuits. All he'd have to buy would be a whiskey or an ale, and he could put that on his bill.

It would be warm there, too, he thought longingly. He could eat and drink, and with so little food in his belly he could perhaps get a bit tipsy and forget his problem for a while. He could certainly rest and prepare for what he must do next.

He rubbed his worn gloves together as he approached the club and started to bound up the short stair. And stopped there. *But there might be old friends inside.* What if they asked him along to dinner? Or invited him to play cards and chance his luck on a foolish wager? He couldn't even afford to bet on a certain thing. Luck was running against him.

He turned and headed back down the stair, feeling like a leper. But without money in London, a gentleman was one.

There was only one logical place to try his luck now. It was the last place he thought he'd go. But apart from the Christmas gift he wanted to buy, he had four other people to feed now—Gwenn and her governess, and the aunts. And John had been his best friend, as they'd helped each other down through the years with everything from school work to sympathy for difficulties life dealt them. John wasn't plump in the pocket, but Max wouldn't ask him for much. Just a pound or two to tide him over until he could find more to pawn. The traveling case, for example. Once he got to Fair Oaks, he could sell it and pay John back.

Mostly, Max admitted as he trudged through the late afternoon as snow began falling again, he needed to know how Lisabeth had taken his letter. John would know everything; she was his sister.

Max knew it might hurt to hear about her reaction. But sometimes pain was necessary. It would be like searing the bleeding end of a swift amputation, as he'd seen the physicians do on the battlefield. He had to close the wound once and for all, or all his heart's blood would keep leaking out of it. It felt like that, at least.

He'd been worrying about money, about how to get a Christmas present for his niece. But all along, like the bass accompaniment to the symphony of anxiety and fears that wouldn't stop running through his head, there was that constant throbbing ache of losing Lisabeth.

Max walked faster, wanting to get there before he could change his mind. *After all, John had a right to know why his sister had been rejected.* Lisabeth had wasted some of the best years of her youth waiting for him, and so if John wanted to plant him a facer for it, Max supposed he had a right. He supposed he would welcome it. It had been a damnable thing to do. But there hadn't been a choice.

Maxwell hurried to his friend's flat, telling himself he was seeking a loan, knowing he was looking for punishment or absolution. But most of all, for word of his Lisabeth—*of Lisabeth,* he corrected himself. She wasn't his anymore and never could be again.

Max arrived at John's rooms as the afternoon eased into twilight. He raised the door knocker and waited, stamping his boots to keep the blood in his feet flowing. It was growing deuced cold. But when the door opened, he stopped stock-still. He felt such a rush of gladness, followed by such enormous shame and sadness, that he was dizzied.

Lisabeth stood in the doorway. With all he knew, even so, he almost started for her. He swiftly crushed instinct and imposed reason and control. He could only allow himself to look at her, drinking in the actual fact of her presence. She was still lovely—no—much lovelier than he remembered. He froze, helpless, waiting for her to speak.

She faltered, too. He saw it happen. When she first saw him, her eyes lit, and she gave out a yelp. She reached toward him; then her hand fell as she saw his expression.

"Max?" she asked breathlessly, her eyes devouring his face. *"Max?"*

He didn't reach for her. He didn't move. He stood in

the snow on the doorstep, his dark face pale, and only stared at her.

She'd been expecting much, she'd rehearsed this minute for five long years. But never this. He stood still and held himself apart, something in his expression that she couldn't read. He was more handsome than she remembered, and she hadn't seen a man to equal him since he'd left. He looked older, wearier; strangely, it suited him. Anything would. Still such a beautiful, distinctive, dark, rousing face. *So much more handsome . . . and so much colder.*

She was suddenly shy, wary, altogether elated, too. There were so many things she wanted to say, but all she could utter was, "Max? It *is* you?"

"You're here?" he asked.

"I came to London to find what happened to you," she said.

"You didn't get my letter?"

"Which one? The last was from Dieppe, the one you sent the night before you left for England. You never wrote again."

"I did," he said dully. "I sent it to your house. What are you doing here?"

"When I didn't hear from you, I worried. Mama said I was fretting her to death. Papa finally agreed I could come stay with John, so I could see you when you returned. But you weren't at your town house, and no one knew . . . Oh," she said, suddenly flustered, "what am I thinking of? Come in. John's not here." As she spoke she raised her chin, because this was Max, and it was not, and something was terribly wrong and she no longer knew what to do. "But it's all right. My Aunt Maude, you remember her, she came with me. So did Nurse. But now that the younger boys are grown, she says time hangs heavy on her hands . . ."

What is it? was what she really wanted to say, as her eyes searched his for a clue. *Why don't you take me in your arms? The way you said you would when we met again. It's been so long. You said that, too. What has happened? Oh, Max, please, what's happened?* Her hands were cold, her smile flat.

"Do come in," she said.

The lantern on the doorstep showed his expression clearly even though the afternoon was coming on to milky dusk. Snow covered his high beaver hat and settled on his wide shoulders. The wind was picking up. But he simply stayed there, standing tall and straight, as aloof from her as the north wind itself. She'd waited so long, she'd expected so much. *So, he'd written, had he.* She'd thought there would be tears and kisses, such kisses that she'd only dreamed of since he'd left. She'd thought he'd swoop her up and she'd wrap her arms around his neck so she could believe he was really here at last. And not let go.

Now here he was. This was Max. And it was not. She shivered.

"You're cold," he said. He stepped into the hall, closing the door behind him. But he didn't move from where he stood. "I told you everything in the letter," he said hollowly. "I suppose you heard about my change of fortune?"

She nodded dumbly.

"And so," he said, "you must understand that things of necessity have changed between us?"

Her head went back. She paled and swayed. He put out a hand to steady her, but she stepped back and put out her own hand to keep him away.

"The inequality of our situations cannot be more pronounced," he went on dully. "You must agree. Your family isn't wealthy. But compared to me now?" He gave a hollow laugh. "You see, don't you, Lisabeth?" But saying her name made his voice catch, and he paused to get it under control.

He stared at her hungrily. She looked even more beautiful than the memories of her that had sustained him through so much. She did up her hair now, the tendrils framing her face. That face . . . it had been charming and fresh when he'd last seen it, but compared to her beauty now he saw it had been unformed, holding only the promise of how lovely she'd become. She had cheekbones now, he thought with tender sorrow. It gave her face definition and made her mouth look even more tempting and full. *Would it taste the same?* He quashed the dangerous thought. Her hair gleamed honey gold, as did her eyes. *Were there tears there?* He hoped not. He hoped so. He wished she'd try to talk him out of his decision. He couldn't give her time to try.

"What I said in the note, I can tell you again now," he said. "Much as it hurts me to say it, in all conscience, I can't marry you now, Lisabeth. It wouldn't be right for you, or of me. Please don't try to convince me otherwise. I have my pride. I won't allow myself to be lured into what I most want, because I know too well what I must do in the years to come. I have different responsibilities now. I thought I'd be free when the war was over. I'm less so now than ever. There's the estate to set in order, my niece and her future to care for—all will be different now. She must be a prime consideration, too. There's no way you can fit into that anymore, you do see?"

She said nothing, only gaped at him.

"Lisabeth, please say you understand, at least a bit," he said a little desperately. "I have obligations now. I can't give you what I thought I could before this all happened to me."

She caught her breath, then recovered. "Yes," she said, nodding slowly. "Yes," she said more briskly, "I see. You're right. Wise of you, I think. It's not what the heart might wish," she murmured, "but it makes perfect sense when you come right down to it. It's all pounds and cents, or pounds and sense, isn't it?" She gave a start of pained laughter at her chance play on words.

"What the heart might wish?" he asked incredulously, before he could stop himself. "No, hardly. It hurts more than you can imagine, I can't deny it. All those years of hoping, waiting, longing. Our letters . . . I'm sorry, but I never thought this would happen. . . ."

"Who could?" she asked. She smiled bravely. "But I quite understand, I assure you. Things *are* very different now, aren't they? Of course, how can you share such a turn of fortune with me? Don't worry. Consider yourself free of any obligation. You always were, you know. My papa was wiser than I knew."

"Your family has every right to hate me. By God, Lisabeth, you do, too!"

"No," she said, avoiding his eyes now. "But it does show my papa was right again. We had quite a to-do when I told him I was coming to London." She laughed unconvincingly. "He didn't want me chasing after you, seeking you out when you didn't send word to me after we heard what happened. You'd told me you improved your fortune, but before we read the paper we didn't know the half of it. I won't go into that. Papa did. He thought—well, that hardly matters. But I thought you might have been hurt. I worried you might be ill . . . Of all the things I imagined, it was never this."

She shook her head to chase the tears. She would *not* let him see her cry. "Clever man, my papa. Good-bye, Max. Good luck. I do wish that to you. And a happy Christmas, too."

It was over, he realized numbly. Just like that. All those years, gone and for nothing, over in a moment. Of course. Very sensible of her. She'd grown up in more than looks. Young love was one thing, committing to a pauper's life another. She was meant for better things. They both knew it, as did her papa. Max was relieved—and crushed. He turned to go.

"Oh!" she said.

He turned back eagerly.

"Since you're not staying at your town house and John's not at home now, do you want to leave my brother your direction?"

He nodded, fumbling a card from his pocket. He'd scrawled the address of his room there to leave at Dan's office, should he ever return. He started to hand it to her, then stopped, suddenly shamed at her seeing what he was reduced to. But she'd given him up because of it, hadn't she? He handed her the card. She pocketed it without looking. He doubted she could with tears in her eyes. *So, she cared. But not enough to change her entire life. Wise girl.*

"Good-bye, Lisabeth," he said, tipped his hat, and went out into the growing evening.

* * *

He sold the hat, feeling lucky to get to the pawnshop just before it closed. He couldn't take off the boots and sell them there and then, but he got an estimate for them, too. Tomorrow, perhaps. But they were closed on Christmas Day. He reconciled himself. He'd need them for traveling.

"You're just in time—it's almost Christmas," the pawnbroker said sourly as he brushed snow from the hat and set it on his shelf. His was a hard business, and he had the heart for it, but it had been a long, busy day with too much human foolishness and suffering finding its way to his doorstep. He wanted to get back to his rooms upstairs and a hot mug of ale. "Seen too many of you young bucks selling off everything just before the holy day," he grumbled. "Remembering their responsibilities at the last moment. I hate to send a man out in this weather with nothing on his head, but I'm thinking there wasn't much in it before. Maybe next time you'll be a little less quick with a card or a wager, eh?"

"I just left His Majesty's service," Max said in clipped tones, gripping the coins the pawnbroker had given him into his white-knuckled fist. "The only wager I made was with myself, setting the odds on my ever coming home. A man can lose everything more easily than you realize, my friend," he said sourly. He looked around the shop. "Like that, for example. That spyglass you've got there in the bin. Belongs in a museum, not a box of oddments. My grandfather had one just like it. My brother sold it for more than you've got in this whole shop. And a Merry Christmas to you, too," he said, and swung open the door.

"Wait!" the pawnbroker shouted. "If that's so, why didn't you buy it and sell it yourself for the profit?"

Max stopped short. He paused, then laughed. It wasn't a merry sound. "By God! There's the reason I'm a pauper! I never thought to cheat you. Lord! It's what I should have done! Happy Christmas," he said and stormed out the door, fumbling for his hat to clap on—recalling where he'd left it too late. He strode away, angry at his honesty, furious with his sense of honor. It was how he'd got where he was, and see what good it had done him?

He soon knew why a gentleman always wore his hat. His close-cropped hair was no match for the snow. All the heat in his body seemed to have left by the top of his head. He hoped the weather would let up soon, and not just because of the cold.

If travel was delayed by the weather, how could he keep his niece and her governess in London? Not in his meager room—he couldn't go back to his town house . . . He supposed he could take them to the aunts. But the roads must be beastly. What if something happened to them on the way to London? And what was Lisabeth thinking now?

Max grimaced. Hunching his shoulders, he made his way toward the meaner streets, heading back to his room.

The snow drove in sheets, so thick he almost bumped into a band of revelers staggering down the street toward him. There were six of them, six drunken fops. They blocked the street like a phalanx of enemy troops—fell one and you incurred the wrath of them all. Max knew their sort, bored young noblemen off for a night on the Town. Their travels had taken them far from their usual haunts. They were looking for liquor, females, trouble of any sort they could find. A scuffle in the street would certainly please them. Max didn't want to be their evening's sport. He could acquit himself well in a fight, but six to one?

However it ended, he didn't fancy bleeding on the snow. He stood aside in silence in the hope they'd pass without incident.

"Whatch where you're goin', sirrah!" one cried as he lurched into Max. "Almosht knocked me flat! What shay you, Dexter? Show the fool the right way to walk down a street, shall we?"

Dexter? Max peered into the milky darkness. How many gentlemen of that height were named Dexter? *Dexter Simms?* He saw the tall lanky man weaving as he tried to stand on his feet. It could be no other. He stared at the man who'd spoken—short as a cord of wood and twice as thick. Dexter's bosom friend—Charlie Rigby. He'd thought that voice was familiar. He knew the men, had known them since he'd been a boy.

He said nothing, hoping they'd forget him. The Dexter he'd known had been a peaceful lad. He still was.

"Never mind," Dexter said generously. "Christmess, dont'cha know? Let's go."

"But you should watch your step, sir, that you should," Charlie admonished Max, shaking a finger in his face. He looked up into that dark impassive face and frowned. "I know you," he said carefully, "Don't I?"

Max bowed—and waited for his opportunity to leave peaceably. The others went weaving down the street. Not Charlie. He stood staring at Max.

"I shay! You're Max, our Max, Evers . . . the Lieu . . . the new baron, y'know. *Max!* I swear it!" Charles called after the others excitedly, "It's Evers! Was just speaking of him, wasn't we? Y'know, the fellow from school? Was in the wars? Got all the medals and then . . . Y'know! The one with that strange turn of fortune? Hold, lads! Least we can do is ask him along and give him a drink? A toast to his incredible turn of luck, eh? 's Christmas, after all."

"Max?" Dexter turned to ask with a puzzled look. "*Our* Max? The one everyone's lookin' for?"

"Aye!" Charles cried.

But when they looked down the street again, all they saw was the snow.

Max pushed open the heavy door and ducked through the entrance. He strode down the aisle, turned, and edged his way along a long pew, then collapsed and slunk down low in his seat. He doubted they'd follow. They were drunk, but not enough to invade a church, looking for him. He wouldn't have come here himself if he'd a choice. It was, literally, the only door open to him on this street. He didn't want company. He didn't want questions. What he wanted was unobtainable. But he was cold and weary, and this was sanctuary, literally. It was an ancient place, and not of his denomination. There would be no one he knew here.

He groaned low in his throat. He could have asked them for money! They'd have given it gladly, along with their pity. He wasn't that desperate yet. Maybe, tomorrow . . .

It wasn't warm in the ancient cathedral; the stone bones of the place made that impossible. But it was warmer than the streets, and so he wasn't the only one in the place. Services would start hours from now, as Christmas approached. But it wasn't empty—far from it. He glanced around and saw his fellow refugees.

He realized he wasn't the only one to find sanctuary here tonight. There were old, poorly dressed men and old women in ragged clothes, as well as weary-looking young men beside careworn women with babies at their breasts beneath their tattered shawls. Children sat as silent as the effigies on the walls around him, or spoke in low whispers that were swallowed up by the thick stones in the floors and walls.

It was peaceful. Candles blazed everywhere. Swags of evergreens gave the place a vital green scent that was refreshing. Somewhere he heard distant chanting, and it slowed his racing heart. Max sat back and rested. It was as good a place as any to wait for his madcap old friends to give up the hunt and stagger on to new diversions. He wished he still had his watch; that was one of the first things he'd pawned. But he had a keen sense of time. He'd give it an hour, then leave and go to his room to wait out the storm. Tomorrow would come soon enough. In the meanwhile . . .

Heartsick and lost, in a place he didn't belong, Max closed his eyes and waited for night to fall.

There was a scent in his nostrils, so cool, pure, and filled with smoky spice that Max breathed in deeply to fill his lungs with it. It refreshed him, soothed him, made him feel at peace. He smelled it and kept drifting in that strange country half on the border of consciousness, too comfortable to wake, too aware of his state to give the sensation up to sleep.

He knew that scent! It came to him along with the words he now heard intoned, lulling him even as they raised him from the sweet short sleep he'd woken from.

Frankincense and myrrh. Rare balms and attars, the first Christmas gifts, along with gold.

Gold—Max's eyes opened to see a blur of it. Candles flared, glinting off the priests' white-and-gold robes as they went in procession down the long aisle to the chancel. The cathedral was awash in light suffused by a blue veil of haze dispensed by the priests as they swung their smoking censers.

Max watched, and thought deeply. Suddenly, he saw clearly, in spite of all the smoke.

The three Wise Men had brought what they thought most valuable. Gold was understood. What use was frankincense and myrrh in a stable? But worth was what you thought it was, wasn't it?

He sat up straight. He'd nothing fitting to give his niece for Christmas. But he'd give her the rest of his life, and that was not nothing. It was, in any event, all he had. So it had to be enough. Pride had made him want to steal a toy for her. He couldn't afford much, and certainly not pride. It was time to trade it for truth, however painful.

He gave a heavy sigh. Forget about his fortune. The truth was he'd lost something more valuable, the best thing he'd ever had, his dream of love and life with Lisabeth. It had been only a dream. But it had been of great value, greater than anything he'd ever owned. And if it had been enough to uphold him through all those dangerous years, then surely his dream of the future would be enough for his niece?

It would have to be. It was his greatest gift. He'd give her himself—his devotion, protection, and vigilance. No man could give more. It wasn't such a bad gift, at that. He hadn't offered it to Lisabeth. It was just as well. She wouldn't have accepted it, but his niece would.

Maybe the smoke had some narcotic in it, he thought. He felt strangely at peace at last. He sat back, loath to leave the place and the fragile content he'd found. He closed his eyes again. It had been such a long, strange day.

Max felt a touch on his sleeve and started up.

"Peace," the priest said gently. "You may stay if you wish, and go back to sleep. But here's something for you. It's not much, because there are so many to share it with, but it will buy you something for Christmas morning." He handed Max a coin.

Max stared at it dumbly. He weighed it in one callused palm. Then he smiled. "Father," he said, rising to his feet, "thank you. But I don't need this as much as some others. I came here to rest, that's gift enough for me tonight. Please take it back, along with some of its brothers for those who may need it more."

Two more shillings gone, he thought as he dug in his pocket and handed them to the priest. Small price to pay for the answer he'd found.

"You're sure?" the priest asked. "Then thanks, but it's no longer night. It's Christmas Day in the morning. Happy Christmas, and luck to you, too."

"I need that most," Max said. "My thanks, and Happy Christmas to you, too."

He strode up the aisle, went to the door, pushed it open, and blinked. It was early, but the sun was blinding on the fallen snow.

He hurried to his room as all the bells in Town began to toll, welcoming the day. He needed to wash and pack. He'd be gone from London by night. Breakfast was out of the question; he'd given that to the priest for those poorer than he was. There was enough money left to buy food for the aunts and his niece and her governess on the trip—that and perhaps an extra sweet for the child. She'd have that and the aunt's gingerbread, and his promise to her.

His step slowed. It had nothing to do with the lack of a material gift. He'd made his peace with that. It had lifted his spirits, but he suspected his heart would always feel empty now. His gift of himself was enough for his niece, but not for his love. He couldn't have asked Lisabeth to share a future of poverty. What he tried to stop thinking about was that she hadn't even considered the possibility.

Max looked around the shabby room to see if he'd left anything, then laughed aloud as he realized he'd nothing to leave. He hefted his traveling bag. It was considerably lighter than when he'd arrived in London. He wasn't leaving London until nightfall, but he was vacating his room now so as not to have to pay another day's rent. He'd use the extra time to walk to the Bull and Mouth to buy coach tickets, then hire a hack and pick up the aunts, and then . . .

Someone rapped on his door.

He hesitated. It couldn't be the landlord; he'd paid to the hour. No one else knew he was here.

"I knows yer there! Could y' open the door?" a strange high voice shouted. "Got me bloomin' hands full!"

Max didn't recognize the voice; it was a young one, filled with exasperation. He opened the door—and looked down.

It looked like a greatcoat standing there, its arms filled with a package. It took a second for Max to realize that a small, gaunt boy occupied the coat. The collar almost hid his face, the sleeves covered over his hands, and the hem trailed on the floor. The coat had obviously been made for a large man. It took another second for Max to recognize the face. He'd last seen it looking imploringly at him as its owner dangled from the arm of an irate rag doll seller.

"Aye, it's me," the boy said. He stepped into the room and set the package down on the one table there. Then he looked around with interest. "Leavin', huh?" he asked when he saw the traveling bag at Max's feet. "Can't say as I blames you. Foul place, this. Well, good thing I came early, in'nit then?"

Max stood back, his arms crossed on his chest. "Good for me, bad for you. If you mean to steal anything else from me, you'll find slim pickings, I'm afraid."

"Got it the other way round," the boy said, "I'm givin' this time. Well, see," he said with a shrug. "It were a mean thing to take the doll after you done me such a good turn, I admits. But you looked like you could stand the nonsense. Then I gets to thinkin'—*eh. Woodenhead! If the gent's got blunt, why's he shopping in the market, huh?* So, I follered you a bit, after. And I seen you ain't got no more than me. I mean eatin' one of Mrs. Peele's pies in the street? Coulda died doin' that! And comin' back to this place? I seen you're a gent down on his luck, but so was I—then.

"But, see," the boy went on with animation, "you changed my luck! Aye, I sold the hankie that were in the doll's pocket. And when I was at the fence's, I seen a set of earbobs he din't know were hot as fire, and so I told him, so he sold 'em to me and I sold 'em to . . . Well, makes no never mind, you changed my luck and that's a fact! Had enough to buy a Christmas dinner for us, enough left over for a coat for my brother and one for me, too. Nice, ain't it?" he said, preening as he stroked one chapped red hand down the front of the greatcoat.

"And so that night at the boozer," the boy went on, "I was sharin' the luck, 'cause that always brings more, and tellin' your story, and up speaks Old Filtch—him that works the gentleman lay at the best shops in town—and he says, 'Hold on! That's the toff what saved my neck at Markham's when he give the Runners the wrong scent!' So I felt even meaner. So this morning I tole my ma, and she tole my pa, and so here I am to share our dinner with you and give you back the doll only without the hankie."

The boy looked at Max with defiance. "I'm sorry, but it paid for the feast, y'see. I owes you one, and Gower always pays his debts, anyone can tell you. So if you're leaving, give me your direction and you'll get the gelt in time, and that's my word on it."

"Your mother and father didn't care that you stole the doll?" Max asked in astonishment.

The boy looked patient and spoke as though to a child. "My pa hurt his back. He used to be a carpenter, but he can't do no heavy work no more. Can't hardly walk. Fixes stuff, and whittles things my sisters sell. My ma got the six of us to tend, plus the knitting she does what we sells. Them of us that can, works. Money's needed, so no one asks no questions when it comes in."

He saw Max about to speak and added, "I ain't no fool. I makes money by keepin' an ear to the ground and my nose in the wind. But I have to take risks, time to time, when the need arises. Christmas is a need, you gotta admit. I mean, porridge for Christmas dinner is a shame and a sin, ain't it? So I done what I could. But see, were I nabbed, I'd hang, and it would go hard for the family, so I'm beholden to you."

"You're welcome," Max said. He was honestly amused,

as well as appalled. "But you didn't have to share. As you see, I'm leaving anyway."

"It don't matter," the boy said stubbornly. "A debt's a debt. And I'll get you your money for the hankie, in time. So, your moniker and address?"

When Maxwell didn't answer, the boy added, "Oh, yeah, I'm called Squirrel, but my name's Gower."

He gave a convulsive movement. Max's eyes widened. For a minute it looked like the coat had decided to swallow the boy, but it became clear he was only bowing.

Max bowed in return. "My name is Maxwell, Maxwell Evers."

The boy straightened. He stared, then laughed. "Sure it is! The bloke everyone's looking for? So, you're the lieutenant major? Well, serves me right for asking. It don't matter. A man's entitled to his privacy. Now . . ." He undid the packet. Looking like a small, thin parody of Father Christmas, he reached in and pulled out a rag doll. It looked none the worse for its rough treatment. "Sorry about the hankie, like I said. But I got the doll for you. You had a need for it once, right?"

Max smiled. "Yes, and still do. Thank you."

"And," the boy said proudly, opening the packet all the way, "here's a pie a fellow can sink his teeth in! My ma's. *And* a slice of the best puddin' in London Town, I promise. I'd of brung you a bit of the turkey we're having this afternoon, too, but it ain't been cut into yet."

"This is more than sufficient. I'm honored—and grateful," Max said, and meant it.

The boy reached into his pocket, "*And*," he said, "speakin' of grateful, here's somethin' from Old Filtch."

He handed Max some coins. "You didn't peach on him at Markham's, and he said to tell you he ain't forgettin' it."

"I didn't mean to have the whistle blown on him in the first place," Max said ruefully. "It was the least I could do. But how did he know? Last I saw of him was his back as he ran away."

The boy laughed again. "Only a clodpole would of kept runnin'! Who's a man to chase? Why, the fellow he sees harin' off! Old Filtch, he got out the door and joined the crowd, lookin' down the street like he was shocked at what was happenin'. One of the Redbreasts actually asked him where the thief had got to! So he heard what you said. He followed you a while, too, to the market at least. Where he seen you save *my* neck. So all round there ain't much that happens in Town that we don't know. And we all thank you and wish you a Happy Christmas."

The boy walked to the door, then turned. "Oh. And if you ever needs me for anythin', just go to the White Cat in Seven Dials and ask for me. They'll get word to me. If you needs anythin' or hear of a good job o' work, I'm cheap—reliable, too. There ain't much I can't turn a hand to. Well, give you good day. And Happy Christmas to you." He bowed again, turned, and pattered down the stairs.

Max shook his head. There was honor among thieves, after all. He was sorry to have to share the boy's largess, and sorry he couldn't help him. But now he had breakfast and luncheon, and a doll for his niece. And enough extra to buy a decent dinner for her and his aunts at the Bull and Mouth before they left London tonight. He felt incredibly rich.

He ate the pie rapidly and had to agree with Gower. It was much better than what he'd bought in the street. He

wiped his hands and carefully laid the doll in his
he could go.

But he heard another knock at his door. *The*
back? He opened the door.

"I don't have much time, and the stairs played
my legs, but I owe you something," the pawnbr
almost angrily. "I'm a man with a reputation to
and I pay my debts. The Squirrel told me you
abouts. Anyway, here's your hat back, sir, and a p
sides, because you were right about the spyglass
obliged to you. And my own lad served at His M
pleasure, only he didn't come back, and he'd have
me to deal squarely with you. Good day, and good
you. And a happy Christmas, too," he added as he st
down the stairs.

Max wanted to laugh. Last night, he'd nothing
morning, he'd little. It felt like a great deal more.

He wondered if he should wait and see what else
tune sent to his door. But he shook his head at his
ishness. One thing he knew about Lady Luck—if
pushed her, she pushed back, hard. He picked up his b
and went to the door.

The landlord stood there, scowling. "You said you'd b
leaving?"

"I am," Max said simply, "as you can see."

"That's good. You din't say there'd be such a coming and going. A body don't get a chance to rest of a Christmas morning. Here's a parcel just come for you. Leave the key afore you go," he added, then handed a package to Max and stalked off to his room downstairs.

All things came in threes, Max marveled, opening the parcel. His hands froze on the wrappings, disbelieving what saw. He picked up the note that came with it and read twice.

You admired it, far more than you admired me. I saw it in your eyes. It's only fitting his daughter have it, you never have to tell her it came from me. If you ever change your mind about the other, however, I will remain, yr. devoted servant, Eloise Wiggins.

Max picked up the snuffbox. He opened the lid. It sang s perfect tiny tune. He smiled. *So she had some grace, fter all.*

A doll and a musical snuffbox, and money to pay for xtra comforts on Christmas Day! Ironic that it all stemmed rom theft or the desire to steal. But he hadn't had to steal anything, after all. He was luckier than he'd been for months. There was only one thing he needed now, the one thing he'd always wanted. But he didn't believe in miracles, even on Christmas Day.

Time to leave, he thought superstitiously, before some awful force came along to take this all away. He packed the box and strode to the door again—and barely missed being smashed in the nose as it flew open.

"John!" Max said, shocked.

His oldest friend stood there, glowering at him.

"There you are!" John said angrily. "Your aunts spoke true. No, you don't!" he said, eyeing the traveling bag. "You don't leave till I have my say. I don't want lies, I won't have paltry excuses, I want all the truth, and I won't be denied. Tell me why you wasted Lisabeth's young life as you did, and tell me so I can understand. If it means we meet at dawn somewhere, so be it. I didn't serve in the army, but I can account for myself with sword, saber, or pistol. Now. Why?"

John was his own height, a pleasant-faced young man with Lisabeth's cinnamon hair and ready smile. The smile was not in evidence now.

"What's there to say?" Max asked with angry sorrow. "The facts speak for themselves. My fortunes changed. That changed everything, of course."

John's fist shot out. Max was unprepared. He was hit square in the mouth and staggered back. The pain wasn't so bad as the shock. He shook his head, gritted his teeth, balled his fists, and counted slowly in his head. He'd learned patience in his years in the army, as well as the need to keep a clear mind, unaffected by anger or pain. His life, and his men's, had depended on it in the past. A lifelong friendship depended on it now. He steadied himself and held his temper in check. And besides, he deserved that blow and more, he thought with immense sorrow.

"Come on, strike back!" John urged as he stood tall, balling his fists.

Max touched his cut lip with his tongue and drew out his last clean handkerchief. "First, tell me why you blame me for circumstance," he said as he dabbed at the blood pouring from his cut lip.

"Circumstance?" John cried. "Is that what you call arrogance? My sister waited years for you. She'd dozens of suitors—rich ones, too. But did she even entertain the notion of letting them woo her? No, she waited for you—you false-hearted, two-faced, contemptuous jilt!"

"Because I wanted to spare her a life of poverty?" Max asked bitterly. "Some love that would be! I can work, have worked since I got home. Loading cargo, laying cobbles, aye, even carrying coal. But not earning enough to feed a cat. There's not much honest labor available these days. Penniless men returned from the war are cheaper than tuppenny whores, and just as desirable in polite company."

He paced a step, then swung around to face John again. "What? You're astonished?" he asked with a crooked smile, because his lip was swelling. "Why? Would you have me offer a gentle, well-bred girl like Lisabeth such a life? I met a lad the other day, a thief, no more than eight, if that. A guttersnipe. He helps support his parents and five siblings because his father hurt his back. What if I hurt mine? Would you want Lisabeth to take in sewing? Her son to steal in the streets? I've a niece to support now as well. By God, man. I tried to *steal* a gift for my niece yesterday, and couldn't even do that.

"That's why I let Lisabeth go, though I'll only tell you, John, it damn near broke my heart . . . no. I believe it did. But a man has to give up his heart when he truly loves. And believe me, I truly love—loved her. *Now* call me a jilt, and I'll meet you now, or later, with fists or swords or what have you."

John stared at him. He frowned. "*What?* What are you talking about?"

"I read the paper on the packet coming here, from Dieppe. It had the story of what happened to Dan Merrick. I invested everything with him, John. I don't have a groat that I didn't. That's why I've got only what you see before you—my clothes and my skin. Oh, yes," he added harshly, "and a stolen rag doll, a music box I tried to steal, and some coins I earned by not being able to steal. Lovely booty, eh? It's all I own now. Enough to offer a bride?

Maybe some. Not a fraction of what I'd want for Lisabeth, John, and there it is."

"When did you read this paper?"

"A week Friday past. No. What day is this? Two weeks past. Or so."

"Oh, my God!" John said, wide-eyed. "That story! Yes! It was in the papers, the talk of the Town. Merrick threatened to sue soon as he heard—a day later, when he got back from France. They retracted all. As well they should. Max," he said, dropping his fisted hands and spreading them wide, "it was all a hum. That is to say, there was an embezzler. But he only stole a bag of money. Merrick caught up with him and got it back, he was that angry about it. But his fortune, his investments, his holdings are too vast for any one man to steal. He's one of the richest men in England now."

Now Max stared. "*Still?*" he asked, unable to believe his ears.

"Still and always. He owns half of Town."

"But the creditors on my town house doorstep when I first returned," Max said, thinking furiously, "they were clamoring for their money!"

"Well, of course the paper immediately printed a correction, and they knew they could get it when you got back."

"And . . . I still have funds?" Max asked, disbelieving.

"I imagine you have more now. Your friend Merrick was looking for you at our house the other day. He heard you had returned and was wondering why you didn't come see him. Especially with Christmas coming, he was having a grand soiree at his house and wanted you there. Lisabeth was so excited. We didn't know where you were either.

She couldn't stop pacing, waiting for you. But when you returned, it was to say good-bye to her.

"You didn't know any of this?" John said, beginning to smile. "So when you told her there was too profound a difference in your states now for you to marry her—that's what you meant? Not that she wasn't rich enough for you now that you're so rich?"

"I could never be that rich," Max said as his heart leapt up. "Now, again, John. Tell me once more. Twice more. Three times. That's my lucky number today. It's true? I still have my money?"

"All of it, and more."

"No, the more is yet to come, and I have to get it for myself," Max said as he strode to the door.

"No," Lisabeth said, shaking her head and clasping her hands tightly together. "I don't want to see him."

"I think you should," her brother said.

"Do you? To get his apology? Or his pity? No, thank you. Of all I've borne, I couldn't bear that! I suppose he apologized to you, and you want him to do the same to me. That may be a man's way. It's not mine. I'm glad you can preserve your friendship . . . or did you fight with him?" she asked, suddenly looking keenly at him. "No matter, it's not for me, John. I heard what he had to say. There's nothing he can add."

"There's much he can. I think you should receive him. He's waiting in the parlor."

"He can wait until next year—no, that's too soon. Forever then, if he wishes. I won't see him." She thought of that dark face and bit back her tears. She was sure she'd no more now anyway.

"It's not just my pride. Oh, John," she said fervently, "I've been thinking about just how I *would* like to see him again since he was here and told me I no longer suited him. I've been doing more than weeping. I've been dreaming of my revenge. I want him to see me looking grand, certainly not with these red eyes. Well," she said on a sniff, "*that's* over with, I assure you! And if I saw him again, I'd want to be dressed wonderfully well, too. Most of all, I'd want to be married to someone who makes him look like the toad he turned out to be. Mind, I'm not vindictive," she added. "It's just that I want to be at my best when he does his worst. And that is *not* now."

Privately, her brother had to agree. Her eyes were red and swollen from weeping, and her nose was pink to match them. He didn't think Max would care.

"I think you must see and hear him," he persisted. "There's something you didn't know. In all fairness, you must hear him out."

She turned her head to one side and looked stonily at the wall.

"I didn't think you were craven," he said.

Her head swung round. "I am *not*. Oh, well, all right. I see I'll have no peace until I do. So if it has to be done, let it be over with. I'll see him."

"Good! That's my girl! I knew I could count on you," he said happily. He went to the door, paused, and looked back. "And, Lisabeth," he added, "hear what he says. And if you don't believe him, look at his hands."

She frowned in puzzlement.

He opened the door, then had another thought, and poking his head back into the room, said, "But not his lip. That was an accident, soon mended."

* * *

Max walked in quietly. She stood by the window, looking out. He clenched his hands and forced himself to stand still.

"Lisabeth?" he said to her defiant little profile. "All right, don't look at me. Just listen. It's simple. It's stupid. It's true. I picked up a newspaper left lying on a bench on the packet while I was traveling home from France. It said my friend Daniel Merrick lost all his money and fled the country. His money—and mine. I came home to find creditors at my door. I believed I was a bankrupt. I sold or pawned almost everything I owned. I worked so I could eat.

"I didn't mind the work. In truth, I didn't mind not having luxuries. I was in the war—I'd done without before. But never without the dream of you. Saying good-bye to you was the most painful thing I ever did. But it was because I believed I couldn't afford to marry. It was like giving up my life. This morning John came to my room to kill me. I didn't blame him. He told me the truth about my finances. I'm still a rich man. I still can hardly believe it."

She didn't turn her head.

"Lisabeth," he said hoarsely, "I never lied to you. I kept you in my heart all these years and never went near another woman. There *is* no other woman for me. I can't believe I didn't actually say exactly what I thought the problem was. I was sure I did. But what else in the world could it have been? Do you think I'd have abandoned you because I was rich? How could you think it? Don't you know me at all?"

Now she swung round. "Don't you know me?" she cried.

"I'd have married you if you sold rags on a cart in the street!"

"Lisabeth," he said with a broken laugh, "if I'd had them I'd have sold them. I'd have sold my skin if it could get me an extra hour with you. But I had nothing. Now they tell me I have so much, but it's still nothing without you. There's no reason for me to lie. And no reason for me to stay now if you don't believe me. But before God! I don't want to leave you. I never did.

"Lisabeth? I told you the truth as I knew it. You heard it wrong. You might have asked me for details. I was ashamed, but I would've told you."

"Huh!" she said, raising her nose, "you think I would *beg*?"

"As I'm doing now?" he asked softly.

She turned her head and saw his expression. She'd never seen him look as though he was going to weep.

He held out his hand. She broke from her rigid stance and rushed into his arms. Their lips met, hard. He drew in a sharp breath of pain. She remembered what her brother said and tried to pull away, but he dragged her back. They tasted salt on each other's mouths, and it wasn't clear if it was from his wounded mouth or her tears. Neither cared. The pleasure of their kiss was so keen it transcended pain.

It was a while before they could talk sensibly again.

She sat on the couch with him, her head on his wide shoulder, one hand on his heart.

"So you and John will come with me, the aunts, my niece, and her governess to Fair Oaks tonight?" he asked.

"I've a better idea!" she said. "Let's share our happiness with my parents. Let's all go home for Christmas.

There'll be time enough for Fair Oaks in the future. Is that all right?" she asked anxiously.

"Too right," he said. "I'll have to go soon," he said, making no move to budge. His arm was around her as he held her close. "I've got some errands to run before I pick you and John up and we get the aunts. Drop in on Dan, see to my town house . . . It may be stocked with servants if Dan followed my request. When I thought I was rich I wrote and asked him to hire on help. But I'll need extra assistance now that I've committed myself to the civilian life. I think I'll need a likely lad to help me, as a secretary in training, a protégé or such, in some capacity somewhere around the house. I know just the fellow. And there's proper gifts to be purchased—and not just for my niece."

"You're my greatest gift," she said honestly, touching his crisp, clean hair, because she couldn't seem to get enough of touching him.

"Lovely sentiment, and you may have me completely, but at least you should have a bright new ribbon to wear around your neck," he joked, feeling light-headed with joy. He kissed her neck to make his point, then sighed. "Now, the problem is to see if I can find any more mundane gifts for sale on Christmas Day . . . but I think that likely lad will know where to get some," he added with a tilted smile.

She gently touched his swollen lip. Her eyes grew dark. "John's work?" she asked.

He nodded. "It'll heal so fast you'll never know it was hurt. Like us?" he asked hopefully.

She picked up one of his callused hands. She turned it over and saw the scratches and scars on his palm. "Only if you realize I'd have worked just as hard for you, had I known."

His hard hand closed over her soft one. "Lisabeth," he sighed, "please understand. I didn't want you ever to be hungry or in need."

"I was both without you," she said seriously.

"As I was without you. But I'd less than nothing else and no way to get anything more," he said. "In fact, I hate to tell you this, but I actually tried to steal a Christmas present for Gwenn. I failed, again and again. I'll tell you about it someday. Lord, it's good my fortune's restored. I'd be hanging as high as a Smithfield ham if I had to make my livelihood that way. I was a good soldier, but I made a miserable thief."

"What a liar," she said tenderly, her lips brushing his. "You're a master thief. You stole my heart, you rogue, and never gave it back."

"Nor will I," he said raggedly, taking her back in his arms. "But beware," he whispered against her lips, "because I can't wait to continue my life of crime."

"How can you steal what I so yearn to give?" She laughed.

"With joy," he said, "the most I ever knew. Believe it. I may be a thief, but I'm not a liar. Happy Christmas, my love."

"The happiest," she said, and it was only true.